to...

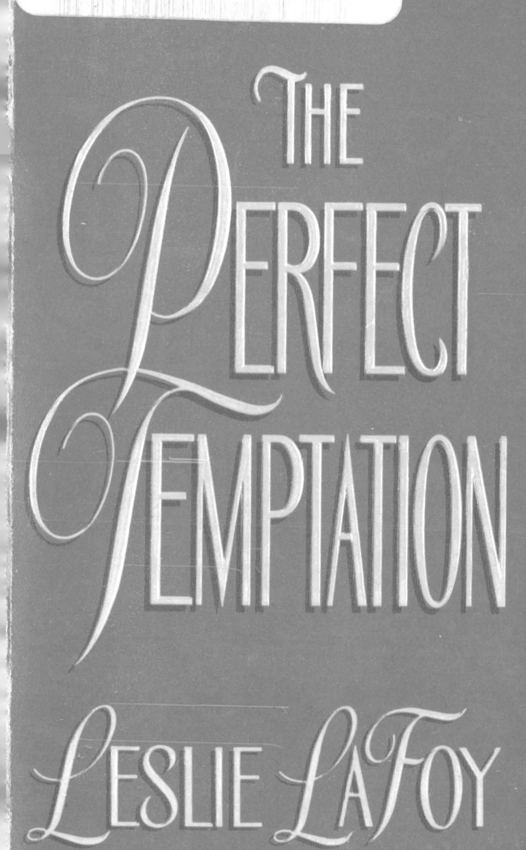

"Leslie LaFoy is intelligent, sexy, fun."
—Kasey Michaels,
New York Times bestselling author

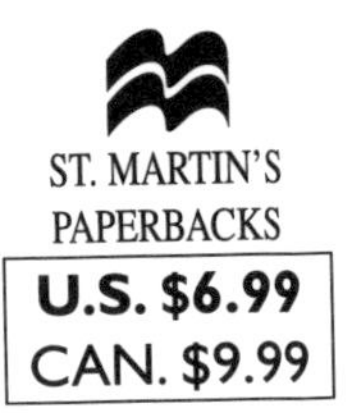

Let yourself be seduced by
Leslie LaFoy's

THE PERFECT SEDUCTION

From St. Martin's Paperbacks

And don't miss her next novel

THE PERFECT DESIRE

Coming soon from St. Martin's Paperbacks

Turn to the back of this book for an excerpt...

Praise for Leslie LaFoy and *The Perfect Seduction*:

"Intelligent [and] sexy. . .you won't be able to resist *The Perfect Seduction*."

—Kasey Michaels, *New York Times* bestselling author

"*The Perfect Seduction* is incredibly delectable and satisfying!"

—Celeste Bradley, author of *The Spy*

"Romance, emotion, marvelous characters—no one does it better than Leslie LaFoy!"

—Maggie Osborne, award-winning author of *Shotgun Wedding*

"*The Perfect Seduction* is a perfect blend of heart and soul and wit."

—Mary McBride, author of *My Hero*

"I was seduced by the first page."

—Marianne Willman, author of *Mistress of Rossmor*

"The lures of LaFoy's writing are not just great characters, fantastic storytelling and heightened sexual tension, but also the subtle ways she plays on your emotions."

—*RT Bookclub* (4½ stars, Top Pick)

"LaFoy's remarkable characters utterly seduce the reader."

—*Booklist*

St. Martin's Paperbacks Titles
By Leslie LaFoy

The Perfect Seduction
The Perfect Temptation

The Perfect Temptation

Leslie LaFoy

St. Martin's Paperbacks

THE PERFECT TEMPTATION

ISBN: 0-312-98764-1
EAN: 80312-98764-0

Printed in the United States of America

St. Martin's Paperbacks edition / July 2004

St. Martin's Paperbacks are published by St. Martin's Press, 175 Fifth Avenue, New York, NY 10010.

10 9 8 7 6 5 4 3 2 1

For
Mary McBride and Kasey Michaels
sister storysmiths
sister Scorps
sisters of my heart

Chapter 1

London, England
Early January, 1864

John Aiden Terrell turned his back to the fire and looked out the office window, watching the snow fall and hating winter. Almost as much as he had lately come to hate Barrett Stanbridge, a man who was, to Aiden's recent way of thinking, an all-around son of a bitch. The things Barrett had asked of him in the name of friendship . . . The last three weeks had been hellish. All the more so because Barrett had insisted that he be sober enough to fully experience every moment of the heart-aching, head-pounding misery.

And the cold. Yes, the bone-cutting, flesh-numbing cold of winter in London. How could he forget that? Just getting from Haven House to Barrett's office each and every morning was an ordeal that usually lingered in his fingers and toes until well past noon. No fire was big enough or hot enough to banish it. This morning there had been the cold *and* the snow; which meant that he'd probably never feel his digits again.

"Do you mind?" the object of his disgust said without looking up from his paperwork.

Aiden stamped his frozen feet again and blew into his cupped, blue hands. "Not at all," he snapped. "I live to meet your every expectation."

Barrett snorted and offhandedly motioned toward the silver coffee service on the far side of the office. Still reading, he said, "Pour yourself a cup and stop your wallowing."

Aiden glared first at his friend and then at the silver pot sitting primly with a sugar and creamer on the sideboard. "I don't want coffee. I want a brandy."

"It's nine-thirty in the morning and you're not having a brandy. Not now. Not later, either. You're reforming."

It was actually nine thirty-eight, but Aiden knew there was no point in correcting his friend. There wasn't any point in protesting the leash Barrett had put on him, either, but he still possessed a bit of pride. Albeit tattered. "As I've mentioned several times already, I'm not the least interested in reformation, thank you very much."

Barrett reached for a pen and scribbled in the margins of the report as he replied, "And as I counter each and every time . . . Your father has asked me to put you back on the straight and narrow. I take the responsibility seriously."

"I've never in my life been on a straight path and you know it just as well as he does," Aiden shot back. "Frankly, I'd rather be dead than live the boring existence you find so comfortable."

"Frankly," his friend retorted calmly, still writing, "when I first found you, I thought you were dead. If a lorry had run over you, you wouldn't have felt a thing."

"Which was precisely my intent."

Barrett finally looked up and met his gaze. "Had you been conscious enough to have seen yourself, you would have been mortally embarrassed. You would have made a pig retch."

Such bluntly honest comments had been constant fare since he'd first sobered up enough to comprehend anything at all. Aiden had had quite enough of it. "I should have known better than to come to London," he snapped.

Barrett cocked a brow but said nothing. He didn't have to. Aiden heard the unspoken rejoinder. *"You should have known better than to go to Charleston."*

Abruptly turning on his heel, Aiden faced the fire and extended his hands toward the flames, trying to forget that day—and failing—yet again.

"Hindsight is always perfect, Aiden," Barrett said quietly. "You can't punish yourself for what you didn't see at the time."

"Oh, but I can," he retorted drolly, hating the sympathy, hating even more the pity. "Just watch me."

A knock on the door spared Aiden from another lecture meant to be inspirational. Instead, Barrett called out, granting his secretary entrance.

The man pushed open the door, then stood stiffly on the threshold to say, "Pardon the intrusion, sir. There is a Miss Radford in the anteroom. I suggested that she make an appointment for tomorrow but she refuses, insisting that it is a matter of considerable urgency."

"Isn't it always?" Barrett quipped with a dry chuckle. He looked past his man and his brow shot up as a smile quirked one corner of his mouth. "Please see to the lady's coat and then show her in, Quincy."

"I'll be going," Aiden declared, seizing the chance and heading off in Quincy's wake. "Wouldn't want to intrude on a private conversation and all that."

"You'll stay right where you are, John Aiden."

It was a command, spoken as only a former army officer could issue one. Aiden stopped in his tracks. Partially out of habit, but mostly out of something else that was deep inside him, nameless but potent nonetheless. He clenched his teeth and turned back.

"Whatever problem she has," Barrett went on crisply, "is

going to land in your lap. You need to be productive for a change. It's time."

There was one good thing to be said for Barrett's sanctimonious pronouncements; they made him mad enough that his blood actually heated. Aiden smiled thinly and made his way to the desk, saying, "Then you should know that I'm going to tell her that there's nothing to be done about her goddamn missing ring until the bloody snow melts."

"We have no idea why she's here," Barrett countered, rising and straightening his jacket with a quick, efficient tug at the hem. "It might be some rare and valuable piece of British antiquity. Or a valuable family member who's gone missing. A wanton niece or a dotty grandfather. And the finder's fee could be considerable. It would be yours, of course. He who does the work, earns the money."

"I don't care about money," Aiden supplied, thinking that all he really wanted was to get the hell out of Barrett's reach for a while. And Sawyer's, too. Between the two of them there wasn't a single moment in his day—or night—that wasn't carefully supervised.

"All right," Barrett conceded with a bare shrug. "So you've thrown away your self-respect and don't care about earning your own way. You might, however, want to think about the considerable pleasures to be had in bathing in the font of gushing feminine gratitude."

Aiden instantly bristled but Barrett didn't give him a chance to retort.

"It's been almost a year, John Aiden," his friend declared gently. "You've been virtuous long enough."

It angered him that Barrett not only didn't understand how deep the pain went, but that he'd never even pretended to care that it existed. Aiden swallowed down the sudden lump in his throat to say, "You're a bastard."

"Which is precisely why your father chose me to salvage you," the other countered, coolly shooting his cuffs.

"For God's sake, I'm twenty-six years old. To be treated like a child in leading strings is insulting. I don't want—or *need*—to be salvaged. All I need is to be left the hell alone."

"You were allowed that course," Barrett pointed out quietly, his gaze arrowing past Aiden to the doorway. He put a polite smile on his face as he added, "You didn't do well with it."

"Miss Alexandra Radford, sir."

Quincy stepped to the side and the woman entered the room. Glided, actually. In a cloud of what had to be outrageously expensive silk. Like the shifting colors of a peacock feather, her morning dress was sometimes green, sometimes blue, and somehow, sometimes both colors at once. Actually, it was a blouse and matching skirt, he noted. Which strongly suggested that she didn't have a lady's maid to assist her in dressing.

The woman herself . . . So very English. Of middling height, with fairish skin and raven dark curls peeking from beneath a stylish bonnet. Her face was nicely shaped and finely featured. And even a dead man would have noticed the decently corseted and curved figure. Not that any man would have dared to openly regard that particular feast. Miss Alexandra Radford might well be deliciously wrapped, but under it all lay the heart and soul of a woman who considered herself the equal of any duchess. A duchess without a maid.

Aiden suppressed a groan and summoned what he could of a civil smile. Women of privilege—and especially those who simply considered themselves privileged—were such a pain in the ass. Well, the vast majority of them, anyway. There was always the rare exception. Alexandra Radford, however, didn't look to be such an exception.

"Good morning, Miss Radford," Barrett offered smoothly as he moved forward to meet her halfway. She stopped and extended her hand. He took it and bowed over it slightly, adding, "Barrett Stanbridge at your service."

"Good morning to you, Mr. Stanbridge," she replied on cue and in perfectly even, cultured English tones. "I deeply appreciate your willingness to see me without the courtesy of an appointment."

"It's no trouble at all." Barrett smiled broadly and moved to the side to gesture toward Aiden. "May I introduce my associate, Mr. John Aiden Terrell."

"Mr. Terrell," she said, barely lowering her delicate little chin in acknowledgment. But her eyes as she met his gaze . . . God, they were the most breathtaking color. Not quite blue, not quite green. With a hint of gray. She blinked, twice. And he saw something flicker in their depths just before she forced herself to swallow.

His long-dormant sense of curiosity stirred. He obviously unsettled her. Why?

"Miss Radford," he said, bowing ever so slightly at the waist as he continued to assess her.

"Please have a seat and tell us how we may be of service to you," Barrett interjected, indicating one of the chairs facing the desk and drawing her attention away from Aiden. "Would you care for a cup of coffee? Aiden will be more than happy to get one for you."

Aiden, the obedient minion, he silently groused.

She met his gaze again for the barest fraction of a second as she seated herself. "If it wouldn't be too much trouble," she answered, looking away to watch Barrett settle into his chair.

"Cream?" Aiden asked wryly. "Sugar?"

She didn't look at him again as she said, "Neither, thank you."

Well, that was interesting. He would have guessed her to be a three-lumps, half-a-cup-of-cream woman. Not entirely because she preferred it that way, just mostly because it meant that someone would have to do her exact bidding.

"I was referred to you by Mrs. Emmaline Fuller," Aiden heard her say to Barrett. "Her brother, Sawyer, is in service to Mr. Carden Reeves, who Emmaline says is a great friend of yours."

"Ah, yes. We know Sawyer. In fact, Mr. Terrell is residing in the Reeveses' home while the family is out of the country."

"Egypt. A bridge project," Aiden supplied, crossing to the desk. Handing her the cup and saucer, he smiled tightly and added, "Carden is an architect."

"Thank you," she murmured, taking the coffee while—quite pointedly—not looking at him.

Whether she was intimidated or dismissive, he couldn't tell. But, in either case, he wasn't about to be ignored. If Barrett, private investigator extraordinaire, intended for him to deal with whatever petty tragedy she'd brought in the door, then he was going to take charge of it all from the beginning. With any luck, he'd so fluster her that she'd change her mind and go away. That or Barrett would decide that he wasn't fit to be let loose in the civilized world and decide to take the case himself.

Propping his hip on the corner of Barrett's desk, Aiden casually crossed his booted ankles and folded his arms across his chest. "And why has it become necessary for you to ask Mrs. Fuller to recommend a private investigator? Has there been a loss or theft of some valuable piece of personal property?"

Her gaze darted to the vicinity of his thighs and then away. To Barrett she said, "I don't quite know how or where to begin, actually."

"Perhaps simply and at the beginning?" Aiden suggested, not caring one whit that sarcasm rippled through the words.

"Please ignore his tartness," Barrett offered in way of censure. "He has no patience in the morning. What is it that you would like us to do for you, Miss Radford?"

She sat up straighter, squaring her shoulders and lifting her chin. The coffee cup sat silently in the saucer, but the surface of the liquid rippled ever so slightly. Slowly taking a deep breath, she finally said, "I need a child protected."

"Your child?" Barrett asked before Aiden could.

"In a manner of speaking. I'm responsible for his care, education, and safety."

"In other words," Barrett continued, "you're his legal guardian."

"Not legally. Not in the strictest British sense of it, anyway."

With a cocked brow, Barrett slowly asked, "In just whose sense of it then?"

"His father's."

At the rate they were *not* progressing . . . "Miss Radford," Aiden said, trying to find a smile of sorts, "I'm afraid that I don't have much patience at any point in the day. Would you please begin at the beginning and spare us the necessity of playing a quizzing game?"

The look she shot him was lethal. Aiden grinned, amused by her obvious assumption that he could be quelled by such feminine censure. She arched a brow and pointedly turned to Barrett before she began, saying, "My father was in the employ of the British East India Company. After his death, Mother entered into the service of an Indian family in the northern provinces as a tutor. When she passed away, I assumed her responsibilities."

Barrett nodded. "And how long ago was this?"

"I came into the position just after the Sepoy Rebellion."

"That was some six or seven years ago," Barrett commented. "You couldn't have been much more than a child yourself when you assumed such a heavy responsibility."

"I was nineteen at the time. And I assure you that I was—and still am—quite capable."

Which made her now twenty-four or -five, Aiden figured

as Barrett droned on, no doubt offering some sort of apology for what she'd obviously perceived as an insult. At that age any *miss* was not only well past her prime, but so was any hope of an advantageous marriage. Alexandra Radford had come out of India too late.

"As you are no doubt aware," he heard her say, "the Sepoy Rebellion dramatically changed the political and economic structures of India. With the collapse of the East India Company, some of its power was redistributed among the native leaders."

"From what we hear," Barrett contributed, "not always in a peaceful and roundly accepted manner."

She nodded and took a sip of her coffee before answering. "Native Indians have always engaged in political intrigue. With power the prize, the ancient game has become one of much higher stakes and thus of much more deadly means. Three years ago, fearing for his son's life, my employer arranged for me to bring the child to London. We're to remain here until such time as he deems India—and his position—safe and sends for us."

"How old is this child?" Aiden asked, hoping to move matters along now that they'd dispensed with her general family and employment history.

She didn't look at him—not that he'd expected her to—and said to Barrett, "He's now ten."

Again Barrett nodded. "And why do you believe him to be in danger?"

"I've noticed that we're being followed when we move about town, Mr. Stanbridge. I'd like to think that it's nothing more than a cutpurse surveying a possible victim, but, given our circumstances, I can't afford to assume that it's anything so benign."

She considered a cutpurse a benign threat? Jesus. "If this . . ." Aiden knit his brows. "What did you say his name is?"

"I didn't," she replied coolly. "It's Mohan."

With a nod, he went on. "If Mohan's father is so concerned about his son's safety, why didn't he send an army with you for protection? Why are you in a position to have to seek it from us?"

She set the cup and saucer on the desk and turned slightly in her chair to face him squarely. She was at a disadvantage in having to look up at him, but she compensated for it well. As though speaking to a dullard, she said with careful measure, "An army would draw attention, Mr. Terrell. Drawing attention to yourself also draws the danger you're seeking to avoid. Mohan's father chose a safer course and sent two of his most trusted men with us, posing as household servants.

"One died of illness while we were at sea. Rather than risk betraying our whereabouts by sending for a replacement, I decided to make a go of it with the one remaining guard. And, as I expected, his protection proved to be quite sufficient. Unfortunately, four months ago he was an innocent bystander caught up in a street altercation. While he survived the assault, he sustained an injury to his head that left him partially paralyzed and with the mind of a child. The doctors said there was nothing to be done to improve his condition and so, three weeks ago, I regretfully sent him back to India and his family. At the time I did so, I also sent word of our situation to Mohan's father and asked that he send replacements. Until they arrive, I'd like to employ Mr. Stanbridge's services to ensure that Mohan is kept safe."

Barrett, not him, Aiden noted. There was a God and He was indeed benevolent. But as long as he had her attention, there was no point in wasting it since—for some odd, unknown reason—he enjoyed the fact that his mere presence seemed to irritate her. It certainly wasn't very gentlemanly to goad her, but then, he'd given up being a gentleman quite some time ago.

"Why didn't you send word to Mohan's father when the

guard was injured?" Aiden asked. "Why did you wait until you were in a desperate situation?"

He saw her jaw tighten, heard her draw a long, slow breath. Her eyes bright with anger, she said with far more calm than he expected, "I had hoped that he would recover, Mr. Terrell. That sending word of any sort wouldn't be necessary. There are people who will be watching for it and attempt to trace it back here to Mohan. Contact is always risky and to be avoided if at all possible."

"If these people were to find the boy," Barrett asked quickly, "what would they do to him?"

"They will initially hold him and make a ransom demand," she supplied, turning away from Aiden. "In the end, though . . . They will brutally kill him."

And you couldn't have guessed that for yourself, Barrett?

"It could take months for Mohan's father's guards to arrive," his friend offered in what Aiden recognized as the opening gambit in the fee-negotiating phase of the meeting.

"I understand that, Mr. Stanbridge." She slipped her right hand into the folds of her silk skirt as she continued. "And I'm prepared to pay whatever your charges will be for the duration."

"They will be considerable," Barrett countered in a soothing, clearly preparatory tone.

"Mohan's father is a generous man who cares deeply for his son," she replied, extracting her hand from her skirt. In it was a black silk bag, drawn closed by a golden cord. Handing it across the desk, she added, "He provided me with the resources to properly care for his son under any circumstances."

Aiden watched over his shoulder as Barrett untied the knot in the cord, pulled open the top of the bag, and poured the contents into the palm of his other hand. It took every bit of Aiden's self-control to keep his jaw from dropping at the sight of the diamond-and-ruby necklace. The setting was gorgeous, the stones brilliant and clear. It was small and delicate, but that didn't mean that London's elite wouldn't kill for the chance to own it.

"If you would prefer cash," she offered as Barrett dropped it back into the bag, "I can see to the conversion of the piece myself."

Barrett shook his head, stood, and slipped the bag into his coat pocket. "That won't be necessary, Miss Radford."

Aiden expelled the breath he'd been holding and considered the creature sitting in front of the desk. In their brief acquaintance he'd learned a few important things about her; one of which was that she didn't provide full answers until she was backed into a corner and forced to do so. There were just a few things he wanted to know before Barrett put the necklace in the wall safe and committed one or the other of them to the case.

"Just out of curiosity," he began. "Are the Indians going to be knocking on our door, asking for the return of their crown jewels?"

"Not at all," she assured him, rising to her feet. "That piece has been in Mohan's family for centuries."

Ah, she hadn't disappointed him; she'd given him a truth but not a full one. "Is Mohan's father the king?" he asked bluntly.

She hesitated before answering. "India has many kings, Mr. Terrell."

"As I'm aware," he countered. "Is Mohan's father one of them?"

Barrett, coming around the corner of his desk, intervened in their contest of wills. "I must say, Miss Radford, that while I deplore Aiden's rather brusque approach, I'm afraid that he has a valid reason for the inquiry. If we're to adequately protect the child, we need to know precisely how much consequence he represents. It makes a difference in what men are willing to do to reach him."

She looked back and forth between them, clearly trying to decide just how honest she was compelled to be. Finally, she said softly, "Mohan's father is a raja."

"And Mohan is the heir to the throne, isn't he?" Aiden guessed.

"Yes."

"And where is Mohan at this moment?" Barrett asked.

"With Emmaline Fuller."

She'd left the boy with an old woman? Good God. "I hope she's considerably rougher around the edges than Sawyer is," Aiden observed. "If she's not, then the only thing standing between the boy and abduction is a firm commitment to protocol."

With an arched brow, she retorted, "I'm not a fool, Mr. Terrell. I hired two men to stand guard outside her shop until I return. They are suitably armed and are rumored to have the necessary grit to use their weapons if called upon to do so."

In other words, Aiden silently summarized, she'd hired a couple of street thugs. "Why not keep them around until Papa Raja can send his own guards?" he asked. "They wouldn't cost you nearly what we will. Why hire us?"

"There are certain standards to be maintained," she explained crisply. "The two men on duty this morning are not the caliber of men with whom Mohan should be associated for any length of time. They will do, however, for the moment."

"I'm sure they will," Barrett agreed smoothly. "Just as I'm sure that you'll find Aiden eminently suitable. He may have his faults, but he's a very resourceful man when he puts his mind to it."

"Mr. Terrell is to see to the arrangement for and the scheduling of guards?"

"No," Barrett corrected. "That's my responsibility. And

I've decided that Aiden is to be Mohan's protector. From dawn to dawn until the raja's man arrives. You and your charge will be in very capable hands."

Aiden could practically hear her mental wheels clicking and whirring. What, precisely, she was thinking, he couldn't be sure. But he could see that her eyes had darkened and that she was chewing on the inside of her lower lip. All in all, the signs indicated that she wasn't the font of gushing feminine gratitude Barrett had envisioned.

"Mr. Terrell will be residing with us?" she said after a long moment and with a smile that bordered on actually being tremulous.

"It's the best way to ensure the child's safety," Barrett assured her. "Unless, of course, such an arrangement gives you a significant cause for concern."

Would she plead her reputation to avoid having to spend the next few weeks with him? Clearly, she was mulling over some dire vision; she was frowning and worrying the inside of her lip again. Aiden decided to give her a bit of a nudge. "Having second thoughts, Miss Radford?"

"No," she answered too quickly and with a little shudder. She recovered her poise and lifted her chin to the haughty angle she'd borne when she'd first come into the office. "I assume that you will return to your residence for your personal items before joining Mohan and myself."

If she thought he was going to play the dutiful minion for her, she was in for a rather rude awakening on the matter. "I'll send for what belongings I'll need," he said, knowing that they had a long list of issues to resolve before the hour was out. "Where should my man bring them?"

"The Blue Elephant Shop in Bloomsbury," she provided, rising with a soft rustle of silk.

Aiden instantly closed his thoughts, afraid that they'd inadvertently give him away. Barrett, however, didn't think quickly enough to hide his surprise, but covered it well, moving to escort her toward the door and saying, "My mother's spoken of that shop frequently and quite highly. Apparently it is *the* place for her circle of friends to shop for silver and Far Eastern bric-a-brac."

The rest of their conversation was so softly spoken that Aiden couldn't hear it. Not that he cared what they said, he silently admitted as he watched them move into the anteroom. If he had a gram of brains, he'd slip open one of the windows and make his escape while he could. Of course if he did, Barrett would come looking for him again, determined to fulfill his obligations as a surrogate brother.

Better, Aiden supposed, to go through the motions and appear to be cooperative. It was the easiest way to avoid living on Barrett's time schedule for a while. If the duchess had any ideas of imposing one of her own in its place, he'd disabuse her of that notion along with all the others.

"Quincy's seeing to her wrap and the hailing of a cab," Barrett announced, coming back into the room and making straight for the wall safe. "I'll send word to Sawyer for you, Aiden. If you need anything else, let me know."

"So tell me," Aiden said, rising from the corner of his friend's desk, "am I working on the silver case, as well?"

"By a stroke of pure luck," Barrett answered, smiling and storing away the precious payment. He closed the door of the safe and then turned toward Aiden. "Be careful," he added quietly. "Our Miss Radford could very well be more than she appears to be."

"Really?" Aiden drawled, heading for the door. "I hadn't noticed."

Chapter 2

Alex took her seat in the cab, folded her hands in her lap, and sincerely regretted that she hadn't had the courage to throw something of a dignified tantrum. Barrett Stanbridge was everything that Emmaline had said he was; urbane, gentlemanly, the epitome of a professional. His associate, however, was another matter entirely. John Aiden Terrell was a man barely civilized.

His hair was too long and too sun-bleached to even approximate fashionable. And it was unruly, too. Most men combed their locks into a deliberate style of one sort or another. But not Terrell; he simply let it tumble wherever it wanted. Which happened, she silently groused, to somehow perfectly accentuate the most beautiful, intensely green eyes she'd ever seen. In the first moments they'd quite simply taken her breath away. And then she'd noticed the sardonic, knowing glint in them. Combined with his easy, graceful movements and his massive shoulders . . . She'd thought of tigers, of the danger that lurked beneath the indolent manner, and it had taken every bit of her self-discipline to suppress the gasp. It hadn't been easy, but she'd studiously ignored him and eventually recovered some measure of her composure.

He, of course, seemed to have spent the rest of the interview trying his best to ruffle it. Positioning himself so that he half reclined against the desk with his well-muscled thighs within casual glance! It was patently obvious that he had abandoned the major tenets that ruled the public conduct of gentlemen. The man was a rake at best. At worst, an unabashed hedonist.

Yes, she should have spoken up when asked if she had any concerns about or objections to the arrangements Mr. Stanbridge had made. She should have said that she preferred to avoid being in the presence of John Aiden Terrell if at all possible, that he made her feel really quite . . .

Well, *frightened* wasn't entirely accurate. He was so very different from all the other gentlemen she'd ever met that she couldn't help but be a bit intrigued by him. Her heart skittered when she met his gaze and she held her breath every time he opened his mouth to speak. And the way he moved . . . Good God, the man was nothing short of a feast for brazen eyes. It was all most unsettling. Yes, Alex decided, "unsettled" was the proper word. John Aiden Terrell made her feel horribly unsettled. She should have said that when Mr. Stanbridge had asked for any objections.

But she hadn't said anything of the sort. Terrell had goaded her until stubborn pride and dignity had seized control of her better judgment. Now she was stuck with him for the immediate future. The only recourse was to make the best of the situation, to remember that protecting Mohan came before all other considerations. If Terrell proved himself to be anything short of stellar at the task, she wouldn't hesitate to send him packing back to his employer. With any luck at all, he'd be on his way before sunset.

The door of the rented carriage opened and Terrell, his sun-burnished head uncovered, bounded in and dropped unceremoniously onto the opposite seat. "I presume," he said, stuffing his hands into the pockets of his greatcoat, "that you've instructed the driver as to your address?"

The vehicle began to roll even as he asked and so she refused to dignify the question with an answer. Instead, having decided that there was no time like the present to firmly establish her authority as his employer, she said, "I wish to be absolutely clear on one point at the very outset, Mr. Terrell. While in Mr. Stanbridge's office you referred to my situation as desperate. It's not. It's merely vulnerable. There's a significant difference between the two."

One tawny brow slowly rose to disappear under the hair tumbling over his forehead. A wry smile lifted one corner of his mouth and dimpled a handsomely chiseled cheek. "The difference, Miss Radford," he countered dryly, "between vulnerable and desperate is generally about a half-second. Which is roughly the time it takes for someone to pull a trigger."

"No one from India is going to use a firearm," she replied, struggling to contain her irritation. "A blade of one sort or another would be the weapon of choice. It's tradition."

"And does that bit of reality make you feel better?"

"I have been trained in the defensive arts," she supplied, meeting his gaze unflinchingly.

"Are you proficient enough that you could turn an attacker's weapon against him?"

It depended entirely on the skill and determination of the assailant. A small child or a cripple might have reason to think twice before launching an assault against her, but no one else would. Still, she wasn't prepared to share the truth with the likes of the tiger in the opposite seat. "I assure you, Mr. Terrell," she said evenly, "that I would be able to delay any attacker long enough to afford Mohan the chance to escape capture."

He considered her as a smile tugged at the corner of his mouth. Finally, he asked, "Would he take it or would he stay to help you?"

The man had all the persistence of a rat terrier. And none

of the charm. "Mohan has been instructed to run away under such circumstances."

"You didn't answer the question," he observed with a slight shake of his head. "You have a habit of doing that, you know." He leaned forward to rest his elbows on his knees. His gaze boring into her own, he firmly asked, "Is Mohan the type of child who thinks of himself before others?"

She had no idea why he considered the matter to be worth such dogged pursuit, but since she also couldn't see any danger in honesty, she answered, "I suspect that in a threatening situation, Mohan would act foolishly and try to protect me."

"There's something to be said for gallantry and bravery," he countered, settling back into the seat again. "Too many young people today think only of themselves."

"Mohan can't afford the luxury of such lofty ideals," Alex felt compelled to point out. "He's to be the raja one day. His survival is far more important than being well considered by others."

"What good is a raja who's a coward?" he scoffed. "Who would willingly follow him? Assuming, of course, that he even possesses the strength required to lead."

And what did Aiden Terrell know of the qualities of leadership? He was nothing more than an underling to be hired out to anyone who would pay. "Mohan will someday make a very competent and courageous leader."

The brow inched up again. "Will he be a wise one, as well?"

"It's my responsibility to see that he has the knowledge and experience necessary to exercise his power for the betterment of his people."

He sighed, compressed his lips, and contemplated the tops of his boots. After a long moment, he lifted his gaze to meet hers. "Is it a custom in India to avoid answering questions?"

"I beg your pardon?" Alex asked, genuinely confused by his sudden change in conversational direction.

"There," he said with a wave of his hand. "You just did it again. You have a very difficult time providing direct answers, Miss Radford. In the short span of our acquaintance, your willing responses have been of three types—half the truth, a truth unrelated to the inquiry, or an overt attempt to change the subject entirely. You aren't fully honest unless you're absolutely forced to be. Why is that?"

Because it's how one survives in a royal Indian household, she silently answered. Pushing aside the jumble of memories and ignoring the odd and unfamiliar sense of melancholy welling inside her, Alex lifted her chin and squared her shoulders.

"I don't see that my personal behaviors are any of your concern, Mr. Terrell," she declared in the voice she used to squelch dissension in the schoolroom. "You've been employed for the sole purpose of protecting Mohan. And while your duty and mine are temporarily the same, our association doesn't require the development of anything more substantive than a purely business relationship."

He tilted his head to the side and smiled ever so softly. "That rather lengthy answer went into the change-the-subject column. Why do you do that?"

This was not going well. Not well at all. She was feeling under siege and she didn't like it one bit. "You are a man with a most inappropriate sense of curiosity, Mr. Terrell," she declared, hoping to at least shame him into a more deferential manner.

"An unrelated truth." Again he leaned forward to close the distance between them, to more effectively pin her gaze with his. "Let's go back to where we were when you attempted to derail me. Will Mohan be a wise leader?"

Clearly, he wasn't going to abide by accepted social conventions. "It's too early to tell," she all but snapped. "He is, after all, only ten years old. His judgment is that of a child."

He made no attempt to contain his smile. "That was physically painful for you, wasn't it?"

"And the possibility of it pleases you greatly."

"A half-related truth." He sat back once more and pushed his hands into his coat pockets, adding, "That makes a fourth way you can answer. I'm impressed."

He had to be the most insufferable man in all of London. In all of England. Perhaps even the entire British empire. The possibility of enduring his questioning and derisive comments for the foreseeable future was more than she could bear. "Is there some particular reason why you have this apparent compulsion to needle me, Mr. Terrell?" she demanded, determined to resolve their contest one way or the other. "Do I remind you of someone you especially dislike?"

"Well, you certainly don't appear to have any difficulty in asking a direct question."

"A related truth, Mr. Terrell," she shot back. "Perhaps even an attempt to change the subject. But not an answer."

His smile was easy and broad, crinkling the corners of his eyes and sending a hard jolt into the center of her chest. "And you don't appear to like evasion any better than I do, Miss Radford. Shall we call a truce? Or shall we just continue to verbally fence until one of us actually succeeds in drawing blood?"

A truce? Dear God, no. Not under any circumstances. She needed to keep as much distance as possible between them; he had a way of undermining her concentration, of stirring feelings that she suspected might grow to be uncontrollable.

"I don't much care for your manner, Mr. Terrell," she admitted. "You're disrespectful, sarcastic, and appear to be, at best, only marginally interested in the task to which you've been assigned."

He snorted softly and his smile widened. "I've been assigned to the task for less than fifteen minutes. The majority of that time has been spent trying to pry straight answers out of you. And not altogether successfully, I might add. Which means that, to this point, anyway, you haven't earned my respect." His smile faded and his eyes darkened to the color of a storm-shadowed sea. "As for sarcasm . . . I don't like being treated like a boot-licking minion, Miss Radford."

"Especially by women," she clarified, her pulse racing in the face of prodding his obvious anger.

"Mostly by spinsters with an inflated sense of self-importance."

There it was; the unvarnished truth of it. He'd accurately concluded that she wasn't the sort of woman who would ever wrap herself around his ankles and beg him to deliver her from evil. And since she didn't meet his standards of femininity, he wasn't obligated to meet the expectations of a modern Saint George. It certainly wasn't the first time she'd been declared insufficiently female, but that truth didn't dull the pain. In fact, inexplicably, the barb seemed to have gone deeper this time than ever before.

Summoning every shred of her dignity, Alex found what she hoped passed as a serene smile and said, "It's apparent that we're not going to be able to work well together, Mr. Terrell. I think it would be best if we had the driver turn back."

"As long as you understand," he countered, "that I'm the closest approximation to a gentleman that Barrett Stanbridge can assign to you. If you're looking for abject subservience, you're going to have to find another private investigator."

Subservience would be perfect. It was the way men had usually treated her. It was one of the more positive benefits of being a royal tutor, the only British member of a royal Indian household. "Mr. Stanbridge himself will do quite nicely," she mused aloud. "He has a most appropriate demeanor."

Terrell glared at her as another of his derisive smiles lifted one corner of his mouth. Alex drew a slow, deep breath and waited.

"If Barrett were the least interested in being the one to

stand between the little raja and harm, he would have stepped up to it and you and I would have ended our acquaintance at his office doorway. But since it's you and me sitting in this rented hack together . . ."

She'd been backed into a corner. Ruthlessly tamping down a swell of fear, Alex calmly announced, "Then I will simply have to find another investigator."

"Where?" he inquired, chuckling. "You've already interviewed all of the reputable ones in London."

"Excuse me?" she asked, stunned that he somehow knew.

He settled his broad shoulders into the corner of the carriage, stretched his long legs out, folded his arms over his chest, and grinned. The pit of Alex's stomach tightened even as her skin warmed and tingled.

"You said that you put the injured guard on a boat for India three weeks ago," he began. "Given your determination to protect your ward, I'm guessing that you haven't spent the last three weeks forgetting to hire a replacement guard. I think you've made the rounds and went to Emmaline for a recommendation only when the obvious, more publicly known choices didn't meet your standards. Barrett is a very private investigator. You only know about him by personal reference. So, following the deductive logic to the end . . . You have two options, Miss Radford. It's me or go it alone."

He might actually do a decent job of protecting Mohan. His mind worked with surprising precision and clarity. Not that she was about to share that bit of appreciative insight with him. And not that she was willing to surrender control of any situation to him, either. "What credentials and experience do you have, Mr. Terrell?"

He laughed silently and she knew that he was thinking, *Change of subject.* Blessedly, though, he found some grace and didn't torment her. "Relatively few, actually. I was once ten years old and have younger brothers, so I do have a basic understanding of what goes through the minds of boys.

Beyond that . . ." He shrugged. "Barrett has decreed that I shall spend my life productively. I've discovered that, for the time being, it's easier to acquiesce than fight him on the matter."

"Do you always take the easiest course?"

"Rarely, actually. I'm reforming at the moment."

Alex arched a brow, wondering just how much of an improvement she was seeing.

"No, not happily and not by much," he supplied, apparently able to read her mind. "But since a child's life is in danger, I'll manage to trudge along."

She understood the edgy resignation she heard in his voice; she'd spent all of her life trudging through one duty after another. Nevertheless . . . "I don't find that attitude very reassuring, Mr. Terrell."

His smile faded slowly and, as they had the last time she'd prodded him, his eyes darkened. "I'll do what I must to protect Mohan for as long as necessary. How you feel about me in the process really doesn't matter one whit."

Why on earth that taunt bothered her—and bothered her deeply—she didn't know. It was, however, quite liberating if not completely honest to counter, "Which sums up perfectly my sentiments concerning your opinions of me, Mr. Terrell."

"Good," he said, openly assessing her. "We have an agreement. Our first."

"And quite likely our only one."

"No. One more is absolutely essential. I'm responsible for the child's protection and I'll make decisions in that regard. You'll agree to respect them."

"Only if I consider them wise ones, Mr. Terrell. I won't surrender my good judgment to you or anyone else."

There was a long moment of silence during which the rented carriage slowed and drew out of traffic. As it eased to a stop in front of Emmaline's shop, Terrell leaned forward in the seat, took the door handle in hand and said, "I'm a fairly reasonable man. I'm willing to discuss whatever issues may arise, but only to a certain extent. When I draw the line, it's drawn and I won't tolerate dissension or resistance from either you or Mohan."

"How very imperial of you," Alex observed icily.

He grinned, dimpling his cheek and sending another jolt into the center of her being. "I can go toe to toe with the best. You've met your match, duchess." Then he winked, popped open the door, and vaulted out onto the snow-covered walk.

Alex sat there, too stunned and angry to do more than blink. *Duchess?* And what precisely was that wink supposed to imply? That he was teasing? That he hadn't intended for the barb to be as sharp as it was? He was standing there, his hand extended, obviously expecting her to accept his assistance out of the carriage.

"When hell's as cold as London," she muttered, gathering her skirts and disembarking on her own. The snow crunched under her boots and pelted down onto her shoulders. She ignored it just as studiously as she did Terrell's cocked brow and frown.

"John Aiden!"

Alex lifted her gaze toward the woman's voice, toward the doorway of Emmaline's millinery shop. Alex had never met the attractive brunette advancing toward them; she did, however, recognize the maid toting boxes and coming in her wake. Alex met the servant's gaze and knew in an instant that there would be no public acknowledgment of their association. Which was as it should be. The woman's employer—Mrs. Geoffrey Walker-Hines—would be mortified to have it known.

"I had heard rumors that you were back in London!" the other cried, extending her hands to Terrell and smiling brightly. As he took them, she fluttered her lashes and cooed, "How lovely it is to see you again, Aiden."

"It's lovely to see you, too, Rose," he replied with what Alex thought was a forced smile and too-careful politeness.

"You look radiant as always. How is Geoffrey? And little Geoffrey?"

The mention of her husband and her son didn't keep the woman from all but abandoning propriety. Using Terrell's hands for balance, she stretched up on her toes and pressed a kiss to his cheek. And her breasts hard into his chest.

"Both are exceedingly well," she answered when she finally drew back. Still holding a blushing Terrell's hands, she added, "We have a daughter now. Elizabeth was born almost two years ago. You must come by the house for dinner one evening and meet her."

Alex watched him swallow, saw his mental wheels spinning at a furious pace. His smile became even more strained. "I promise to do so at my first opportunity."

"I'll tell Geoffrey so that he can be sure to have your favorite brandy on hand for the occasion. Please feel free to bring your companion."

And with that pronouncement Alex found herself skewered on the woman's gaze. It was direct, certainly, but it was also decidedly hostile. All the conversations she'd had with the woman's maid and housekeeper, the transactions they'd made, flashed through her mind. No, there was no reason for animosity of any sort. Discretion had been their watchword.

"My apologies, ladies," Terrell said, quickly freeing himself of her grasp. He took Alex's elbow in one hand and, gesturing with the other, said, "Mrs. Geoffrey Walker-Hines, Miss Alexandra Radford."

Rose Walker-Hines gave her a smile that only another woman would recognize as venomous. "If you're with Aiden, you must have the patience of a saint."

"Hardly," Alex answered honestly before summoning an utter lie. "It's a pleasure to make your acquaintance."

"And I yours," she lied in return before turning her full attention back to Terrell. "The invitation is open and standing,

Aiden. As always, at your convenience. It's so nice to have you back. We've missed you."

The smile that had been strained was most definitely edging toward brittle as he bowed slightly. "Do give my regards to Geoff."

"I will," she promised, turning and moving toward her waiting carriage. Climbing in, she paused to wave and call out, "Until then, Aiden dear."

Terrell waved with his free hand. His stony smile didn't falter and his lips didn't move as he said quietly, "Just as a point of information, Geoffrey Walker-Hines is a waste of a good suit."

"We agree on a second issue," Alex admitted as the driver closed the door on both the carriage and the encounter. "I never would have imagined the possibility."

He looked down at her, his hand still cradling her elbow. "How is it that you know him?"

"I don't personally. Their servants have been selling off heirloom silver pieces for the last six months to pay the household bills."

"How do you know that?"

"I happen to be a silver broker," she supplied, thinking that he asked more questions than most three-year-olds.

"That was half an answer," he observed with a slight shrug. "But I can deduce the rest. It doesn't take any mental prowess to know why the Walker-Hineses are in such unfortunate circumstances. Geoffrey is a miserable gambler. And he's always had a fondness for mistresses whose tastes he can't afford."

Did John Aiden Terrell keep mistresses or did he prefer brief liaisons with married women? Judging by the kiss Rose Walker-Hines had planted on— Alex mentally shook herself, appalled at the nature of her musing. Terrell's personal life and proclivities were absolutely none of her concern.

"One can't help but wonder why she married him," she ventured, hoping to mask the true direction of her thoughts.

"She decided that it was better being Geoffrey's wife than being a—"

He bit off the rest, but she knew the words nonetheless. She'd heard them countless times before. "Spinster," Alex finished for him, pointedly drawing her arm from the warmth and security of his grasp. "On that point, we will never agree, Mr. Terrell. Better no marriage than spending eternity in a state of misery."

His eyes instantly went dark and the lines at the corners of his mouth deepened as he struggled to take a breath. His voice strained, he retorted ever so quietly, ever so somberly, "There are worse fates to endure than that of an unhappy marriage, Miss Radford." With a motion of his hand, he indicated the shop door and asked, "Shall we go in?"

Alex nodded and gathered her skirts. She didn't know him, didn't much care for him, but cruelty, whether unintentional or not, was unacceptable. Troubled by his obvious pain, she ventured to ease it, saying, "I'm sorry if I prodded a heartache, Mr. Terrell. I didn't mean to."

His smile was weak but genuinely appreciative as he took her elbow back in hand and pulled open the door. "Does Emmaline know that Mohan's an heir to a throne?" he whispered as he guided her into the shop ahead of him.

"She's the only one who does," she supplied, pausing to stamp the snow off her feet. "I had no choice but to tell her. Otherwise she wouldn't have known how desperately I needed the services of a socially acceptable private investigator."

"So you have gone through all the others."

"I didn't say that."

From behind her he laughed softly. The sound rolled over her, bathing her in a gentle, comforting warmth. Her body relaxed as her mind dully warned that Aiden Terrell's ability to understand her was a danger unlike any she'd ever encountered. A warm shudder slowly cascaded down the length of her, and she savored the depth of it, trying to identify the feeling it stirred. It most definitely wasn't apprehension. Neither was it anything even slightly akin to repugnance. It was almost a hunger of sorts, a rather pleasant kind of . . .

Anticipation, she realized, her heart jolting and her breath catching. Dear God in Heaven, what was wrong with her? Distance. She needed to keep as far away from the tiger as she possibly could. If only she'd spoken up when Barrett Stanbridge had given her the chance. If only there was someone else she could hire.

Alex drew her elbow from his grasp yet again and resolutely set off toward the back of the store, saying crisply, "Follow me, if you please," hoping that by some great miracle he'd turn around and walk out of her life.

Chapter 3

Aiden didn't want to notice the seductive sway of her skirts, didn't want to follow her. But he did and he went, telling himself that merely looking wasn't a betrayal in the truest sense of the word and that he did, after all, have to meet the boy he was charged with protecting. The assurances went only a small way toward the easing of his conscience as he moved through the displays of hats, gloves, and reticules. There was a curtain covering an apparent doorway at the back of the store and it was through it that Alexandra Radford disappeared without so much as a backward glance.

He paused and was eyeing the curtain, thinking about heading for the docks, when he heard a squeak of what could only be described as stunned outrage.

"What are you doing?" the duchess demanded.

"His Excellency wanted tea and biscuits," answered a woman whom Aiden assumed to be Emmaline Fuller.

"Mohan!"

Aiden smiled and proceeded, parting the divider curtain just as he heard a child say in an incredibly pompous tone, "Yes, Miss Alex?"

"Miss Alex" was temporarily unable to reply as she had her hands full in trying to help a rather frail elderly woman rise from her knees. The task was made even more difficult by the fact that the older woman had a death grip on a silver tea tray with a full service and wasn't about to turn it over despite her rescuer's efforts to take it. Mohan, a slight and ever so lightly bronze-skinned boy, watched it all with a smile from his seat in the office chair. With his feet, Aiden noted, propped up on a stack of velvet-covered pillows.

"Emmaline, for God's sake, you're British," the duchess admonished gently. "You know better. You don't bow to anyone but our own queen."

Emmaline froze in mid-rise and looked up at the duchess, incredulous. "But His Excellency said that you bow to him all the time."

"Mohan is his name—*not His Excellency*—and he's a great fabricator," she hotly countered as Aiden moved to the other side of Emmaline and resolved the contest over the tea tray. The duchess did give him a nod of thanks but went on speaking to her friend, saying, "I've never bowed to him. Or to his father. And Mohan will suffer consequences for humiliating you."

Aiden had the tea service set aside and a firm grip on Emmaline's elbow when the child snorted and said, "I did not humiliate Mrs. Fuller. I graciously and kindly provided her an opportunity to express her reverence for my person and my station."

Biting his tongue, Aiden decided that—for the moment, anyway—wisdom lay in, first, getting Emmaline firmly back onto her feet, and then in letting the duchess manage the discipline of her unruly and decidedly pompous ward. The former task was eventually accomplished with coordinated effort on his and Alex Radford's part and a second or two of unsteady swaying on Emmaline's. The latter . . . Aiden stepped back as the duchess let go of her friend and turned, arms akimbo, to squarely face the little tyrant.

"We will discuss this incident in considerable detail once

we return home. At the present moment, however, you will apologize to Mrs. Fuller."

The child wanted ever so badly to tell his keeper to go to blazes. Aiden could see the resentment in his dark eyes, could feel the anger radiating from his small, regally held frame. If ever there was a child who represented big trouble in a little package, this one was it. The duchess certainly had an imperial attitude about her, but even on her best day she couldn't hold a candle to the one being sported by the child.

"Mohan?" she said crisply.

Aiden silently gave her credit for firmness and then watched in dismay as a sly smile lifted the corners of the boy's mouth.

Instead of meeting Emmaline's gaze, he mutinously held that of his tutor and said flippantly, "Mrs. Fuller, I sincerely regret that Miss Alex considers your actions inappropriate."

Miss Alex's chin came up but she seemed too shocked by the defiance to otherwise respond. Aiden held back, willing to let the woman manage the situation as best she could. Until the boy smiled in victory.

"All right, young man," Aiden declared, stepping forward and drawing the child's attention to him. "Let's try that again."

A dark brow cocked and an ebony-thatched head moved as he disdainfully looked him up and down. "And you are?"

Aiden tamped down the impulse to snatch the boy from the chair by the lapels of his finely tailored wool coat. With every measure of his restraint, he smiled thinly and quietly replied, "I'm the man who will turn you over his knee and pummel your backside if you don't apologize."

With a snort of laughter, the boy replied, "You would not dare."

Good God Almighty. If he'd ever spoken to an adult in the manner this child was . . . "If you want to stand to eat for the next week, go ahead and defy me."

"Miss Alex, this man," he said with a disdainful wave of his hand, "is churlish."

"Brutish and mean, as well," Aiden supplied, determined to keep the woman from muddying the contest. The boy had crossed the line and wasn't going to be allowed to get away with it. "This is the last time you're going to be given a chance to be gracious. Now, stand up and offer Mrs. Fuller an apology as Miss Radford instructed you to do."

Mohan glared at him. Alex Radford looked as though she'd like to wring someone's neck but wasn't sure who should be the first. Emmaline glanced between all three of them, nervously twisting the fabric of her skirt and finally saying, "Oh, dear me. It really isn't all that important. It's certainly not worth this kind of fuss."

"Yes it is," Alexandra Radford said before Aiden could. She fixed her ward with a steely look. "Mohan, your apology is required and we'll stay here until such time as it's rendered in a satisfactory manner. You will have neither food nor drink for as long as that takes."

It was Mohan's turn to glance assessingly between them. Aiden watched him decide that Emmaline wasn't a viable ally and then set about evaluating the more tactically important resolves. The boy met his gaze for a mere fraction of a second. Aiden smiled thinly and Mohan instantly looked toward his tutor. Aiden couldn't see her face, but Mohan's slowly wilting carriage suggested that she wasn't going to falter, either. The boy studied the floor for a moment and then, without looking up, said softly, "I regret—"

"No," Aiden interrupted. "You will stand and look Mrs. Fuller in the eyes while you speak."

It took Mohan several long moments of additional contemplation but he eventually—and ever so slowly and painfully—rose to his feet. It took a few more seconds of preparation before he lifted his gaze to meet Emmaline's. She smiled encouragingly and the boy drew a deep breath.

"I regret having abused your good nature, Mrs. Fuller. It will not happen again," he offered in a rush and on a single breath.

Emmaline sagged with relief. "Thank you, Mohan. Your apology is accepted."

"Now that that bit of business is done," Alex Radford declared, as visibly relieved as her friend. With graceful sweeping motions of her hands, she continued, saying, "Mohan, this is Mr. John Aiden Terrell. He has been employed to protect you until your father can send a replacement for Lal. Mr. Terrell, this is Mohan Singh. And, of course, Mrs. Emmaline Fuller, proprietress of this shop, Sawyer's sister and my friend."

He gave the boy a curt nod that was more warning than acknowledgment and then turned to offer Emmaline a smile and a courtly bow. "It's a distinct pleasure, madam."

"Sawyer speaks very highly of you, Mr. Terrell. It's nice to finally meet you. I'm relieved to know that Alex and Mohan are now in such capable hands."

It occurred to him that Emmaline was undoubtedly feeling better about the situation than any of the rest of them but he kept the observation to himself. The road was rough enough already without throwing additional obstacles onto it.

"And I'm sure," Miss Radford said while edging toward the curtain and the shop beyond it, "that you'd be even more relieved to have us leave you in peace, Emmaline. My deepest thanks for having kept watch over Mohan this morning."

Emmaline moved in her wake, clearly intending to escort her guest to the front door. "It was no problem at all, Alex. Should you need me to do so again, you have but to ask."

Mohan darted forward just as obviously intending to lead the way for everyone. Aiden caught him by the collar of his coat and brought him to a skidding stop. Leaning down, he said quietly, "You're going to exercise good manners even if it kills you. Ladies always go first. Only when they reach the door will you beg their pardon to step around them to open it and hold it for their passage. Is that clear?"

His "yes" was closer to resentful and grudging than to accepting, but Aiden released him anyway and motioned for him to precede him out of the office. The ladies were standing a few feet from the front door; Alex Radford's brows knitted as she looked over her shoulder at her friend.

"Emmaline? I just realized . . . Where are the guards I hired?"

"I have no idea. One moment they were there, lounging about in front, and in the next there was only a constable poking his head inside asking if we were quite all right. I assured him that we were and he departed with a tip of his hat. They haven't returned."

With a shrug, his employer said, "Well, should they eventually do so to request their payment for services, please send them to me."

If they returned? Aiden rolled his eyes. Newgate would be the only thing that kept them away. Recognizing the tone of a conversation winding to an end, Aiden motioned Mohan toward the door as Emmaline said, "I'm so very glad that you won't have to resort to hiring such unsavory types again. You will exercise prudence should they make an appearance, won't you?"

"I'm always prudent, Emmaline. Always," she assured her jauntily as she smiled approvingly at Mohan and then exited the shop.

Oh, yes, Aiden thought, following along, hiring thugs in the first place had been such a very prudent thing to do. Now every petty criminal in this part of London knew there was a child valuable enough to be worth the snatching. He bowed to Emmaline and made the necessary noises before taking his own departure.

Alex Radford didn't say anything as he joined her and the boy. She simply turned and walked away. Mohan fell in beside her, leaving Aiden to his own decision. If he weren't absolutely sure Barrett would hunt him down and not only make his life utterly miserable again, but also break a bone or two just for good measure . . .

"Between a rock and a hard place," he muttered, stuffing his hands into his coat pockets and watching their progress. Some distance beyond them, extending out from a building on a metal pole and suspended by lengths of heavy chain, was a blue-painted sign that had been cut into the shape of an elephant. For those who couldn't deduce it on their own, the sign's lettering identified the establishment as the Blue Elephant Shop and the source of things Indian and Far Eastern, of silver and other finely crafted domestics.

Aiden sighed and resigned himself to the various tasks at hand. Tasks, he silently groused as he went, that were compounding with each and every minute that passed. First had been the protection of a future raja. Not too terribly complicated up to that point. But of course the simplicity hadn't lasted any longer than five minutes. The first kink in things had come before he'd even left Barrett's office and with the realization that the beautifully curved Miss Radford owned a shop on the list of those suspected as being active in the fencing of recently stolen silver.

She didn't seem the type for that sort of activity, but then, she had known where to hire thugs for a day. And his instincts had certainly failed him before. Rose Walker-Hines came to mind as a perfect case in point. He'd never guessed her to be so sexually predatory. Although, once he'd had his perceptions otherwise informed, he'd enjoyed the hell out of the next few months. But that was all in the past, he reminded himself. And there was absolutely no chance whatsoever of the prim and aloof Miss Alexandra Radford ultimately entertaining him in such delightful, utterly wicked ways. Not that he wouldn't be willing to introduce her to—

Aiden froze, scowling, disgusted for having so absently discarded not only his resolve, but his honor, too. He'd made a sacred pledge, for God's sake. And held to it without so much as a twinge of temptation or regret for the better part of a year. Now, suddenly, his mind was taking him down the most inappropriate paths. Back into wild nights, forward into delectable possibilities.

He needed to keep his mind focused on the purely intellectual tasks at hand. Thinking of Alexandra Radford as anything other than an employer and possible thief simply wouldn't do. Yes, he needed to keep his mind honed on the business at hand, on the very real unpleasantness around him rather than on imagining Alex Radford naked and tumbling about with—

Unpleasantness, he sternly reminded himself. Mohan Singh. Yes, there was something sufficiently awful. Where had he been in his grousing? Oh, yes. And then, as though juggling protection and a discreet theft investigation weren't quite enough for him to manage at once, the universe had added in the rudest, most impossible-to-ignore child he'd ever encountered. There was one good thing about the latter bit of unpleasantness, though. His efforts to protect Mohan from kidnappers weren't going to be all that critical. Anyone stupid enough to take him would very quickly bring him back. And while the boy was gone and he and Alex were alone . . .

"Goddammit," he snarled, furious with the unerring direction of his thoughts, unsettled by the clarity of the mental image of Alex Radford lying happily naked in his bed.

"Mr. Terrell?"

He blinked, clearing his vision to find himself standing in front of the Blue Elephant's display window with Alexandra Radford coolly appraising him from the doorway of her shop.

"Are you planning to come in soon, sir? Or shall I close the door for now?"

Alex saw his hesitation and swallowed down her hurt. It

was bad enough that he obviously hated the window arrangement she'd spent so many hours making, but to have him be so openly reluctant to set foot inside . . .

She quickly turned away, determined to bring her feelings under control. What did she care of his opinion, anyway? It wasn't as though he were a customer. And he most certainly wasn't a friend or even a social acquaintance. He was a guard for Mohan; nothing more than an exceedingly male presence whose only purpose was to discourage would-be kidnappers. She blindly started to push the door closed behind her, reminding herself that Aiden Terrell needn't be appreciative of anything except for the fact that she was the one ultimately paying his wages. Well, the raja was the one actually—

"Excuse me."

Alex started at the sound of his voice so near, at the sudden resistance against the door. She looked back over her shoulder to find him with one foot in, one foot out, and his large hand gripping the edge of the door. His gaze, warily searching, met hers and she instantly abandoned her position, retreating with a foolishly racing pulse to the other side of the welcoming rug. Behind her, the doorbell jangled as he stamped his feet and closed away the outside world.

Mohan, two steps up the staircase, stopped and turned back. "I do not like your manner, Mr. Terrell. It is disrespectful."

"Those who don't respect others have no right to demand respect for themselves," Terrell countered calmly. "You earn it only by giving it."

A definite truth, Alex silently admitted, stripping away her gloves in a deliberate effort to keep from looking at him. Why on earth was he so easily capable of rattling her sensibilities? "Now is not the time to have this discussion," she said, glancing up at her charge. "Please go."

"It was no more than a harmless prank."

"Lying and humiliating others is never harmless, Mohan," she replied, frustrated with his obstinacy. "They're the actions of a petty person. You're better than that. Please do as I've instructed and retire to your quarters to reflect on the fundamental elements of good character. I'll be with you shortly to discuss this morning's lack of them."

He hesitated for a second, looked past her, and then with a royal huff, turned and stomped up the stairs. Alex closed her eyes and began to undo the buttons of her coat, wondering if one could possibly declare a day done before noon. She'd already had quite enough for it to qualify as one of the longest of her life.

"Is he usually so imperial?"

No, the day couldn't be done yet. There was still Terrell. Alex sighed softly and began to shrug out of her coat. She'd barely moved when he stepped behind her and laid his hands on her shoulders. The gesture was gentlemanly, the effect anything but. Her breath caught high in her throat and her heart jolted up to lodge painfully hard just beneath it.

"He's especially high-handed today for some reason," she replied, desperately trying to distract herself as he slid the wrap down her arms. It wasn't supposed to be a sensual feeling at all, but it was. Deeply, disconcertingly so.

"But I assure you that I'm perfectly capable of bringing Mohan back into line," she went on, putting some distance between them in what she hoped passed as a completely nonchalant sort of way. "It's inappropriate to threaten him with physical harm, Mr. Terrell. One simply does not pummel the backside of a future raja."

He casually draped her coat over the back of the upholstered chair and then began unbuttoning his own while saying, "You don't know much about raising boys, do you?"

"I'll remind you that Mohan is not an ordinary boy," she

countered, thinking not of the particulars of raising children, but of those that made for sensitive hands. Terrell's were positively breathtaking.

He dropped his coat over hers on the chair, then absently shot his cuffs as he cocked his brow and met her gaze. "It may well be covered with a royal attitude, but underneath it all Mohan's a boy just like any other the world over. And, having once been a ten-year-old boy myself, I can tell you with absolute certainty that all of them want to have the lines drawn for them as clearly and firmly as possible."

Yes, firm lines were most desirable. Especially personal ones. Establishing them with Aiden Terrell was an absolute necessity. But since she didn't have the slightest inkling as to how to go about doing that without sounding like a frightened little mouse, she decided to confine their present discussion to Mohan. "You're certainly entitled to your opinion, Mr. Terrell. But I'm his guardian and I'll be the one who sets the parameters for discipline."

"I'm just the temporary hireling," he summarized, his eyes flashing green fire.

"Bluntly put, but accurate." She motioned toward the stairs, undaunted by his anger. "If you'd follow me, please, I'll show you to your living quarters."

She led the way, not looking back but nevertheless very much aware of him behind her. He was furious, judging by the way he was apparently sucking each of his breaths through clenched teeth. And every now and then he made a strangled sound that suggested he would like nothing more than to somehow catch her hems under the heel of his boot.

Tomorrow, she told herself. By tomorrow she'd have found a way to keep herself under control in his presence. With that would come the energy and presence of mind to be a peacemaker and to find some common ground with him. If she had to, she'd even swallow her pride and apologize for having been so abrupt and prickly today.

"This will be your room for the duration of your employment," she announced, stopping and throwing wide the door. He stepped into the opening but went no farther. As he surveyed the interior, Alex added, "The second door connects to Mohan's room. My personal quarters adjoin his from the other side."

Aiden blinked away another too-clear carnal image. "It's . . . interesting," he offered, hoping it was a diplomatic enough reply. The last thing he wanted to do was ruffle her feathers any more than he already had. Alex Radford gave as good as she got, and that, he'd discovered on their way up the stairway, seemed to trigger the most incredibly forceful fantasies. And a silk-covered pallet on the floor, silk pillows and silk drapes—all of it in the deepest shades of red and black—didn't do a damn thing toward diluting them, either. Good God Almighty. He'd never seen a room so perfectly, decadently, and unabashedly appointed for seduction.

"I understand that it's not decorated to Western tastes," she said, her voice just barely audible over the sound of his thundering heart. "But the room was Lal's and so to his liking. I sent his personal belongings back to India with him, but, since his permanent replacement will also be Indian, I see no reason to change the basic nature of the room itself. I hope you'll be able to find some degree of comfort in it."

Jesus. Comfort? Only if there was a naked, willing woman behind the carved screen in the corner. If there wasn't, he was going to spend his every waking moment thrashing about the silks, consumed with thoughts of finding one. Damn Barrett to hell and back. If it weren't for him, Aiden would be blissfully, blindly drunk in some dockside tavern. He sure as hell wouldn't be fighting to control his baser impulses.

"Is there something you find objectionable, Mr. Terrell?"

He started and quickly summoned both a smile and a lie. "Not at all. It's a striking room and I'm sure I'll be very comfortable in it."

"Good. I'll leave you to privately explore it."

Christ Almighty, he needed to escape the fantasies, not wallow in them. "That can come later," he said, catching her wrist as she started away.

Her eyes were huge, and even if he hadn't been able to feel her pulse racing under his fingertips, he could see it thrumming frantically in the delectable little hollow below her ear. His own heartbeat traitorously quickened to match the cadence.

"I need a tour of the house," he quickly explained. "Both the public and the private areas of it. The sooner it's done, the sooner I can identify the weaknesses and correct them."

"But Mohan is waiting."

Her voice was a lush whisper that feathered over his every sense. He released his hold on her, afraid of what he might do if he didn't. He took a step back before he felt safe enough to counter, "Let Mohan wait. He has a great deal of reflection to do. He can use the time."

She wanted to escape; he could see the fear in her eyes. Why, he couldn't guess, but he instantly regretted having cornered her for his own attempt at evasion. He was about to withdraw his request when she lifted her chin.

"Very well," she said, her voice still soft, still dangerously enticing. "I suppose we should start at the front door and work our way back and then up."

And then she gathered her skirts so that they didn't brush him as she swept past and headed for the stairs. Aiden expelled a hard breath and sagged against the door frame of his room. He'd promised Mary Alice there would be no other. Ever. He'd promised.

A familiar voice rumbled from his memory. *It's been a year. You've been virtuous long enough.* Aiden pinched the bridge of his nose. A year. He'd pledged an eternity. God, he was going to kill Barrett Stanbridge for this.

Chapter 4

Alex stood in the center of the front shop, her hands pressed to her midriff and willing her heartbeat to slow. It was absolutely ludicrous to run away from a man in your own home. Especially a man who was there to protect you and those for whom you were responsible. She simply had to gain some measure of control over her reactions to Aiden Terrell. She was the employer and he was the employee. She'd been the royal tutor, for heaven's sake; she'd had hundreds—perhaps thousands—of relationships with subordinates before. This one was no different from any of the others. She closed her eyes and took a deep, steadying breath. "Cool distance," she whispered. "Cool, cool distance."

The sound of his footfalls on the stairs sent her heart back into her throat and shattered her mantra. Letting her hands fall to her sides, Alex opened her eyes and faced him squarely, resolved to take command of the situation before he could.

He was just coming off the last step when she gestured to the goods surrounding her and crisply said, "As you've no doubt surmised, the main floor is devoted to the sale of goods. I've tried to arrange things so that my customers can easily visualize the various objects in their own homes."

He nodded and let his gaze wander over the displays. "Did

you bring all of this with you when you came out of India?"

"Very little of that initial shipment remains," she supplied, vastly relieved by the distant and impersonal tone she heard in his voice. "I receive replacement goods from a trader in Dwarka on a regular schedule. One is, in fact, due any day."

Casually rubbing a paisley cashmere shawl between his fingers, he said, "If he knows where you are—"

"He's Mohan's favorite uncle and can be trusted."

Again he nodded. This time, though, the gesture was accompanied by first a humming sound and then a pronounced silence. After several moments, he turned to face her, crossed his arms over his chest, and asked, "May I pose a more personal question?"

"I suspect that refusing wouldn't make any difference in whether you ask or not."

"True," he admitted with a grin that sparkled all the way to his eyes. "Let me more accurately restate the question. If I asked you a personal question, would you give me a straight and honest answer?"

"I can't know the answer to that," she countered warily, "until I know what the question is."

"Fair enough." He picked up an ornately carved picture frame and studied it as he asked, "Why the shop? Why London? Mohan's father could have bought a country estate and tucked you both neatly away in safe seclusion. Why didn't he? Why did he choose to establish his royal tutor as a merchant in the heart of a huge city?"

He considered this a personal subject? God was indeed merciful and caring. Alex leaned her hip against the writing desk and relaxed, suddenly much more confident in her ability to manage both the conversation and Aiden Terrell.

"While, in recent years, the East India Company may have crumbled as a governing body of India," she said, "it's apparent that British control isn't going to be surrendered anytime soon. The rajas know this, of course, and believe that in order to effectively exercise their power within those parameters, they must understand the ways of Britain herself."

He set aside the one frame and picked up another without comment or—most surprisingly—another question.

"Part of the reason for bringing Mohan to England," she went on, watching him caress the carving with the pads of his thumbs, "was to immerse him in British ways so that he can be a better leader when his time comes. Ensconcing him at a country estate wouldn't have accomplished the larger goal. London is the center of the empire and so it's London that Mohan must experience in order to learn what he must to rule effectively."

"A partial answer. A quite acceptable one, actually." He put down the frame and selected yet another. "Now if you'll just as ably answer the other part. Why did he establish you as a merchant? Why not simply put you in a house and support you and Mohan in royal fashion?"

"That was his intention at the beginning. I suggested that Mohan would learn more of what he needs to know if he were to experience a more common reality. In the end, the raja saw matters my way."

"Do you always get your way?"

"No, not always." He set down the small frame, but this time didn't select another. Still, he didn't look at her. She found it most odd; it didn't seem at all like him to approach matters in this way. "Just usually."

His gaze snapped up to meet hers as another of his heart-jolting grins lit up his face. "I'm not the least surprised by that."

Something had surprised her, though. Aiden could see it in the nervous edge to the smile she gave him in return. Despite an apparently determined effort to appear unaffected, her gesture was a bit vague and shaky when she indicated the back of the main floor and said, "If you'll come this way, I'll show you the other rooms."

There was nothing vague about the way she turned and walked off. He'd seen squads of royal sailors make less obvious retreats. He followed, puzzling over what he'd done that had set her into flight. She'd been answering his questions easily and forthrightly up until . . . He'd given her a compliment. Well, of sorts, anyway. That's when she'd gotten flustered. And he'd smiled at her, too.

"This is one of the three fabric rooms," she said, interrupting his musing.

Aiden stopped with the space of the doorway separating them and looked inside. There were shelves against all the walls from floor to ceiling, all of them packed with neatly folded fabric. The floor was covered with a dark blue, richly patterned rug. A huge library-type table sat in the center of the room and a discreetly draped dress form had been placed in the corner. Everything was blue, green, purple, or a variation thereof.

She didn't say anything but he followed when she moved to the next room. As the first had been stocked with fabrics at the cooler end of the rainbow, this one decidedly displayed the warmer. Reds, yellows, oranges. From bright to the merest hint of color. Another coordinating rug, another table, another dress form.

The third room she showed him was, to his surprise, something of a disappointment after the first two. It was visually divided in half. Blacks and grays were on one side. Whites to light camels on the other. The rug was white, the dress form draped in black. He frowned, realizing that, as strange as it was, the general absence of color made him feel somehow cheated.

He was still pondering his reaction to the room when she moved to the next. This one she actually entered and he dutifully stepped in behind her. There were shelves in this one, too. But it wasn't fabric she displayed. It was silver. Tea and coffee services, trays, bowls, platters, pitchers, and silverware. God Almighty, there was enough silverware in that room to set the table at Windsor Castle. There were wooden storage boxes of it everywhere; some stacked one upon the other, some of them opened to display the gleaming contents. If there was any stolen silver in the mountain before him, he'd have one helluva time trying to find it.

"I don't think I've ever seen a collection of silver this . . . extensive," he ventured.

She tweaked the angle of a tea service on one of the shelves, saying, "It is a bit overwhelming, isn't it? I didn't set out to be a silver broker, but the opportunity presented itself and the profits are so attractive, I couldn't resist. It's been very instructional for Mohan, too."

"I can't imagine a raja being all that concerned over what spoons are used on the royal table," he offered, hoping that it was a neutral enough comment. The very last thing he wanted was for her to make a retreat into silence.

"Actually," she replied, moving objects around the shelves as she spoke, "the lesson comes in weighing public appearances and private realities. Mrs. Walker-Hines is a perfect example. Publicly she presents her situation as being the epitome of financial solvency. Just this morning she had her maid carrying purchases out of Emmaline's shop for all to see. Privately, however, she's selling silver to pay those bills and many others."

"With the servants doing the actual selling," Aiden supplied, watching her, noting the easy smile on her face. It was serene and yet somehow bursting with life and energy.

"Of course. She has appearances to maintain. If the selling somehow becomes public knowledge, she can always claim that she knew nothing of it and have the servants charged with theft."

"A rather low tactic," he observed, leaning his shoulder

against a shelf support and crossing his arms over his chest. Damn if she wasn't fascinating to watch. She didn't touch things, she caressed and cajoled them.

"To the Rose Walker-Hineses of this world, appearances often matter more than loyalty," she explained, apparently unaware of his appraisal. "It's a lesson Mohan is finding particularly difficult to understand. Pretensions are quite foreign to his native philosophies."

He disagreed; so far Mohan had given him the impression of being quite wedded to pretenses. But he knew better than to share that view. Alex Radford tended to be a bit protective of her tyrannical charge. "Philosophies?" he repeated, deciding it might be a safer topic of conversation. "He has more than one?"

She nodded and went on with her rearranging. "Hinduism is a complex and ever-so-flexible system of beliefs and practices. We maintain one steadfast religious prohibition in this household, though, and that's regarding the consumption of beef. If you find yourself yearning for it, you'll have to dine out. Other than that concession, my objective is to make Mohan's daily life as English as possible."

"How does he like it?"

"He's a typically tolerant child. With the typical Indian view of the world."

"Enlighten me as to what that might be," he pressed, genuinely curious, genuinely liking—to his surprise—the sound of her voice.

She pursed her lips for a moment as though concentrating and then smiled serenely. "In its simplest form . . . The universe—and all that's in it—is in a constant state of change. What there is, is and there is nothing more at the moment. What comes, comes. What goes, goes. Within that acceptance, one can shape one's destiny for the next lifetime through the exercise of good thoughts, words, and deeds. The tasks, lessons, and challenges of this lifetime are set at birth, determined by the actions of the life lived before, and thus inescapable."

"Sounds rather fatalistic to me," he confided.

"Only on the surface."

He drew a deep breath and stepped out on a limb. "Do you subscribe to that perspective?"

She laughed. Softly, lightly. And like her whisper in the upstairs hall, it washed over him, igniting his senses. "I'm British," she said, mercifully not looking at him. "And like all Britons, I believe that I'm the complete master of my own destiny. My task as the royal tutor is to attempt to infuse some of that perspective into Mohan's Indian one."

"Is he learning?"

"There are good days and bad days, Mr. Terrell."

As with all things. If he only considered the last few minutes, he could call it a very good day, indeed. They seemed to have stumbled on a way to converse without outright conflict. "Do you suppose you could call me Aiden?" he asked, trying to strengthen the tenuous bridge. "When it's just the two of us, of course. 'Mr. Terrell' always makes me think my father's about somewhere and that possibility tends to make me a bit nervous these days."

"I'll give the matter some thought," she replied. Her smile brightened by a degree and she slid a look his way. "I gather he—your father—disapproves of something you've done."

"There's an understatement," he answered. Unwilling to expand on the particulars, he indicated the room's rear window with a nod of his chin and changed the subject. "Is that the kitchen?"

She looked up from her silver to gaze out the window. "Yes," she said, picking up a cloth and wiping her hands. Laying it aside, she turned and walked past him, saying, "Come along and I'll introduce you to Preeya. She's our cook and housekeeper."

There was only a few feet of hallway between the door of

the silver room and the one that led out into the rear yard and the kitchen beyond. A brass coat tree sat in the corner, laden with various wraps, but she didn't pause to take one of them. She'd stepped outside when Aiden felt the compunction to be a gentleman. "Wouldn't you like a shawl or something?" he called after her. "Tell me which you'd prefer and I'll bring it along."

She laughed again, precluding his need for a coat anytime soon. "It's only a short distance and it's really not all that cold. At least not by Himalayan standards."

Expelling a hard breath to steady himself, Aiden left the wraps behind and hurried to catch up. "I've heard that the Himalayas are an especially beautiful part of India," he offered as he fell in beside her on the cleanly swept walkway. "Is it true?"

"It's paradise. A bit closer to the English version of it in the warmer months, though. A good number of the British military commanders spend their summers in the region to escape the horrible temperatures of the south. Winters are rather snowy, of course. One has to expect that in high mountains."

"Do you miss it?"

Her smile faltered, and despite her effort to keep it in place, he could tell it was now forced and empty of any real happiness. He'd inadvertently hit upon a topic that troubled her and he regretted it immensely. He liked the relaxed Alexandra Radford ever so much better than the wary, defensive one.

"You're a man of a thousand questions, Mr. Terrell," she predictably replied as she stepped ahead of him and seized the kitchen door handle before he could. "Preeya," she called out as she entered, "I've brought someone to meet you."

And that was the last he understood of anything she said. Alex Radford rattled on in what he presumed to be a flawless stream of Indian, gesturing to him and to a plumpish, short, gray-haired woman working at the stove. The woman—who wore a pair of flat, heavily embroidered fabric shoes and what looked like a dozen yards of draped cloth—abandoned her cooking to face him, put her hands together before her, bow slightly, and say something that sounded like "Namastay."

He had no idea what it meant or even if he'd heard it right. But returning the greeting seemed to be the polite thing to do and so he mimicked her. His reward was a huge smile from her and an approving nod from Alex Radford.

And then they promptly ignored him. Preeya went back to stirring whatever was in her cook pot and Alex went on talking in Indian. No, he corrected himself, remembering a long-ago school lesson. The most commonly spoken language in India wasn't called Indian. That would have been logical. Hindi? Yes, that was it. They called it Hindi. Of course, for all he knew, she could have been speaking one of the less common ones. His personal knowledge of India was limited to having once seen a set of navigation charts for the Indian Ocean.

And he knew just as little about Indian cuisine. One thing was certain, though, the scents were sharp and strong in Preeya's world. He couldn't identify any of those swirling around and seemingly through him. Well, maybe except for the hint of cinnamon and cloves he was catching every now and again. There were dried peppers hanging on a string over in the corner. He'd seen those in kitchens throughout the Leeward Islands. His mother had some in hers on St. Kitts. Under the peppers, on a table, was a basket of rice. Other than those few things, it was all quite foreign.

It was also warm. Uncomfortably so. With the fire roaring in the hearth and the one in the stove, the condensate was streaming down the windowpanes. Aiden resisted the urge to loosen his stock and collar but couldn't help looking longingly at the door and wishing he were on the other side of it. At the edge of his vision he saw Preeya pat Alex Radford's arm and laugh. Alex rolled her eyes and shook her head.

Preeya said something, grinned, and then waved a huge slotted spoon in a gesture that didn't need any translation. *Get out of my kitchen* was universally understood. Especially by males. He grinned, wondering how many times his mother's cook had ordered him out of her way. Thousands, probably.

She barely gave him time to bow in farewell to Preeya before his hope was realized and he was back outside in the wonderfully cold, crisp air. And hurrying to catch up with her. Yet again. Something inside him rebelled at the notion of complying, of dutifully following along and letting her always set the course and the pace.

The movement was quick and at the very edge of her vision. Alex whirled about, her heart racing, her hands instinctively positioned to fend off an attack. One part of her instantly relaxed at the sight of Aiden Terrell hanging, slightly swaying, from a lower limb of the apple tree.

Another part of her wasn't relaxed at all. Stretched out as he was, his hands wrapped over the top of the branch, his feet well off the snowy ground, his clothing was pulled taut over his body and revealed in great detail every one of his rippled, corded, and bulging muscles. Dear God in heaven, the man was marvelously sculpted. From his broad shoulders to his abdomen to his—

Heat flooded her cheeks and she quickly lifted her gaze to his face. His grin was huge, sparkling brilliantly in his gorgeous green eyes. The effect, as always, was devastating. Her heart skittered and her pulse raced hotly through her veins.

"Mr. Terrell?" she began, unable to keep from watching his display, desperate to get him to stop.

"My father isn't here," he replied, arching his lower body to increase the speed and power of his swing. And the tautness of his clothes.

"Aiden," she quickly allowed, watching him pump higher and faster. "I'm chilled to the bone. May we please go inside?"

Chilled, my great-aunt Fanny, Aiden thought, grinning and shifting his hold on the branch. It wasn't cold coloring her cheeks. He knew a purely feminine response to unexpected infatuation when he saw one. He arched higher, pleased by the sound of her strangled gasp. No, the duchess wasn't cold at all. And she obviously wasn't made of stone, either. That was just a façade. One that, judging by her blush, had the potential to crumble rather quickly and nicely.

His conscience prickled ever so slightly, but the rebellious spirit again surged forward, ruthlessly tamping it down, firmly telling him there was nothing wrong with a general appreciation of a woman's willingness to be seduced. Willing women were wonderful things.

Deciding that he'd best leave those kinds of thoughts no further developed than they were, he selected a suitable landing place some distance out and arced backward to gain the momentum necessary to reach it. She actually squealed and covered her eyes as he released his hold on the branch and launched himself forward.

He landed perfectly, laughing and looking back over his shoulder to see if she'd surrendered to curiosity. She had and a deeper flush swept over her cheeks as she realized he'd caught her at it.

"So tell me about Preeya," he said jauntily, deliberately taking control of the conversation as he buttoned his jacket and moved to join her on the walk. "How did she end up here with you?"

Alex swallowed down her heart and headed off for the rear of the house. "Preeya was the third wife of one of Mohan's father's uncles on his mother's side," she provided, hearing the speed of the words but unable to do anything to slow the tide. "When he died, she came under the raja's protection. It's all rather complicated and I'm not sure that I fully understand the set of social and family obligations that led to it. Frankly, I think the obligation has more to do with his having lived with his uncle as a young man and Preeya befriending a homesick youth. But, in any case and for whatever reason, she considers it an honor to have been sent to England with us. Her room is opposite yours."

"She seems like a grandmotherly sort," Aiden Terrell observed, dashing ahead to open the door for her.

Her skirts in hand, Alex stepped past him and into the hall saying, "An Indian grandmother, perhaps. She's not the least interested in adopting even the smallest of British ways."

"I gathered that." The door clicked shut behind him as he chuckled dryly and added, "I'm not nearly as stupid as I look, you know."

The comment was offhand, but deliberately designed to be disarming. It rankled that he would so blatantly attempt to manipulate her, that he thought she couldn't see through it. They'd been getting along relatively well for the past few minutes and it was a shame that he'd put the tenuous peace at risk, but she wasn't about to let him think her either blind or spineless. She took a deep breath and turned to face him, determined to correct his misconceptions. "I hardly consider you a stupid-looking man, Mr. Terrell. And—"

"We've progressed to Aiden," he inserted with a gentle, eye-twinkling smile. "Let's not move backward."

She ignored the suggestion and plunged on. "And I sincerely doubt that there's a woman alive who would consider you anything but devilishly handsome. I'd also hazard to guess that in the course of your life quite a number of them have freely shared with you their compliments. Verbal and otherwise."

His brow shot up and his smile quirked and she tried to ignore all that, as well. "As for your mental prowess . . . I can honestly say that I have no doubts whatsoever concerning your intelligence, Mr. Terrell. You strike me as a man who finds very little in life that challenges or requires the full use of his mental abilities. I think that, for the most part, you merely dabble at the activities involved in living each day."

He instantly sobered, his eyes darkening as he considered her in silence.

"If you'll excuse me," she went on, knowing she'd struck a nerve and seizing the chance to retire from the field while she had the small victory. "I think Mohan's had all the time for contemplation that might be productive. Preeya will bring the noon meal up when she's ready to do so. There's never a set time so please don't wander out of earshot. The room across from mine is the dining room. I'll see you—"

"I'll need to survey each of the upstairs rooms before the day is out," he interrupted coolly.

"I'll make myself available for the task after lunch," she promised, silently adding that it would be as brief an excursion as she could make it. "As you might have noticed, we don't have a butler or a doorman, Mr. Terrell. You might want to—"

"Stay close to the front of the house to let in Sawyer when he arrives with my belongings," Aiden suggested, knowing full good and well that what she really wanted was to put as much physical distance between them as she could and that any excuse would suffice.

"Precisely."

"Uh-huh," he said, noting the tension easing out of her shoulders. It rather pained him to realize that she wanted to be away from his company, but, all in all, he understood exactly how she felt. He needed the distance and time, too. The cause and reason of it were, at the moment, undefined, but the reality was quite clear: it was damn hard to think straight whenever she was near.

"I'll see you again at luncheon then," Alex announced. Turning on her heel, she left him standing there in the rear hallway.

Her heart thundering, she made her way to the stairs and up to the second floor knowing that she'd been incredibly wrong in her earlier self-assurances. Her relationship with Aiden Terrell wasn't the least bit like any of those she'd ever had with a subordinate. It couldn't be. Because Aiden Terrell wasn't like any other man—or person—she'd ever met. He wasn't abusive as her father had been. He wasn't royal and therefore infallible as was the raja. He wasn't regally self-absorbed as were the members of the royal family and court. And Lord knew that Aiden didn't have so much as one single subservient bone in his beautifully sculpted body.

He was curious and bluntly spoken, sinfully handsome and intriguing. He could be breathtakingly, recklessly impulsive. Yet he was always clear-headed, always thinking. He honestly didn't care what anyone thought of him, didn't measure his words or actions or opinions in consideration of what others would think of him. And, under it all, he was a basically decent man who didn't particularly want to be a gentleman but simply couldn't keep himself from it.

And to think that she'd initially seen him as nothing more significant than Barrett Stanbridge's minion. She'd never been more wrong about anything. Aiden Terrell was most definitely his own man.

There was one early perception that had proven to be spot-on, though. Aiden Terrell was indeed very much a tiger. He liked the hunt, liked the thrill of playing a good and spirited game. Which meant that, unless she was able to exercise extreme caution, she was very much in danger of being consumed. Because, Lord help her, she found everything about him incredibly attractive.

Chapter 5

Alex paused in the upstairs hall, gazing longingly at the closed door of her room. To lock herself away in silence and shadows, to climb into her bed and take a long nap, would be heavenly. Unfortunately, that sort of indulgence wasn't possible at the moment. There was duty to attend. It didn't matter that the very last thing she wanted was to have a confrontation with Mohan. It had to be done. He'd been a terror this morning, embarrassing her in front of both Emmaline and Aiden Terrell.

That Aiden had been forced to step into the situation had been horrible. That he'd had to employ a threat of force to bring Mohan into compliance had been truly awful. And his decision to do so was perfectly understandable. British children simply weren't allowed to run roughshod over others. Especially adults. Lord knew that she'd tried time and time again to explain that to Mohan. And, despite her obvious and rather significant past failures, she was obligated to attempt it yet another time.

Before what little resolve she possessed could desert her, Alex knocked on the door of Mohan's room. He didn't call for her to enter. Neither did he open the door. She knocked again, her temper rising. The response was the same as before and she abandoned good manners.

He was sitting cross-legged on his bed, facing the doorway with his arms folded over his chest. Glaring at her, he said, "I did not grant you permission to enter."

She ignored the rebuke. He wasn't a raja yet. "Do you recall the conversation we had—just last week—regarding the importance of creating positive first impressions?"

"I do not like that man."

"He doesn't much care for you either, Mohan," she countered. "And *your* decisions and actions are the reason you've gotten off on the wrong foot with each other. Therefore, it's *your* responsibility to undo the damage you've caused."

He barely shrugged one shoulder. "I want him sent away."

Alex clung to the shreds of her patience. "In the first place, that simply isn't possible. There's no one to replace him until your father's own guards arrive. You have no choice but to make the best of the present situation. Which, I must add, includes being polite, hospitable, and finding something approximating a friendly demeanor.

"In the second place," she went on, ignoring his scowl and narrowing eyes. "Pushing one's difficulties off to where they can't be seen, doesn't eliminate them. They're still there, still requiring a solution or redress. Having them at a distance only complicates the task of making matters right. You have—however inadvertently—created a poor impression of India in the mind of Mr. Terrell. If you don't correct it, don't demonstrate that you come from a people of kindness and grace, he'll not only carry away a wrong view of India, but will pass that view on to others, compounding the misunderstanding. Surely, you don't want—"

"I want to go home," he interrupted. "Now. Today."

Of course he did. What child wouldn't want to be with his parents, his brothers and sisters, his aunts, uncles, and cousins? "I can understand that, Mohan," she offered sincerely. "I truly can. Hopefully soon your—"

"I command you to make the necessary arrangements."

"I will not," Alex rejoined, her sympathy for him withering under the increasing heat of her anger. *Patience,* she silently instructed herself. *Patience.*

"England is full of dirty people."

She took a deep breath and counted to five. "You've seen little of England outside of London," she calmly reminded him. "Therefore, your statement is an opinion based on nothing more than ignorance. I'll further point out that dirty people are found all over the world and that India too has its allotted share."

He snorted and tilted up his nose. "I never saw any in India."

"That," she snapped, her toleration completely undone, "is because you lived in a royal palace and dirty people weren't allowed in. Is there a specific reason for your contrariness today, Mohan?"

He sat up straight and lifted his nose another degree. "I am a prince. I am not required to explain or justify my actions."

And she wasn't required to restrain Aiden Terrell, either. At the moment his approach to discipline had enormous appeal. "That sort of attitude is what leads to palace coups, Mohan," she pointed out, resolved to hold the higher ground. "But since you're a considerable number of years away from that reality, let me provide you with a more immediate one. Your present behavior is unacceptable, making you truly unpleasant to be around. That being the case, you will take your midday meal in here, in solitude. Further, you will remain in here until such time as you think you're capable of conducting yourself in a civil manner."

With that pronouncement, Alex turned and walked across

the threshold. She was turning back to pull the door closed when he made one of his own.

"I will not eat."

"Suit yourself," she shot back, pausing with the doorknob in hand. "I'll remind you that it takes twenty-one days to starve a child and suggest that unless you plan to discover a font of self-control in the next few minutes, you'll be wasting not only the food, but also the infantile demonstration."

"I hate you!" he screamed as she confined him. "I hate England! And the queen!"

Alex rested her forehead against the door frame and closed her eyes. He was only ten, she reminded herself. He was far from his home and his family, awash in a world so very, very different from his own. She knew exactly how he felt, remembered all too well how she'd felt when her mother and she had found refuge in the raja's household.

She'd been a bit older than Mohan when her world had been upended. But she'd adjusted and endured. With grace and hope. Unfortunately, those were the two qualities Mohan seemed to lack entirely. If only she knew how to impart them to him, how to instill in him the kind of vision and strength necessary to look past today to a distant, brighter tomorrow.

Setting an example hadn't worked. Neither had very carefully and clearly explaining it. Attempting to go at it through the instruction of manners had produced no discernible change in him, either. But was locking him away the only course remaining? It felt like such an admission of failure. If she were a competent teacher, she wouldn't have to resort to such drastic, cold-hearted measures.

Of course, she added, straightening and walking toward her own room, she hadn't yet been reduced to the use of corporal punishment. Alex slipped inside, pressed the door closed, and dropped into the soft cushions of a rattan sofa. No, to her credit, she hadn't turned matters of discipline over to Aiden Terrell. Or even suggested that they might share them. There was something to be said for that, wasn't there?

Wasn't there?

Alex blinked unseeingly into the farthest corner, stunned. She couldn't think of a single reason why she should be pleased by the prospect of continuing to bear the burden all by herself. She was bone weary from the effort to be mother, tutor, mentor, father, and friend. And she was beyond exhausted by the futility of her every effort on every front. Would it be so horribly, unforgivably weak of her to surrender a small part of the responsibility? For just a little while?

She didn't care what Aiden Terrell thought of her, she quickly assured herself. He was here, a reluctant part of their lives, for the next few weeks, a month at the most. As soon as Lal's replacement arrived, Aiden would be gone and she'd never see him again. What did it matter if he thought she was weak and ineffectual?

It didn't matter at all. Except to her pride. Which left her with two clear choices; she could either swallow it or she could soldier on as she had for the last five years and as her mother had before her. Preeya's suggested course wasn't a realistic choice at all. Make Aiden Terrell her lover and husband? Mohan's surrogate father? Ha!

With an aggravated sigh, Alex leaned her head back against the cushion and closed her eyes. Just a short nap, she promised herself. The world always looked kinder and brighter through freshened eyes.

Aiden sat in the wing chair—the one piece of English furniture in the entire shop—and surveyed the rest of the contents of the front store. It was said that homes reflected the innermost nature of the owner. If that was true, what did the Blue Elephant Shop say about Alexandra Radford?

There was absolutely nothing the least straightforward or

simple about the place. There were so many things in it; carefully placed layers and layers of every kind of decorative merchandise imaginable. It was impossible to see it all at even a long glance. Each time you came back to a particular spot you saw something you'd missed the time before. On the table across the room, a little mirror, edged with an intricate silver filigree, had been hidden among a cascade of extravagantly embroidered reticules. Off to the right of that, amid a collection of teakwood chargers and gold-edged china plates, sat a brass candlestick with a fringe of semiprecious beads twinkling in the afternoon sunlight.

Not a bit of it was pretentious and yet it all felt rather elegant and rich. None of it was arranged in any formal way, but there was no denying that there was a deliberate order to the chaos. There was a sense of frustration that came with considering it all, a sense that you were being denied something you desperately wanted and needed. And at the same time there was a thrill in that, an anticipation of a grand, thoroughly accidental discovery.

The Blue Elephant, Aiden decided, was a study in contradictions. Not that that conclusion told him much about Miss Alexandra Radford. It was a store, a public presentation of herself and her wares. She didn't strike him as the sort of woman who would willingly lay bare her soul for any stranger coming in off the street.

No, Alex Radford didn't readily trust people, not even those with whom she was allied. Was she wary because of her concerns for Mohan's safety? Or was it more deeply and broadly rooted than that? Aiden cocked a brow. Or was it that she simply didn't trust *him*? A wry smile lifted one corner of his mouth. Judging by the way her eyes had brightened and her cheeks had flushed out in the yard, it might be that she didn't even trust herself.

His amusement evaporated. Whether or not Alex Radford

was willing to be seduced was an evaluation he didn't need to make, much less ponder. What was worth considering, though, was her apparent distrust. He had a job to do, and if she didn't trust him, protecting Mohan would be all that much more difficult. He needed to find a way to prove himself worthy.

Aiden frowned, irritated by both the burden being his to shoulder and the certainty that accomplishment wouldn't come easily. And Lord knew that his motivation to make the effort wasn't helped any by the fact that Mohan had given every indication so far of being a most unlikable child. He'd be willing to bet the necklace in Barrett's safe that Alex was upstairs desperately wanting to beat her head against a wall in frustration.

The sound of someone tapping against glass brought his attention back to his immediate surroundings. Sawyer stood on the walkway, peering at him through the front window. Aiden pushed himself out of the chair and went to the door to let him in.

"Welcome to hell, Sawyer," he said as the Reeveses' butler stepped inside.

"You seemed quite at home in it, sir," Sawyer observed as Aiden locked the door behind him. "Wouldn't Lady Lansdown adore spending a day in this establishment."

Aiden, standing shoulder to shoulder with the man, looked over the displays again and shook his head. "It doesn't look at all the way Sera decorates."

"It is the breadth and arrangement of color of which she would most heartily approve, sir. She would most definitely appreciate the artistic spirit of your present employer."

"Alexandra Radford with an artistic spirit?" Aiden scoffed. "Sawyer, you have no idea how far off the mark you are on that. She's nothing at all like Seraphina. Miss Radford is very rigid and committed to propriety and maintaining distance."

"If I might point out, sir," Sawyer countered, "those qualities do not preclude her from possessing an artistic nature."

"Then it's buried deep," Aiden grumbled.

"As still waters usually run, sir." He lifted the valise he clutched in his right hand. "I have brought your belongings as Mr. Stanbridge instructed. Where are they to be placed?"

He could have offered to take care of it himself, but he really wanted Sawyer to see the outrageously decorated quarters. Shocking Sawyer was always the best entertainment. "Follow me," he said, leading the way to the stairs and up.

Throwing the door wide, Aiden stepped back to let Sawyer have a full view. One gray brow twitched slightly. "Well? What do you think of it?" Aiden prodded.

"It would appear, sir, that when not formally engaged in your duties, you are expected to spend the hours . . ."

Ah, the man was struck speechless. Aiden grinned and pressed, "Doing what?"

"Lolling about, I believe," Sawyer replied easily. "In what seems to be, at first glance, considerable comfort and luxury."

Aiden's smile withered in disappointment. He gestured toward the silk-covered pallet. "I haven't lain on the floor since . . . Since . . . Well, it's been at least twenty years."

"That would have made you six at the time, sir," he said, advancing into the room with the valise.

God. Ever unflappable. "Thank you, Sawyer."

"If I may ask a question, sir?" the man inquired, bending down to open the lid of an ornately carved trunk that sat beneath the windows on the far wall.

"Go ahead," Aiden replied, sighing and propping his shoulder against the doorjamb.

"Have you any general knowledge of the Indian culture?"

"Absolutely none. If you do, I'd appreciate the sharing of it."

"Personally," Sawyer said, moving items from the valise to the trunk, "I've never been to the subcontinent, but in the course of my service in Her Majesty's Army, I encountered several men who had been garrisoned there for a time. While they expressed some reservations concerning the overspicing of food, they appeared to be quite taken with other aspects of Indian life. In particular, they described in most favorable terms the natives' appreciation for earthly pleasures."

"What kind of earthly pleasures?" Aiden asked, intrigued.

"An abiding appreciation for food, drink, and . . . ah . . . comfort, sir."

That was the thing with Sawyer. You had to listen carefully. The hesitations often had more meaning than the words. "Could you define 'comfort,' Sawyer?"

"It would be sufficient, I think," he said, closing the lid and turning to face him, "to say that physical satisfaction on all levels is considered an appropriate quest and the regular attainment of it a most desirable state of being."

Well, Sawyer might have considered it sufficient, but he didn't. Physical satisfactions covered a very broad range of human activity. "That last part sounded a great deal like something the duchess would say," Aiden groused, knowing that when Sawyer declared a pronouncement sufficient it was pointless to ask for an expansion. As habits went, it was one of his more frustrating ones.

"The duchess, sir?"

"Miss Radford," Aiden supplied. "Trust me, it fits. And just in case you're wondering, her ward shows every sign of being the Spawn of Satan."

Sawyer cleared his throat softly. "Be that as it may . . . I gather that she's spent some considerable time in India. Those who have tend to develop a unique way of expressing themselves that clearly identifies their experience."

"She's lived there all of her life," Aiden supplied, coming off the jamb and moving into his room. "Except for the last three years here in London," he added, prodding the pallet with the toe of his boot.

"Then I would say, sir, that the general appointment of your room is a clear testament to the fullness of Miss Radford's understanding of the Indian approach to life. Were I so fortunate as to be in your shoes, Mr. Terrell, I do believe that I'd be tempted to fully wallow about in the rare and exceptional opportunities I've been afforded."

"Rare and exceptional?" he repeated, looking up to meet Sawyer's gaze.

Sawyer started to respond but his gaze suddenly shifted to a point over Aiden's shoulder. A fraction of a second later he snapped his mouth closed and drew himself up to his full height.

"Pardon the intrusion, Mr. Terrell," she said from the doorway. "I wasn't aware that your man had arrived."

Thanks to his man, he'd known she had. Bless Sawyer. He turned and, indicating the butler with a genteel sweep of his hand, began the formalities. "Miss Radford, may I present Sawyer. Sawyer, Miss Alexandra Radford." *The duchess,* he silently added.

"Emmaline speaks most highly of you, sir," she replied, seemingly frozen to the spot in the hall. "It's indeed a pleasure to meet you."

"And I you, Miss Radford." Sawyer gave her a respectful bow and then a genuine smile. "May I say that your store is a delightful feast for the senses."

She beamed back at him. "Why, thank you, Sawyer. That's most kind of you. I work constantly to keep it vibrant and interesting. Would you care to join us for luncheon? Preeya always cooks more than enough."

"My sincerest thanks, Miss Radford, but unfortunately I cannot today. I paused briefly at Emmaline's on my way here and promised that I would share the noon meal with her."

"Perhaps some other time then." At his slight bow and

nod, she added, "I'll look forward to it." Her smile wasn't nearly as radiant when she turned it on him and said, "When you are free, please join us, Mr. Terrell."

She'd barely walked out of sight when Sawyer said softly, "She seems to be quite down to earth and amiable, sir."

Yes, she could be delightfully pleasant when she wanted. Which, so far, seemed to be when in the presence of anyone except him. "I'll walk you down and let you out," Aiden offered, scowling.

They were standing on opposite sides of the front door when Sawyer cleared his throat and spoke again. "I stand by my earlier observations and recommendations, sir."

Something in his expression must have adequately conveyed his confusion.

"Do make a point, sir," the butler said, a touch of exasperation edging his tone, "of exploring the wonder of deeper waters while you have the chance. You'll never forget or regret the immersion. If you need anything I've neglected to bring, send a runner and I'll see that the matter is rectified immediately."

"Thank you for toting it all over here, Sawyer," Aiden replied, knowing that Sawyer meant well with his advice. "I'll be dropping by the house from time to time, I'm sure." He gestured toward the display table at his side, and with a weak smile added, "One can only take so much of all this for so long."

"Very good, sir. If you'd let me know when you'll be visiting, I'll have Cook prepare you a beef dish." He bowed and then turned crisply on his heel and strode off in the direction of his sister's store.

Aiden closed the door and locked it, his mind racing. Sawyer knew about the Indian proscription of beef. Somehow that realization placed all of what he'd said in a different light. Aiden considered the rich array of color and texture and pattern that surrounded him. It *was* a feast for the eyes. And more. It somehow made the soul feel good, too. Full and maybe even . . . He studied the feeling in his chest and decided that "liberated" came closest to being the right word. There was a quality to it all that seemed to say, "You may indeed."

The thought came as a slow dawn, creeping over him, gradually brightening the darkness that had been troubling him before Sawyer's arrival. When he'd promised there would be no other, he'd meant that he'd never love another woman. There was a significant difference between making love to a woman and actually loving her. Only very rarely did the two go hand in hand. God knew he hadn't had one flicker of true feeling for Rose beyond a wicked appreciation for the fact that she was willing to do anything, anywhere, anytime he wanted.

Of course it was a given that Alex Radford wouldn't be the wanton Rose had proven to be, but if she was willing to be seduced, then far be it for him to turn his back on the opportunity. It wouldn't mean anything beyond a brief physical relationship. Bedding her wouldn't compromise his pledge at all. He could plumb the depths of still waters without so much as a single twinge of guilt.

And it was all the simplest of logic. Why he hadn't seen it before now . . . He sighed and half smiled as he shook his head. He hadn't seen it because he'd spent the last year so blindly, roaringly drunk that he hadn't been able to see so much as his own hand in front of his face. It was galling to have to admit that maybe his father and Barrett were right about the benefits of sobriety, but right was right.

He headed toward the stairs and lunch with a widening grin. Just because you'd realized that someone had been right all along didn't necessarily mean that you had to share that bit of news with them. At least not right away. What did matter was that you used the newfound understanding to improve the general conditions of your existence. To be . . . Aiden chuckled, remembering Sawyer's choice of words. Yes, one should strive to be well and truly comfortable. As often as humanly possible.

Of course, there were a good number of steps to be taken before that was even remotely possible. Gaining Alex's trust was the first. That wasn't going to be easy. And to make matters ever more frustrating, he didn't have a clue as to how to go about it in any sort of deliberate fashion. Being nice to Mohan might be an effective avenue, but the idea of gritting his teeth in silence didn't appeal in the least. In fact, just thinking about it made his jaw ache.

He'd come up with something else, he promised himself as he stepped into the doorway of the dining room. Alex sat at one end of a linen-covered table, a silver dome-covered plate before her. Preeya sat in the center of one side with her own covered plate. Places had been set opposite them both. The one opposite Preeya consisted only of a linen napkin and a set of silverware. The other had all that and a covered plate. Aiden paused, uncertain as to which place was his. Preeya solved his dilemma by gesturing to the seat opposite Alex.

Smiling his thanks, he took his seat saying, "My apologies for having kept you waiting, ladies."

Preeya said something and a rapid exchange in Hindi ensued. At the end of it, Alex said in English, "Preeya says that she doesn't at all mind waiting for the company of a handsome man."

"Did you tell her that she was unnecessarily feeding my already grandiose sense of self?"

"Something along those lines," she replied, removing her plate cover and setting it on the brass holder.

Preeya did the same and Aiden followed suit, confused yet again. "Is Mohan not joining us?"

Alex didn't look at him as she placed her napkin in her lap and replied, "He's dining in confinement today."

If she'd taken him food, she was far more lenient than his parents had been. The belief in the Terrell household was that if you'd behaved badly enough to warrant being banished to your room, you'd also behaved badly enough to miss a meal. In his experience, the second part of it made the first part hellish enough to bring about—and rather quickly—the required change in attitude. Aiden knew, however, that sharing that perspective with her wouldn't go toward garnering her trust.

"I gather," he said, hoping to be blandly conversational, "that his time of personal reflection wasn't all that productive."

Her smile was taut. "Today is shaping up as one of his more beastly ones."

And the odds were that the boy was just beginning to cut his teeth where defiance was concerned. Ten-year-olds were like that. Deciding that she probably didn't want to hear that bit of reality, either, he considered his food and the direction he ought to take the conversation. The fare was some kind of steamed fish with a rice side dish that looked to have bits of fruit in it along with a heaping portion of a spice that not only made it a bright yellow but perfectly suited for clearing any stuffiness his nose might have been suffering. He picked up his fork and flaked off a bit of the fish, asking, "How does Mohan usually spend his days? In formal studies?"

"Generally the mornings are spent with the books and slate boards," Alex answered. "The afternoons are typically devoted to the conduct of Blue Elephant business. The evenings to reading and various board games."

God, he felt sorry for the child. If there wasn't anything more than that, the boy was utterly and completely bored out of his . . . That was it! he realized. The way to take control of this entire mess. Alex would be grateful and out of that would come trust. And trust was the key. He didn't have to grit his teeth and endure Mohan. He simply had to take control of the boy's existence. It was a brilliant plan. Absolutely brilliant.

Barrett was right; when he put his mind to something . . . Lord, it was going to be so incredibly easy.

Chapter 6

Alex's stomach turned to lead even as her heart swelled and flip-flopped in her chest. Good God, the man had a smile that could tatter pantaloons at fifty paces. And those green eyes when they sparkled with devilment . . . If she didn't steel her resolve, she was going be lunch instead of the fish.

"Well, no wonder the boy's beastly," he said with a flourish of his fork. "I would be, too. In fact, if you made me live like that I'd either run away or slit my wrists."

He didn't give her a chance to say that she considered the assertion overdramatic. "He's bored out of his skull, Miss Radford. Books, business, and board games? Little boys have to run and play. They have to go and do. They have far too much energy to be contained inside four walls every hour of the day."

"Mohan's hardly a prisoner," she protested, aware of Preeya's quick glancing between the two of them. "We frequently venture out into the city."

"To do what?"

"We attend auctions," she supplied. "We watch the ships come into port and the lords and ladies parade along their avenues. We go to the market daily. From time to time we attend a play."

"Be still my heart," he countered dryly. "I can scarcely bear the excitement of it all."

No, it wasn't exciting, but it wasn't meant to be. It was safe and largely designed to fulfill the tasks required for daily living. "And what would you have him doing with his time instead?" she asked, not really sure she wanted to know, but unwilling to back away from his open challenge.

"Has anyone taught the boy to ride a horse?"

Of all the silly notions. "We don't have a horse, Mr. Terrell."

"Does he know how to play cricket?"

"With whom would he play?" she asked. "And where? In the street, between the passing carriages?"

"What about football? Or rugby?" he persisted.

"Good God, no," she exclaimed, appalled at the very notion of Mohan being involved in such violent, dangerous sports.

He took a couple of bites of his food, but what hopes she had of the interrogation being over were dashed when he asked, "What about sledding and ice skating? They're not terribly manly pastimes, but they're something children usually find amusing. Especially in the dead of winter when there isn't much else to do."

"Mohan isn't interested in sports of any kind," she announced with all the firm politeness she could muster. "It's pointless to inquire after any others."

"Does he have any pets? A dog? A cat? Maybe a lizard or a snake or two?"

Slithering things? As pets? Alex suppressed a shudder. "He's expressed no interest in having one. Or two. Of anything."

Again he paused to eat. This time she knew better than to hope. The man didn't relent, he simply shifted directions ever so slightly. She consumed some of her own lunch, waiting for the inevitable resumption of their contest.

Preeya continued to look back and forth between them,

slowly eating, but saying nothing. In the aftermath, the first time the two of them were alone, Preeya would want a summary of all that had been said. She'd also remember specific words and ask what they meant. Not that she'd ever do anything with them. Which, in this particular situation, was most definitely a blessing. Preeya's refusal to learn English meant that she didn't know just how inept her mistress was at fending off persistent men.

"He doesn't know how to hunt, to fish, or to sail either, does he?"

Well, he was indeed predictable. "Mr. Terrell," she said on a sigh, "Mohan is going to be a raja someday. He doesn't need to know how to do those things."

"He'll be the most boring—and bored!—man to ever occupy a throne," he countered, his tone that of a man of clear and unshakable convictions. "More importantly, at the moment he's an exceedingly bored little boy. He behaves badly simply because it's something to do that affords some degree of excitement. God knows there's nothing else that qualifies in his existence. Why has he been so boxed up? Is it that you can't afford to hire a riding or a sailing instructor?"

What was it about the men who came through her life? Were all men determined to be overbearing? Or was there something about her in particular that attracted such men? "We have considerable financial resources, Mr. Terrell," she answered, squarely meeting his gaze across the length of the table.

"It's a matter of Mohan's safety. Lal—the guard who recently returned to India—maintained that Mohan would be considerably easier to kidnap or harm if he were out and about in the city, that he was far safer when within the walls of this house. I happen to think that he's correct."

"Well, if I were bent on kidnapping him," he quipped, "I'd certainly appreciate knowing where I could always find him."

"And there is the matter of protecting him from accidental injury," Alex went on, committed to making him see the wisdom in the pattern of their lives. "He could be thrown from a horse and break his neck. He could fall out of a sailboat and drown. We will not even venture into a discussion of the types of injuries commonly suffered by the reckless, self-destructive fools who play football or rugby. I promised his father that I would keep him safe from *all* harm."

"Then you'd best tell Preeya to put out the cooking fires," he instantly countered, his smile wide and altogether too confident, "because every time she lights one the kitchen stands a chance of going up in flames that could very well spread to the house and kill the boy."

Preeya, in hearing her name, looked back and forth between them in obvious distress. Alex hastily assured her that the argument had nothing to do with her and then turned her full attention back to Aiden Terrell. "You're being ridiculous," she accused. "Absolutely ridiculous."

And, just as she expected, he was ready with a rejoinder. "No more so than you are, Miss Radford. Life is risk. You can't avoid it. Simply opening your eyes and climbing out of bed every morning is fraught with peril. You could slip on the rug, fall, and bash your brains on the bedstead."

"Did you not notice the bed in your room?"

"Don't split hairs," he countered, cocking a brow. "You're an extremely intelligent woman and you know full good and well the point I'm trying to make. You can't—and most importantly, *shouldn't*—treat Mohan as if he's some fragile piece of porcelain. He needs to be treated as a normal child and allowed to take reasonable chances. If you do, his general attitude will be much improved and you won't be nearly as frustrated with him."

"I'm not frustrated," she lied, putting down her fork, afraid that he'd notice that her hand was trembling.

"The hell you aren't."

She blinked at him, not so much shocked by his language, but more for the fact that he so clearly understood how she felt deep down inside. She'd tried very hard to keep it locked away, hidden from the casual observer. That she'd failed was more than disturbing, it was frightening. Alex swallowed and forced herself to take a breath. With what she hoped passed for a serene smile, she shrugged and said, "We'll simply have to agree to disagree on that point. And on the matter of Mohan's daily activities."

All right, Aiden thought, *so it's not easy.* He'd underestimated her sense of independence. And her mother-hen tendencies. But if she thought he was going to give up the voyage because he'd encountered a little patch of rough sea, then she was underestimating his tenacity. As well as his abhorrence of boredom. He and Mohan had common ground in that.

It might well turn out to be the longest damn day of his life, but he was going to keep pushing until she didn't have the wherewithal to fight him another step, until he'd so worn her down she'd have to trust him if for no other reason than to get her exhausted, curvaceous little body home.

"Tell me, Miss Radford . . . Do *you* know how to ride?"

She sighed and closed her eyes for a second before she said, "No, I don't."

"Hunt, sail, or fish?"

She looked as if she wanted to pick up her fork and throw it at him. "Of course not. Nor do I sled or skate. And I wouldn't play cricket, football, or rugby even if you held a gun to my head."

"Would you care to learn?" Her eyes widened and he couldn't keep from chuckling. "Not the rougher sports. Those are strictly for men. I was thinking of the others. We could start with riding. Teaching two doesn't require much more effort than teaching one."

"You've presumed that I've given my consent for Mohan to engage in these activities. I thought I made it clear when—"

"I haven't presumed anything of the sort," he interrupted, smiling at her. "And you did make your position clear. Now let me make mine just as understood. I don't care whether you give your consent or not. I've made a decision and it's going to stand."

She stared at him, her eyes wide again and her lips slightly, invitingly parted.

"Yes, Miss Radford," he assured her, placing his napkin on the table beside his plate. "This is indeed one of those occasions I mentioned in the carriage earlier today. I decide. You and Mohan acquiesce without protest. There is no discussion."

"You are positively . . . dictatorial," she sputtered.

He shrugged and nodded. "I was born to command. I happen to do it well and you happen to be in no position to defy me." Rising from his seat, he added, "I'd like to finish our tour of the house as you promised. Whenever you're ready, of course. I'll wait for you in the hall."

He didn't give her a chance to object. Turning to Preeya, he bowed, and said, "Preeya, thank you for the meal. I have absolutely no idea what it was, but it was delicious."

Still smiling, he left the dining room thinking that, all in all, the exchange had turned out precisely as he'd envisioned. So far, anyway. There was always the possibility that Alexandra Radford would follow him out for the sole purpose of summarily dismissing him.

Alex glared at her half-eaten lunch, wondering what he'd do if she refused to get up and trot obediently after him. Preeya leaned forward to place a hand on her arm and say in Hindi, "It is never a good thing to argue with a man, dear. They do not like to think of women as being as strong as they are."

"Women are every bit as capable as men in every respect," Alex maintained angrily.

"Agreed." The older woman patted her hand. "But that does not mean men like to know it. And there is much to be gained in keeping them contented and blissfully ignorant of that fact."

"Such as?"

"Aside from a quieter house and smoother digestion, it makes them much more attentive lovers."

For heaven's sake, she'd met the man only a few hours ago! Yes, he was handsome and incredibly well built. Yes, he was well spoken and for the most part gentlemanly. But those were hardly the basic criteria for establishing an intimate relationship. "As I said the last time you spoke of this," Alex replied, trying to be kind about her dismissal of the notion, "I have no intention of making him a lover. He simply doesn't interest me in that way."

Again Preeya patted her hand. This time a quiet chuckle accompanied the gesture. "My dear, you are the worst liar in the world. You really must stop trying. You're embarrassing yourself."

It wasn't the first time she'd had that fact pointed out. Rather than continue an obviously failed protest, she changed the avenue of approach. "He's far too full of his own viewpoints to be even marginally tolerable."

Preeya considered her for a moment, a smile tickling the corners of her mouth and her dark eyes shining. "I've been listening to the sounds and watching your faces. It feels and looks very much like a lovers' quarrel."

"Well, it's not."

"What is it that you are arguing about so passionately?"

They were, thankfully, to the summary part of the exchange. Alex sighed in relief. "How to properly parent Mohan. He contends that the days should be filled with riding, hunting, fishing, sailing, and all manner of wild, uncontrolled sports."

"Ah," Preeya said, leaning back in her chair and nodding.

"Your gentleman wants Mohan to be a boy. You want him to be a prince."

"He *is* a prince," Alex righteously countered.

Preeya laced her fingers and stared at the dining room wall. Quietly, her gaze still focused in the near distance, she said, "Mohan is both a boy *and* a prince. You are both right. Perhaps you might seek a way by which Mohan can benefit from the wisdom and vision you both possess."

As always, Preeya was right. Alex barely kept herself from sagging as her anger evaporated in a single instant. In its absence, she felt nothing but overwhelmed and beleaguered. The threat of tears tightening her throat, she struggled for control of her wildly careening emotions. "He's not *my* gentleman," she asserted, clinging to the only real certainty she could see.

"He very much wants to be," Preeya replied softly. "For what other reason would he make the effort to assist you in the guidance of Mohan? Nothing requires that effort of him. He is offering it out of his desire to be meaningful to you."

She didn't want him to be meaningful. She didn't want his help with anything beyond guarding Mohan. She didn't want to need him for more. Needing people made you weak and vulnerable; it obligated you to them. And she had enough obligations already.

"While you ponder that truth," Preeya went on, "you should also consider another, Alex, my dear. He knows that you're only pretending to find him unattractive. His are the eyes that can see through a thousand veils. Perhaps you should ask yourself if it might be pointless and foolish to continue to wear them."

Pointless, no doubt. But foolish? It would be even more foolish to let them fall, to consciously allow Aiden Terrell to look fully into her soul. Better that he only suspect that she lacked any moral depth than to blatantly display the unflattering truth for him.

"Alex, dear?"

She recognized the tone. Part of her relaxed in the knowledge that the personal inquisition was over. Another part braced, wondering which word Preeya had picked this time.

"What does 'manly' mean?"

Yes, it would be that one. Preeya had an uncanny ability to pick the most sensitive words out of any English conversation. "It means virile," she explained matter-of-factly. "Masculine. Very much a man."

"Like your gentleman."

"Yes, but he's not *mine*," she corrected weakly.

Preeya arched a brow and smiled broadly as she rose to her feet. Gathering up the plates, she said, "He is standing in the hall. It is not wise to make men wait too long for you. But for just long enough that they do not take your appearance for granted."

Alex had the distinct and uncomfortable feeling that Preeya's last bit of wisdom was intended to apply to more than just her promise to show Aiden Terrell the upstairs rooms. But she was too battered to think clearly and so she set aside any immediate consideration of it, placed her napkin beside her plate, and rose from the table. Thanking Preeya for the meal, she left the dining room to fulfill her duty and a promise she wished she hadn't made.

Aiden had no idea what the two women had talked about, but the effect on Alex was obvious. He'd seen sailors adrift on a raft who had more spark in them. She wasn't going to send him packing, that was certain. She didn't have the energy for it. This wasn't quite the surrender he had in mind, though.

"As a point of information," he said, hoping to bring a bit of her starch back to the surface, "I enjoy a good game of rugby."

She rewarded him with a delicate snort and a roll of her eyes as she walked past him. "That doesn't surprise me in the least," she quipped over her shoulder as she halted in the doorway just down the hall. "This is the salon, sitting room, parlor, whatever you choose to call it. It serves for our communal gathering."

She disappeared inside and Aiden followed her into a most curiously appointed room. Unlike the dining room, this room wasn't purely English. A camel-backed settee, a wing chair—the mate to the one downstairs, he realized—and a few carved wooden pieces paid tribute to traditional English tastes, but that was the sum total of it. The rest of it looked a great deal like his quarters.

Thick, fringed, intricately patterned carpets covered the floors. There was a chaise of sorts, draped with what looked like paisley shawls. And there were pillows. Lots of pillows. Large and small and in between. Plaids, stripes, solids, damasks. In all kinds of colors. Fringed and tasseled, embroidered and plain. What he supposed were lamps were nothing more than brass cylinders punched full of holes. A short English chest of drawers sat against the far wall to the right of the crackling fireplace. In the center of the top was a statue of a woman with what looked like four painfully bent arms. Little pots of sticks sat around her.

"It looks very comfortable," he offered cautiously, not wanting to offend. "An interesting combination of English and Indian styles."

Nodding, she bent to retrieve a pillow from the carpet. "With the Indian part of it being ever so much more inviting and comfortable," she said, tossing it casually toward the chaise.

Since she'd opened the conversational door and he was curious as to how she thought, he ventured, "You sound as though you've been a bit let down by your countrymen."

Going about tidying the room, she answered, "It's difficult to maintain that British ways are superior when your back is aching from sitting on an unforgivingly stiff English settee."

"Then why not admit the obvious truth and throw yourself into the pillows?"

"I'm employed because I'm British," she answered, peering inside one of the brass tubes. She extracted a squat candle stub as she went on. "And because I'm British, my ways are considered to be worth knowing and emulating. If I suggested that Indian ways might be better than mine there'd be no point in keeping me about."

Watching her put the candle remnant in a basket beside the chest, he took a chance. "So you live a lie?"

Shrugging, she got a new candle—a tall, fat, brown one—from the chest under the statue. "I've never claimed it to be an ideal existence," she answered, carefully placing it into the cylinder. She looked up and met his gaze, adding, "It is, however, a reasonably secure one."

"As long as you can keep up the pretense."

"It helps if one doesn't dwell on the incongruities."

"What is, is," he guessed, remembering what she'd told him earlier about Mohan's beliefs.

"You learn quickly, Mr. Terrell," she offered as she glided past him. "I'm most impressed." She stopped in the center of the hall and turned back, nonchalantly but effectively blocking his exit from the parlor. "My room, of course, is down there," she said, gesturing to the hall on her left. She lifted her right hand toward the other end of the hall and Aiden saw her intention.

"I'd like to see it, please."

Her arm falling slowly to her side, she looked at him for a long moment, clearly weighing a decision. "My private quarters are none of your concern."

There was no fire in her assertion, just a quiet wariness that he found utterly intriguing. "I beg to differ," Aiden countered gently but firmly. "There are three rooms on this side of the hall. I've seen one of them, mine. It's on the end and has five windows and two doors. One door comes in from the hall, the other opens into Mohan's room. Two of the windows overlook the rear of the house, three overlook the city to the east. If I wanted to gain illegal access to this house, all I'd have to do is climb any one of several trees on the east side, lean out on a limb, break the window glass and crawl inside."

She continued to study him, one delicate brow arched and her wariness apparently unaffected by his explanation. Undaunted, he pressed on.

"Your room, Miss Radford, is undoubtedly—British architecture being the predictable creature that it is—configured exactly as my own. I need to see what lies outside your windows that can aid someone bent on getting to Mohan. And yes," he added before she could suggest it, "I could very well go out and stand at the side and rear of the house to make that survey. However, I'm here and it's a simple matter of opening the door and letting me in to look from the perfect vantage point."

"I assure you that my windows are perfectly secure."

Still no fire; still wary. He held his ground. "I want to see that for myself. Please."

She caught the inside of her lip with her teeth and he knew that in the end she would relent. He waited, willing to be patient for the sake of earning her trust. God, she was beautiful standing there, loose ringlets of dark hair framing her face and looking a little confused, a little wary, and so very determined to keep him from knowing that. So young, so vulnerable. So at odds with the duchess she pretended to be.

Without saying a word, she turned and walked off in the direction of her room. Aiden expelled a hard breath in relief and went after her before she could change her mind.

Her hand on the doorknob, she looked up at him and said, "There will be absolutely no comments of a personal nature."

Aiden resisted the urge to laugh, drew a quick *X* over his heart, and held up his hand, palm out.

And regretted the casually made vow the instant she flung wide the door. The windows were shuttered with panels of intricate wooden fretwork that threw a thousand delicate swirls of shadow and afternoon sunlight over the contents of the room. Which were, with the exception of the four-poster bed and a rattan sofa, most decidedly non-English. The coverlet was a deep, deep gold. Almost an amber. An intensely rich rainbow of pillows had been invitingly piled about the bed and every corner of the room, all of them plump and full, covered in rich silk fabrics of one sort or another. A thick carpet of reds and golds and greens covered almost the entire surface of the wood floor. Gleaming silver and gold pieces sat on her dressing table, a true masterpiece of hand-carved artwork.

But all of that paled beside the fact that Preeya had apparently done the washing that morning. On the bed, lying in brilliant contrast against the dark coverlet, was a white corset of sheer, sheer fabric and trimmed with lace and ribbons in all the right places. A saffron-colored nightgown of impossibly transparent fabric had been draped over the foot of the bed. Between it and the corset was a pair of equally seductive pantaloons.

Clearly none of it was made of English fabric. And it was equally obvious that the garments didn't reflect so much as a hint of typical English reservation. Alexandra Radford had excellent taste. As well as what appeared to be an excellent understanding of what men considered irresistibly erotic. Who would have guessed? Hc certainty hadn't. But, as unexpected discoveries went, it was definitely the best one he'd made in a long, long time.

And it was probably wise to keep that pleasure to himself. With monumental effort, he reined in his appreciative grin and moved toward the windows. Flipping open the latch, he pulled the fretwork aside and gazed out over an unobstructed western view of the city. No trees. No nearby buildings, just the street below and the houses on the other side. No one was going to gain easy egress to this room unless Alex Radford opened one of the doors and invited them in.

Which she wasn't at all likely to do, he reminded himself as he rehooked the latch. All those delicious wrappings going to waste, hidden away and unseen. Untouched by male hands. Damn. There was a true, heartbreaking tragedy if ever there was one. He needed to do something about rectifying that.

"Have you seen enough?" she asked as he moved back to the door.

God no, he silently answered, fighting his smile again and bringing his gaze up to meet hers. His amusement ebbed away and his steps slowed until he stood in front of her. So many emotions in her eyes. Uneasiness and courage, hurt and hunger. He wanted to reach out and gather her into his arms, to pull her close and rub his cheek against her dark curls. Just to hold her; that's all he wanted. It wasn't much to ask, much to give or to take. But it was too soon.

And yet . . . She knew. It was there in the quick rise and fall of her breasts, in the way her lips were parted as she struggled to breathe. He could see it in her eyes, too. Temptation, curiosity, a flicker of trepidation, of uncertainty.

A kiss would be all it took. He could banish the doubts in seconds, make her forget she had them. Until he let her go. And then she'd remember and distrust him all the more for his having so callously pushed her fears aside. No, when the apprehension was gone, when she searched his face without asking silent questions . . . Only then. Only when she was absolutely sure.

And it was only right that he give her fair warning of his intentions. He cleared his throat softly and moistened his suddenly too dry lips. "Enough," he said quietly, firmly. "For now."

Chapter 7

Alex forced herself to swallow, but breathing . . . The look in his eyes made it impossible. If she moved, if she tried to speak, he would lean down and kiss her. Gently, deliciously, and thoroughly. There would be no resisting him. She knew that to her marrow. In the center of her soul a quiet hope whispered of risk and sweet reward.

"Mohan's room," he said softly, still watching her face. He quietly cleared his throat again before adding, "If you please."

He'd offered a reprieve. All she had to do was turn her head, look away, and the spell would be broken. All she had to do was reach for him and he would take her in his arms. He dragged breath into his lungs, took a full step back, and mercifully kept her from making a fool of herself.

Turning away, filled with a curious mixture of relief and disappointment, Alex moved with weak knees to Mohan's door. As before, he didn't respond to her knock and she opened the door without asking again.

And, as before, he sat cross-legged on his pallet, his arms folded over his chest and his chin raised defiantly. This time, however, the floor between his bed and the doorway was strewn with what had been his lunch.

She gasped in shock. From behind her came Aiden Terrell's

low growl. "Mohan!" she began, furious. "You will clean up this mess immediately."

He raised his chin another notch. "Preeya can do it."

"She's perfectly capable of doing so," Alex snapped, "but she won't. She has enough work to do without following behind you with a broom and pan. You alone created this disaster and you alone will rectify it. Now."

Mohan glared at her in silent defiance. Alex mentally ticked through the punishments she could impose as leverage. Continued confinement, she decided. With no more meals. Not until it was cleaned up. "Very well," she began. "Then I have—"

"We're going out," Aiden Terrell said coolly, firmly from over her shoulder. "You have five minutes to make yourself publicly presentable, young man. Don't waste it."

Alex looked back at him, stunned that he would presume to override her attempts to discipline the boy. "Mr. Terrell—"

"It'll wait for a bit," he declared, his brow cocked, the light in his eyes resolute. "Preeya's room, if you would, please."

Now wasn't the time and in front of Mohan most certainly wasn't the proper place to challenge his usurpation of power. Alex wordlessly promised him a contest at a later point and went to open Preeya's door.

He stood in the doorway and looked around, nodding.

"Will you also want to see the attic?" she asked, hoping he did. The attic would be the perfect place for them to set matters straight.

"Does it have windows?"

"Six dormers," she supplied. "Three on each side, front and back. And a small round window in each end. I don't recall the views from each. That you'll have to ascertain for yourself."

His brow inched slowly higher as he considered her. A tiny smile curved the corners of his mouth as he said, "For now, the description will suffice. In what sort of condition is your carriage house?"

She blinked, confused by his sudden change of direction. "I beg your pardon?"

"Your carriage house," he repeated patiently. "The stone building out back, the one not the kitchen. It has the wide Dutch front door."

"I'm well aware of which building it is," she countered. "Why are you asking of it? There's nothing in it and I can see absolutely no reason to be concerned about its general security."

"We'll take a look at it before we go," he declared as he moved past her and back toward Mohan's room.

"You haven't answered my question, Mr. Terrell."

He didn't look back at her, but grabbed the doorjambs in his hands and said, "Time's up. Let's go, Mohan." After a slight pause he added darkly, "If you don't get your rear end up off that bed and out this door in the next two seconds, I'm going to turn you over my knee and you won't be able to sit on your royal fanny for a month."

Alex was about to step forward and intervene when he released his grip on the jambs and said, "Bring your coat. You'll need it."

Mohan had surrendered. Alex exhaled the breath she'd been holding as her ward stepped into the hall, roughly yanking his coat into place and demanding, "Where are you dragging me?"

"On an adventure," Aiden Terrell replied, pointing to the stairway. "I'll meet you at the base in just a moment. Go."

Mohan stomped off, his hands balled into fists at his sides. They were both watching him when the man beside her quietly asked, "Your bank account . . . Is it in your name or Mohan's?"

Her mind raced through the possibilities and the ramifications. Knowing the truth gave him no power. It took her signature to spend any of what they had. "We each have one," she supplied. "I put the money from the silver trading in mine. The monies from the Blue Elephant go into Mohan's. I'm its legal custodian."

"Perfect." He moved toward the stairs, saying, "We'll be in the carriage house when you're finished buttoning coats, finding reticules, pulling on gloves and pinning hats. Try not to take forever. We have a lot to do this afternoon." He was halfway down when he added, "And don't forget to bring Mohan's letter of credit."

Alex stood there, considering the space his shoulders had filled only seconds before. It was just after two o'clock . . . It had been just before ten when she'd walked into Barrett Stanbridge's office. Just over four hours ago she'd had complete authority over this house and all the people in it. Now . . .

How could one man so thoroughly, effortlessly seize control in so short a time? He barked and Mohan obeyed. He made requests and she acceded. Grudgingly, yes, but acceded nonetheless. He issued pronouncements and she accepted them. What protests she mustered, he dismissed and moved around as if she hadn't bothered. And as if all that wasn't bad enough, he looked as though he might want to kiss her and she wasn't the least bit insulted, much less repulsed.

It was as if he'd walked in the door and she'd taken immediate leave of her senses. How could he do that? What was wrong with her? At court she was renowned for her refusal to be submissive to any man. She'd sent officers of Her Majesty's Army running for cover. Even the raja walked softly around her, for God's sake! But not Aiden Terrell. Oh, no, he just plowed his way in and through and over and didn't give her resistance so much as a passing note.

What was it he'd said? That he was born to command? That he did it well? He certainly hadn't been lying or even stretching the truth. He'd also said that he could go toe to toe with anyone and that she'd met her match when it came to being willful. That also appeared to be true. He really was a most infuriating man. It didn't help that he was also devilishly handsome and thoroughly charming when he wanted to be. That just-out-of-bed tousled hair of his, that dimple when he grinned . . . Those incredibly green eyes. How wondrously the light danced in them when he laughed.

Alex mentally shook herself to dispel the debilitating images. If she had any self-respect left at all, she'd walk back into the salon, sit down, and pick up a book. She'd refuse to find her coat and trot dutifully and obediently down to the carriage house. And if she did that, he wouldn't bother to come looking for her. No, he'd simply look back at the house, shrug, and then take Mohan off to God only knew where to do God only knew what.

He'd managed to very effectively strip away her choices. With an exasperated stamp of her foot, Alex gritted her teeth and went to get her things.

Aiden pulled open the latches, swung open both sections of the carriage house door, and then paused, watching Mohan peer into the shadowed interior.

"It is a dirty place."

And the boy was trying hard not to be fascinated by it. Grinning, Aiden walked past him, saying, "It's actually in very good condition. A bit of sweeping up and an airing out would do wonders." He motioned off to his left. "If you'll open the windows on that side, I'll get those on the other." Holding his thumb and forefinger about three inches apart, he added, "Roughly this wide."

"What is this place used for?"

Aiden lifted the window sash, his smile broadening as he heard Mohan doing the same on the other side. "It's a carriage house and stable."

"We do not have a carriage. And, as you can see, there are no horses, either. Why is it that we are opening the windows of an empty building?"

Because, Aiden silently answered, *I have a plan.* "Well, if you were a horse," he posed, "would you want to go to a new home that was stuffy and stale?"

"We are acquiring horses?"

Ah, the sound of too studied disinterest. Aiden moved to the next stall, the next window, the next step of his course. "Five of them. Three for riding and two for the carriage."

"Are we acquiring a carriage, too?"

Moving on down the line of stalls, Aiden didn't look at the boy as he answered, "It would be rather pointless to have carriage horses and no carriage, wouldn't it?"

"Will it be an open one so that we can be admired when we drive about town?"

A little less restraint than before. Aiden chuckled, remembering how easy he'd been at that age. "If that's what you want. But do bear in mind that, if that's what you choose, it's going to be a cold ride for the next few months."

"I am to be allowed to choose the carriage?"

And the restraint was gone, evaporated in the gleaming allure of whirring wheels and adult power. "With a bit of guidance," Aiden qualified.

"Miss Alex knows nothing of carriages," Mohan offered, a decidedly wary note shading the observation.

Aiden opened the last window on his side. "Then it's a good thing that I do, isn't it?"

"Does Miss Alex know this is what we are about?"

And it was done. They were now fellow conspirators, united against the practicality and feminine fears of Alex Radford, Duchess and Mother Hen. He'd have to make sure it didn't go too far, of course; he was the adult in this. But it was time for the boy to let loose of the apron strings and, one way or another, Alex needed to let him go. Aiden came out of the stall and leaned his shoulder against the upper rail. "She has some idea. In a general sense."

"Does she approve?" Mohan asked, climbing up to sit on the railing on his side of the stable.

Aiden shrugged and smiled. "She'll eventually come around to seeing things my way."

Mohan looked as if he wanted to be optimistic. "Miss Alex can be somewhat stubborn, you know."

Somewhat? "I've noticed that."

"My father says that until she learns to be less stubborn she will not make a good wife."

"Then it's probably best that she hasn't married," Aiden offered diplomatically.

"My father says that she would make a most acceptable mistress, though."

Aiden chuckled. "I just can't imagine her being interested in such an arrangement, can you?"

"My father is a raja," the boy countered in all seriousness. "People must obey his commands. Even Miss Alex. Even if she does not agree with him."

Mohan thought the raja could command Alex Radford to be his mistress? Obviously the boy had no realistic idea of how those sorts of relationships worked. A scrap of conversation fluttered from his memory and he smiled. "So tell me, has he ever commanded her to bow to him?"

Mohan beamed. "He did Mrs. Radford, Miss Alex's mother. She explained the British customs and my father, being a wise and honorable man, decreed a solution. Miss Alex continues with the decision and lowers her chin to acknowledge my father's presence and authority."

"How very accommodating of her," Aiden replied dryly, thinking that the raja, to his credit, had emerged from the battle with as much of his dignity as any man could have hoped to salvage.

"There are some in the court who think Miss Alex is disrespectful and resent her presence."

Aiden's amusement ebbed away. Mohan had offered the words blithely, but the look in his eyes was wary and assessing. "Then I'll bet they were happy to see her shipped to England for a while," he offered, testing the waters into which Mohan seemed to be drawing them.

"They will oppose her return. Strongly."

"If you're trying to tell me something, Mohan, just come right out and say it."

It took him a moment to choose his words. "Miss Alex fears that my father's enemies will come here to harm me. I think my father's friends will also come to London and that they will kill Miss Alex."

His stomach slowly knotting, Aiden turned the information over in his mind. "Does she know about these people? Does she suspect that their opposition is that strong?"

"If you have noticed that she is stubborn," Mohan countered, hopping down off the railing, "you have also no doubt noticed that she is very intelligent and observant."

That she was. And so, surprisingly, was Mohan. And in ways far beyond his years. "Do you think anyone's here already?" Aiden asked, willing to trust the boy's assessment.

"My father's enemies, perhaps yes. My father's friends, not yet."

"They'll come when you're summoned back to India," Aiden mused aloud. "Until then, their larger interests are served in keeping her around."

Mohan slowly smiled. "You are a very intelligent man, Mr. Terrell," he said, the buoyancy back in his voice. "I believe that I may be persuaded to think that it was wise of Miss Alex to hire you."

"Persuaded?"

"I would like a white stallion to ride about London."

Aiden chuckled. "What you'd like and what you'll actually get are two very different things."

Mohan studied him for a moment and then shrugged his shoulders. "One should at least try."

"True. Nothing ventured, nothing gained. Let's see if we

can find some brooms and clean this place up a bit while we wait for Miss Radford to join us."

He half expected Mohan to say that cleaning the stable was Preeya's work, and when he didn't and headed to the tack room instead, Aiden counted it as a sign of sure success. He let the boy go to explore on his own, knowing that Mohan would appreciate and do well with the freedom. Still leaning against the stall railing, he stared down at his dusty boots. How long would it be before the raja called his son and the royal tutor back to India? A week? A month? A year? Would the assassins arrive after the missive or would Alex be dead before she could receive it?

Next week would be on his watch; he could protect her. Maybe he'd still be here even a month from now. But if the summons was issued after Lal's replacement arrived . . . He'd just have to make sure, before he left, that the new guard understood that Alex needed to be protected every bit as much as Mohan did. Yes, that's what he'd do. It would be enough and he could go away without his conscience bothering him. But why the hell hadn't she said something to him?

It was the most disconcerting ride she'd ever taken. Aiden Terrell sat opposite her either staring out the window or appraising her as if she were some sort of rare and exotic bug. She'd thought several times to politely inquire as to what was concerning him, but hadn't been able to find so much as a pause in the steady stream of commentary that had been pouring out of Mohan since the moment the rented carriage had started to roll.

Lord only knew what had transpired in the stable before she arrived there, but clearly something rather momentous had. Mohan was more excited and happier than she'd ever seen him; leading her to think that whatever had happened was generally good. On the other hand, Aiden Terrell was quiet and decidedly pensive. She didn't know what to think of his behavior. It was so different from any she'd seen from him so far. Although, she admitted, as the carriage turned and slowed, there was a certain deliberate quality to his silence that seemed to be typical of him. As far as she could tell, nothing Aiden Terrell did was less than wholehearted.

The carriage eased to a stop and Mohan bolted for the door, throwing it open and bounding out before she could catch him.

"Mohan!" she called after him. "Slow down and be careful!"

Aiden stepped out and turned back, offering his hand. Alex took it and allowed him to help her to the ground, her gaze arrowing past him and her stomach filling with dread. They had arrived at a snowy field filled with rows and rows of carriages of every sort. And Mohan was running headlong into their midst. The ground was so slippery underfoot. He was going to lose his footing in the snow, fall, and crack open his head.

"Let him run and climb," Aiden said softly, releasing her hand to offer his arm instead. "He isn't going to hurt anything."

"Other than himself," she protested as she accepted his assistance and her ward disappeared into the maze of wheels and big black boxes.

"Boys not only bounce, they heal quickly. Besides, the only way he'll ever know his limits is to push them." He looked over his shoulder as he led her off toward the carriages. "Please wait for us, driver."

"And if he hurts himself in the process?" Alex pressed, trying and failing to catch a glimpse of Mohan.

"Then he'll have something interesting to talk about with other boys. Never underestimate the social value of a good scar. The grislier, the better."

"Men are very strange creatures, Mr. Terrell."

He chuckled and the arm under her hand relaxed a bit. "Do you have a preference for a carriage style? Mohan wants an open one so he can be admired as he careens through town."

Careen? God help London if Mohan was ever truly given the reins. "I think a closed one would be much more practical from a number of standpoints."

"What?" he teased. "You don't want to be admired as you ride about London?"

"In the first place," she countered, glad that his pensive mood had lifted, "only the most outrageous of the ladies are noticed or admired by anyone. I'm a shopkeeper and not worth anyone's attention. And in the second place, the fewer people who notice Mohan, the better."

"Well, we could put a sack over his head and be done with it."

"You're being ridiculous again."

"That would require a lead rope around his waist, though," he continued, undaunted by her censure. "Otherwise, he's going to charge headlong into something and damage it. And of course, sacked, he'd never be able to ride a horse or drive a carriage. Not that that would make *you* unhappy."

"Mr. Terrell," she began. "I know that you think I'm—"

"What is it going to take to get you to call me Aiden?"

"A great deal more familiarity than is prudent."

He drew her to a stop and turned to squarely face her. He cocked a brow and smiled, dimpling his cheek. "Prudence is highly overrated, *Alex*."

"I haven't given you permis—"

"I know. I haven't asked for it either, have I?"

The presumptuous man! "Must you always inter—"

"Yes. I've discovered it's the quickest and easiest way to end the resistance." His eyes twinkled. "Which is utterly futile, you know. You may as well give up the effort and enjoy the fact that someone else is taking the lead for a change. If it helps any, pretend that you're dancing."

"I don't dance," she declared flatly, firmly.

He blinked and rocked slightly back on his heels. "Why ever not?"

"Because I don't like to be led. I tend to step on toes with great regularity."

His smile quirked higher. "You just need a bit of practice and the right partner. It's all a matter of trust and conviction."

The effort to hold her own against his relentless press was exhausting, but she was determined to try for as long as she possibly could. "I've always wondered," she countered, "why it's the man who is allowed to maneuver by conviction and the woman who is expected to follow on blind trust." *There,* she silently taunted. *Explain that, Aiden Terrell.*

He laughed quietly, boldly meeting her gaze. "Because, generally speaking, we can see over your heads. That's a distinct advantage when trying to shepherd someone through a crowd of people, you know.

"Since you don't dance," he went on, ignoring her quiet groan of frustration, "I assume Mohan hasn't been taught. We'll have to add dancing instruction to his activities. Not that he's going to be any more thrilled by the prospect than you are. Boys hate to dance. It's not until they're a bit older that they can appreciate the tactical aspects of it."

"Tactical?" she repeated. Her mother's instruction on European dances hadn't included the slightest hint that there was anything more to it than proving oneself socially and physically graceful.

"I'll show you later."

"I think not," Alex countered, remembering the power he'd had over her in the doorway of her room. To actually step into his arms would be the greatest folly of her life.

He laughed and his eyes sparkled as he gazed down at her. "Have you always been so headstrong?"

"Mr. Terrell! Miss Alex!"

They both looked toward the sound of Mohan's voice. He

was some distance down the row, his stance suggesting that he'd slid to a halt. "Over here!" he called, pointing off to his left. "It is the perfect carriage! Come see!"

Aiden Terrell offered his arm again. As Alex took it, he said, "You're not off the hook. We'll finish this conversation later."

No they wouldn't, Alex silently vowed as she walked at his side. She wasn't going to give him the slightest opportunity to push her in a direction she didn't want to go, into concessions she didn't want to make. If there was one thing she'd learned about him in the hours since he'd moved into her life, it was that to give Aiden Terrell even the tiniest of openings was tantamount to surrendering.

No, she was done trying to be amiable and accommodating. He could smile all he wanted. He could laugh and his eyes could twinkle and she wasn't going to let it affect her. He was an employee. A temporary one at that. It didn't matter how charming he could be or how pleasantly persistent.

And, most importantly, it didn't matter that simply looking at him warmed her blood and stirred her desires. She could resist. She was strong. She was of independent mind, body, and spirit. No man was ever going to own her. Especially John Aiden Terrell. He was too handsome, too confident, too sure of his ability to seduce any woman he wanted. She wasn't going to be another of his Rose Walker-Hineses. It would be entirely too embarrassing to be casually bedded and then just as casually discarded.

Thinking to steel her resolve, Alex stole a glance at him. He caught it and held it, his smile soft and somehow knowing, his brow cocked in silent amusement. Her mind said that she should be outraged by his manner. Her heart whispered that he was the most fascinating, magnificent man she'd ever met.

It took every bit of her will to look away. But there was absolutely nothing she could do about silencing the thundering, traitorous beat of her heart, nothing she could do to squelch the certainty welling up and filling her soul.

"Is it not beautiful, Miss Alex?"

She blinked, startled back to the snowy field with a breathtaking jolt. Just ahead of her, Mohan sat in the box pretending to drive what had to be the biggest, brightest, most outrageously garish carriage ever built.

"My, it's certainly . . ." She hesitated, searching desperately for something even remotely kind to say about Mohan's choice. "Red," she finished lamely.

"And with enough gilt," Aiden muttered, "to qualify as a rolling French—" He exhaled long and hard and then called up to Mohan, "I thought you said you wanted an open carriage."

Mohan beamed down at them. "People will surely be able to see me in this one. Will they not?"

"I don't know how they could possibly miss you," Alex answered, feeling slightly queasy. She turned her head and fastened her gaze on a nearby carriage—a sedate and conservative black brougham. "For God's sake," she said softly, "don't let him choose that thing. Do something. Change his mind."

"Just how desperate are you to avoid being seen in it?" he asked, suppressed laughter rippling through each and every word.

She looked up at him and into green pools sparkling with mischief. "That's blackmail," she accused, keeping her voice low.

He grinned. "And that's really ugly. How desperate?"

The certainty overfilled her soul and flooded into the center of her bones. At least he was a kind man; her dignity would be intact when he walked away. "Name the price," she said, knowing that the words were sealing her fate. "Within reason, please."

"You'll call me Aiden."

Such a seemingly benign request. But clearly recognizable as the first brick being taken from the wall he intended to fully dismantle. "Only in private. There are standards to be maintained for Mohan."

"Of course." His grin edged toward wicked. "And you'll let me teach you to dance."

On a surge of panic, she retorted, "I don't want to learn to dance."

He glanced toward Mohan's carriage and then smiled down at her. "Do you not want to dance *more* than you don't want to be seen in that?"

"You're ruthless."

"Absolutely. Is that a 'yes'?"

What would be would be. Whatever lesson there was to be taught would have to be learned. Intentions and logic and rationality were pointless exercises; destiny wasn't going to be evaded or denied. "God help me," Alex whispered, closing her eyes and putting herself in the powerful hand of fate.

It was as close to a "yes" as she was going to give him. Aiden resisted the urge to plant a grateful kiss on her cheek. Instead, he covered her hand with his. "You won't be sorry," he offered softly, sincerely. "I promise, Alex."

She managed a tremulous smile but didn't look at him. Her obvious doubts gently tugged at his heartstrings and added to his resolve. She wasn't going to regret letting him past her reserve. He'd make sure of it. In the end, Alexandra Radford was going to think he was the very best thing that had ever happened to her.

"Why don't you have a seat?" he said, leading her to a nearby carriage and depositing her on the running board. She glanced up at him and he winked and added, "And watch a master at work."

"Mohan!" he called, turning away. "Climb down from there for a minute."

"Is it not perfect, Mr. Terrell?"

Alex leaned her back against the carriage door, waiting and watching. A master? A master at what? she wondered.

"Well," Aiden drawled, "looks are only part of perfection, Mohan. If it doesn't roll right and true, it doesn't matter how pretty it is. It's always wise to inspect the structure before you make a decision. Let's walk around and take a careful look at it, shall we?"

They made a slow circuit, neither of them saying a word, both of them seemingly intent on memorizing every hideous turn, curve, and filigreed scroll.

"Oh, now this is troubling," Aiden said as they returned to their starting point. He reached out and traced a fingertip across the top of the wheel. "Look here, Mohan. See the dent in the band?"

Mohan moved closer and ran his fingertip over the wheel, too. "There must have been an object in the road."

"It could be from that," Aiden agreed, nodding. "Or it could be from something a bit more serious." He pointed to the spokes of the same wheel. "Notice how the paint's a slightly different color on some of those?"

"Yes. Does that mean something of great significance?"

"It could," Aiden replied, squatting down so that the wheel was at eye level. He trailed his fingers over the length of the spokes and shook his head. "Oh, that's not good. Not good at all. Feel along this spoke, Mohan. And this one, too."

Mohan did as instructed, knitted his brows, and then examined several others before saying, "These three are bumpy. These others are not. Why?"

"I can't say for certain, of course, but I suspect that they were broken and not mended very well."

"It must have been a very large object in the road."

Again Aiden noddcd. "Let's crawl underneath and take a look at the axles."

A master manipulator. That's what Aiden Terrell was. Smooth and flawless, he chose his path and moved others along to the destination he wanted to reach. Mohan was completely unaware that the carriage was being pulled out from beneath him inch by deliberate inch. Alex smiled, knowing that by the time Aiden finished the inspection, Mohan would abandon the notion of owning it and think that the decision was his own. And that it had been freely made.

Yes, absolutely flawless. She considered the wheel and the two of them rolling under the carriage to peer at its underside. Odds were good that Aiden had noted the dent in the wheel the instant they'd walked up to it. Which, of course, meant that he'd negotiated terms with her knowing full good and well that the carriage was unacceptable whether she surrendered or not. She'd been manipulated, too.

She should be angry about it. She certainly had every reason to be. And yet she wasn't. In fact, if anything, she admired his ability to achieve his ends without being the least bit heavy-handed. Where so many men were bullies, Aiden was charming. Where so many would have smirked and decreed, Aiden had smiled and cajoled. Yes, he was indeed a master. She'd have to remember that in the future.

"That bend is not good, is it?" Mohan asked.

"No, I'm afraid it's not. It rather strongly suggests that this carriage has been wrecked. And look along here. Do you see this crack? That's not good, either."

She watched them climb out from under the carriage to stand side by side, their arms folded across their chests, studying it in silence.

"Can it be repaired?" Mohan finally asked. "Better than it has been already?"

"Not without a great deal of expense," Aiden answered, sounding ever so regretful. "And, quite frankly, it hasn't really been repaired at all. They've done nothing more than try to hide the problems in the hope the buyer won't notice the damage until after the sale is done."

Mohan's jaw slowly sagged and he looked up at Aiden, his eyes huge. "They hoped to cheat me?"

"Not necessarily you personally," he qualified with a shrug. "Anyone who comes along and doesn't look past the red paint and the gilt will do."

"I will not be duped."

Alex grinned. Aiden was far more controlled in recognizing his victory. He nodded solemnly. "A very good attitude to have, I think. Perhaps we should look a bit further?"

"I shall go over this way," Mohan announced, moving down the row, "and report what I find."

Aiden turned to her, his smile broad and his eyes sparkling, and bowed ceremoniously.

"Very well done, Mr. Terrell," she offered, clapping in sincere appreciation of the performance. "Very well done."

"Aiden. Remember?"

"Aiden," she corrected, gaining her feet. He was instantly in front of her, presenting his arm. "You've not only spared me the embarrassment of being seen in a rolling monstrosity, but given Mohan useful knowledge in the process. If your career as an investigator doesn't go well, you might consider teaching. You're very good at it."

"Well, the truth is that I'm not an investigator. And I'm a temporary protector only because I owe Barrett a favor. A rather large one, in fact. When the debt's paid . . ." He shrugged and snorted softly. "I'll probably have to go back to sea."

"You don't sound too terribly excited about the prospect."

"It's a long story," he replied, his voice suddenly taut. His smile was still in place but the brightness of it was gone and it no longer reached his eyes. Looking over his shoulder, he said, "I think he's found something that might actually be worth a closer look. Shall we?"

Alex allowed him to guide her through the maze, sensing that he'd opened a personal door without thinking. Then, realizing what he'd done, neatly sidestepped the blunder and slammed it closed again. It was an artful dodge, but certainly not perfect. She decided it was rather nice to know that he wasn't always in control. It made him decidedly human and quite likable.

"I hope this next carriage is a bit more appropriate than the last," she ventured. "As for stories . . . I've always found that longer ones are always so much more interesting than shorter ones."

"Not in this instance."

Firm and final. He wasn't going to willingly share it with her. Alex studied him askance, noting the hard line of his jaw, the way the muscle at his temple pulsed in hard, steady rhythm.

"Miss Alex! Look over there!" Mohan called.

She found him off to their right, perched in the driver's box of an old-fashioned carriage. He was pointing off toward a copse of trees and a little cottage tucked deep into the shadows.

"At the very far edge of the field!" he added, fairly jumping up and down. "In the low growth! It is Preeya's peacocks!"

Peacocks? Alex let go of Aiden's arm and quickly stepped around him, straining to see, trying to find amid the underbrush the birds Mohan said were there. A quick movement, a flash of bright, familiar color.

"Of all the places," she whispered, her heart racing. She whirled about and grabbed Aiden Terrell by his arms. "Preeya wants a peacock in the worst sort of way. I have no idea whether she intends to keep it for a sentry or to have it for a main course one night. But she's asked me for ages to find one for her and . . . I have to have that pair of peacocks, Aiden. I don't care what it takes. I don't care what it costs. I have to have them. Today. Now."

God, she was beautiful. Such excitement, such open happiness and hope. Her eyes were bright blue with it. "Peacocks," he said, moistening his lips. Catching the birds, trussing them, and getting them into the rented hack and back to the house was going to take some time. Time he'd planned to use for finding and buying horses. But if Alex wanted peacocks and getting them for her made her happy, then he'd make what adjustments were necessary. He'd get to the horses tomorrow. It was a small thing compared to having accomplished his most important goal of the day. Alex had not only come to trust him, but she had just thrown herself and a heartfelt desire on his good nature.

It was good to know that life could still offer the pleasures of a game well played. It was even better to realize that, despite having been to hell and back, he hadn't lost his touch.

"All right, Alex," he said. "If Preeya wants peacocks, we'll get her peacocks."

Chapter 8

Ah, Alex groggily thought, rolling over and burying her face in her pillow. The unmistakable notes of outraged peacocks at dawn. It was like being back in India. Except in India, of course, one of the servants would be bringing her breakfast in bed. Here, she was going to have to get up, dress herself, and walk to the dining room if she wanted something to eat. Preeya might well be thrilled beyond words to have peacocks, but she wasn't going to let the raucous reminder of home sweep away her common sense.

Flopping onto her back, Alex sighed and stretched, then sat up, struggling to keep her eyes open. She stretched again, long and slowly, trying to draw herself from the edges of one of the deepest sleeps she could ever remember. She smiled and let her arms drop into her lap. A day with Aiden Terrell would make anyone sleep like the dead.

The man simply didn't sit idle for a single second. He and Mohan had been playing a spirited game of Parcheesi last night when she'd had to put down her needlepoint and admit that she couldn't keep her eyes open another minute. What a day it had been. Hopefully, today would be a bit less frenetic. No, she amended, pushing the coverlet down and sliding to the edge of the mattress, a *lot* less frenetic.

The knock at the door gave her pause. She arched a brow, wondering if perhaps Precya was even more grateful than she'd known. "Yes?" she called out.

The door opened and, without the slightest preamble or apology, Mohan marched in, jauntily saying, "Good morning, Miss Alex."

Right behind him came Aiden Terrell. "Good morning, Miss Radford."

Mohan, dressed in a clean, crisply pressed suit, was carrying a secretary's portable desk, the quill pen tucked behind his ear. Aiden was without his suit coat, his shirt sleeves rolled up to his elbows, and carrying a folded wooden tape. He smiled at her and winked.

"Excuse me!" she gasped, snatching up the coverlet and using it as a shield. "What are you—"

"Oh, it's no problem at all," Aiden assured her, grinning as he followed Mohan to the windows. "As long as you keep that coverlet in place."

Scrambling back into the bed and well under the covers, she asked, "What are you two doing?"

"Is it not apparent?" Mohan asked, making a notation on his paper as Aiden unfolded the tape. "We are measuring the windows."

"Why?"

"Mr. Terrell and I will take our numbers to a blacksmith this morning and commission iron covers for each and every window," he supplied, leaning forward to note the numbers as Aiden held the measure flush against the window frame.

As they continued to work in tandem, her ward went on, saying, "Mr. Terrell has designed a most attractive pattern. You will like it immensely. And when that task has been completed, we will begin our search for horses. Two for the carriage I selected and three for riding. And when that task is completed we will bring them home and then construct a more substantial pen for Preeya's peacocks. They have destroyed the one Mr. Terrell attempted to make last night."

"I'll remind you that it was dark and cold and I was under attack," Aiden retorted good-naturedly, refolding his tape as Mohan made further notes.

"How is your leg this morning?" Alex asked, struggling to contain her laughter, amusement overriding her embarrassment.

"Sore. He took out a couple of good-sized chunks."

Good-sized? Ha! He'd barely been nipped. "Perhaps you'll have scars to share with the other boys."

He was biting back a rejoinder; she could see it in the devilish twinkle in his eyes. He had to look away and gain control of his smile before he could say, "With what we have to do, I'm guessing we'll be gone all day. I'll tell Preeya before we leave so she doesn't cook for an army at lunch."

"Am I not invited to go along?" *Please, dear God, have mercy on me.*

He looked a little startled and he sounded apologetic when he answered, "Mohan said that you wouldn't want to because your crates have arrived."

"Well, then he's right," she hastened to assure him, relieved. "There's work to be done here." She started and studied the light filtering through the fretwork. "What time is it?"

"Just after nine," Mohan supplied, marching toward the door. "We have been up for hours. We have much to do today."

"I've never slept this late in my entire life," Alex whispered.

"It's hardly a sin, you know," Aiden said on his way out the door. He grinned at her over his shoulder, winked, added, "But that nightgown certainly is," and then disappeared from sight.

With a mortified squeak, Alex buried her face in her hands. Maybe, just maybe, Hope quickly suggested, he hadn't really seen anything before she'd pulled the coverlet over her. Checking the open doorway with a nervous glance, she took a deep breath and slid to the edge of the mattress again. The opposite one this time. The side nearest her dressing-table mirror.

"God," she moaned, knowing there was no point in scooping up the coverlet to see how fast she could hide herself. A single moment—a mere fraction of a moment!—would have been more than enough. Gossamer silk didn't hide a thing. And the cinnabar shading only made the curves and the peaks of her breasts all that much darker, all that much more noticeable. Her only remaining hope, tattered and slim as it was, was that her nipples hadn't been hardened then as they were now.

Flannel. She needed to make herself a nightgown of thick, heavy flannel. In black. With buttons all the way up to her chin. And then pray that he'd have a chance—just once—to see it and realize that she wasn't a complete wanton.

Aiden blew a stream of cheroot smoke into the fading daylight and considered his accomplishments. By any standard of measurement the day had been an absolute success on almost every single front. The one less-than-sterling achievement . . . He glanced toward the enclosure he'd fashioned out of poles and a huge fisherman's net. Inside were the peacocks, hale, apparently happy, and, to his irritation, very much alive. Whoever had originally thought to clip their wings should have been shot. And the sound the damn things made at first light . . . Jesus. He'd come straight up off his bed, scrambling for his revolver and thinking that Mohan was being murdered by inches in the back yard.

How Alex had managed to sleep through it was a mystery. So was the fact that the neighbors hadn't stormed the yard and, in the name of public peace and order, dispatched the obnoxious beasts. He'd sure as hell been tempted. But he hadn't.

No, he'd gotten Preeya feed grain from the stable before he'd left and then built the pen when he'd returned.

Aiden sighed, shook his head, and deliberately set it all aside, reminding himself that the positive notes in the day's ledger had considerably more weight than a pair of peacocks. Mohan was no longer a sullen, abrasive brat. In fact, he was downright pleasant company. The boy had a quick mind and a rather impressive ability to focus on not only the larger tasks but the finer, essential details within them. Aiden knew adults who couldn't claim the same abilities.

The horse trading had gone exceptionally well, too. The two black ones for the carriage had been pulling together for years. They'd stepped in the traces without so much as a hint of resistance and then brought the carriage home as if they'd already known the way. And the three horses for riding . . .

Aiden smiled and blew another stream into the evening air. Mohan, in addition to his other fine qualities, had a healthy amount of good sense, too. It had firmly and instantly crushed the desire for a white stallion as he'd stood there with the saddle in his hands and the animal pawing the ground in front of him. The Irish palfrey gelding had been his next choice, one Aiden had let stand. His own was a gelding, as well. A tall Arab bay with an incredible spirit and a beautifully smooth gait. He'd picked a bay for Alex, too. A little gelding with a gentle disposition and a willingness to do anything for a slice of apple. Aiden grinned, hoping yet again that Alex might follow the horse's lead in certain respects, and flicked ash onto the patchy snow at his feet.

Then there'd been the trip to the blacksmith's. The man had been thrilled with the size of their order and had promised to set aside all of his other work to see the commission finished in days instead of the weeks he'd expected it to take. Not, Aiden admitted, that he could see any real necessity for the window covers. If there was anyone following Mohan as Alex had said, he hadn't been able to detect them. They either were a figure of Alex's Mother Hen imagination or they were very, very good at blending into the shadows. Which would have been some trick if they were Indian. London might well be a hub of nationalities, but the non-European ones tended to be a bit more noticeable than most.

No, the odds were that no one was actively stalking Mohan at the moment. Or Alex, either, for that matter. Which was fine by him. The lack of any real threat meant that he could focus on more personal concerns. Aiden grinned. Like getting another peek at Alex in her nightgown. That had been as much an unexpected treat as it had been a truly wonderful compensation for the peacock start to the day. And the memories that had kept him inspired all day after that . . .

Chuckling, he tossed down the stub of his cheroot, ground it beneath his heel, and then headed toward the house. He stopped just inside the back door, brought up short as a stranger, a petite, well-curved female, stepped out of the silver room. She seemed vaguely familiar and he had a feeling that he should know who she was. His eyes strained to adjust to the dim light of the hall, to see her face.

"Mr. Terrell!"

He relaxed, instantly recognizing the voice. "Well, hello, Polly," he replied, his mind racing back through the past. "What brings you to the Blue Elephant?"

"Business for her ladyship."

Silver business, he guessed. "And how is Lady Tyndale doing these days? Is she well?"

Polly sighed and shook her head. "She's still living apart from his lordship. Has been for over two years now. Since the last time we saw you in London."

"I'm sorry to hear that," he offered politely. *Not at all surprised, though,* he mentally added. "Hopefully they can reconcile one day soon." *Not that there's much chance of that.*

"His lordship tends to be the kind to hold a grudge."

And all of London knew it, too. Charlotte had been playing with fire. Which made the temptation of playing with her all that much more irresistible. "Well," Aiden drawled, "that's not a sign of good character, is it?"

She smiled and then arched a brow to ask hopefully, "Shall I give her ladyship your regards?"

Not as long as he had the slimmest of hopes of making his relationship with Alex more intimate. And not even if he didn't, actually. If Charlotte knew he was there, she'd turn up on the doorstep if for no other reason than to exact revenge for his role in the debacle. Minor though it had been.

"I think it's best to let the sleeping dog lie, Polly," he answered truthfully. "No sense prodding it with a sharp stick if it's not necessary. His lordship isn't the only one who can carry a grudge."

"I understand completely, Mr. Terrell," she said solemnly. She offered him a little curtsy, adding, "It was a real pleasure to see you again, though."

"And I you, Polly. Take care of yourself."

She smiled prettily and then turned to the silver room to say, "Thank you for your assistance, Miss Radford. I'll show myself out."

Aiden watched her make her way to the front door of the shop, his shoulder propped against the wall, keenly aware that Alex had stepped into the doorway and was watching him. The tiny pucker of her mouth . . . Oh, and were her eyes gray! With the brightest telltale flecks of green.

"What?" he asked in wholly feigned innocence.

"Just out of pure curiosity . . . Is there a woman in London that you *haven't* bedded?"

He tried to look as though he were ticking through a list. "Polly," he finally provided.

Alex's hands went to her hips and the green sparks in her eyes danced. "If you offered, she'd accept."

"Really?"

"Ugh!"

And with that disdainful comment, she turned on her heel and disappeared back into the silver room. Aiden followed her, laughing and realizing that he'd truly missed her company that day.

"Since Polly left here empty-handed," he said, propping a hip on the corner of the central table, "I'd guess that Charlotte Tyndale is selling off silver to pay her living expenses."

Taking a tissue-covered object from a silver chest, she unwrapped it, saying, "I have no idea what she's doing with the money, but yes, she's selling silver. An especially ornate set of Roberts and Belk, a design they created just last year. The set looks as though it's never been used." She handed him a fork, adding, "It's gorgeous, isn't it?"

It was both gold and silver and far too fussy to be to his liking. But he knew that diplomacy lay in silence. He simply nodded and checked the balance of the piece. It was finely made and no doubt horribly expensive. Which made perfect sense.

Handing it back, he said offhandedly, "Knowing Charlotte, she received it as a gift from an ardent admirer."

Alex chuckled softly and quipped, "She apparently didn't admire him enough to invite him to stay for dinner."

"He probably wasn't interested in dinner, anyway. That's not why men give Charlotte gifts, you know."

She looked up from her silver to meet his gaze and arch a dark brow. A tiny smile tickled the corners of her mouth and she replied, "No, I didn't know. But thank you for so freely sharing what has to be—at best—dubious knowledge."

Lord, he didn't know when it had happened, not precisely, anyway, but Alex Radford had somehow become one of the most adorable women who'd ever crossed his path. And dubious knowledge was what Barrett Stanbridge was operating under if he thought she could be involved in a fencing operation.

It was so far from the realm of even remotely plausible as to be laughable. But, just for the time when Barrett would ask if he'd so much as bothered to pursue the investigation, he'd make a show of it now and then be done with it.

"Speaking of knowing . . ." he began, pointedly looking around the room. "How do you know that the silver you're asked to buy isn't stolen?"

"Very easily, actually," she replied, taking an oil lamp and a small silver box from one of the shelves. "You can tell which is honestly acquired silver by the caliber of the person coming in to sell it. Ladies' maids, housekeepers, butlers, and footmen are of noticeably better quality than your average thief."

Placing the lamp in the center of the table, she opened the box, took out a phosphorus stick, and proceeded to light the wick. Adjusting the flame and fanning away the smell of the igniter, she added, "When I first started brokering, though, a good number of people tried to sell me stolen goods. But the word soon spread that I wasn't willing to be a party to such things and they seldom come around anymore. Occasionally, but not at all often."

"Those that do are probably very new to the thieving business," he ventured, hoping she might know something about the illegal side of the brokering street. A description—or even better yet, the name—of a potential buyer would be far more than Barrett had at present.

She nodded and put the silver box back on the shelf. "They tend to be very young and haven't the foggiest notion of the silver's worth. I'm always tempted to take them by their ear and drag them home to their mothers."

"An admirable consideration, but it wouldn't do any good," he counseled. "More than likely their mothers are counting on the money to go to market."

"Which is why I don't do it," she agreed with a sigh. "It's horrible to live so hand to mouth."

Aiden frowned. East India officers made handsome wages. And then, as first the daughter of the royal tutor and then the tutor herself, Alex never should have wanted for anything in her life. "And how does Miss Alexandra Radford know about a meager existence?" he pressed gently.

She studied the maker's mark on the back of a fork as she replied, "My father had many vices, the worst of which were drinking and gambling. Mother would wait for him to stumble in during the wee hours of the morning, and when he finally fell unconscious, she'd search his pockets. What money she found would be what we had to take to market and to pay the rent that week."

"So she left him and went to teach in the raja's court," Aiden supplied.

She shrugged and picked up the wrapping tissue she'd removed earlier. "More or less."

The fact that she'd been vague was telling. "It's considerably more, isn't it? Was he abusive?"

A sad smile touched her lips. "Have you known very many drunks who were jolly, lovable people?"

She'd answered a question with a question, one of the defensive strategies she'd employed early yesterday and then abandoned along the way to sunset. That she'd resorted to evasion again suggested that he was prying into areas that troubled her. The gentleman in him urged him to cease his questioning and let her keep her secrets. But something else insisted even more strongly that he'd never understand her unless he could get her to share her story. He didn't know why understanding her was so important, but it was.

"Did your mother kill him?" he asked bluntly, hoping to force her into an equally direct answer.

"No." He was about to ask if she knew where her father was when she expelled a hard breath, put the fork back in the box, and added, "But she didn't shed any tears when one of his gambling associates did. The man came to us for the money my father owed him and since we didn't have it and had no way of getting it, Mother and I fled Bombay."

"And went to the raja," he offered, thinking to make the telling easier for her.

"Eventually. Where's Mohan?"

Eventually? Aiden cocked a brow, watching her put the chest on a shelf and debating whether or not to press her for more. The simplicity of her answer and the abrupt change in subject, however, suggested that he wasn't going to be successful at it a second time. At least not right now.

"Preeya's supervising his bath," he provided. "He's gotten a bit piggy today. I came in for his clean clothes. Mine, as well. I'm next in the queue."

"I would hope so," she laughingly said, picking up the lamp and moving past him.

He came off the table and followed her out into the hall. "Then I gather that a torrid affair with the stable master is out of the question?" he teased.

She laughed outright and put the lamp on the desk in the front store. "Judging by your appearance, I'd guess that you managed to acquire the horses you wanted."

Change of subject. He wasn't surprised. A bit disappointed, yes, but not surprised. "Yes, and then we went to take delivery of the carriage," Aiden explained, noting that while the wooden crates remained where the delivery crew had left them that morning, they were now surrounded by a shallow sea of packing straw.

"It's been cleaned and polished and the horses are happily munching on sweet oats, all settled into their new home," he continued as she leaned into one of the boxes and he tried not to stare at the attractive curve of her backside. "Tomorrow we'll saddle the horse we bought you and start your riding lessons."

"We'll see. I'm sure Mohan made you start with his today." She straightened with a wad of straw in her hands. Wiggling her fingers, she let the golden bits fall slowly away. "How did he do?"

"He's very good. Not at all afraid or put off by their size. He's going to be one of those riders who looks as though he was born in the saddle."

She stopped and looked over at him. "You will make an effort to keep him from taking unnecessary chances, won't you?"

It was a momentous step for a confirmed mother hen. "He's on a palfrey and a lead rope until he proves himself competent several times over."

"Thank you, Aiden. That makes me feel better."

And the appreciation of her smile was making him feel decidedly too warm. He nodded his acceptance of her gratitude. "Well, I'd best be getting those clothes and back to the kitchen," he said, backing toward the stairs and beyond the persistent whisper of temptation.

Alex watched him leave and then went back to work, thinking that he was a far more fascinating man than was good for her. Thankfully, he didn't seem to be a callous predator like so many of the British Army officers her mother had taken pains to see that she encountered. And while Aiden obviously wasn't opposed to taking opportunities that presented themselves, he didn't strike her as the sort that went out of his way to deliberately create them. Placing an otherwise virtuous woman in a compromising situation just so that he could take advantage of her . . . No, Aiden was decent and honorable. He'd never do such a dastardly thing.

But, by the same token, he clearly wasn't opposed to accepting an offer freely made. And if the woman of the hour expected a payment of sorts in exchange for her favors, he'd pay it. If one man had given Charlotte Tyndale a set of Roberts and Belk's latest and most expensive flatwear, then what had Aiden given her? Horses and carriages?

Not that he would have had to give so extravagantly; he was a handsome, charming man and no doubt the sort of lover women like Lady Tyndale preferred. But he didn't seem like the sort to stint on quality or value just because he could. For Aiden, providing a special, memorable gift would probably be a point of pride.

And, she admonished herself, to spend so much as a second of her time thinking about such things was beyond foolish. It was unseemly. Ladies didn't entertain such musings. If they even occurred to them in the first place.

"A pair of sapphire rings."

She looked up to find Aiden standing at the base of the stairs, clothing draped over his arm and his smile wicked. How long had he been standing there? she wondered. And had she been thinking aloud? Lord, she hoped not. She knitted her brows, trying to fathom what sapphire rings had to do with anything.

"You were wondering what I gave Charlotte."

Of course he'd known what she'd been thinking. He always did. At least it didn't overly surprise her anymore. "Rings are a very expensive, personal gift," she observed. "Weren't you afraid her husband would notice them at the breakfast table?"

The devil danced in his eyes and his smile broadened. "They weren't for her fingers. Charlotte has certain—intimate—parts of herself pierced for jewelry."

Alex stared at him, stunned and slack-jawed mute. She'd heard of such scandalous practices, but to actually know of someone who engaged in them . . .

"It was interesting," he admitted, nodding appreciatively. Apparently feeling as though he'd sufficiently shocked her, he turned to leave, adding, "But I'm certainly glad I'm not the one who married her."

She couldn't resist the impulse. "Aiden?"

He stopped and turned back, his brow cocked in silent question. And to her dismay, her wits and courage picked that very moment to desert her. One really didn't ask such things, her conscience virtuously intoned. It was truly none of her business or concern.

"No," he said, chuckling softly, "I had nothing to do—directly—with the fact that Lord and Lady Tyndale have been living separately. The responsibility for that one belongs to Barrett. And it was absolutely spectacular."

Oh, God. She most definitely didn't need that information. Wanting it was nothing more than a sign of prurient interest and low moral character. Which, of course, meant that she was a really, really terrible person.

"We'll be in shortly," he said, still grinning as he walked off again. She let him go, grateful that he'd had the decency to save her from herself.

Aiden toweled his hair, decided there was nothing to be lost in asking a few questions, and stepped from behind the bathing screen. Preeya was by the stove, stirring something steaming and aromatic. The boy was perched like a long-legged bird on a stool beside her, "Mohan," Aiden began, "what do you know about how Miss Radford and her mother came to your father's court?"

"They arrived when I was just a baby," he replied with a shrug. "I do not remember then or the time before."

That was an odd statement, but he wasn't going to be sidetracked by pondering it. "Would Preeya know?"

Again he shrugged but he chattered away in Hindi for a moment and then looked back at him to smile and say, "Preeya wants to know why you ask."

"Tell her because I want to understand Alex, why she is the way she is, why she does the things she does."

Again Mohan spoke to Preeya in their native tongue. The

older woman looked over her shoulder at Aiden, smiling broadly and then began answering. Mohan nodded throughout and only when she'd finished did he translate.

"Preeya says that my father saw Miss Alex in one of the temples. She was a child then and stealing the offering food. He had his men follow her to bring her and her mother to the court for justice. Once my father heard their story, he took pity on them and brought them under his protection. Preeya says that if you seek the story of her life before and after that, you must ask Miss Alex for it yourself. It is her story to tell."

"I don't think she's likely to share it with me," Aiden admitted. "No matter how nicely I ask."

Again Mohan and Preeya conversed and Aiden watched the spirited exchange, relieved that Preeya didn't seem the least put off or hesitant to discuss what were—to his mind, anyway—rather personal questions.

"Preeya says that Miss Alex tries very hard to make people believe that she needs no one, that she prefers to move through the world alone. Preeya says Miss Alex would be happier if she were to abandon her illusions. Preeya says that she believes this must be done and thinks you are a most capable man in this regard."

"Thank her for her confidence in me," Aiden instructed while thinking that Preeya had no real reason for such certitude.

"Preeya wants you to know that Miss Alex was raised in the women's quarters after she came to the court."

Aiden knitted his brows. "And that's important because . . .?"

Another exchange transpired, this one far shorter than the others. "I think that you must ask Miss Alex that question. I do not know the answer and Preeya says she cannot tell you any more without betraying her friendship with Miss Alex."

Which was fair enough, he knew. She'd already told him a great deal. "Thank Preeya for her help, Mohan. I appreciate what she was able to give."

But only in certain respects. The mental image of Alex, young, barefoot, dressed in rags, and stealing food to live bothered him deeply. No wonder she didn't trust easily; her life until the raja had taken them in had been one hard, painful lesson after another. Actually, it was a miracle that she was able to trust at all. For that the raja had to be respected and commended.

Alex angled her needlework to better catch the light from the fire. From the other side of the salon came the gentle clicking sounds of the chessboard being arranged. She cast a quick glance at Preeya, who rolled her eyes and smiled. *Yes,* Alex thought, *this is going to be interesting. Best of luck to you, Aiden.*

"All right," Aiden began. "We'll start with the fundamentals. You always move to protect your king, Mohan."

Just as Alex expected, her ward crisply said, "The king is most important. He is all that matters."

"Not in chess. When the queen's captured the game's fairly well over."

"Why?" Mohan demanded. "Men are more important than women."

"What would men do without women?"

"Whatever they wanted."

"Which would rarely be intelligent, thoughtful, or appropriate," Aiden pointed out. "There would be no such thing as civilization without the influence of women, Mohan."

The boy snorted, and at the edge of her vision Alex could see that he'd punctuated the derisive sound with a dismissive wave of his hand. "My father does not ask my mother or his other wives or his mistresses for their opinions or advice on his actions. He is the raja and they are his subjects."

Alex put in a stitch and waited.

"Well, just guessing, Mohan," Aiden drawled, "but I'd say that your father's always aware that what he does is noted by the various females in his life and that he's going to have to answer for his actions one way or another."

She smiled and laid in another stitch, thinking that, for an unmarried man, Aiden Terrell had a surprisingly fine grasp of domestic politics.

"Ha!" Mohan scoffed with another wave of his hand.

"Am I right, Miss Radford?"

"Very much so," she offered.

Aiden nodded in vindication and then went on. "There's something else you need to know about women, Mohan. They talk to each other. And in a way that's very different from the way men do among themselves. Women are masters of the coordinated action. Should they ever decide to create armies of their own, men are going to be in very serious trouble."

"How do you know this?" her ward asked, clearly skeptical.

"I have a mother and six sisters. Thankfully, they're kind women because my father, my brothers, and I are completely at their mercy. My father makes pronouncements, but unless my mother seconds them, they're largely empty in the end."

"Then your father lacks a spine."

It was Aiden's turn to snort. "If he were here, you'd be pinned against the wall and sincerely regretting having suggested he was anything less than a force to be reckoned with."

"Your mother would intervene and make him apologize for so roughly handling me."

"No she wouldn't," he countered, every bit as firm in his convictions as Mohan was in his. "She'd let him go, figuring that you were getting what you deserved and learning a valuable lesson about keeping your mouth shut and your uninformed comments to yourself."

"Then she is the puppet."

Alex wasn't at all surprised when Aiden heaved a sigh of frustration and turned to her. "Could you possibly have a go at explaining this? I'm not doing too terribly well with it on my own."

Of course he wasn't. Mohan wasn't a child who accepted pronouncements; he had to reason his way to conclusions. Especially those that significantly challenged his view of the world's natural order. She smiled at Aiden and placed her needlework in her lap. "Mohan," she began. "Do you remember when your father brought Kali into his household?"

"Yes."

"What was it like in the palace while she was there?"

He thought a moment. "There was no laughter. The women did not smile and my father was . . ." He paused another moment and then stridently finished, "He was most angry with the women for their treatment of Kali."

She let the assertion go, holding to her course. "And where is Kali now?"

"She is the wife of one of my father's minor administrators."

"And the consequences of her marriage were . . .?"

"She left the palace and the women laughed again," Mohan said slowly, contemplatively. "My father stopped being angry and brought Chun into the household."

"And did the laughter stop with Chun's arrival?" she pressed.

"No."

The groundwork successfully laid, Alex smiled at him and began the actual instruction. "That's because the women approve of Chun and accept your father's choice of her. They didn't Kali. For a variety of reasons you're far too young to understand. It's sufficient for our purposes this evening to say that your father was made aware of the women's displeasure and took steps to see that harmony was restored. No one was the puppet of anyone else. The decisions were made for the benefit of everyone's happiness." She gave him a moment to consider what she'd said and then asked, "Do you understand the lesson in all of that?"

"I think so."

No, he didn't, but he would in time. "Perhaps you could ponder on it some more as you drift off to sleep. It's time for bed."

"But Mr. Terrell and I have yet to begin our game of chess," he protested, gesturing to the board.

"We can begin it tomorrow night," Aiden assured him. "If Miss Radford says it's time for you to retire, it's time for you to retire. And you won't argue about it."

Mohan cast a quick glance between the two of them and then rose to his feet with a disgruntled but resigned pout. At his wishes for their pleasant evening—in both English and Hindi—Preeya laid aside her embroidery and rose from her cushions beside the fire, announcing that she would retire, as well. Alex bade them both sweet dreams and watched them leave for their rooms. It was only in the silence afterward that she realized that she'd been left alone with Aiden Terrell.

"If it's not prying to ask," he said, carefully moving the chessboard from the pillowtop to the floor. "Why was Kali unacceptable to the women?"

"How to put this delicately . . ."

"Don't worry about battering my sensibilities," he hastened to assure her, grinning as he stretched out on his side, his head propped in his hand. "They're not all that tender."

"I assumed that. My concern is for my own," she laughingly countered, picking up her needlework again. Her vision suitably focused *not* on him, she explained, "There's a general attitude in the women's quarters regarding their individual relationships with the raja. It's of the moment, what it is for that moment, and nothing more or less. There's no jealousy over who's called to his chambers for the night.

"Kali, however, attempted to change all that. Her entire existence revolved around working to set us against each other and on restricting the raja's favor only to her."

"In other words, she didn't share well."

"She didn't want to share at all," Alex clarified, pushing the needle through the canvas and drawing the yarn into place. "Mohan doesn't quite understand the dynamics of what happened and I'd prefer not to enlighten him just yet, but the truth is that his father wasn't unhappy with the way we treated Kali. He was unhappy because of the way we treated him for bringing her into our midst. The raja doesn't like to be treated coolly."

"Ah," Aiden said, his smile radiating through the sound. "The coordinated action I warned Mohan about. I can almost feel sorry for the man."

"Almost?"

"Almost," he reiterated. "Any man who has more than his fair share of companions doesn't really merit too much pity for the complications that come along with it."

She could feel his gaze on her, could sense the bright light of curiosity in his eyes. "No," she said softly. "I wasn't one of his companions."

The edge of her vision lit up with his grin. "Well, since you broached the subject . . . Why—"

"Because I'm British," she supplied simply. Before he could ask another question and before she had to refuse to answer it, she rose from her chair and laid the needlework on the seat, saying, "I do believe it's time I retired, as well. Good night, Aiden. Pleasant dreams."

He scrambled to his feet. "If you must, I certainly understand." His gaze was assessing as he met hers and added, "Good night, Alex. Sleep well."

"And the same wish for you, Aiden," she offered, her heart

skittering as he searched her face. It took a substantial measure of her self-discipline to gracefully, calmly, move past him and out the door. It took every bit of the rest of it to keep from looking back over her shoulder in the unsettling hope that he'd come after her.

Chapter 9

Better, Alex reminded herself for the countless time, to rise before the peacocks and miss breakfast than to risk being caught in her nightgown again. She dug her hands into the straw, feeling for the mate to the candlestick she'd just removed. And it wasn't as though she'd been sleeping soundly anyway. The night just past was one of the most restless she could ever remember having. Twice she'd awakened, short of breath and her heart pounding, certain that she'd find Aiden Terrell lying beside her in reality. And instead of feeling relieved . . .

The sound of footfalls on the stairs quickened Alex's pulse and brought her attention up from the packing crate. She relaxed at the sight of Mohan and smiled.

"Good morning, Miss Alex," he said, beaming as he bounded toward her. "Mr. Terrell asked me to tell you that he will be downstairs directly."

"Thank you. Is there any particular reason why I need to be informed of that momentous event?"

Mohan looked at her as if she had the mental acuity of a brick. "Your first riding lesson is this morning," he said with extreme patience.

"Oh. I'd forgotten," she lied, resuming her search in the packing straw. "I'm really terribly busy, you know. I have to finish unpacking these crates and then, of course, there's the putting away and proper displaying of everything. Followed by the tidying up of the shop itself. I just don't see how I have time for a riding lesson, do you?"

"Is it the horse of which you are afraid, Miss Alex? Or is it Mr. Terrell's instruction? I assure you that he is most competent."

As though Mohan had anyone against whom to compare him. "I'm not afraid of anything," she assured him, finding and taking the candlestick from the crate. Turning to place it on the desk, she added, "I simply have work to do. And work must come before pleasure."

"Why?"

"Because if I don't work there won't be money with which to buy carriages and hor—" She instantly recognized the two men coming down the walk, heading for her door. "Mohan, go upstairs and stay there until I call for you. Go!"

Thankfully he obeyed and she had just enough time to seize a single deep breath before they pushed open the door and sauntered in.

"Top o' the mornin' to ya, mum," said the one called Rupert.

She found a smile and dipped her chin in acknowledgment. "Gentlemen."

The other one—Willie—stepped from behind Rupert. Openly surveying the shop, he said, "There's some business to be finished 'tween us."

"Yes, there is, isn't there?" Alex managed to say pleasantly. "You disappeared before I returned the other day and could pay you for your services. The amount was four shillings, as I recall."

Rupert shook his head. "We've decided eight would be more fittin'. Took a big chance for ya, we did."

Yes, lolling about in front of a millinery shop was incredibly dangerous work. Alex bit her tongue and forced herself to smile. "Eight shillings it is, then," she said, willing to pay whatever it took to get them out of her store. "Kindly wait where you are and I'll return with your payment in just a moment."

Hoping that they wouldn't pocket everything small enough to fit while she was gone, Alex gathered her skirts and retreated to the silver room. She'd barely stepped inside and scooped up her cash tin when she heard footsteps behind her. Her heart thudding, she spun toward the doorway. And found it blocked.

"I distinctly recall," she said with all the calm she could muster, "having asked you gentlemen to wait in the front shop."

Rupert looked around, his eyes narrowing. "Lots of pretty stuff in here, isn't there, Willie? Look at all this plate. Too awkward and heavy to be cartin' out of here all at once, though. But still . . . It has to be worth a king's ransom, don't ya think?"

"Aye," his companion agreed. He smiled thinly at her and wagged an eyebrow. "Or a chit's."

She couldn't breathe, couldn't make her feet move, couldn't hear anything over the thunderous roar of her heartbeat. As though from a great distance she saw herself hold out the tin, heard herself say, "Take the cash box and whatever plate you want and go."

Willie's lips moved but she didn't hear the words. Hope flickered when he reached for the tin with both hands. It was extinguished when he took the tin in one and clamped the other hard around her wrist. Instinctively, she pulled back, trying to break his hold, trying to twist away.

Her flesh burned and the cry caught painfully in her throat as she was flung forward. Spinning and stumbling, her heels caught in her hems, she fell hard against the body of the second man. An iron band instantly slammed around her, high above her waist, driving the air from her lungs and another strangled cry past her lips. And then there was only the sensation of cold metal and deadly sharp pressed hard against her neck. Alex froze, holding what little breath she had remaining.

"Scream and it'll be the last sound you ever make," Willie snarled in her ear as he hauled her toward the door.

Alex dragged her feet, her every instinct telling her that if she let them get her out of the house, she'd never see it again. Never see Mohan. Preeya. Her knife was on the desk in the front shop. Beyond her reach, beyond usefulness.

"Pick up your feet!" he commanded, tightening the band around her midsection and giving her no chance to comply on her own before lifting her clear of the floor and carrying her into the hall. Willie came on their heels, exhorting his partner to hurry.

"Let go of her. *Now.*"

Aiden. At the entrance to the hall. A gun in his hand, held level and steady at arm's length. The sight of him, the sound of his voice, clear and strong . . .

"Let her go," he said with steely calm, "or I'll kill you."

So tall, so lethal, so absolutely determined. It would be all right. Aiden was there. For her. Her knees weakening with relief, Alex sagged downward and then choked back a cry as the arm around her crushed the air from her lungs again and the blade pressed closer to her throat.

"Close your eyes, Alex."

She obeyed, trusting him, knowing that she should and could.

There was the sudden jangle of metal—the change in the box she dully realized—and then there was only a soul-pounding blast and a sudden, wrenching weight slamming against her legs, pulling at her skirts and hauling her down. The band tightened yet again and she stumbled, trying to keep herself upright as she was hauled backward. Her lungs were burning; she couldn't breathe. Scalding tears poured through her lashes. And her heart . . . Her heart was going to explode.

"Throw the gun away, guv'ner, or I'll open her up. I swear I will."

Alex winced at the voice, the threat, issued against her ear. Aiden kept his gaze steady along the length of the barrel, knowing that her best chance of survival lay in dropping the bastard where he stood. "If you so much as twitch," he warned, "I'll put a bullet in your brain."

Squeezing a cry out of Alex, the man smiled. "You can't shoot me without hitting her."

"Last chance." He slowly drew the hammer back until it clicked into place. "Let her go."

The smile disappeared, replaced by a dark scowl, as, for a fleeting second, the man's gaze passed over Aiden's shoulder and into the front of the shop. Aiden strained to hear, but refused to be drawn into looking, into surrendering what slim advantage he had.

"Reach behind you," Alex's captor growled into her ear, "and open the damn door."

Aiden saw her force herself to swallow, watched as she carefully turned her head away from the pressure of the knife blade and stretched her right hand back to blindly search for the doorknob. *Just a bit more, darling,* he silently coached her. *Just a fraction more. Give me a clean shot. One's all I need.*

He seized the opportunity in the same second that she gave him that precious space. The blast was deafening, the smoke acrid and thick. Through it he heard Alex scream, saw the man's head snap back, saw him stagger and the blade fall away from Alex's throat. His stomach churned, but he ignored it, knowing that he had to reach Alex before she either collapsed onto the body at her feet or fell back onto the one sliding down the wall behind her.

The revolver still tight in his fist, he covered the space between them, catching her about the waist just as her knees gave out. "Gotcha," he rasped, hauling her hard against him. Her face buried against his shoulder, she sobbed his name and he pressed a quick kiss to her temple before he bent, swept her up into his arms, and carried her out of the hall.

"Miss Alex!"

The top of the stairs. A frightened Mohan. "She's all right," Aiden assured the boy. "Stay up there! Do you hear me?"

"Yes, sir."

One problem averted. Alex so close was the next one he needed to solve. His senses had been sharpened by the danger and were still too raw, too aware, to have Alex in his arms. She felt too good, too inviting, and he didn't trust himself not to take advantage of her confusion. He glanced toward the chair in the front shop, thinking to take her there.

He froze at the sight of a face peering in the front window. A pair of obsidian eyes in a burnished male face met his gaze for an instant. They both started at the unexpected contact and the hairs on the back of Aiden's neck prickled as a cold shudder rippled down his spine. Then the stranger turned and was gone.

And, in that moment, so was his strength. He dropped down on a lower step, Alex cradled in his arms and across his lap, and dragged a deep, ragged breath into his lungs as he struggled to banish the bloody images from his mind.

"Oh, God," Alex brokenly whispered, lifting her face to gaze up at him, tears still coursing down her cheeks. "Aiden."

He wanted to kiss her. Long and slowly. Until they both forgot what had just happened. He managed to exercise self-control and find a smile. "I'm afraid that I've made a mess in your rear hall. Sorry about that."

"I don't care," she replied on a shaky breath. A fresh wave of tears spilled over her lashes even as she swiped a trembling hand across her cheek. "I'm sorry," she offered, her voice on the verge of breaking. "I'm trying not to cry. Really, I am."

"It's all right, Alex," he assured her, pulling his handkerchief from his pocket and gently dabbing her cheeks. "Go ahead and cry all you'd like. I intend to later."

She sniffled and took the cloth from him to vigorously scrub her eyes and demand, "How can you be so damn calm?"

Damn? The duchess could swear? He smiled and allowed that if any situation merited a few curses, this one was it. He pushed a tendril of tear-dampened hair off her cheek and gently tucked it behind her ear. "I wouldn't be doing you much good if I fell to pieces, now would I?"

The look in his eyes as she gazed up at him . . . Gone was the cold, lethal man who had squarely dealt with her attackers. This Aiden Terrell, the one holding her, comforting her, was compelling in an entirely different way. It would be so easy to melt into him and surrender all of her fears, all of her self. He wouldn't hurt her, wouldn't take advantage of her lack of courage. She knew that to the very marrow of her bones.

The tender searching in his eyes was gone in a blink. As was the gentleness with which he held her. All of his muscles instantly taut, he turned his head and lifted the gun, pointing it at the slowly opening front door. Alex held her breath and pressed herself closer to him, her heart racing in cadence with his.

"Ah, Mrs. Fuller," he said, lowering the weapon as she poked her head inside. "Perfect timing. Would you please be so kind as to find a constable for us? Tell him it's a bit urgent."

The older woman met Alex's gaze for a second, then she nodded crisply and withdrew, closing the door smartly behind her. Aiden expelled a quick, hard breath and offered Alex a smile that was both reassuring and apologetic.

It served both intentions well. And also fueled the temptation of him. "Thank you for coming to my rescue," she offered, sensing the danger in silence and desperately hoping to distract herself.

"I specialize in saving damsels in distress," he replied, his eyes twinkling with amusement. "I thought you knew."

She hadn't, but then, she hadn't known that a man's laughing eyes could be so powerfully seductive, either. And at the moment, that particular piece of knowledge was far more important than any other. She needed to put some physical distance between them before she blithely threw herself into the enchanting trap. She turned her head to look at the step, thinking to move herself off his lap and onto it if space permitted.

"No, Alex," he said, gently taking her chin in his hand and drawing her back to face him. The amusement was gone from his eyes, replaced by a gentle resolve. "Keep your attention focused right here, on me. Don't look anywhere else. And talk to me, Alex. Let what's whirling around in your head tumble out. It doesn't matter if it makes sense or not."

He didn't want her to see the carnage and she appreciated his kindness, his continued protectiveness. But if she were to give voice to what she was honestly thinking, truly feeling . . .

What would he do if she stretched up and just grazed his lips with hers? Lightly, just for a moment. If he asked why, she could say it was a kiss born of gratitude. It would be a partial truth; she was grateful beyond measure or words for his intervention. But in her heart she knew there was far more to it than that. She wanted to know what his lips felt like, how they tasted. It was the sweetest, most gently compelling hunger; a need that unless met would always linger among her life's regrets.

To satisfy the yearning was to risk opening a Pandora's box, though. Aiden might expect more than she was willing to give. Might? It was a given. Tigers never nibbled at their prey and decided to abandon it. Never. If she offered only a little of herself, she had to be willing to offer all.

It was an odd, deeply unsettling mixture of emotion, trepidation, and hunger. Part of her wanted to scramble out of his arms and away from temptation. Another part boldly urged her to act on desire and accept whatever consequences came of it. And deep down inside she hoped that Aiden would make the decision for her. She forced herself to swallow, to think of something reasonably appropriate to say.

"How did you know I needed help?" she asked, focusing her gaze on the second button of his shirtfront.

Aiden considered her, frowning and knowing that the question had nothing whatsoever to do with the confusion he was seeing in her eyes. "Mohan told me your rented thugs were here and I acted on a gut feeling," he supplied, wishing she'd trust him as much now as she had in the hall.

"They were going to ransom me for the silver."

It was a reasonable thing, a believable claim. But doubt niggled at him and he glanced back to the window, remembering how Alex's assailant had looked that way, and the man who had been standing there in the immediate aftermath.

"Hiring them in the first place was a foolish thing to do," she went on, pulling his thoughts back to the present. "Horribly foolish."

He wasn't going to argue with her. She'd asked the bastards into her world and they were both dead for having pushed the invitation too far. But there was no reason to agree with her, either; she felt bad enough already. She shivered and he tightened his arm around her shoulders, drawing her closer and asking, "Are you cold?"

"I don't know," Alex admitted, tears inexplicably welling in her eyes again. Her thoughts were suddenly swirling, jumbling together, careening over and through fragments of recent memories. Her body trembled with each flash of recollection and she couldn't stop the mental torrent or stem her reaction to it.

"It's nothing more than shock settling in," he assured her, putting aside the gun and opening his coat. Drawing her closer, wrapping her inside it and the circle of his arms, he softly promised, "It'll pass in time, Alex."

And when replaced by other, more powerful sensations, she realized. His heart was pounding hard and fast and she could feel the heat of his skin through his shirtfront. And he smelled so good. Like earth and wind and heady spices. She breathed deeply, bathing her senses with him, letting his strength fill and settle her spirit.

"And how do you know that it's shock?" she asked, shifting in his arms so that she could see his face. "Have you done this sort of thing before?"

"Yes."

So simple an admission, so full of quiet, aching regret. And also an acceptance that filled her with awe even as it tattered her heart. "Oh, Aiden," she whispered, freeing an arm to reach up and touch his cheek.

His conscience didn't even bother to put up a fight. Between her sweet invitation and his simmering desire, there wasn't any point. Aiden lowered his head and brushed his lips over hers, gently, reverently. Her sigh was sanction, her hand slipping to his neck an undeniable command. His heart racing, he accepted and obeyed, deepening his possession of her mouth, savoring the soft fullness of her lips and the heady wonder of her genuine compliance. Long-dormant embers sprang to flame and he gasped as the heat surged through his veins.

Aiden drew back, reluctantly releasing his claim to her mouth, knowing that it was the wisest, sanest course. But God, he didn't want to be sane where she was concerned. Her eyes fluttered open and in her dreamy gaze what remained of his good judgment was almost undone.

"You," he whispered, his voice raspy, "are an incredibly tempting woman, Alexandra Radford."

"And you're not a tempting man?" she countered, arching a brow and trailing her fingers through the hair at his nape.

He considered her and struggled to find a bit of chivalry. "Which makes this a most decidedly dangerous situation, my darling duchess. If we don't put some distance and common sense between us in the next few seconds, I'm likely to thoroughly ravage you right here on the stairs."

He expected her to start, to squeak in protest, and then claw her way out of his arms and off his lap. Instead, she pursed her lips for a second and then gave him a grin so bright, so utterly and delightfully wicked, that his toes practically curled.

"Christ Almighty, no," he choked out, his breath catching as his heart slammed into his throat. "Don't do this to me."

She laughed softly and straightened in his arms, letting her hands fall into her lap. "Then let me up."

She'd granted him a reprieve and part of him was extremely grateful for the kindness. Another part of him, though, was sorely disgruntled about placing her on her feet. And that part reminded him of its long slumber as he rose to his own feet and took a step back. He nonchalantly drew his jacket closed and buttoned it, hoping to at least hide from Alex the proof of his frustration.

Remembering his admonishment not to look into the hallway, Alex allowed her gaze to skim the width of his shoulders as she drew a deep, steadying breath. All those years spent listening to the raja's women talk. Nodding but not truly understanding what they were saying about the intoxicating power of physical desire. She did now, though. Thoroughly, completely, and ever so personally. It thrummed through her, deliciously warm and persistent, undeniable in its simplicity and yet mysterious in its fullness and complexity. And Lord help her, she wanted to explore—to taste and feel—every last measure of its potent promise.

All from one gentle, brief kiss. It wasn't the first kiss she'd ever had, but all the ones before it certainly paled in comparison. Oh, she was in terrible, terrible trouble. She had to stop smiling at him. Really, she did. Unless she could gain some control over her outward behavior, Aiden was going to think her the most easily acquired woman he'd ever met. And he'd have every right to make that assumption.

What a curse it was to have come of age in India, in the women's quarters. If she'd been raised in England, she wouldn't be struggling with any of this. She could huff and puff and be truly, righteously offended at the liberty he'd taken. But her past was her past and any protest she mustered would be nothing more than a bald-faced lie.

Oh, yes, she was fascinated by Aiden and what he offered. Which put her in a most serious predicament.

He moistened his lower lip with the tip of his tongue and gave her a smile that seemed nervous. Then his gaze slipped past her and he straightened. "Hello, Constable," he said, his smile suddenly easy and confident. "We've had a small crisis here this morning."

Alex turned to the door as Emmaline came inside behind the officer and Aiden added, "Oh, Mrs. Fuller. I'm glad you're here. Would you please take Alex upstairs and get her a cup of hot tea? And keep her and Mohan and Preeya occupied while I speak with the constable?"

Aiden was in command again, Alex realized. Smooth, unruffled, capable.

"I'd be glad to, Mr. Terrell," Emmaline assured him, bustling forward to take Alex's hand and turn her toward the stairs and adding, "Come along, you poor dear."

She glanced back over her shoulder to see him already speaking with the constable, his voice so low that she couldn't hear his words. Yes, very much in charge. And while she appreciated his ability to do that when necessary, she liked the very human, very unbridled side of him ever so much more.

"I knew, *I knew,*" Emmaline said, drawing her up the staircase, "that day they were going to be trouble. I saw them go past my shop just a bit ago and suspected they were on their way here and I *knew* again. I'm just very glad that Mr. Terrell was here to so ably dispatch them."

Alex's knees buckled without warning. Grabbing the banister, she barely kept herself upright. Emmaline made comforting sounds as she slipped her arm around Alex's waist and supported her, but it didn't make matters any better. Alex closed her eyes and took a deep breath, sternly reminding herself that she couldn't afford the luxury of collapsing whenever someone mentioned what had happened.

She was made of sterner stuff than that. She'd faced tragedy and danger before. And without Aiden Terrell there to hold her in the aftermath. There would be other tragedies and dangers in the future. That was the nature of life. And when they came, Aiden wasn't likely to be there for her. As much as she appreciated his intervention now, as much as she was drawn to his strength, his calm, and his charming irreverence, she couldn't come to depend on his presence. He was a wonderful man, but he was also the most temporary feature of her existence. She had to be able to stand on her own when he walked away.

Lifting her chin, Alex opened her eyes and gave Emmaline a reassuring smile. Then, with clenched teeth, she forced herself to take another step.

The smile he gave them from the salon doorway didn't reach his eyes. Alex didn't know what to say, what she could do to ease his obvious sadness, but he didn't give her a chance to fumble her way along the path of good intentions.

"The bodies have been removed," he said without preamble. "The cleaning woman is here and almost done with her work and the constables tell me they think there'll be no further investigation. We're free to go about our regular lives."

Emmaline rose from the settee, smoothing her skirts and saying, "Then I should be getting back to my shop."

Aiden dipped his chin in acceptance. "I'll walk you there, Mrs. Fuller."

"Oh, that's hardly necessary."

"I'll do it anyway," he countered firmly. His gaze swept around the room, touching each of them briefly, somberly, before coming back to Alex. "While I'm gone, the three of you need to get ready to leave the house."

"Where are we going?" Mohan asked, scrambling up from his pillow nest, his book tumbling onto the carpet at his feet. "To buy more horses?"

"There are some matters that need to be attended," Aiden supplied. "And I'm not willing to leave any of you here alone while I take care of them. So we're all going."

Mohan momentarily looked dejected and then brightened to ask, "May I walk with you and Mrs. Fuller?"

"Go get your coat."

"We'll be right back," Aiden assured her as Mohan bounded toward his room and Emmaline glided toward the doorway in his wake. "I'll lock the door behind us when we leave."

She nodded, worried for him, troubled by the tautness of his body and the coolness of his distance. He'd comforted her when she'd needed it and it only seemed right that she offer the same kindness in return.

He'd barely disappeared when Preeya said quietly, "He is very much disturbed by what happened."

"And determined not to let it get the better of him," Alex agreed, laying aside her needlework. *Just as I'm doing,* she silently added, suddenly understanding how she should approach him when he returned. She had a fairly good idea of what a "regular daily life" with Aiden entailed and resuming it certainly seemed to be the best course possible. Their kiss might have changed matters a bit but she'd simply adjust to whatever signals he gave her in that regard and go on. What mattered most was that he have a reason or two to smile in the hours ahead. Maybe even to laugh.

"I am grateful that you had the wisdom to hire him, Alex. Had he not been here—"

"I'd prefer not to think of the possibilities," she interrupted, determined to keep her newly restored—and still fragile—sense of control from being undermined. "Perhaps we should get ready to leave."

"We?"

Alex frowned and then relaxed. "I'm sorry. I forgot to translate for you," she offered, hoping that the functioning of her brain improved as the day wore on. "At the moment, Aiden and Mohan are walking Emmaline back to her shop. When they return, we're all going somewhere. Where, I don't know. But Aiden says he isn't going to leave any of us behind and unprotected."

"He is a good man, your gentleman."

"He isn't—" Alex bit off the rest of the protest. He *was* her protector. And more. A friend, perhaps? Somehow that didn't seem to be an adequately meaningful distinction. A confidant? Confessor? No, hardly that. And yet it didn't feel all that odd to think of him as being a central part of her life. Given the resolve she'd found on the stairs no more than two hours earlier, that was a disturbing realization. Alex sighed, abandoned the effort to sort through the jumble, and announced, "I'm going to get my things."

Aiden thanked Emmaline one more time and then followed Mohan out of her shop. And stopped dead at the sight of Rose Walker-Hines advancing on him. Sweet Jesus. What other nasty, god-awful things were in store for him today?

"John Aiden!" she cried, reaching out for him with both hands. "Why is it that I'm always meeting you in front of a millinery shop?"

"Pure coincidence, Rose," he answered, taking her hands

in his in an attempt to get her to halt a respectable distance out. She didn't, of course. Her breasts impacted his chest full on and he had to take a half-step back as she kissed his cheek just to keep her momentum from toppling him onto his back.

The instant she drew away enough to look at him, he cleared his throat and cast a quick glance toward Mohan.

She took the cue beautifully, but not in the vein he'd hoped. Instead of circumspectly stepping away, she tightened her hold on his hands, smiled at Mohan and asked, "Who is your young friend? Aren't you going to introduce us?"

"Rose, Master Mohan Singh," he began, resigned to making the best of it and then getting away as quickly as he could. "Mohan, this is the wife of a friend of mine from years past, Mrs. Geoffrey Walker-Hines."

"Madam."

"Well, aren't you a darling little boy," Rose crooned at his polite response and bow. And then, like a spigot being shut off, she promptly dismissed the boy's presence.

She reached up and ran the edges of Aiden's jacket lapels between her fingertips. "You haven't sent word of when you'll be coming to dinner, John Aiden." She looked up at him, pouted, and fluttered her eyelashes. "You promised that you would."

And he'd once been attracted to such a coquettish performance? He'd been insane. Barrett and Carden should have had him locked away for his own good. "My apologies for the oversight," he offered tightly. "I've been busy the last few days and it slipped my mind. I'll attend to it tomorrow."

"What about today? Right this moment?" she pressed. She patted the center of his chest and wrinkled her nose in what he supposed she considered a flirtatious smile. "That way it can't slip your mind again or be postponed. How does this Saturday evening sound to you? And please don't tell me that you've already made plans."

He had no idea what Alex intended to do Saturday evening,

but, whatever it was, he wasn't going to miss it to be with Rose Walker-Hines. "Actually, I do have an engagement already."

"And for Saturday evening next?" she asked, irritation lacing her words as she pointedly arched a brow.

"I'm sorry, Rose, but it's a standing engagement."

"Well, surely she lets you off the leash one night a week," she snapped. Then, apparently thinking better of her tone and approach, she sighed and summoned a more honeyed manner. Leaning closer, she said softly, "Geoffrey always plays cards at his club on Wednesday and Friday evenings. Would either of those be possible for you?"

"Not at this time," he replied, trying his best to look at least a little regretful. "Perhaps in a few weeks. And then again, perhaps not. I'd be reluctant to make a promise today that I might not be able to keep. I hope you understand."

"Oh, I do indeed," she quipped, her brow arching again. "And I also understand how such commitments can quickly change. Especially with you."

He thought about reminding her that the shoe fit her dainty little foot too, but decided against it. Trading insults would only prolong his agony. Instead, he smiled and shrugged roguishly.

"The invitation remains open, John Aiden." She stepped forward to press her breasts against him again and plant another kiss on his cheek. "Please don't be boorish and ignore it forever," she admonished, furiously fluttering her lashes as she inched off toward Emmaline's door.

One last lie . . . "It was nice seeing you again, Rose."

"It's always a *pleasure* to see you, John Aiden," she countered, pausing halfway across the threshold. "And I'd dearly love to see more of you. Soon."

She turned away and he instantly did the same, his heart thundering in relief to have escaped largely unscathed. Scrubbing his hand over his face, Aiden expelled a hard breath and shook his head in wonder. Had Rose always been so incredibly, tactlessly predatory?

"If she is the wife of your friend," Mohan drawled as they started back toward the Blue Elephant, "why did she invite you to dinner the evenings her husband is not home?"

"You noticed that, huh? I was rather hoping you hadn't."

"Is she your companion?"

Aiden winced. "That was delicately put." But, he realized, if the boy was perceptive enough to guess the truth, the time had probably come to discuss such matters openly. And considering that this very necessary part of his education was well outside Alex's expertise, he should be the one to address it. He knitted his brows as a riddle presented itself for consideration. He wasn't the first man to have kissed Alexandra Radford. And she wasn't one of those skittish women who bolted at the merest suggestion of physical attraction. God, no. If he lived to be a hundred, he'd never forget the way she'd looked up at him when he'd threatened to ravage her on the stairs. And yet he'd bet his soul that Alex was a virgin. How she could be so obviously innocent and yet so breathtakingly carnal at the same time was beyond him. It did, however, make him curious. A long road stretched between kissing and lovemaking. How far had Alex traveled before she'd met him? How far would she let him take her?

"Was I too delicate?" Mohan asked, intruding on his speculations. "Should I now attempt to be less subtle?"

Aiden chuckled and allowed the boy credit for persistence. "Just between us men, Mohan . . . Rose was a lover. We parted ways a good long while ago."

"Before she became the wife of your friend?"

"One, he's not really my friend," Aiden clarified. "You say things like that just to be polite. And two . . ." He took a breath and committed himself to providing Mohan with what

Alex would undoubtedly consider an unseemly education. "No, it wasn't before she married him. It was after."

"If she was one of my father's wives, my father would have had you killed for that."

"Those sorts of . . . transgressions are viewed differently in England," he explained. "It's fairly common practice for husbands to have affairs. Sometimes the wives do, too. As long as everyone's discreet, it's considered acceptable."

Mohan stuffed his hands into his coat pockets and considered the near distance with narrowed eyes. "Why," he asked slowly, "would a man marry a woman and then let her lie with another? If he cares for her enough to bring her into his household, would he not care enough about her to keep her for only himself?"

It was a damn good question. One that he hadn't thought to ask until he had been quite a few years older than Mohan. "Some people marry for reasons other than love, Mohan. Wealth and social standing being the most common. They don't so much care about the person they marry as they care about what can be had from the union in a tangible sense. As long as that isn't threatened, they're willing to overlook physical affairs." He shrugged and added, "Personally, I think it's a shallow life."

"Yet you engage in the affairs with married women?"

So much for delicate. But it was an honest question and deserved an honest answer. "Yes, I do. Whenever possible, actually."

"Why?"

"I knew you were going to ask that," he admitted with a rueful smile. The boy was naturally curious about matters of casual sex and just as obviously wholly uninformed. How to tell him what he needed to know without telling him more than he could use at the moment? "Look, Mohan," he began, remembering how his own father had explained it to him years and years ago. It had served him well enough to be worth passing on. "There are several distinct categories of women. The first one is those you just don't think of in any physical way at all. Your mother and your sisters, for example."

"And the queen."

"Exactly." Aiden relaxed, pleased and thinking that their discussion was going to go extremely well. The boy was quick. "And then there are the ones you do notice that way, but know better than to touch. For example, Seraphina, the wife of my friend Carden. Seraphina is a beautiful, exceptional woman and if she weren't Carden's wife I'd be willing to stand in the queue to court her. But she's devoted to Carden and I know that if I ever so much as touched her . . . Well, if she didn't kill me on the spot, Carden would, and it would mean the end of two friendships that I value very much. It's not worth the risk."

Mohan nodded but didn't say anything. Aiden took it as a sign of his understanding and went on. "And then there's the kind of women that someone like you and I would marry. Women like Seraphina was before she married. Their interest and attentions will someday belong solely to their husbands and they don't go around passing out their favors before they meet him. You respect women like that for their strength of character and good virtue. You don't pursue them unless you fully intend to pledge your life and fidelity to them."

Again Mohan nodded but kept his silence. Aiden took a deep breath and let it out slowly. "And that leaves the last group of women," he began, "married or not, who make themselves available to you without strings or any conditions beyond a bit of discretion and an ability to please them in bed. I call them the giving women. It's either them or nothing at all."

The boy tilted his head to the side and asked, "And nothing is not an acceptable condition?"

"It's all right if you're a monk or too drunk to notice,"

Aiden admitted. He laid his hand on Mohan's shoulder and continued, saying, "You're not quite old enough yet to appreciate the kind of drives men have, Mohan. Trust me, you will in another four or five years. When you find yourself there, just remember that the giving women are a relatively safe outlet. As long as you keep your wits about you and employ precautions."

He nodded again and then stopped abruptly. "What kind of precautions?"

It was a good question, a perfectly logical and understandable one. But the answer was more than the boy needed or could use at the moment. "Let's save that discussion for another day, shall we? I've probably gone way too far already. And for God's sake don't mention any of this conversation to Alex. She'd have my hide for it."

"In which category of women does Miss Alex belong?"

"Well . . ." The answer was as instant and clear as it was infuriatingly painful to see. He had no business whatsoever kissing her, much less hoping to draw her into his bed. "She's like Seraphina," he admitted aloud, the words thickening in his throat. "She's the kind of woman that a man marries for love."

"I thought so," Mohan countered, nodding enthusiastically. "You sometimes look at Miss Alex like my father looks at my mother. Are you hoping to marry her?"

"Your mother's already married," Aiden pointed out, dodging the issue, furious with himself for having been so blinded by desire.

"I meant Miss Alex, and you very much know that. You are attempting to evade giving me an answer."

Angry with being pinned into a corner, angry at Alex for not being what he wanted her to be, he replied, "The answer's no. I'm not planning to marry Alexandra Radford. Is that definite enough for you?"

"That is good. My father would be most displeased if she were to marry someone else."

It took a second for the words to fully penetrate his resentment. "Whoa right there!" he demanded, catching the boy by the collar of his coat and hauling him to an abrupt stop. "What are you saying? That your father intends to marry her?"

Mohan shrugged. "Perhaps my father. Perhaps some other raja."

"But you told me just yesterday that your father considered her too stubborn to be a good wife."

"She is greatly improving by the day, is she not?" Mohan asked, smiling broadly. "My mother has always said Miss Alex would. In time. And with the right man."

He didn't want to think about the possibilities. Not in any sense directly connected to Alex, anyway. "How many wives does your father have?"

"When I left India, he had four. And a dozen mistresses. He is a very wealthy man. With, as I understand what you have told me today, much of the man's drives."

Sixteen women at his beck and call? Sixteen to keep pleased? "God, I guess. Either that or he's just plain crazy."

"You will say nothing of your knowledge of this future to Miss Alex, will you?"

He blinked, pulled from his imaginings. "Why? Is it a secret?"

Mohan knitted his brows and pursed his lips. After a moment he said, "I think so. It is a matter never spoken of in the presence of Miss Alex." He brightened a bit to add, "I spoke of it now only because I like you and do not wish you to build hopes for something that you cannot have. I do not want to see you disappointed at their collapse."

In certain respects, it was too late for that. "Thanks," he groused.

"You are upset."

"Not about anything in particular," Aiden lied, starting down the walkway again. "It's just been a helluva day so far, Mohan. One helluva day."

"And it is very early yet."

Yes, it was. And if the rest of it went as the hours just past, he'd have to seriously think about shooting himself. God, what a damn inconvenient time not only to remember that he'd been raised to be a gentleman, but also to remember what had to be the one and only scrap of useful information his father had ever given him. He'd opened a door with Alex he shouldn't have. How the hell he was going to get it shut again without hurting her feelings or insulting her . . . Christ, doing the right thing would be ever so much easier if he even remotely wanted to do it.

Chapter 10

It was the third stop of what Alex was coming to think of as their tour of London's highs, lows, and in-betweens. The first place had been a rather seedy boardinghouse where Aiden had gone to look for a man named O'Brien. No explanation had been given as to why they were looking for him; not as they'd alighted from the carriage and not as they'd climbed back in without having seen him.

The second stop had been the offices of Barrett Stanbridge. Only Quincy had been there and he'd been none too happy to see them all traipsing in to deposit three-day-old snow on the anteroom carpet. Aiden had spoken with him in hushed tones and Quincy had gestured wildly to a stack of papers on his desk before throwing his hands up in a gesture of obvious frustration. Aiden had growled in response, then marched them all back to the carriage. Again without an explanation. He'd sat silent, the reins in hand and frowning, for a few moments before sighing and then resolutely setting them in motion.

Now Alex stood on the front walk of a huge brick mansion, waiting patiently for Mohan to finish assisting Preeya from their carriage.

"It's a beautiful house," she ventured, hoping he'd finally

say something, anything, that might give her some idea of what they were about.

"Carden's an earl and an architect," he supplied, offering his arm. "Seraphina's a well-known artist. It's amazing what one can do with unlimited amounts of money and talent, isn't it?"

Carden, the man for whom Sawyer worked and who was currently in Egypt, she recalled. This was the place where Aiden had been living prior to being sent to guard Mohan? "The Blue Elephant must seem like a hovel to you," she posed, feeling decidedly out of her element.

"Not in the least," he assured her as he led their procession toward the front door. "The Blue Elephant's charming and comfortable in a way I didn't know a house could be."

"You certainly didn't think that at first sight."

His cheeks colored slightly. "Well," he drawled, "I'll admit that all the colors, all the touches of India, were a bit off-putting at first, but I've come to like and appreciate it. Quite a lot, actually."

"Why?" she pressed, determined to know whether he was being honest or merely polite.

"I don't know," he answered, leading her up the steps. From the other side of the massive door came the unmistakable sound of several wildly barking dogs. Apparently unaware of it, he went on. "I suppose there's a refreshing lack of pretension about it. And Lord knows that it's not the least predictable or boring." He drew her to a halt and, blindly using the door knocker, smiled broadly as he added, "Now that I think about it, it's a lot like you."

Her cheeks flooded with heat but she resisted the impulse to hastily assure him that she hadn't been in search of either a compliment or a declaration of his feelings. Any sort of protest—however brief or spirited—couldn't help but be painfully awkward. Better, she knew, to let it pass as though unnoticed. But the silence stretching between them was becoming noticeable and she felt a need to fill it before it could become strained.

"How many dogs do your friends have?" she asked, grateful to the raucous beasts for the timely diversion.

He looked at her as though puzzled by the question and then turned his head to stare at the door, seeming to have suddenly become aware of the commotion on the other side. "Six, but they took two of them along to Egypt." He reached for the latch, saying, "Sawyer probably can't hear us knocking over the welcome committee. Either that or he can't get past them to open the door."

He pushed the door wide. Straight ahead of them, in the center of the foyer, was a large round table centered with a crystal vase holding a lush arrangement of exotic, freshly cut flowers. It was the perfect welcome, a serene island whispering of perfect hospitality. The rest of the foyer, however, was bedlam in progress.

"Good God Almighty, Sawyer!" Aiden shouted over the din of the dogs as he advanced into the chaos.

"My apologies for not letting you in, sir," Sawyer called back from atop a ladder teetering in front of heavily draped windows. "As you can see I'm putting down a rebellion in the zoo."

A zoo? Well, yes. Four good-sized dogs leaping, barking, their tongues lolling and their tails wagging furiously would have surely qualified. But adding in the cat and the five kittens—all of them perched on the valance, puffed up, hissing and spitting—took the pandemonium well beyond anything Alex had ever seen. She glanced back over her shoulder, afraid that Mohan would be frightened by the anarchy. His eyes were wide; almost but not quite as wide as his grin. Preeya was clearly just as amused. Her concerns allayed, Alex turned back to consider Sawyer and how she might help in bringing matters under some semblance of control.

Aiden spared her the effort. "Well, the cats might come

down if the dogs weren't threatening to eat them," he advised, taking the ladder in his hands and steadying it. "Climb down off there before you're knocked off and let's impose some order."

"The dogs were confined but broke loose just as I had the first blasted kitten in hand," the butler explained over the din as he carefully inched his way toward the floor. Once safely there, he tugged his suit into place, lifted his chin, and slipped into his official role. "Welcome to Haven House, Miss Radford."

"Hello, Sawyer," she replied. Half turning and gesturing, she added, "This is Mohan Singh, my ward. And our housekeeper, Preeya."

"A pleasure, Master Singh. Madam," he said with a perfunctory bow. It was to Preeya that he said, "If you would excuse me for just a few moments while I incarcerate—once again—the hounds of hell."

"I'll get Lucy and Tippy for you," Aiden volunteered, snagging the heavy leather collar of one of the beasts as it charged the window. A second later he had another one in hand and was hauling them both toward the opposite doorway and the hall beyond. The cat hissed and howled epithets after them. The kittens sang the chorus. It took Sawyer a bit longer to apprehend his pair of culprits, but eventually he too moved off, his departure noted with additional commentary from the still outraged cat.

"I like this house, Miss Alex," her ward said in Hindi. "Might we have some animals of our own?"

"We have peacocks," she pointed out, remembering her conversation with Aiden about Mohan's general state of boredom and, specifically, his lack of pets.

"I meant an animal that could live in the house with us and provide for our entertainment. A cat. Or a dog. Or perhaps several of each."

"It's you who provide for them, Mohan," she cautioned.

"Yes, they can make one feel better and laugh. But animals are also a responsibility. One that can't be taken lightly or forsaken once the commitment is made."

"I will be a good caretaker and a kind friend."

Not Preeya, she noticed. Just days ago it wouldn't have occurred to him to assume the obligation himself. At least not without having first attempted to pass it off to someone else. "I'm willing to consider the proposal," she ceded, assessing the little fur balls lined up along the high ground.

"Perhaps Sawyer knows where we can acquire a cat of our own," Mohan mused.

If she were inclined to wager, she'd put a few crowns on which cats Sawyer would suggest they take home with them. "Perhaps," she countered, "he might need to be convinced of your willingness to be responsible and caring before he would offer his advice in that regard. Do you suppose that coaxing the cats down off the valance might be a way of demonstrating those qualities?"

To his great credit, he didn't hesitate. "If you and Preeya would steady the ladder for me, please."

Neither she nor Preeya said a word as they took up their stations on opposite sides of the ladder and Mohan scampered up the steps. But then, words weren't the least bit necessary, Alex realized. They were both thinking the same thing: Mohan had become a different, far happier, and more likable child in the last few days. Since the day that Aiden Terrell had been drawn into their lives. In the larger scheme of things, adopting a family of cats was a very small reward for the very significant changes Mohan had willingly undergone. She could only hope that Aiden wasn't one of those sorts who got near a cat and sneezed.

"Since they apparently were able to slide the bolt on the pantry door," Sawyer said from behind him, "I think they'd best be placed outside in their kennel, sir."

Aiden nodded and continued past the pantry door and out the back of the house. With their wrought-iron enclosure in sight, the dogs strained to race him there and he released them, allowing them to run the last measure of yard. He'd no sooner done so than the other two bolted past him, dashing to catch up, vying to be the first inside.

"Where did the kittens come from?" he asked, closing the kennel gate and drawing the chain around to secure it. "They weren't here the last time I was."

"Actually, they were, sir," Sawyer corrected, giving the chain a good yank to be sure it would hold. "In the carriage house. But when the snow started falling, the mother cat brought them to the rear door and demanded warmer shelter."

Aiden grinned, stuffed his hands in his pockets, and leaned his shoulder against a bar. "And you couldn't refuse."

"Of course not, sir." He cleared his throat softly. "Although I did attempt to confine them to a well-appointed box in Miss Beatrice's room. As a strategy, it worked well enough until Mrs. Blaylock inadvertently failed to fully close the door after feeding them this morning."

"Then all hell broke loose."

"Yes." He cocked a silver brow as he added dryly, "But not until after she'd left for her day out, of course."

Yes, it was a good plan. Sawyer was the perfect solution. "How would you like a chance to avoid all this for a while?"

The silver brow moved slightly higher. "Are you suggesting that I take a holiday, sir? How very kind of you."

"Well, it would be something like a holiday."

Sawyer's brows came together as he lowered his chin. "Do go on, Mr. Terrell."

He knew how to play Sawyer. Leading with the trump card always did it. "This morning," he said coolly, matter-of-factly, "two thugs came into the Blue Elephant and attempted to kidnap Alex at knife point."

As Aiden expected, Sawyer started, blanched, and glanced back toward the house. Just as predictably, the man blinked twice, then straightened his shoulders, turned back, cleared his throat and said, "Obviously, and most thankfully, they failed to do so."

Aiden nodded. "That's because I shot them both dead."

Sawyer considered him somberly and then gently offered, "I'm sure it was absolutely necessary to do so, Mr. Terrell. I sincerely hope you also view it in such a light and have no remorse over the course of events."

"I'm working on it," Aiden admitted with a shrug. That was the one problem with knowing Sawyer so well; the man also knew him.

Rather than dwell on the regrets, he deliberately moved to the next phase of his plan. "But it occurred to me in the aftermath that I can't adequately protect three people all at once. If I'm out and about with Mohan, then Alex is alone in the house and Preeya's alone in the kitchen. I can't very well confine everyone to one room of the house to keep watch over them. The boredom would be unrelenting. For all of us."

"And you do so loathe being bored."

Aiden smiled, knowing that if Sawyer were being honest he'd have to admit to the same predilection. "So what would you say to being my second for a few weeks?" he posed, already knowing that the deal was done and all but sealed. "Just during the day. I'd take full responsibility for Mohan's safety and you could be a daunting male presence hovering along the edges of Alex's and Preeya's worlds. You could step in and diffuse any number of situations that might arise. At night, we're always together in the salon until we retire. I can manage that on my own and you could come back here to sleep in your own bed. So what do you think? Would you be interested in helping me protect them?"

"I am hardly a professional at such efforts, sir."

"And I am?" Aiden countered with a snort. "I thought I might press O'Brien into duty, but I couldn't find him. Which is just as well. He's a bit rough around the edges. Then I went looking for Barrett to see if he had someone else he could assign to help me. His secretary says that he thinks Barrett has gone off to Wales on a case. Not that he'd know. Barrett never tells anyone what he's going to do. The inconsiderate bastard. I swear to God, Sawyer, the man will be dead in a ditch somewhere for a week before it occurs to anyone that he might be missing."

"You sound slightly harried, sir."

"That's probably because I am," Aiden supplied, knowing that they were mere seconds away from Sawyer's formal enlistment.

"If you truly believe that I would be of more help than hindrance—"

"Bless you, Sawyer," he declared, clapping a hand on the man's shoulder in genuine gratitude. "I'll make sure Barrett pays you for your trouble."

"But I can give of my time only until I hear word of the family's imminent return. At that point, my duties here would have to take precedence over any others."

"Of course. I wouldn't have it any other way. Can you start tomorrow morning?"

"I believe that will not be a problem, sir. At what time should I arrive?"

"Nine?"

"Very good, sir. Nine o'clock it will be."

"Thank you, Sawyer. You're a saint. Now," he added, looking back at the house and sighing. "Let's go see what we can do about the cats and salvaging Sera's curtains."

"If you have any hopes of becoming a saint yourself," Sawyer muttered, "you'll take them home with you. The cats, I mean. Not the draperies."

Aiden grinned. "If no one's sneezing or blotting red eyes

when we get in there . . . A boy should have pets, don't you think?"

Aiden started awake and stared into the darkness, hearing only the rasping of his breath and the frantic pounding of his heart, feeling only the searing heat in his shoulder. He reached up and laid his fingertips over the scar, letting the smooth familiarity of the circle ground him. As always, the burning slowly began to subside, retreating back into the realm of his nightmares. And as usual, the stark, horrifying clarity of the images started to fade with it. But not completely. This time the memory of them hauntingly remained and his heart refused to slow.

He swallowed and deliberately considered the changes. Her eyes had been blue, her hair golden in the sunlight. She'd been a tiny slip of a thing; so feminine, so delicate, that he'd called her his china doll. God, he could remember all of that so clearly. So why couldn't he just as clearly conjure the actual image of her from his memory? Why had the crumpled body on the bloody deck of his nightmare been raven haired? Why had it been Alex's hazel eyes that had stared unseeingly up at him?

He couldn't have forgotten, couldn't have let such a precious thing slip away. It was unforgivable. More so than having failed her that day when the sun had glinted so brightly off the sea and all the world had been full of hope and promise.

Aiden sat up and scrubbed his hands over his face. With a hard breath, he willed his awareness on the moonlight spilling in through the windows of his room and the world slumbering around him. It took a long time, longer than it ever had before, but eventually the harshness of his breathing eased and the desperate cadence of his heartbeat slowed.

He needed a drink. The darker and more potent, the better. Not much, he promised himself as he raked his fingers through his hair. Just enough to dull his mind so that he could sleep without being haunted. Maybe Alex kept something suitable in the parlor, he thought, quickly pulling on his trousers. Brandy, perhaps, for when she entertained. Most likely it would be in the chest, the one with the statue. Probably the bottom drawer. He snagged his shirt as he climbed off the pallet and onto his feet. He wouldn't have much of it. But even if he did, he'd replace it for her tomorrow.

A flutter of white at the edge of her vision told Alex he was there just before she heard him gasp in surprise. She glanced down past her open book to be sure she was adequately covered, stroked a kitten once to calm herself, and then looked up to smile at him. "I see that you can't sleep, either."

For a second he looked panicked and his gaze darted to the chest against the far wall. Then he expelled a hard breath and moistened his lower lip with the tip of his tongue. "Would you mind some company?"

She should say that she was just planning to try to retire again. She really should get up and let him have the salon to himself. And she most certainly shouldn't be noticing the bare chest clearly visible between the open edges of his shirtfront. And neither should she be so keenly aware of the roguish tilt of the waistband around his narrow hips. But, dear God, it was such a fine expanse of flesh and well-defined muscle and she was only human. What harm was there in looking? As long as she didn't act on her baser impulses, there wouldn't be any at all.

"I'd love to share your company," she assured him, closing her book and laying it on the floor beside her. "Please come in and be comfortable. I can loan you a kitten if you'd like one."

His conscience told him that he was going to be sorry if he didn't make some excuse, turn around and leave. Another voice, a far more strident one, countered that one more regret on the heap wouldn't matter one whit to either his happiness or the destination of his soul.

And, the hedonistic voice went on, peeking out from under the hem of that caramel-colored dressing gown was a bare, delicately curved foot and a wisp of cinnamon gossamer silk. All curled up on her side in the pillows as she was, her hair unbound and fanning around her shoulders, kittens nestled into the curve beneath her breasts, the flickering light of the fire, of the candles . . . He wasn't dead. Not by a long shot. In fact, at that particular moment, he was truly glad to be alive. His conscience could just be damned for the next little while. As long as Alex didn't curl into him, purr, and ask to be petted, everything could be kept quite under control, quite circumspect.

Alex tilted her head, hoping to give the impression that she was deeply engaged in deciding which kitten to offer him. The truth, however, was that she didn't want to be caught openly watching him move toward her. But there was no way to keep from doing so altogether. He was positively magnificent, a true feast for a wanton appreciation of sensuous form and grace. No wonder he'd had his choice of London's women. The wonder was that any of them had ever let him go.

Not that they'd been given any choice in the matter, she reminded herself as he settled into the nest of pillows beside her. Like all big cats, Aiden Terrell enjoyed the hunt too much to be willingly, completely domesticated. She'd do well to keep that bit of reality in the forefront of her awareness. And she'd be equally well served if she could manage to keep both her gaze genuinely fixed on the kittens and their conversation lively and light.

"It occurs to me," she ventured, trailing a fingertip along a fuzzy little spine, "that you know considerably more about me than I do about you."

"So tell me about yourself, Aiden Terrell?" he supplied, cradling his head in his hand and mercifully allowing the front of his shirt to drape over his chest.

"Yes, please." She risked meeting his gaze to add, "Graphic details aren't necessary, of course."

His smile was instant and as wicked as the devil dancing in his eyes. "Well, if I leave out the more sordid and debauched parts, there's really not all that much left to tell. I'm the oldest of twelve children."

"Twelve?" she repeated, tearing her gaze away, a little embarrassed by how easily he could make her heart race.

He knew his limits and watching Alex stroke the kittens was well beyond them. He rolled onto his back, cradling his head in his hands and pinning his gaze safely on the ceiling. "Six sisters, five brothers," he supplied. "My parents believe in order and careful planning. I was educated by the best private tutors money could buy and with an eye always on the fact that I would someday take the helm of the family business. I'm excessively educated, actually. And truth be told, I hated every minute in the schoolroom. I figure—if I'm truly fortunate—I'll be disinherited someday soon. I've certainly been working on it anyway. Quite diligently as a matter of fact."

She settled more comfortably into the pillows, saying, "Your family . . . Do they live in London?"

"No. St. Kitts. In the Leeward Islands."

"The Caribbean Ocean? That's as far west of here as India is east. How on earth did you end up in London?"

"The family business is shipping. Mostly in the Atlantic. A few years ago my father brought the entire family here so that I and my three next youngest siblings could accept delivery of four ships he'd commissioned. One was delayed in the yards and I stayed behind to wait for it. While idling away my days and nights, I met Carden and Barrett."

"Are you still waiting for the ship to be finished?"

If only. "I accepted delivery just over two years ago," he answered, "and sailed it home like a good and dutiful son."

"So you're not just a sailor, you're a ship's captain."

"Part owner, too."

"I'm sure Mohan would love to see your ship sometime."

It was more question than statement. A request for what she obviously considered a large favor. "Well, that would be rather difficult," he admitted ruefully. "I managed to very effectively sink it a year and a half ago."

"Oh." Disappointment. Hope bloomed again as she asked, "And are you back in London now to take delivery of another vessel?"

All he had to do was say yes and they'd move on to another subject. It would be a lie but she'd never know it. He didn't have to be honest with her. And Lord knew that the truth wasn't at all flattering. "I'm in London because it was as far as I could stumble before I fell flat on my face."

"You don't strike me as the sort of man who stumbles very often, Aiden."

He chuckled darkly. "But when I do, it's done in a grand way."

"What happened? Was it the loss of the ship?" she pressed gently. "Is that why your father's angry at you?"

Angry? He rolled his eyes. "Livid might be more accurate."

"Surely, if he's been in the shipping business for any length of time, he knows that sometimes accidents happen, that ships are lost through no fault of the captain or the crew."

"And sometimes," he added, "they're lost because the captain does something unforgivably stupid."

"What did you do?"

So soft, so caring. If he changed the subject, she wouldn't protest. If he handed her a lie, she'd realize it, but accept it because it would be the kindest thing to do. "As you've no doubt heard, the Americans have been having a bloody set-to between themselves for the last few years. The northern states have thrown a naval blockade around the southern ones. I tried to run it."

"For any particular reason?"

"In hindsight it wasn't a good one."

She was searching his face, he could feel the tender caress of her gaze. He decided that he had no choice except to tell her everything. He'd come this far and she deserved to know the rest. "Her name was Mary Alice Randolph. Of the South Carolina Randolphs. She'd been in London since the start of their war and wanted to go home to Charleston. And I wanted her to marry me, so I promised to get her there." He had to swallow and take a deep breath before he could force the final truth of it out. "She was killed in the first barrage we took. She was gone by the time I could get to her. I didn't get to say good-bye."

Alex felt her heart tear. "Oh, Aiden," she whispered, fighting back tears as she touched his arm, hoping to comfort him in some small way. "I'm so very sorry. How deeply you must hurt. And how horrible your regrets must be."

He rolled onto his side and met her gaze squarely. His brows knitted as an unsettling mix of sadness and wonder darkened his eyes. "You're the only person who's ever said that to me, Alex. The only one." Then he leaned forward to graze her forehead with a kiss as he murmured, "Thank you."

She didn't know what to say, what to do. Which was, she realized as he settled back on his side, how she usually felt when around Aiden. Always at something of a loss, always off kilter and uncertain. And yet, in the oddest way, it wasn't a disconcerting feeling. Under the confusion was an unshakable sense that he wouldn't let her flounder or make a fool of herself.

"Anyway," he went on, a reassuring degree of buoyancy back in his voice, "I managed—largely through miserable luck—to survive the assault and the sinking. Those of us left were pulled out of the water, thrown into a hold, hauled to New York, and processed as foreign enemy combatants. It took six months and cost my father a fortune to ransom us out of the Union prison."

"But I'm sure your parents were relieved to have you home again, safe and sound," she offered, hoping to take his memory down a happier path.

His laugh was dry and mirthless. "The joyful family reunion lasted all of fifteen seconds. Somewhere in the midst of the roaring lecture that followed, I walked out the door and haven't looked back."

She wasn't doing this at all well, but she felt an obligation to keep trying, to keep hoping that she could make him feel better. "What made you decide to come back to London? To be with your friends?"

This time there was, blessedly, a hint of real amusement in his chuckle. "I honestly don't know. I can't tell you how I got here, either. The last four weeks have been the longest stretch of time since that day that I've been sober. I can only guess that at some point I decided to get as far away from my father as I could and headed this way. And as I said, I got this far before I fell down and didn't care enough to get up and keep moving."

"The favor you owe Barrett Stanbridge . . . The one that led you to accept the task of protecting Mohan . . . Is it for his insistence that you stop drinking?"

"He said that a year was long enough for any man to soak in misery. That's one of the very few things he's said to me in recent weeks that I can repeat in the presence of a lady. I wasn't inclined to think of him as a friend for a while, but I'm beginning to see that perhaps he's right."

"I'm glad he intervened to bring you up short. If he hadn't, I'd be at the mercy of those two men right now."

"If I hadn't been here," he said solemnly, "you'd be dead right now, Alex."

"Then I'm especially appreciative of your newfound sobriety."

He should be gallant. Self-effacing. Actually, he really should get up and leave. But he couldn't. In the soft flickering light she was so exotic, so deliciously tempting. Her dark hair framed a face that wasn't as English fair as it was softly kissed by a distant, foreign sun. Her eyes were dark; not blue, not green, not gray. They were sultry shadows, inviting him to search for answers to ancient mysteries, to discover treasures beyond compare. No, he wasn't about to leave her. Common sense could be damned, right along with his conscience.

He grinned roguishly, knowing full good and well that she always melted in the face of it. "Just how appreciative are you?"

Oh, the master was truly at his best. Alex quickly considered her choices and daringly discarded all but one of them. Two could play the game and while she certainly didn't have the worldly experience he did, she did have the element of surprise to her advantage. It was a reckless gambit, to be sure, but somehow that didn't matter to her nearly as much as the chance to gently rattle his cool composure.

Studiously avoiding his gaze, she reached out, slowly trailing her fingertips along his shirt collar before moving down ever so slightly and taking the open edge of the front gently but firmly in hand. Deliberately drawing him toward her, she leaned forward and lifted her gaze to his lips.

He swallowed. Or rather tried to. His breath came shallow and quick, from between slightly parted lips. And then, just before she touched his lips with hers, he stopped breathing altogether. She lingered purely for the pleasure of it;

fully savoring the softness of his lips and the sweet taste of his absolute acceptance. Only when he murmured her name and slipped his hand up the length of her arm did she stop and draw away.

"Thank you, Aiden," she whispered, releasing him, her pulse racing and her senses overfilled. "For being here."

Aiden knew it was the moment, the quality of the light. It wasn't real. And he didn't care. He was consumed by a hunger, a desire so compelling that it took his breath away and left him quaking with need. His conscience prickled, reminding him of how he'd vowed just that morning that he'd be a gentleman and close the door with Alex. Now . . . It was irrational. Unjustifiable and indefensible. Nevertheless, he had to know if there was a chance. Even the slimmest one would be enough. He could be patient if he had to be.

"May I ask you a very personal question, Alex?"

"You may ask anything you like as long as you understand that I reserve the right to refuse to answer."

"Do you see yourself ever marrying?" he asked without further prelude.

"Honestly? No." She shrugged a slim shoulder and gave him a shy smile. "Oh, from time to time, I dream about being swept away by a handsome prince on a white charger. But I know that it's never going to happen."

"It could."

With a soft laugh she replied, "On the very remote chance that it does, he'll promptly drop me. I don't have the temperament to be a good wife, Aiden. I'm stubborn, opinionated, rigid, and far too independent. And as if that's not bad enough, I've never learned how to flutter my lashes, faint in a timely fashion, or dither helplessly over minor decisions. The world is full of women who are far more suitable for marriage than I am. There's no reason for a man to choose me over them."

He disagreed but it wasn't in the interest of his more

immediate hopes to share that with her. "Does the idea of being alone forever bother you?"

"I'm never truly alone," she blithely countered. "Here in London I have Preeya and Mohan. Emmaline. You. And starting tomorrow, Sawyer as well. And in India . . . It's a very full and busy household."

"That's not exactly what I meant," he grumbled, frustrated but unwilling to risk shocking her by more clearly stating the question.

"Does the idea of never lying with a man bother me?"

He blinked, stunned. "That was . . ."

"Frank?" she supplied impishly. "Indians are much more open about such matters than the English are, Aiden. And the answer is sometimes yes, but most of the time no. And this is the point in our conversation where I refuse to say anything further."

Everything he really wanted to know lay on the other side of "further," beyond the current limits of her trust. "Fair enough," he acceded. But only because he really didn't have any other choice.

"Do you hope to someday marry?"

"No," he replied, feeling oddly dispassionate about the assertion. Of course, he reminded himself, it was a decision he'd made quite some time ago and then put away from further consideration. It was done and it was final. There really wasn't any great emotion wrapped up in it anymore.

"That's truly a pity. You'd make a wonderful husband and father. You've done wonders with Mohan. He's become a completely different, much happier child."

"I had my chance. And I destroyed it."

She considered him in silence for a long moment and then nodded slowly. "I can see how you'd feel that way. My mother's marriage was a painful disaster in every sense. Like you, she thought that her chance for happiness was lost forever." A smile lifted the corners of her mouth ever so slightly. "Life and the raja proved her wrong."

Aiden chuckled. "Is there a lesson in that for me?"

"I hope so."

"To keep my eyes open for a raja? No, thank you."

The smile ebbed away. "The lesson, Aiden," she said gently, "is that sometimes what you least expect comes to you from where you least expect it, when you least expect it."

It was a lovely sentiment, but she'd missed the point. "I don't want anything to come my way," he countered. "Expected or otherwise."

"So deliberately living your life without hope is your penance for not being God?" she posed, her brow arched. "For not being able to lift up your hand and brush aside the salvo that killed the woman you loved?"

"More or less," he agreed, disliking the way she'd put it and sensing something ominous closing in around him.

"How very British of you," she remarked somberly, openly studying him. "If you were an Indian, a Hindu, you'd view it completely differently. You acted in the belief that you were doing a good deed, a true and loving kindness for another human being whose soul was in pain. Your good intentions, however, were thwarted by the gods and the power of the universe through no fault of your own. To love and to lose was your fate. To rise above the failure and engage in further good deeds, to risk failing again, is your challenge."

"But I'm not Indian or Hindu. I'm British to the core," he pointed out, trying to tamp down his inexplicably rising irritation. "Blaming the outcome of something on fate is nothing more than an excuse for the lack of sufficient will. Fate is mine to shape as I desire."

"So you didn't truly, in the heart of your heart, want to successfully run the blockade?" she asked gently. "You didn't strongly enough want your Mary Alice to live and become your wife?"

He didn't like the way she'd framed that issue, either, but he supposed that it was the fundamental truth of how he looked at it all. "And there you have the foundations of an abiding guilt."

She hummed softly, looked down at the kittens, petted one, and then looked back up at him to ask, "So now your great challenge in life is to be as alone and miserable as humanly possible?"

Damn if she didn't have a way of making the most rationally arrived-at decisions seem downright featherbrained. And, he had to admit, there was the tiniest kernel of truth to the point she was making. Being with her, kissing her, definitely didn't fall in the category of human misery and he certainly wasn't the least bit interested in abandoning either pleasure. Accepting that reality, he willingly conceded, "Not all the time."

Her smile bright and her eyes twinkling, she replied, "Well, that's a relatively healthy sign. Apparently you haven't given up the struggle altogether. Which might suggest—to an open mind—that you're not really fated to spend this lifetime wallowing in regret."

He didn't like the culmination of her logic any more than he had the process of getting there. The promise he'd made was a solemn one, a noble, honorable sacrifice for his having failed. While he could still make the argument that it was well within the bounds of noble and honorable, he wasn't quite so sure anymore about the fundamental intelligence of it. Lord knew the qualities didn't necessarily go hand in glove. The world was full of honorable, noble fools. And he didn't particularly relish the notion of being one of them.

Alex and her way of looking at the world . . . He hadn't had a single second thought about his course until he'd met her. Not one. Not so much as a twinge of doubt. But, having spent less than a week with Alexandra Radford, his world was, if not turned fully upside down, then at the very least severely tilted on its axis. Had she done it to him deliberately? Or was it just the natural consequence of his having been immersed in her decidedly unique existence?

"Which are you really, Alex?" he mused aloud. "Indian or British? Deep down inside."

She gave him the slightest of shrugs and a cryptic smile. "I can see the strengths of each way."

As usual, she hadn't really answered the question. Undaunted, he pressed in a more roundabout manner. "What's your fate in this lifetime?"

"Today it's to educate Mohan so that he can better serve his people. What it will be tomorrow, I don't know. What comes, comes. I'll accept the challenge as best I can and try to do good whenever and however possible."

What comes, comes. "That would be very Hindu of you," he observed, feeling smug for having maneuvered her into revealing the truth.

"It wouldn't be an approach frowned upon by Christians, either," she countered, her eyes still dark, still inviting him to search. "Or Buddhists."

He had no idea about Buddhist beliefs; he'd have to take her word on it. What he did know, though, was that she had perfected avoidance and resistance to a fine art. That and she intrigued him in so many ways. Far more than was good for either of them at the moment.

"I should let you get back to your reading," he suggested, reaching out to pet one of the sleeping kittens.

Alex willed herself to keep breathing, willed herself still as his fingertips grazed the curve of her breast and a thrilling current of heat arced through her. If she confessed that the book wasn't nearly as interesting as he was . . . If she invited him to stay . . .

"Good night, Alex."

There was a solace of sorts in seeing the reluctance in his eyes as he eased out of the pillows. It was nice to know that she wasn't alone in regretting a commitment to good judgment and the dubious value of sterling virtue. "Good night, Aiden," she bade. "Sweetest of dreams."

His smile was quirked as he winked and walked off into the shadows. Alex watched him go, feeling suddenly adrift and sadly incomplete.

Chapter 11

Three consecutive days in the saddle, Aiden silently grumbled as they made their way into the rear yard, would make one, if not weak, then at least acutely aware of discomfort. Especially if it had been well over a year since you'd last thought about saddles, stirrups, reins, and using certain muscles in your body. Thank God for long hot baths and whatever was in the tincture that Alex had been giving him before dinner every evening.

There were two consolations in it all; the first being that Mohan was well on his way to becoming an excellent rider, the second that Alex was a delightful caretaker who winced every time he did and spent considerable effort seeing to his physical comfort. The only drawback was that he'd been too tired too soon in the evening to reap the larger rewards of her tender caretaking.

Although, he reminded himself, there was something nicely domestic about having her gently wake him, help him up from the pillows, and send him off to his own bed. It would be even nicer if he ever had the presence of mind to ask her to come with him.

"Perhaps we should put my horse back on the lead."

Aiden looked over at the boy and cocked a brow. "Do you think we need to?"

"I am quite comfortable without it," Mohan assured him. "It is Miss Alex's comfort which concerns me. She is not likely to be pleased to see the lead gone. She has a habit of worrying about me unnecessarily."

That she did. And the last three days of riding in the parks of London had brought that home in a way he hadn't expected. "We won't tell her that we've taken it off."

"And you do not think that she will be at a window, watching through the new iron covers for our return?"

"If she is and if she protests, I'll assure her that you deserve the freedom and can manage it ably."

"And you believe that she will accept your word on this?" he posed, clearly skeptical.

"Yes."

Mohan snorted and countered, "Then you would be the very first man to have such an influence on her."

"And just how would you know that?" Aiden asked as he reined in his mount and swung down. "You're only ten. You couldn't have seen too many men try to sway her on anything."

"British officers come to see my father all the time," he retorted, climbing down as Aiden pulled open the doors of the stable. "They notice Miss Alex. And when Mrs. Radford was alive, she took Miss Alex to parties at their summer headquarters. Always one or two officers would come back after them. I have seen many men talking sweet to Miss Alex. She is always polite but unaffected by them. Eventually they go away and do not return."

Which, when it came right down to it, was exactly what he was doing now, what he was going to do in the end. Aiden frowned, not liking that he was falling into the same pattern as the other men who had passed through Alex's life.

"Fairness compels me to admit that you are different,"

Mohan added as they led their mounts inside. "She does not keep the same distance with you. You may have a chance the others did not. So perhaps it is all right to leave the lead off my horse after all."

As though it weren't far too late to put it back on. "Sometimes," Aiden grumbled, "I think you're an old man in a child's body."

"Perhaps I am."

The movement was in the lengthening shadows outside the stable door, furtive and silent. Aiden pulled the revolver from the small of his back even as he whirled and stepped between it and Mohan.

Hands instantly went up. "Kindly don't."

Barrett. Aiden exhaled in relief and dropped the muzzle toward the floor, muttering, "Well, look what the cat dragged in."

"The cat is out?" Mohan asked, looking around quickly, clearly panicked at the possibility.

"It's an expression," Aiden clarified as Barrett sauntered toward them. "It means that something unexpected has turned up rather unceremoniously." He nodded toward Barrett while tucking the gun back into the waistband of his trousers. "That would be, in this particular case, one Barrett Stanbridge."

Mohan bowed but never took his eyes off Barrett. "Sir."

"Since you appear to be hale, hearty, and reasonably happy," Barrett said, looking the boy up and down with a smile, "I'll assume that Mr. Terrell is doing his job to your satisfaction."

"My satisfaction is of no consequence, sir. It is Miss Alex who passes judgment on the situation."

Barrett cocked a brow and Aiden seized the moment to turn to Mohan and say, "Speaking of Alex . . . Please go tell her and Preeya that we'll be having a guest for dinner. Mr. Stanbridge and I will take care of the horses before we come in."

"Yes, sir."

"And then stay in the house."

Mohan nodded crisply and took off. Aiden waited until he'd disappeared before he turned to loosen the girth of the gelding's saddle and ask, "Where have you been, Barrett?"

"In the country," his friend supplied, stepping up to Mohan's animal and beginning to work. "My father summoned me for the annual lecture on accepting my various obligations to the Stanbridge name. Quincy said you'd been by the office looking for me."

"Four damn days ago," Aiden griped, pulling the saddle and blanket away. He flung the tack over the top rail of the open stall, adding, "And your secretary told me you were in Wales."

"I never tell Quincy where I'm really going. If I did, he'd send people like you trotting right after me. And he'd send a huge satchel of papers to be signed with you." He tossed the saddle over the railing. Mohan's horse strode into its stall on its own as Barrett asked, "What do you need?"

"Nothing now," Aiden supplied, leading the gelding in. He removed the bit and bridle. "I solved the problem myself by hiring Sawyer. He's my second, keeping an eye on the flock when they split up from time to time. Nine to five every day. I trust you to pay him appropriately."

"What was wrong with O'Brien?"

Working a brush over the animal's back, Aiden shrugged. "I considered him and then decided against it. I wanted someone suitable for being inside the house. O'Brien isn't exactly the coat-and-stock variety."

"True enough. Why do you need the second man? You're only guarding the boy."

Aiden paused. How to put it all into words? He hadn't tried before this moment. Just knowing it was out there was enough for him. For Barrett, though . . .

He'd put two scoops of grain and an armload of hay into the stall feeder before he crossed to Barrett's side of the stable, leaned his arms on the top rail, and admitted, "Something isn't right about all of this, Barrett. I've spent days parading Mohan around London in plain sight. If someone's after that child, I haven't caught so much as a hint of his shadow. The one assault was on Alex and by the two thugs she hired to stand watch over the boy the morning she came to us. At least that's what it appears to be on the surface."

"Quincy saved me the *Times* account of it all," Barrett replied, running his hand over the combed coat. He stepped out of the stall, handing Aiden the brush and asking, "What makes you think that it's something more than an overly complicated attempt at robbery?"

"In the aftermath, I happened to glance to the front window of the shop," Aiden supplied as he took the brush back to the tack room. "There was an Indian man standing there, looking in. The instant I met his gaze, he was gone."

"Maybe he happened to be passing by," Barrett suggested, "heard the gunshots, and couldn't resist a morbid curiosity."

"He wasn't curious."

"Then what was he?"

"Well, not coolly detached," Aiden mused aloud, returning with feed for Mohan's horse. "Resolved, maybe."

"Might you be stretching it just a bit? You'd just killed two men, you know. The brain tends to be slightly overactive when under such stresses."

"Perhaps," he offered noncommittally.

"But you don't think so."

Aiden leaned his back against the stall, crossed his arms over his chest, and stared down at the toes of his boots. "Mohan tells me that there are members of the royal court who oppose Alex's presence."

"Because she's British?"

Aiden frowned. "I think it's more complicated than that, but being a Brit is probably at the root of it. Alex hasn't come right out and bluntly said so, but she's strongly implied that her mother wasn't just the royal tutor."

"She was also one of the raja's consorts?" Barrett said, clearly intrigued. "Is Alex their daughter?"

An image flashed though his mind, a memory of sun-kissed skin and inviting eyes in the flickering candlelight. If it had been the only one he had of her . . . Aiden shook his head, dispelling the exotic fantasy. "They were taken into the royal court when Alex was a child," he supplied. "Mohan seems to think that when they return to India his father's going to either make Alex one of his mistresses or another of his wives. Either that or marry her off to someone else."

"So tell me, did hearing that bit of news put a kink in your tail?"

He heard the amusement, the friendly taunt in Barrett's tone. "That's neither here nor there," he answered, refusing to be drawn into a personal discussion. "All I'm looking at are the puzzle pieces and trying to understand the whole picture. I can see why there would be some opposed to Alex's returning. Say he made her a wife and they had children, a boy or two. There would be a half-British heir in line for the throne."

"Way down the line, though," Barrett countered, beginning to pace, his hands clasped behind his back. "Any children she might have with the raja would hardly be a significant threat to the older heirs."

"I know. That's why it doesn't make sense to consider Alex an imminent threat in any way. Hell, you can't even really make the argument that she imposes strict British standards on their way of life and makes them uncomfortable from that standpoint. In many ways, she's really more Indian than she is British."

"That could be interesting in certain respects."

He wasn't about to share any of those particular details

with Barrett. Keeping to his professional concerns, he asked, "So why would anyone be so opposed to her return that they'd travel to London and try to kill her?"

Barrett shrugged. "You're assuming that they are, John Aiden. You don't have any proof that it's actually happening. All you have is the boy's assertion that there are some who don't like her presence in the court and don't want her to come back."

"And an Indian stranger peering in the window the morning someone tried to kidnap her."

"Which could simply be a coincidence. Have you seen him again?"

No, he hadn't. And the fact that he'd been keenly looking somehow reinforced the sense that all wasn't right in Alex's world. "All right, I don't have any proof. I'll give you that. But I've got a feeling, Barrett. It's crawling under my skin."

Barrett stopped his pacing and sighed. "It's called lust, John Aiden," he said, his tone a mixture of both patience and amusement. "The more you resist it, the worse it gets. Bed the woman and you'll feel ever so much better."

Aiden considered ignoring the comment but decided that Barrett wasn't likely to abandon the issue until it had been squarely addressed. "In the first place," he said coolly, meeting his friend's gaze, "I know the difference between the feelings of lust and danger. And in the second, Alex isn't the sort of woman you toss down, thoroughly rumple, and then leave with a tip of your hat and a pleasant thank-you."

"My," Barrett drawled, his brow cocked high, "a little touchy about that, aren't you? It would seem that you have some genuine feelings for her."

"Whatever they might be," Aiden replied easily, firmly, "they're none of your business. The only reason I'm mentioning any of this to you is that I'm hoping to pick your brain as to why she's in apparent danger and how the hell I'm supposed to protect her."

Barrett smiled. "And I don't have the slightest notion that would be of any help to you. Other than to suggest that you keep her tied to your hip and ankle while clutching a loaded gun in your hand. Sleeping with one eye open might not be a bad idea, either."

As though, with Alex physically tied to him, he would sleep at all. "Why does anyone ever spend good money to hire you?" he mused aloud.

"Hell if I know," Barrett admitted, his grin broadening. "But they do. Time after time. Amazing, isn't it?"

Aiden snorted in disgust.

"And speaking of investigations," Barrett went on. "What have you been able to learn about her silver trading? Or have you even bothered to make an effort in that direction?"

The inquiry had been couched in just the tone and terms he'd known it would be. Aiden was ready with the answer. "Alex doesn't trade with street people. Every transaction she makes is with those she knows—mostly the trusted servants of people we're likely to meet at one of your mother's social affairs. It's discreetly done, but it's always aboveboard and perfectly legal."

"You're absolutely certain?"

That Barrett would even think to question his assertion and Alex's inherent honesty was profoundly irritating. "Absolutely." *Prod again,* he silently threatened, *and I'll put your ass on the floor.*

Barrett considered him, his brow slowly rising. "Do you think," he finally ventured, "she'd know where to get stolen silver if she were of a mind to acquire it?"

As insults and implications went, it was borderline. "Why are you asking?"

Barrett checked a smile. "I hear the distinct notes of suspicion in your voice, John Aiden. I'm thinking about being offended."

"Go right ahead and be offended," Aiden countered. "I don't give a damn if you are. Why are you asking?"

Apparently deciding that matters would go much more smoothly if he didn't take offense, Barrett smiled and started pacing again. "I'm thinking that she might be able to help me find where Lord Westerham's silver went and perhaps even get it back before Lady Westerham returns from Paris to discover it's gone and starts asking questions that his lordship would really prefer not to answer."

"Well, if he'd been a little more careful in who he brought home and dropped his trousers for, he wouldn't be in this particular mess."

"True. But that doesn't change the fact that he needs his silverware back. And is willing to pay whatever expense is involved to get it." He looked over to meet Aiden's gaze. "Do you think Alex Radford would be able to help in that regard?"

It was a logical request. Of a person who was in a position to better solve the problem than anyone else they knew. He wasn't particularly happy with the idea of Alex taking on the task but understood that it wasn't his right to make the decision. "You'll have to ask her."

"You'll let me?"

The surprise, the suppressed laughter irritated him anew. Aiden glared at him. "I'm her guard, not her keeper, Barrett."

His friend tilted his head to the side and considered him somberly for a long moment before carefully asking, "May I give you a piece of personal advice, John Aiden? As one friend to another?"

"No."

"Well," Barrett drawled with a bare shrug, "I have to anyway. Conscience being the nastily persistent thing it is and all."

"I don't want to hear it," Aiden announced, unfolding his arms and coming off the stall. He'd taken two steps toward the stable door when Barrett blocked his path.

"You don't really have a choice," Barrett said, sounding—surprisingly—regretful. "Your sweet Mary Alice is dead, Aiden." He went on blocking his attempt to step around him. "There's nothing you can do to change that."

Aiden gritted his teeth and resolved himself to enduring the lecture. The sooner it was done, the sooner he could walk away and forget it. "I assume there's more," he growled, meeting his friend's searching gaze. "There always is."

Barrett nodded slowly. "Look, John Aiden," he said kindly, "it's not a dastardly betrayal of her memory for you to find Alex attractive. Hell, if you didn't, I'd be worried about you. Nine-tenths of the reason I sent you off with her was because I was hoping she'd be the perfect temptation for you. And I'm glad—no, I'm over-the-moon happy—that she apparently is. Just remember: Sex is certainly nice, but it's just sex. It's nothing more than that."

Aiden's stomach was knotted and his pulse pounded through a tumult of jumbled, heated emotions. Anger. Hurt. Regret. And most frighteningly, an overwhelming, soaring sense of relief. "You're treading the line, Barrett," he warned, hoping it would be enough to make Barrett drop the matter entirely. "Be careful. There are limits to friendship."

"I know that I'm pushing," his friend replied solemnly. "If I didn't think it important, I wouldn't take the chance. But I'm not sure that the distinctions between lust and obligation are really all that clear to you these days. They have to be, John Aiden. I need to know that you've finally regained a solid, healthy perspective on things."

"Why?" Aiden demanded.

"Because the last time you fancied a woman," his friend retorted, "you damn near got yourself killed for the wonder of riding her."

Anger surged through him. But so did the feeling of being utterly besieged. "You're over the line now," he declared, his voice rough with barely contained desperation.

"And the choice to cross it was deliberate," Barrett said even more kindly, even more regretfully. "I'm also afraid that you expect Alexandra Radford to step into Mary Alice Randolph's shoes and take up the grand and glorious illusion where the love of your life dropped it. Bed Alex if you want to—and God knows you'd be human if you do—but understand that you don't have to marry her for the privilege.

"Never love a woman more than you love yourself, John Aiden. Never. Keep your head firmly on your shoulders and your wits about you. Tell me that you can do that with Alexandra Radford and I'll leave you alone. I'll never mention any of this again."

Jesus Christ! That's what all this had been about? It was about what he was thinking in wanting to bed Alex?

"I know the difference between love and sex, Barrett," he said firmly. "I don't love Alex. Yes, I like her and find her an interesting person. Yes, I'll admit to wanting to bed her. I think about it all the time, actually. But I have no fanciful illusions as to what she means to me beyond that and no intentions whatsoever of offering her forever. My head is firmly on my shoulders and I have full possession of my wits. You don't need to worry about me. Thank you for doing so, but it's not necessary."

Barrett visibly relaxed as he expelled a hard breath. His smile was apologetic. "I do believe you might have turned an important corner. Thank God."

Aiden shook his head in amazement and walked past his friend saying, "Dinner's probably ready."

He'd been set up. So had Alex. Barrett had deliberately put the two of them together, hoping he'd want to seduce her and willing to sacrifice Alex in the name of . . . In the name of what? Aiden wondered, leading the way toward the kitchen and the washbasin. For what grand and glorious cause was Alex supposed to surrender her virtue? So he could feel better? To draw him back into the world where bedding women was nothing more than an evening's casual pastime?

Absolutely nothing about Alex was casual. And, Barrett's hopes be damned, he liked her just the way she was and wouldn't change one damn thing about her even if he could.

Alex couldn't recall any other time when she'd been so grateful to see a meal come to an end. Maintaining a steady, smooth flow of conversation had been excruciatingly difficult. Barrett had certainly held up his end of the effort but Mohan had been occupied with translating for Preeya and Preeya had been too busy listening and watching to contribute anything. And Aiden . . .

Aiden had been largely lost in his own thoughts. Every single time they'd tried to draw him into their conversation, the question had had to be repeated. And then his answers and observations had been so skeletal that they'd eventually given up trying. Asking him what troubled him had produced only a shrug and a terse assurance that it wasn't at all significant.

Alex rose from the table, intending to gather up the remaining plates and follow Preeya and Mohan down to the sanctuary of the kitchen. At least the three of them wouldn't be at a loss for something to talk about.

"Miss Radford?" Barrett said as she picked up her plate. "I'm wondering if perhaps you might be able to help me with something."

She paused. "If I can."

From the inside pocket of his suit coat he removed a butter knife and handed it to her asking, "What can you tell me about this particular piece of silver?"

"It's sterling," she supplied, thinking that this was the

oddest after-dinner exchange she'd ever had with a man. Aiden was standing beside his friend, staring off into the distance as he had throughout dinner.

"The pattern is simply called 'Fiddle' for obvious reasons," she went on. "It's a fairly popular one these days. You can tell by the feel of it that it's extremely well crafted." Turning it over, she looked at the back side of the handle. "Ah, James Ross's mark. He's one of the more noted silversmiths in Glasgow. That makes it an expensive piece." She turned it back to the front and then returned it to him, adding, "Unfortunately, the monogram reduces the trading value by a good bit."

"Would you happen to have any matching pieces to this one?"

Why would Barrett Stanbridge want pieces of silver monogrammed with a *W*? she wondered. And how . . . ? Alex knitted her brows, considering him, suspicion niggling at her mind. "How is it," she finally ventured, "that you know I deal in silver, Mr. Stanbridge? How did you know to bring a butter knife with you tonight?"

Aiden shifted on his feet, threw a quick look her way, and then went back to his contemplation of the far wall.

Barrett smiled. "I was telling my mother over dinner the other evening that John Aiden was working with you and she mentioned that a friend of hers had purchased some replacement pieces for her formal set from you. Luncheon forks, I believe she said."

She couldn't recall any such transaction. Warily, she prodded, "And you're looking for replacement pieces for this set?"

"Actually, this is the only piece that I have at the moment. I'm looking for the rest of the set that goes with it."

And he thought she had it? The implication was clear and it made her angry. Aiden didn't look at her, but he shifted his stance again and took a long, slow breath. It might have been wordless, but it was an admission if she'd ever seen one. None of this conversation was coming as a surprise to him. Was the knowledge of Barrett's suspicions what had preoccupied him during dinner? Did he suspect her of trading in stolen silver, too?

No, she instantly admitted. He knew her better than that. He would have dismissed the possibility out of hand. Had he been worrying that she would feel insulted and hurt and angry? He was right, but the apparent fact that he'd known how she'd react was most decidedly to his credit.

Deciding there was nothing to do but to address the matter squarely, she faced his friend and bluntly inquired, "Was the rest of the set you're looking for by any chance stolen?"

His smile studiously pleasant and his brow twitching ever so slightly, Barrett explained smoothly, "A recent guest of Lord Westerham walked off with it while he was sleeping. Lady Westerham is due back from Paris before the week is out and he'd prefer to avoid having to explain its absence."

"And he's hired you to find the set in time," she guessed.

"And I, in turn," he said before she could ask her next question, "would like to hire you for the task. Would you be willing to consider it? The finder's fee is considerable."

"So is the risk," Aiden said quietly, meeting her gaze. "Understand that if you decide to accept Barrett's offer, you won't go looking without me."

There were so many emotions in his eyes. Irritation. Resolve. It was the depth of his regret and embarrassment that spoke the loudest, though. He didn't like this at all. Not one little bit. "And who would guard Mohan in your absence?" she asked, thinking that he might be wanting her to provide them an excuse to evade the task. "He's most certainly not going with us. Not where we have to go and not among the kinds of people we'll have to meet."

He nodded and gave his friend a tight smile. "The boy

needs a riding suit and a decent pair of boots. You can see to getting him outfitted while Alex and I are conducting your investigation."

"I suppose—"

"Good," Aiden declared, cutting him off and effectively out of the conversation. "Is tomorrow all right with you, Alex? The sooner it's done, the better."

She sensed that his desire to have the task behind them had nothing whatsoever to do with Lord Westerham's desperation. "There's an auction at Christie's I had hoped to attend in the morning but given the circumstances, I—"

"I don't see any reason why you should miss it," he interjected. "We'll go and then see what we can do about finding the missing silver. We'll make a day of it. Barrett will cover any of our incidental expenses." He turned to his friend. "Won't you? And the cost of the silver when we find it."

"*If* we find it," she corrected before Barrett could answer. "There's a reasonable chance that it's been melted down. The monogram makes it both more identifiable as stolen and more difficult to sell. Even unscrupulous buyers have certain standards. A monogram matching their own surname initial being a primary one. Whoever acquired it from the thief would have a better chance of a faster profit in melting it all down and moving it back into production. When was it stolen?"

"A fortnight ago," Barrett supplied.

Well before she'd met either one of them. They'd had to have begun looking for it immediately. Had to have developed a list of people they suspected of having purchased it from the thief. Had she been on that list? Aiden had a good many answers to provide. God help him if they weren't good ones.

"We'll be diligent in our efforts," she told Barrett. "But I think it's only fair to warn you that the odds of finding the set intact are very slim, Mr. Stanbridge. If I might make a suggestion?" She didn't wait for his permission. "If we can find a set of Ross Fiddle without monograms, they could be engraved and Lady Westerham might never know the difference."

"How likely is it that you'll find even a plain set?"

She smiled weakly. "I hope Lord Westerham isn't holding his breath and has somewhere else to live. If you'd come to me for help the day it was stolen, you'd have had a far better chance than you do now."

"I didn't know then that you could be of help. I sincerely wish I had."

No, at the time he'd considered her suspect. A fence. A dealer in stolen goods. Had Aiden thought of her in a similar light? He had asked her about stolen silver that day Polly had brought in the set of Roberts and Belk. Had his question been an idle one based on passing curiosity as he'd said? Or had it been grounded in genuine suspicion?

"Well, as much as I hate to eat and dash," Barrett announced, "I really must be going. Having been gone from the office for the better part of a week, I'm behind in my paperwork and desperately need to catch up as quickly as possible. Thank you for the lovely dinner, Miss Radford. My compliments to Preeya."

"I'll see you out," Aiden offered crisply. "What time is the auction tomorrow, Alex?"

"It starts at nine in the morning," she provided, feeling almost sorry for Barrett. Aiden was angry and she suspected that his friend was going to get a solid lashing the moment they were alone. "We should leave here by eight to get a number and good seats."

"You have a lot of midnight oil to burn, Bare." He motioned toward the dining room door. "You probably shouldn't tarry another moment."

Barrett took a step in that direction before he paused and offered her a slight bow. "Thank you for being willing to help me with the investigation, Miss Radford. I trust you to come up with a solution one way or another. And to further that end, I'll be here well before eight tomorrow morning."

She nodded her acceptance of it all and watched him walk away. Aiden, glowering at his friend's back, followed. He'd reached the threshold before she couldn't stand the wondering any longer.

"Aiden? Before you go, might I—"

He wheeled around and came back, stopping only when he was standing in front of her, so close that she had to tilt her head to meet his gaze. "Yes," he said firmly, "you were a suspect. And yes, he asked me to look into the possibility. I did only because I knew he'd turn up and press the issue just as he did. But I knew the truth before I even broached the subject, Alex. You don't have a dishonest, deceitful bone in your beautiful body. Not one. Anyone who knows you knows that."

She believed him. To the center of her honest, reputedly beautiful bones. And she wanted, just as deeply, to slip her arms around his narrow waist and hug him tightly. Resisting the urge, she said instead, "I should be offended that I was ever under even the slightest suspicion."

The tension in him disappeared in an instant, replaced by an impish smile and slightly cocked brow. "Should be?"

It was impossible to even pretend to be angry with him. And no real reason to, either. "I think we're even."

"You had suspicions of *me*?"

"Not so much suspicions," she admitted, "as unflattering assumptions."

"Such as?"

It was amazing how easily he could lift her mood, how effortlessly he could banish even the darkest thoughts. Just by being himself. She smiled up at him and slowly shook her head in appreciative wonder. "I thought you were uncommonly arrogant for being a toady."

"A toady?"

His amusement prompted her to add to her confession. "And that you were no gentleman."

"Well," he drawled, his smile quirking, "since I do actually work at that when I remember to, I'll allow you that one as being fairly accurate."

"I also thought that you were a brazen rogue, an unabashed hedonist."

"I certainly can be," he admitted, his eyes twinkling. "If you're attracted to that sort of man."

Had temptation ever been wrapped in a package more handsome and captivating than Aiden Terrell?

"You are, aren't you?"

Her heart shot into her throat as her blood sang with hope and desire. Dear God, when he smiled like that her good judgment turned to pudding. "No," she managed to lie. She moistened her lower lip and then raggedly, honestly, added, "Not as a general rule."

"If you also assumed that I'm exceptional," he whispered with a wink, "you'd be right."

She didn't have a doubt. Not even the tiniest one. Not about him. "I'm sure you are," she agreed breathlessly. "However, such magnificent abilities would be utterly wasted on someone like me."

She saw astonishment flicker in his eyes, saw him swallow and take a slow, even breath. The roguish edge slipped away from his smile. "If Barrett wasn't likely to come back through that door at any moment looking for me," he said softly, "I'd prove you wrong right here on the spot."

Alex summoned every shred of her tattered common sense to keep her arms at her sides. "No one is ever going to accuse you of lacking self-confidence."

His good humor unaffected, he shrugged and eased away, saying, "We'll address your lack of it when I get back."

A vivid image, intoxicatingly carnal, instantly filled her

mind. "No we won't," she countered hastily. "I'll bid you good night now, Aiden."

He stopped and slowly turned. The look in his eyes stole her breath and filled her with heart-thundering certainty.

"What about Barrett?" she reminded him as he came back to her.

"He can wait," he replied, slipping one arm around her waist, the other around her shoulders. He drew her closer and, his gaze searching hers, lowered his head.

It wasn't a light, tentative kiss as the others had been. No, this one was slowly, heatedly deliberate and undeniably possessive. Her senses instantly, blissfully reeling, Alex wrapped her arms around his waist and melted against him, abandoning reserve and surrendering conscious thought. When he traced her lips with his tongue, she sighed with pleasure and granted him admission. When his arms tightened around her and he tasted more deeply, she clung to him, reveling in waves of heady sensation. And when she boldly sought a taste of him in return, his moan swept through her like liquid fire, igniting a hunger that pulsed and flared through every fiber of her being.

From the farthest recesses of his awareness came the tiny voice of reason warning that he was teetering on the edge, telling him that he had to do the right thing, had to let her consciously choose to tumble into oblivion with him. It hurt to heed the wisdom, but he forced himself to ease his claim to her mouth and shift her in his arms. Holding her close, her head tucked under his chin, he sucked in greedy breaths and marveled at the furious beat of his heart.

God, she was the most amazing woman. His abilities wasted on her? He closed his eyes and breathed in the scent of her hair. Never. Such genuine acceptance, such a complete lack of artifice. It was so utterly, extraordinarily foreign to his experience. He craved more of her. All of her. He could only hope that she didn't reduce him to a pile of smoldering ash. And if she did . . . Aiden smiled, knowing that she was worth that risk and ever so much more.

But his conscience spoke the truth. The choice to give was hers to make. Sweeping her unknowingly past the point of no return wasn't right. She deserved respect and he'd honor her even if it killed him to let her go. He opened his eyes and deliberately focused on the world around them, on the reality of where they were and the tasks needing to be done.

"I have to leave. Now," he whispered, his voice rough, his hands gentle as he set her from him and steadied her on her feet. He trailed his fingertips along the curve of her shoulders, up the slim column of her neck. Her pulse thrummed beneath them and almost undid his resolve. Clinging to the tattered remnants of it, he stepped away and let his hands fall to his sides.

Her eyes were inviting shadows as she looked up at him and his heart wrenched at the sacrifice. "Yes, now," he said, more for himself than her. "Or I won't be able to go at all. Good night, Alex."

Alex choked back a cry of protest. Then there was only the thundering of her heart and the desperate, aching want in the center of her soul as she watched him leave. And in those moments a realization budded and bloomed full. For as long as she could remember, she'd lived one day at a time, fulfilling the expectations of others as best she could and always assuring herself that someday there would come a reward for enduring. That reward, a tangible thing she could hold, would magically make all the loneliness, all the emptiness of the days that had gone before, worth bearing.

Alex stared into the shadows of the hall. She'd never known, never guessed that it was possible to feel as magnificently alive as she did now. How incredibly naïve she had been. The reward wasn't a thing at all; it was a feeling from deep within her. It was joy and wonder and a wanting to dare to reach for more. It was in discovering a vibrant path, in making the journey. Where it ended . . . Alex took a steadying breath. Where it ended didn't matter nearly as much as being able to travel along it—even for just a short while—with John Aiden Terrell.

Chapter 12

The peacocks, Aiden resolved as he strode down the upstairs hall, were going to die. The means by which early-morning peace and tranquility was restored was all that remained to be decided. Wringing their necks promised more satisfaction than putting a bullet in them, but it would take longer. And considering the hue and cry rising from the rear yard for the second time that morning, the speed of their dispatch was all that truly mattered. By the time he got there, Preeya would be done feeding them and back in the kitchen. Which was good; it would go much faster if he didn't have to shoot around her.

He was on the third step down when a tiny streak of butterscotch shot past his right foot. Instinctively, he hopped to the left. And would have landed on a streak of calico if he hadn't immediately and desperately thrown his entire body back to the right. He froze, barely on his feet, just as three more blurs of color dashed past and downward.

"They're out!" Mohan shrieked from behind him, testing Aiden's grip on the banister as he bounded past in pursuit of the kittens.

Gazing after the reckless parade, he saw Alex in the front shop, a kitten in each hand, her head tilted back as she laughed at the chaos racing around the hems of her skirt and cloak. The center of his chest clenched, trapping his breath and warming his blood. And then, out of the blue, a wave of melancholy washed through him. How he'd missed the sound of laughter. How he'd missed the brightness of hope and the thrill of little, unexpected joys. He wanted to go home. He wanted to pack up Alex and Mohan and the kittens and Preeya and her damn peacocks and take them home. Today. On the evening's tide.

And it wasn't going to happen, he sadly admitted. It couldn't happen. Not today. Not tomorrow. Not ever. And, he sternly added, only a fool would spend another moment thinking about it. Resolved, he focused his sight on the present reality, noting that Alex had placed the kittens in a shawl. She was smiling, trying to transfer the squirming bundle to Mohan while keeping the determined kittens from popping out the folds.

His chest tightened again and he quickly looked away, forestalling another painful bout by doing a quick appraisal of the shop. He blinked and frowned. Where the hell had everything gone? And when had it disappeared? There were a few things left, certainly, but the vast majority of her merchandise had vanished. He glanced toward the rear of the house and into the blue fabric room. The shelves were practically stripped.

"Good morning, Aiden."

He looked back at her as Mohan raced up the stairs with his lumpy sack of cats.

"Were you robbed?" he asked, resuming his trek downward. "When did it happen? And why didn't you say something to me?"

"You've spent the last three days teaching Mohan to ride," she supplied, her smile radiant. "And when not answering the blacksmith's endless questions about the window grates, I've spent them dealing with a flood of customers. It happens every time a new shipment comes in. It's almost magical. I don't have to do a thing to bring them here. They simply appear. If the auction weren't today and if there weren't some specific items I've been asked to find for one of my customers and if we weren't off to find stolen silver . . ." She threw out her hands in a gesture of good-natured frustration. "As you can see, I desperately need to spend some time imposing order on the remains."

His chest was tight but he couldn't take his eyes off her. She was so happy, so beautiful. He forced himself to swallow, to again put away the impossible. "You need another shipment already, don't you?"

She nodded ruefully and glanced around her with a delicate sigh. "Mohan's uncle has regular trading routes and England is a significant departure from them. When he does come this way, there isn't much room in the hold for my things. I could easily sell three times what I usually get but I can't impose on his kindness any more than I already do."

The idea came, bold and bright, from out of nowhere. "Maybe," he drawled, liking it more with every second, "you need another supplier, another shipper."

"Are you offering your services, Mr. Terrell?"

He liked how her eyes sparkled, too. And the way she arched a brow when she joined his games. "I think we can come to an arrangement we'd both enjoy." *For a few days at a time, every few months,* he silently added. *The perfect relationship with the perfect mistress. But only if she stays in England.*

"Aiden? Mr. Stanbridge has arrived."

He blinked and grinned sheepishly, knowing he'd been caught dreaming. Hoping to keep her from asking about what, he extended his hand, saying brightly, "Then we shall depart."

Barrett was just climbing out of his carriage when they stepped outside onto the walk. Handing Alex up the carriage steps, he passed the key to the front door of her shop to his friend, saying crisply, "Remember to always lock the door behind you, old man. Sawyer should be here shortly. Kindly stay until he arrives to keep watch over Preeya. And if you don't mind, we're going to appropriate your carriage and driver for the day. It'll make our logistics ever so much easier. Feel free to use whatever transport you fancy in our carriage house."

Before Barrett had a chance to either accede or protest, Aiden looked up at the driver and called out, "Christie's, my good man. We need to be there before nine." Then he vaulted inside, pulled the door closed, and dropped into the rear-facing seat. Through the open window, he could see Barrett standing on the walk, the key in his hand, chuckling as he nodded to his driver.

"That was rather presumptive of you," Alex chided softly.

"That's the thing with Barrett," he explained as they pulled out into traffic. "You have to presume before he does or you'll end up on a leash of his design. It's the army officer in him."

"And resisting is the ship's captain in you."

"It's a friendly contest. And, truth be told, I haven't won that many of them lately. I'm due one or two. His nose isn't out of joint over it. Barrett's a good sport. If he weren't, we wouldn't be friends." He settled back into the squabs and the prospect of a wonderful day. "What are we going to buy at Christie's this morning?"

"It's an estate sale, so there's really no telling what, precisely, will be there. Which makes it far more fun, I think. It's something of an adventure. In addition to purchasing whatever might be appropriate for the Blue Elephant, I'll be acquiring artwork for one of my regular customers who has asked me to find some things suitable for display in her private quarters."

"Why doesn't she go buy it herself?"

"She has horrible taste, knows it, and defers to mine."

"Given what I've seen in some homes," he mused, "she's

not the only one who could benefit from assistance. You could probably make a profitable business of that, too."

"I've given it some thought," she admitted, smiling. "If I were staying in England permanently I'd likely do it. It's really quite entertaining to spend other people's money. And to be paid for doing it is absolutely astounding."

He saw the potential in the comment and seized it. Trying to sound as though the idea had never occurred to him before that instant, he asked, "Why don't you stay? With all your enterprises, you'd surely make more money here than you will as the royal tutor in India."

Her smiled faded and there was a faint sound of resignation in her voice when she replied, "Money isn't everything, Aiden."

"True," he admitted, his mind racing in search of another tack. "What draws you back to India? Your mother's gone. Do you have other family there?"

She shook her head and looked out the window of the carriage for a long moment before sighing and saying, "It's very complicated, Aiden, and would take forever to explain."

"I'm a patient man."

Laughing, she looked back at him. "You are not."

"I beg to differ," he instantly countered, enjoying, as always, the challenge of her and knowing the perfect gambit to play. "Haven't I nodded every single morning and accepted your excuse *du jour* not to go riding with Mohan and me? Have I once pressed the issue?"

"All right, in some things you can be remarkably, admirably patient."

"And this is one of them," he assured her. "The longest story begins with a single word, Alex. Why do you want to go back to India?"

It took her several long moments, but finally she said softly, slowly, "They took me in when I had nowhere else to go. They gave me a home. I have a place there. I belong to people. It's not a family like yours by any means, but they care for me and worry about me. That doesn't exist for me in London. There's only Preeya and Emmaline and Mohan."

"And me."

"And you," she agreed with a sufficient amount of hesitation that Aiden suspected she was doing so simply for the sake of being polite. "If I didn't go back . . . If I stayed, I'd never again see Preeya and Mohan. With Mohan no longer needing your protection, you'd go on with your life. There would only be Emmaline left. And I'm afraid that she would very quickly become very tired of mothering me."

Her concerns were legitimate and completely understandable. But he wasn't about to cry quits in the face of them. "You could make other friends, Alex. Easily."

The smile she gave him was patient. "I don't belong here, Aiden. I'm English and yet I'm not."

It wasn't what he'd expected her to say, but he had to admit that if ever there was one absolute truth about her . . . "Well, you're certainly not Indian," he pointed out, grasping at the only counterpoint he could see.

Again she surprised him. Laughing quietly, she shook her head. "Being Indian is more than a matter of race, Aiden. It's a way of looking at the world, at life. And you'll have to concede that I tend to approach matters in ways that aren't thoroughly, typically English. Other people realize it, too. They know that I'm different, that I'm not really one of them. You're the rare exception in being intrigued by it. The usual reaction is to establish a polite but decidedly cool distance."

"Then their ignorance and bigotry is their loss."

While she smiled in shy appreciation, Aiden silently groaned. Could he have offered a comment any more sophomoric? And as counters went, it was worse than pathetic. He'd not only all but openly accepted her point, he'd also left himself no room to maneuver in the process. Of all the short-sighted, brainless—

"And yet," she went on, interrupting his internal diatribe, "being perfectly honest about it, there's a part of me that very much wants to stay here."

His relief was as profound as his surprise. With reignited hope, he cocked a brow. "Why? The Blue Elephant?"

"In small part. But mostly because life here is so predictable."

"Predictable?" he prodded as her gaze slipped to the world beyond the carriage. "How so?"

"The boundaries are very clear, Aiden," she replied, looking into the distance. "The proper thing to do, to be, to feel, to think . . . One doesn't have to think, actually. All one has to do is follow along with everyone else and meet the very clearly defined expectations of society. And those expectations are as narrow as they are universal. Which is what makes them attractive. Living life by the rules is safe."

Safe. His conscience boldly thrust his hopes and intentions forward for scrutiny. Inwardly, he winced. His fantasies were dependent on her living anything but a safe and rule-bound life. Yes, he could manipulate her. He was perfectly capable. But it would be callous and wrong. Alex deserved respect, deserved to make her own decisions, and to choose—on her own—the course of her life.

"Living and dying by the rules is also boring," he countered honestly, sensing that he was casting loose something precious. "Is being safe worth a mindless existence?"

Slowly, her gaze came back to his. "If you'd asked me that the morning I walked into Barrett Stanbridge's office, I would have answered you with an unequivocal 'yes.' But now . . ." The tiniest of smiles touched the corners of her mouth. "Sometimes, under some circumstances, with some people . . . As you said the day we met, life is risk. I'm learning that deliberately taking one from time to time doesn't always lead to disaster."

A moment's hesitation, a moment of open assessment. As

the carriage slowed she smiled ruefully and added, "Unfortunately, that realization only makes the choice that much more difficult. The only compromise I can see is to spend my life sailing back and forth between England and India."

"There's a good number of people who do just that," Aiden pointed out, vivid images playing across his mind. The popping of the sails, the spray of the water. And Alex. Standing in the bow, the wind threading through her hair as she laughed up at the sun.

"Yes, but I'm not an especially good sailor."

He knew better than to entertain possibility. His conscience was squirming, telling him that the new hope was separated from the old by only a few degrees. It wasn't safe. Not by any stretch of his imagination. He knew that from bitter, heart-wrenching experience. "Then we'll have to think of another solution for you," he declared, reaching for the door handle and the timely salvation of having to exist in the real world.

In a good many ways bringing Mohan to an auction was easier. All he did was squirm in boredom and there was nothing wrong with placing her hand on his knee to still him. Aiden, on the other hand . . . He wasn't bored at all. In fact, she'd have to say that his mind was clicking furiously. But along a track that was miles and miles away from Christie's. It was equally clear that whatever it was that occupied his attention wasn't a particularly pleasant thing. He was decidedly somber, as though he were weighing the scales in trying to make some great decision on the fate of mankind.

And nothing she'd done had been able to bring him out of his distraction for very long. Not even entrusting him with her personal bidding paddle. His mind tended to wander between bids, even on the same item. She'd lost an ormolu clock because she hadn't been quick enough in nudging him back to the auction floor.

"The next item up for bidding is a pen and ink drawing by the contemporary British artist D. Terrell."

Beside her, Aiden snapped to attention, his gaze riveted on the carefully draped picture being set on the stage's easel. Intrigued by his sudden attention, Alex considered the piece. It was large enough to nicely fill the space over a mantel. The frame was thick, ornately carved, and gilded with heavy, Spanish silver. The subject, as much as the drape of black velvet permitted her to see, was a man who appeared to be half looking over his shoulder. No doubt at a lover. The artist had beautifully captured the seductive—

Alex gulped a startled breath. She knew the curve of that smile, that delightfully wicked sparkle in the eyes.

"Ladies," the auctioneer intoned, "we caution you and suggest you avert your gazes for a brief moment."

A few feminine heads turned away as the drape was lowered by two attendants. A few feminine ones and Aiden's. She heard him groan, felt him slump down in his chair.

"Aiden?" she asked under her breath, staring at the picture and knowing with every fiber of her being that those were Aiden's shoulders, his torso, his waist, and—dear God in heaven—his buttocks and thighs. Her heart was pounding and the temperature of the room seemed to have spiked several hundred degrees. "Who's D. Terrell?"

"My mother," he supplied, sounding as though he were strangling on every syllable. "*D* is for Darcy."

She leaned closer to keep their conversation private. "And who is the subject?" she pressed as the drawing was discreetly covered again. "His build is much like yours. So is his smile. The face is different, though. Harder."

He seemed to choke back a whimper before he replied, "I favor my mother."

"As I favored mine. People always knew we were mother and daughter," she admitted, thoroughly amused by his mortification. Who would have thought Aiden could be embarrassed by anything sexual? "So is the man in the picture your father?"

"He'd die before he publicly admitted it."

And his son would, too. Alex turned her attention back to the front and the opening round of bidding. The impulse was wicked. And it was absolutely irresistible. She nudged Aiden with her elbow and whispered, "Bid."

"No!"

She had to swallow down her laughter. "Wouldn't you like to have it?"

"God, no! Why would I want to look at my father naked?"

Oh, she would pay in her next life for so enjoying this moment. A bid was accepted, another solicited. She raised her paddle and joined the fray. Beside her, Aiden gasped and practically came up off his chair.

"Alex!"

"I'm buying it for my customer," she explained, artfully playing the soul of cool acquisition.

In response, he closed his eyes and moaned, "Oh, God."

She bid, said, "Aiden, you're blushing," and bid again.

A memory flitted across her mind, no less clear for the brevity of its presence. The man who had stood in her hall and calmly killed two men was the same one now sitting beside her clutching a bidding paddle for dear life and blushing more deeply than any maiden bride. There were so many facets to John Aiden Terrell. And every single one of them fascinated her. He awed her, entertained her, and Lord knew he challenged her. Being with him made her smile at first light and happily scramble out of bed, made her regret the inevitable setting of the sun and their parting greetings each night.

Realization came over her in a slow swell. She held her breath and focused her attention on holding her place in the swirling current of bidding, hoping the distraction would drive it back and away from acknowledgment and acceptance. The truth wouldn't be denied.

The gavel banged. "The D. Terrell goes to bidder three-thirty-eight."

Alex looked down in amazement at the paddle in her hand. Three-thirty-eight. What were the odds, she wondered, of buying a painting in the same moment you realized you had fallen in love with the artist's son?

Another realization rolled over her in the wake of the first. What price she paid in the next life for torturing him this morning would be minor in the grand scheme of things. Loving Aiden, though . . . That was going to cost her dearly in this one. She blinked at her paddle, trying to catch her breath, trying to control her smile, and desperately, rationally trying to make herself believe that if she didn't protect her heart she was going to spend the rest of her life regretting the day she'd met him.

Chapter 13

Aiden dragged a deep breath of cold, crisp air into his lungs and held it, letting it cool his blood. There was much to be thankful for, he told himself as he led Alex toward the line of waiting carriages. The picture had been one of his mother's more circumspect pieces. There were a few that wouldn't have been undraped in public. And he wasn't having to haul it out the door of Christie's himself. That was good. Even better, he wasn't going to have to ride around town with his father trying to seduce Alex from the opposite seat. Blessed be the deliverymen of Christie's.

He was scanning the line of carriages and groups of drivers chatting along the walkway, looking for Barrett's, when Alex sighed happily and said, "I think that went exceedingly well, don't you?"

"If your idea—" He blinked and looked back. The man at the rear of the carriage was gone.

"Aiden? What is it?"

"I'm sorry." He summoned a chagrined smile and a lie as he searched for another glimpse of the man. "I was looking for Barrett's carriage and driver and thought for a moment that I saw them. Would you like to get something to eat now or after we do a bit of silver hunting?"

"I'm not really all that hungry."

He had to be there somewhere. He couldn't disappear into thin air. "Then we'll be dutiful for a while."

"There he is," Alex exclaimed, sending his heart into his throat. "Two carriages past St. Bart's Tavern."

The driver. Aiden swallowed down his heart and made one last sweep of the line. Nothing. Not so much as a shadow. "Where shall I tell him to take us?"

"Whitechapel Road."

A good choice, he decided as he and Alex made their way down the walk. Whitechapel was poor, but it was decidedly Anglo. An Indian man would be far more likely to stand out in a crowd there. He'd slipped twice now. There was bound to be a third. And when that happened, the bastard was going to find himself staring down a gun barrel and answering some hard questions.

"Since I don't know anything about silver," he began, handing Alex into their vehicle, his plan made, "I think you should take charge of the search."

"Sensible," she replied as she settled onto her seat.

"I'll pretend to be your beleaguered, utterly bored husband and spend my time gazing longingly out the shop windows."

Laughing, she took up his game. "And at what will you be gazing, my poor, dear husband?"

Hopefully a startled Indian face. But until then . . . Damn, if she didn't have the most lusciously inviting smile. Lips made for kissing and an openness that always made his blood sing. God, what he wouldn't give to say to hell with the Westerham silver, have the driver take them to Haven House and spend the rest of the day making love to her. Which, now that he thought about it, might, with the right touch, be within the realm of possible.

"The hope," he said, grinning roguishly, "of being wildly, passionately rewarded for my incredible patience."

Her smile was instant and brilliant, her laugh full and

throaty. Delight shimmered in her eyes as she wagged a finger at him and declared, "That, Aiden, is exactly the same wicked look as your father's."

"It worked for him on my mother. How do you feel about it?"

"You are *such* a temptation."

"And you're not? I'll surrender if you will."

"We have silver to find. We promised Barrett."

But if he pressed, she'd abandon it. He *knew* it. "All right, my dutiful darling," he teased. "We'll look for a couple of hours so that your conscience isn't bothered. After that, the rest of the day is ours to spend as we want."

"What do you have in mind?"

"We'll think of something," he answered, knowing the value in letting her imagination run on its own. With a grin and a wink, he added, "We're both resourceful people."

She laughed and in it he swore he heard the angels sing.

He'd done just fine with his pretending for the first forty-five minutes or so. He'd followed her into one shop after another and in each one done the same: he'd milled around a bit and then stationed himself by the front window, crossed his arms over his chest, and rocked back and forth between his heels and his toes while gazing out on the street and the people. And for a while he had seemed genuinely interested in life on Whitechapel Road.

It was at the forty-five-minute mark—and after the sixteenth shop by her count—that he'd sighed, struggled to smile, and suggested that they were wasting their effort, not to mention their very precious time.

At the hour, his hands were stuffed in his trouser pockets and he'd abandoned the effort to smile altogether. At an hour and fifteen, he not only gave up the milling around part of his performance, he quit the rocking, too. He simply walked in behind her, stalked to the window, and stood there glowering out, apparently giving serious consideration to turning Whitechapel Road into smoldering rubble.

Alex, for her part, was giving serious consideration to killing him. Not that he'd noticed her increasing frustration, she privately groused, moving along the walkway with him in reluctant tow. She passed a tiny doorway and slowed just enough to give a passing glance to the clutter on the other side of the rippled, thickly hazed front window. Two steps beyond, an object registered in her brain. Whirling around, she headed for the door.

"No, Alex. Please," Aiden practically moaned, spreading his arms to block her access to the door. "It's nothing more than a junk shop."

"There's a silver teaspoon in the window," she countered. "Where there's one piece, there could be more."

"A *pathetic* junk shop."

"With a silver spoon in the window."

He sighed and dropped his arms. "This is the very last one, Alex. I mean it," he announced as she stepped around him and pulled open the door for herself. "This is a complete waste of our day."

Alex silently disagreed. She'd learned something of incredible importance in the last hour or so. Aiden was a wonderful man. He was handsome and brave and kind and strong. He had a wonderful sense of humor and a delightfully devilish charm. But he also had the lowest tolerance for tedium of any human being she'd ever met and she was never, ever, ever going to take him shopping with her again no matter how long she lived.

"Can I help ya?"

Alex looked around, trying to find the woman who belonged to the voice. The store wasn't much larger than a single room in her own shop but it was ten times as full. There were piles and mounds and heaps everywhere. And all of it without any discernible arrangement or order or readily apparent value. Aiden had been kind in calling it a junk shop.

"Is anyone there?"

Alex pulled her skirts through a narrow passage in the warren, moving toward the rear of the shop and the voice. There, behind a counter made by placing a warped plank across two rickety produce crates, sat an old woman dressed in a worn dress and tattered knit shawl. Hunchbacked, her eyes hazed white, she held a teacup in one gnarled hand as she tilted her head to hear.

"Good morning, madam," Alex began, and the woman's attention came instantly to her. "My sister is marrying and I want to present her with a set of silverware. I saw the spoon in the window and thought perhaps you might have more. Would you by any chance have a set for sale?"

"Got three sets, honey," she said, pointing off in the general direction of Alex's left. "Complete ones they is, too. Fine pieces."

It took a few moments to find them, but they were there; three sets of silverware, each badly tarnished, haphazardly bundled, and tied with a frayed piece of twine. One set was on the floor, having obviously tumbled away from the two remaining on the precarious tower above. Alex retrieved all three and laid them on the counter. A large Shell pattern engraved with an *A* and a *C*, a small Shell pattern engraved with a *K* and . . . Alex stared in stunned disbelief. And the Westerhams' Fiddle.

"How much are you asking for this set?" she asked casually, holding the set out so that the woman could touch it and identify it.

She didn't move. "It's what you're lookin' for?"

"It might do," Alex began cautiously, afraid that it was going to cost the moon and stars to ransom. "Her married name will be Timmons. If the price is right, it would be worth having a silversmith remove the current monogram. The *W* would hardly be appropriate."

From the window, from the other side of the maze, she heard Aiden softly swear.

The shopkeeper instantly cocked her head. "Is someone else here?"

"My husband," Alex supplied as Aiden slipped sideways into the narrow corridor and shuffled toward them. She leaned closer to the woman and added in a whisper, "He's the worst shopper in the world."

The old woman chuckled. "Never been a man any good at it. How does five pounds sound to ya?"

New, it had cost close to twenty pounds. Melted down into bullion it would have been worth between twelve and fifteen. Anyone with any knowledge of silver would have asked ten for it. "For the entire set?" Alex asked, dumbfounded.

"Is it too much? My granddaughter brought 'em to me. Said they was gifts that she didn't know what to do with. From admirers. I don't get silver often 'nough to know what folks is payin' for it these days."

Obviously. And that ignorance was costing the woman a profit she just as obviously needed. Desperately. To offer her a fair market price would require doubling her request. Which would be a decidedly strange thing to do. People didn't shop in secondhand stores unless they were in search of bargains. And the woman might take the increase as an offer of pity and charity. Alex didn't want to insult her. But she didn't want to rob her, either.

Aiden came out of the tunnel, squared up, and stepped toward the makeshift counter, saying, "Five pounds is quite acceptable, madam."

Even as Alex met his gaze in frustration and consternation, the old woman nodded and said, "Sold."

He cocked a brow and mouthed, *"What?"*

"Look at this place," she answered in kind, gesturing broadly. *"Look at her!"*

Frowning, his brows knitted, he shook his head and

reached into the inside breast pocket of his coat, saying, "May I ask your name, madam?"

Alex sagged in defeat. The woman stared unseeingly at Aiden and warily asked, "Why would ya want to know?"

"I never do business with people I don't know by name. An odd quirk these days, I know, but business has become so coldly impersonal in recent years. I prefer the older way of conducting such affairs."

"Dora Elmore," she supplied, nodding. "And you be?"

"Reginald Majors. And this is my wife, Millicent."

Millicent? Reginald? Why was he making up names for them?

Aiden took Dora's free hand and laid a five-pound note in her palm, saying, "It's a pleasure to do business with you, Mrs. Elmore."

"Yes," Alex added, watching the woman rub the bill between her fingers. "Thank you for having what I needed. I'm so glad to have found it."

"Would you be needin' the other two sets?" Dora asked. "Don't get many people in here lookin' for silver an' with the money to ac'ly buy it."

Aiden glanced down at the other bundles on the counter. "Five pounds for each of the others, as well?"

"Would be 'nother ten pounds together."

"Millicent?"

Like the Westerham silver, they were badly underpriced. But better that Dora Elmore make a little something today, Alex told herself, than having the silver tossed into the refuse bin when she died. "Your sisters will someday marry," she said, continuing the unnecessary charade. "We could save the sets for them."

Aiden winked, pulled two more five-pound notes out of his wallet and turned back to the woman. "Very well, Mrs. Elmore," he said brightly, pressing the additional bills into her hand. "We'll take all three. And thank you for sparing me the ordeal of looking for wedding gifts in the future. You can't know how very grateful I am."

"I'm even more so," Alex muttered under her breath.

Dora chuckled. "Thank ya, Mr. Majors. Mrs. Majors. God bless you both."

They took their leave, scooting down the pathway, Aiden carrying the silver bundles, Alex holding her skirts close and watching the old woman grin toothlessly at the cash in her hand. *Fifteen measly pounds,* Alex thought sadly as she followed Aiden out onto the walkway. It should have been thirty.

"Did you see the look on her face?" Aiden said softly as they made their way toward Barrett's waiting carriage. "She's never in her life held fifteen pounds in her hand at one moment."

"She's never held so much as two, Aiden. And the saddest thing is that all this silver is easily worth twice what she asked for it. I was trying to think of a way to offer her a fair amount when you stepped in and accepted."

He stopped abruptly. "Is that what all that was about?" he asked in genuine surprise and obvious regret. "Aw, Jesus. I'm sorry, Alex. I thought you were thinking about talking her down, not up, and I didn't care what we paid for it as long as we got it back and were done."

"That's all right," she acceded on a sigh. Glancing back at the shop, she added, "I just feel sorry for her. Old and blind and crippled and poor. With a granddaughter who's apparently not only a tart, but also a thief and a not very bright one at that."

"Why do you say that?"

"In the first place, she stole monogrammed silver, which is the easiest to trace and so the most difficult to fence," she explained as they resumed their course. "And when she couldn't find a fence willing to buy it, she gave it to her grandmother to sell in a junk shop instead of melting it down and selling it as bullion."

"You know," he mused, chuckling, as they reached the coach, "the world should be glad that you're an honest woman, Alexandra Radford. You'd make a very good thief." Opening the door, he looked up at the driver. "Seaman's Mercantile Bank, please."

Alex managed to contain her curiosity until they were under way. "If I might ask . . . Why are we going to a bank?"

"Lord Westerham gave Barrett two hundred pounds just for buying back the silver."

"Dear Lord, Aiden. I didn't know that anyone could be that desperate. Two hundred? That's a positively *insane* amount of money."

He nodded. "And handing one hundred and ninety-five back to him rubs against my grain. It's money he'll never miss."

"You're not going to keep it," she said, appalled at the only course she could see and unable to believe that Aiden would do something so underhanded.

"In a manner of speaking, yes, I am," he replied happily. "I'm going to place it in trust with instructions that two pounds be sent in the name of Mr. and Mrs. Reginald Majors to Mrs. Dora Elmore in Whitechapel on the first day of every month for the rest of her life. If she passes before the funds are exhausted, the balance can go to an orphanage."

"That's why you made up the names!"

"I hope they really don't exist. I was thinking on my feet and picked the first names that popped into my head."

She forgave him for the horrible behavior while shopping, for giving her a name like Millicent, for everything. "What if Dora outlives the funds?"

"Then I'll replenish the coffer myself for as long as necessary," he said with a shrug. "Twenty-four pounds a year isn't much."

"You're a very good man, John Aiden Terrell."

His eyes sparkled and his smile tripped her heart. "I was

hoping you'd think so. It's all part of my grand strategy, you know. I'm figuring that if you think I might be in the queue for sainthood, you'll let down your guard."

"You are so very good. Has any woman ever been able to resist you?"

"Lady Ogden. But I really don't think she should count against me. Rumor has it that she prefers women."

Alex considered him, her heart fluttering and light. In the part of her brain that ordered and aligned the world, she knew that he wasn't good for her. He was temptation without commitment, joy without restraint. When the paths of their lives inevitably diverged, her soul was going to ache with missing him. But it was too late to avoid that consequence; she'd come too far already. There was nothing to be gained in turning back. Nothing at all. She wasn't sure what good was to be ultimately gained in going forward, but she knew Aiden well enough to suspect that the journey to discovery would be magnificent.

"What are you thinking, Alex?"

Ah, so silken, so seductively smooth. He knew precisely what she was thinking. "That neither one of us is ever going to be a saint."

He rakishly cocked a brow. "Disappointed?"

"Not in the least."

He shook his head slowly and expelled a long, slow breath. "If we weren't just a half-block from the bank . . ."

Alex smiled and looked out the window, wondering how long it took to set up a trust and hoping she didn't lose her courage somewhere in the lobby.

In the distance, a bell chimed the half hour. Aiden grinned as they headed back to their waiting carriage yet again. Half past noon. An auction attended, the Westerham silver recovered, a trust established, and Alex on the verge of surrender. It was amazing what one could accomplish if one really tried.

The only disappointment so far was in spending all that time surveying Whitechapel Road and not seeing so much as a hint of the Indian stranger. It would have been nice to have that end neatly tied up before the day was done, but he wasn't willing to abandon his plans for it. Let the bastard try to get into Haven House.

"Terrell!"

His hand on the door, he turned. "Hawkins," he said, handing Alex in as the man rushed forward, his hand extended. "Good to see you again. It's been a long time," he added as they shook hands.

"Talk about divine intervention!"

"Were we?" Aiden chuckled.

"Crumb's out with a broken leg. Fell off a ladder last week. Which leaves us short a right wing three-quarter back for the annual Off-Season Challenge. Would you play?"

"I'd love to," he admitted. "When is it?"

"One o'clock at Pritchard's Field. I'm on my way there now. Running late, as always. And here you are. If I'd left my office on time, I'd've missed you entirely. It's a sign from God."

"Today?" Aiden repeated, realizing that he'd fairly well backed himself into a corner. "I couldn't even begin to guess where my uniform might be."

"I'll go by Crumb's on my way there and borrow his. It should fit you well enough."

Oh, God. His afternoon with Alex . . . "I haven't played in ages."

"It doesn't matter," Hawkins assured him. "One never forgets how. Say you will, please. If you don't, we'll have to take the field a man short. And we're up against Blackthorn this year. Please, Terrell. Just once I'd like to send Blackthorn home humiliated. We won't have a chance if you don't play."

Blackthorn. Damn. If ever there was a game worth playing, Blackthorn was it. He turned back to the carriage and poked his head inside. "Alex, would you mind a diversion? It'll take the better part of two hours."

"What will?"

"A rugby game."

Hawkins poked his head in to contribute, "And Blackthorn tends to think they're cut from a better cloth than anyone else. It's an old, old rivalry. We desperately need your man to play."

She smiled softly, ever so patiently and understandingly. "I can see that you're drawn to the prospect of getting yourself mangled. I wouldn't dream of standing in your way."

"I could go with Hawkins and have the driver take you home," he suggested, trying to be magnanimous. "I know you have other things you want to do."

She arched a brow and he could have sworn she intended to say something wicked, something other than, "And who would see that you're hauled to a doctor in the aftermath? I'll go along."

Aiden straightened and met Hawkins's gaze. "One o'clock at Pritchard's Field. We'll be there."

He instantly bolted off, shouting over his shoulder as he went, "You're a good man, Terrell!"

Aiden smiled weakly and nodded, then looked up at Barrett's driver.

"I heard, sir," the man said. "Now it's Pritchard's Field. If you are to arrive there by one, we will have to hurry."

The carriage rolled forward before he got the door closed behind himself. He fell into his seat, feeling conflicted and more than a little frustrated. "I'm so sorry, Alex. I committed myself without thinking. I really should have—"

"Don't apologize, Aiden," she interrupted gently. "Life has its own rhythm. All things come in their destined time."

"I suppose so," he reluctantly agreed, staring out the window as the carriage slowed for traffic. There, just behind them, standing on the walkway, his hand raised in hailing a cab, was the stranger.

There wasn't time to leap out and confront him. And the financial district wasn't the place to do it, either. Aiden did the next best thing. She landed on the seat beside him with a startled squeak and was still too stunned to resist when he turned her, slipped his arm around her waist, pulled her back against his chest, and laid his other arm over her shoulder and pointed. "Over there. Climbing into that cab. Do you know that man?"

"No," she supplied breathlessly as their coach picked up speed and the other disappeared from sight. "I've never seen him before."

Still holding her close, he sighed and began. "I've seen him three times, Alex. First at the window of the Blue Elephant the day you were almost kidnapped. And twice today."

"All I can tell you is that he looked to be Kshatriya."

"Explain, please."

"There are four castes in India." Holding up her hand, she ticked them off on her fingers. "From high to low and in the most simplistic terms . . . The Brahmins who are the teachers and the religious leaders. The Kshatriyas who are the warriors and the rulers. The Vaishyas who are tradesmen and businessmen. And the Shudras who are servants and do menial work." She paused and then added offhandedly, "Well, and then there's the Untouchables, but they're considered so low that they have no caste status at all. Mohan's family is obviously of the Kshatriya caste."

"How do you know by looking who belongs to what caste?"

"Generally speaking—and always aware that there are exceptions—by skin tone. The lighter the color, the higher the caste. That and the occupations in which they're engaged and how they dress. That man looked Kshatriya on all apparent counts."

"Why would he be following you?"

"To find Mohan?"

"I don't think so," he gently disagreed, his mind turning over all the puzzle pieces he'd collected. "If someone wanted to find the boy, all they'd have to do is ask around the docks either here or in India. You receive regular shipments of goods. There are countless men who could tell them where the crates are delivered and wouldn't know the danger in sharing that information."

"Mohan's uncle's men are very loyal," she countered, relaxing into him. "Whether because of family ties or fear doesn't matter. They wouldn't talk to strangers about such things."

"I've had Mohan out riding in the city for the last three days, Alex. From sunup to sundown. In plain sight of anyone who wanted to find him. No one has come out of the shadows. But I take you out and about just once and there he is. It's you, Alex. You're the prey. Why?"

"I think you're imagining dangers that aren't there, Aiden."

He wanted to think that, but couldn't. "Mohan tells me that there are some in his father's court who oppose your presence. Is that true?"

"He's far too young to fully understand such things."

Aiden closed his eyes for a moment, then kissed the top of her head before shifting her around to face him. "We've come too far together, my darling duchess," he said softly, taking her hands in his, "for you to go back to evading my questions. Talk to me, Alex. I can't protect you if I don't know where the danger's coming from."

Her smile was bittersweet. "One of the most central realities of life in the royal court is that you're never absolutely certain from which direction the danger will come. Intrigue is an art, Aiden. Those who aren't very good at it die early in the game. Those who are left to plot and scheme are the very, very best at disguising their intent and hiding their allies."

"Why would someone want to harm you? Jealousy?"

She blinked and a genuine smile spread over her face.

"For heaven's sake, Aiden. Why would anyone be jealous of me?"

"Because," he supplied crisply, "you're a Brahmin and they envy your status?"

"I'm not a Brahmin," she countered, chuckling. "Some would tell you, if they were willing to stretch the caste system enough to include me at all, that I'm Vaishya because my father was in trade. There are others who argue that I'm an Untouchable simply because I'm British and Christian. There's absolutely no reason for anyone to envy me anything."

He had no choice but to play a high card. Mohan could just be angry about the betrayal. "Perhaps someone thinks you might someday be the raja's wife or one of his royal consorts."

Her smile disappeared in a heartbeat. "There are strict rules about relationships—especially intimate ones—outside one's caste. Violating them isn't done without great personal and social risk."

"Mohan says differently."

She arched a brow. "Mohan has been saying a great deal lately, hasn't he?"

"Change of subject, darling. It's not going to work. Mohan thinks you'll marry his father."

Her jaw dropped. And for some insane reason his spirits soared.

"I don't know why he'd tell you such a thing, Aiden. He knows full good and well that would never happen." She pursed her lips for a second, then took a deep breath. "What I'm going to tell you must remain between us, Aiden. It goes no further. Promise me."

He nodded and she went on. "If Mohan's father had been willing to take an English woman as either a wife or a mistress, he and my mother would not have had to maintain the clandestine nature of their affair for all the years they did. But the price of openly admitting it would have been too great for Kedar."

"Kedar?"

"Mohan's father. His name is Kedar."

"What would have been the consequences?"

Alex sighed, knowing that only a Briton would have to ask the question. "Congress with a woman some consider an Untouchable? Those that want the throne for themselves would have been delighted to have that weapon to use against him."

"So why would he risk even a secret affair?"

"They loved each other, Aiden," she said, squeezing his hands. "They dared as much as they could. Kedar had to outwardly pretend otherwise, but he was devastated when Mother suddenly fell ill and died."

"Who wants the throne? Who opposes Kedar's rule?"

"It's India," she replied with a quiet snort. "The easier question to answer would be who doesn't want his throne?"

"A related truth. If you had to come up with a short list of likely plotters, who would be on it?"

There was no point in trying to divert him. He was going to persist until he simply couldn't go any further. "At the top of it would be his cousin Kalin and his younger brother Hanuman."

"Do you have any idea of where they might be?"

"When I left India, they were at court. I assume they're still there. Kedar doesn't dare let them out of his sight."

"Are they wealthy men in their own right?"

"I can see the lines along which you're thinking, Aiden. Yes, they have the resources necessary to reach all the way to England. But it's Kedar's and Mohan's deaths that would benefit them, not mine. I'm of no consequence to them whatsoever."

He frowned and stared down at their hands. "So, we're back to the original question, Alex. Who wants to harm you?"

"No one, Aiden. Absolutely no one."

"What about those who resent a British presence in the court on general principle?"

She groaned and slumped back against the seat. He could be so relentless, so exhausting. "In the first place," she began with all the patience she could muster, "their protests are largely hollow. As much as they dislike being under British rule, they're realistic enough to know that there's an advantage in understanding the ways of the rulers. And in the second place, they lack the power and wherewithal to do anything more than verbally rail. As long as Mohan's father remains firm in his commitment to working with the British, the worst they can do is be unpleasant."

"Alex," he instantly countered, his gaze coming up to meet hers, "I have never believed that those two thugs came into the Blue Elephant to steal the silver. That might have been the pretense or the second thought, but it wasn't the primary reason. I think they were sent in with instructions to either take you to someone—our shadow warrior—or to simply take you out and kill you. There has to be a reason why."

"If there is, I have no idea what it might be, unless it's to make getting to Mohan easier."

"If that's what they wanted, then I'd be the prey. And I'm not. It's *you*."

Heaven forbid that he ground supposition on reality. She studied him as he stared out the window. He was so determined to see. So very worried that he couldn't. Her heart swelled and her irritation melted away.

"I understand," she said, shifting on the seat so that she reclined against his chest again, "that rugby uniforms are really quite form-fitting. Inspirationally so." His arms slipped around her and she added, "Not that you need the assistance of clothing to do that, of course."

"You're flirting dangerously close to the edge, darling. You have been all afternoon."

"I know," she replied, reveling in the warmth of his body against hers, the rich rumble of his voice as it passed into her.

"At some point I'm going to draw the line and dare you to cross it."

"I know that, too."

He nibbled the edge of her ear, whispering, "Ask me not to play."

"No," she replied, a lusciously warm shiver cascading through her. "You promised Hawkins you'd be there."

"Which I sincerely regret."

"All things happen when they're meant to. And not a moment before."

Moaning quietly, he gently pushed aside the hair at her nape. "Patience," he said, brushing his lips over her skin, "isn't my long suit."

Savoring another delightful shiver, Alex tilted her head to afford him better access, certain that, despite his claims, he was the most remarkably, gently patient man she would ever know.

Aiden stepped out of the carriage acutely aware that James Crumb was a considerably slighter man. The only possible salvation lay in the condition of the field. After the first slide or two through the mud and muck, the fabric might give enough to allow him to breathe.

"Oh, my."

He looked over his shoulder. Alex stood by the front wheel, her brow arched as she slowly looked him up and down. Jesus. What she could do to him with a wicked little smile. Add in the devilish twinkle in her eye . . . "Darling," he said, turning away before she could do any further damage to his self-control. "These breeches are entirely too snug for you to be looking at me like that."

Suppressed laughter rippled brightly through her voice. "I'm sorry. Have fun, but do be careful out there. If you tear something, you're going to reveal what precious little you've left to my imagination."

Walking onto the field was both an act of supreme denial and desperate self-defense. At the edge of his vision, he saw movement and the colors of the Blackthorn team. He fixed his vision on the knot of his teammates and kept going.

"How on earth did you manage to find yourself such a pretty little half-caste?"

He knew the voice, the son of a bitch who went with it, and that he was talking about Alex. Being half English and half something else didn't matter to Aiden in the least. Purity of ancestry did matter to other people, though, and clearly Geoffrey Walker-Hines was one of them. His teeth clenched, Aiden ignored him and kept walking, hoping he'd go away.

"Did you bring her out of India yourself?" Walker-Hines persisted, falling in beside him. "Is that where you've been these past two years?"

Damnation. He'd been in such a good mood. And now, just one narrow-minded bastard later . . . Deciding to put an end to it, Aiden stopped and faced the other squarely. "Not that it makes any difference," he began, "but for the record, Geoff, my mother's American Irish. Strictly speaking, I'm the half-caste mongrel. Alex's parents were both British."

"And you believe that story?" the other snorted, smirking. "I spent my entire two-year enlistment garrisoned in India. She looks British, but the way she carries herself is Indian. She's a half-caste. You're slipping, Terrell. You used to be one of the best at seeing through pretenses and façades."

"You, on the other hand," Aiden countered, "have always been and remain to this day a complete ass."

"I do, however, have standards." He leaned closer, lowered his voice, and looked back toward Alex. "But I might consider making some temporary allowances for her. She looks positively delicious. Is she?"

Anger, white and searing, shot through him. His hands balled into fists, he required every shred of his quivering self-restraint to keep them at his sides. Slowly, so there was no mistaking the line being drawn, he said, "You've stepped past decency and this conversation is over."

Ever the undaunted brick, he posed, "When you decide you're bored with her . . . I've got a Frenchie at the moment. We could trade."

Trade? As though Alex were a horse or a hunting dog? Turning and walking away before he lost what little control he possessed, Aiden tossed over his shoulder, "Go to hell, Geoff."

"Damn you, Terrell. Always the businessman."

Businessman? Christ Almighty. What did that have to do with anything? Aiden walked on, shaking his head, and willing his anger down. Geoffrey wasn't just an ass, he was a first-rate ass. But as sorely tempting as it was, putting him in his place wasn't worth the pain of split knuckles.

"All right. A business proposition," Walker-Hines said, trotting up and falling in beside him again. "After the game. Ten minutes, ten pounds. That's a pound a minute for her. While you ride Rose for free. What do you say?"

Say? He was well beyond words, well beyond enraged. He stopped dead, and as Walker-Hines skittered and turned back, Aiden swung his fist. It connected with a satisfying crunch of flesh against flesh, bone against bone. The ass landed on his, howling and spitting blood and teeth into his lap.

Aiden absently flexed his fingers and leaned down. "Stay well away from my lady. If I ever see you within ten meters of her, I'll geld you right then and there. You'll wish I'd killed you. That's a promise, Geoff. Remember it."

Walker-Hines was struggling back to his feet when Aiden turned on his heel and walked away, resuming his course across the field toward his teammates. *My lady.* He glanced back over his shoulder. Alex was standing beside their coach, obviously listening to the three women who stood in a semicircle before her. In seeing his attention, she smiled and waved. He waved in return, then faced back to his teammates and, grinning, broke into a trot.

She was an incredible woman. And out of all the men in the world, she'd chosen him. His lady. Her lover. Soon. Damn, life was good.

Chapter 14

"Oh, Aiden," she whispered as he dropped onto the opposite seat and they started toward the sanity of home.

He grinned, pulled a strand of dried, muddy grass from his hair and said, "A hot bath and I'll be as irresistible as ever," as he leaned over and tossed it out the carriage window.

"It's not the mud that concerns me," she countered, leaning forward to take his chin gently in hand. Ignoring his cocked brow and his rakish smile, she turned his face so that the right side was angled into the fading afternoon light. "Your cheek is skinned. So is the corner of your jaw."

"They don't hurt."

Alex ignored his assertion and went on with her appraisal. Releasing his chin, she took his open collar and pulled it slightly aside. "Your shoulder's scraped, as well."

"Really? Never felt a thing. Still don't."

Heaven only knew what damage had been done through the cloth, damage that she couldn't readily see. At least there weren't any obviously broken bones, she consoled herself as she swept her gaze down the length of his arms. "Aiden!" she cried, cradling and lifting his right hand, horrified by the wide, bloody, dirt-encrusted splits across the first three knuckles.

"I'll admit that those smart some."

"And you wanted to know if I allowed Mohan to play this beastly game. And calling it a game is being generous. I've never seen such a long and constant stream of utter chaos and deliberate violence."

He grinned. "We won."

"Is that worth getting yourself battered and torn?" she asked, gingerly placing his injured hand on his knee and resuming her assessment.

"Well, yes. On two counts," he countered buoyantly. "The first being that today was the only defeat Blackthorn's been given in over four years. That's no small accomplishment. And the second is that I need a bit of minor doctoring. There's some potential in that."

"Potential for what?" she asked, meeting his gaze, her brow arched. "More pain?"

Amid the dirt stains and the smears of dried blood, his eyes twinkled with mischief. "Pleasure, actually. Especially when we get to the part where you kiss everything to make it better."

"You are such an optimist," she teased, amazed by the resiliency of his spirit.

"Not really. I know that you have the biggest, softest heart in England." His smile mellowed and he added, "Thank you for being a good sport about the game and the time it took, Alex. I used to play practically every day. Having another go at it . . . It felt like yesterday, like the last two years hadn't happened. That was nice."

"Then I'll allow that it was worth the scrapes and cuts," she admitted, her heart wishing that he could have that kind of peace all the time, wishing she had the power to give him that gift.

Leaning his head back onto the cushion, he gazed up at the ceiling of the carriage as his smile faded. "If you could go back in your life and erase one thing you've done, Alex, what would it be?"

He was thinking of his Mary Alice, of his ship and crew and all the losses he hadn't been able to prevent. She searched her brain, sorting through memories, desperately hoping to find something of equal magnitude to share with him, something that would let him know that he wasn't the only one in the world who bore the burden of remorse.

"I can't think of anything," she finally, sadly, had to admit.

His gaze snapped down to hers. "You have absolutely no regrets in your life? None?"

"Well, regretting something I've done rather depends on when I look back," she explained. "A month ago I would have said that I regretted having come to England with Mohan. If I hadn't, there wouldn't be a difficult decision to make about returning to India or staying here. Looking back today, though . . . If I hadn't come to England, I never would have met you. That outweighs everything else. So rather than regretting coming here, I'm now very glad that I did."

"You still have the decision to make."

"Yes," she admitted. "but that doesn't change the fact that I'm now glad I came to England. Knowing you is a greater pleasure than the decision is a difficulty."

He considered her for a long moment and then shook his head, saying, "You have the most unique way of looking at life, Alex. If it's even possible, it's going to take me a while and a good deal of thought to see matters your way."

Another puzzle for him to solve. "Heaven help me. Has anyone ever mentioned that you tend to be something of a rat terrier?"

"If you think I'm bad," he countered, chuckling softly, "you should see my father."

He spoke of him so seldom, but always with strong feeling. Alex debated silently for a few seconds and then decided that the greater kindness was to intrude. As gently but as firmly as possible. "You know, Aiden, it's obvious that you really do like your father. At some point, you should probably make an effort to breach the gap that's come between you. If you don't, it could well be another of your regrets."

With a dismissive nod and shrug, he grinned and countered, "But it isn't one today. If I hadn't stumbled to London to escape him, I never would have met you. And since you're shaping up to be one of the best things that's ever happened to me, I'm damn glad that he and I had that falling-out."

She'd been addressing the longer term, but couldn't be displeased that he'd seized the shorter. "Proof that some good comes of everything. And proof that you can—and without great effort—bend your thinking when you want."

He made a quiet humming sound as his brows knitted and his gaze shifted out the window. Alex let him wander off into his thoughts, suspecting that he was looking back into the last two years and trying to shift the way he perceived all that had happened. It wasn't an easy task for him; focusing on the positive wasn't a natural inclination.

She so hoped he succeeded in changing that. If he could, his life would be a happier one. And then maybe, just maybe, he would someday look back at their time together and declare that her decidedly unconventional way of going through life had changed the way he viewed his own, and that because of that, she was *the* best thing that had ever happened to him.

Which was such a shallow and self-important hope, she chided herself. And a not very realistic one, either. Of the two of them, she was the only one in love. For Aiden, she was just another interlude, another woman in a long, long parade of them. She'd have to consider herself fortunate if he simply remembered her name in five years.

Alex turned that likelihood over and over in her mind, examining it, trying to understand why it didn't distress her. Intellectually, she should have recoiled at the realization that she was nothing more to him than a casual, convenient conquest. She should be sending him away or at the very least working on a steely speech that would put a firm end to any thought of an affair. But she wasn't doing any of that. And more importantly, she honestly didn't want to.

No, the plain truth was that she was willing to accept that Aiden didn't love her. She loved him and that was sufficient. She wanted to make love to him, wanted to pour all of her heart and soul into him. Whatever he could give back would be enough. Loving him was a gift she was giving herself. A very special, once-in-her-lifetime gift.

A gift that needed to remain a secret, she decided, studying him askance. Yes, it was best if he never knew, never even suspected that she loved him. She'd remove herself from his conscience before it could even think to cringe. Her gift to Aiden would be a clear assurance that she fully understood and accepted the transient nature of their physical relationship. How to go about doing that without sounding as if she were buying used silver, though . . .

To the accompaniment of screaming peacocks, they made their way across the rear yard toward the kitchen. "I'm going to kill them one of these days," he shouted over the noise. "You'd better warn Preeya about getting too attached to them."

Alex laughed and traded the key to the kitchen door for the note Aiden had pulled from the jamb. Juggling his clean clothing so that she could hold her skirts close, she stepped past him and into the moisture-heavy heat.

"Please tell me that it's not a ransom note," he asked from behind her, pulling the door closed and shutting away the sharpest edges of the peacocks' cries.

"It's from Preeya," she explained as she read. "She says that Mohan left with Mr. Stanbridge shortly after ten this morning, that they're planning to return around four-thirty, and that while we're all gone, Sawyer has taken her to market. She doesn't say when they left or when they plan to return."

"I'd imagine fairly soon," Aiden suggested, putting the extra bundles of silver on the kitchen worktable. "It's getting late. She still has to fix dinner. Unless, of course, she already did and left it on the stove or in the oven. My mother's cook does that on her days out."

Alex laid the note and his clothes beside the silver, stripped off her cloak, and went to look. "No dinner that I can see," she announced, closing the oven door. "But bless her, she did leave water on the stove. Enough for bathing. And it's hot. If you'll draw a bucket of cold, I'll meet you at the tub."

"Are you going to join me in it?"

Her pulse skittered and sang and for a split second temptation bloomed bright. Common sense seized control in the next. "With Barrett and Mohan, Preeya and Sawyer likely to come through the door at any minute?" she laughingly, regretfully countered, carrying the steaming pot toward the screened area of the room.

From the pump, he taunted, "Live dangerously, Alex."

God, how she wished she could, how she wished they had even a little more time than they did. Pouring the water into the copper tub, she answered, "I'll go so far as to prepare the bathwater for you and then I'll go into the house."

He came around the screen, the bucket of cold water in hand, and blocked her exit. "I'd prefer if you didn't go off alone, Alex," he said, all the teasing gone from his voice. "Not where I can't see you or hear you if you call for help."

The stranger, she knew. The nonexistent mystery he couldn't solve. "All right, I'll stay. The silver has to be cleaned anyway. I'll see to that while you bathe."

"Thank you." He stepped back and let her pass, adding as she went, "With the screen between us, it couldn't shock your sensibilities too deeply. Not if you don't peek."

"I'm not going to peek," she assured him, bringing him the clothes he'd worn earlier in the day. "That sort of behavior is for schoolgirls."

. . .

Schoolgirls peeked, Alex silently amended from her stool at the worktable, but grown women watched. Discreetly, of course. From a distance. While pretending they were polishing silver. Not that there was too terribly much one could see through a carved fretwork screen. Still, what details were lacking were supplied by her imagination and the kitchen had become uncomfortably warm. Rolling up the sleeves of her blouse and opening the first two buttons on her bodice had provided some measure of relief, but not nearly enough.

"I've been thinking," he called, rising from his bath, "about your returning-to-India/staying-in-England dilemma."

"Of course you have." Why hadn't she ever noticed just how wide his shoulders were? And how lean he was?

A flutter of white as he pulled the bath sheet off the wall peg. "I think you're approaching it from the wrong direction. It isn't which you want to do more, it's which you'd like to do less."

Alex put her elbow on the table and propped her chin on her hand, watching him dry off. "I don't see that the change in perspective really makes all that much difference, Aiden."

"Yes it does. Which frightens you more? Going back to India? Or staying here?"

The answer was surprisingly clear and stunningly immediate. "Going back to India." Knowing what his next question would be, she supplied the answer before he could ask. "There's a quality to life there. A rather terrifying kind of freedom. Expectation, actually."

"To . . .?"

"Feel."

"Feel what?" he pressed, casually draping the bath sheet over the top of the screen and reaching for his trousers.

"Everything. All emotions are considered part of the

divine. Happiness. Sadness. Love. Hate. Desire. To deny feeling is to deny God's intention."

"I like that desire part."

"You would," she called back, laughing, watching his legs disappear into his dark trousers and thinking that it was silly to feel deprived by it. "Actually, you'd do very well in India. You wouldn't even try to resist the temptation of it."

"You were right, Alex. This is very complicated. Let me see if I'm understanding so far." He picked up a boot and pulled it on. "Being born English and raised in India, you're certainly not Indian, but neither are you completely English. And while you have a foot in both worlds," he went on, pulling on his second boot, "you feel as though you really don't fully belong in either. How am I doing?"

He plucked his shirt off the peg and she sighed, resigned to enduring propriety. "Quite well so far."

"Yes, but that's the easy part. There are tens of thousands of English men and women who share that particular dilemma with you," he said, walking out into plain view, carrying the rest of his clothing, absolutely breathtakingly bare from the waist up. "What sets you apart is how deeply you feel the conflict and the courses you see for resolving it."

She wasn't feeling the least conflicted about anything at the moment. Good God, he was magnificently sculpted. "You're disgustingly rational," she declared absently, fascinated by the hard ripples in his abdomen. And the chiseled planes of his chest, the corded ropes in his shoulders and arms . . . Oh, if ever there was perfection in human form, it was John Aiden Terrell. Somehow even the circular scar high on his chest added to it. And he was in her kitchen, sauntering toward her, practically begging her to touch.

He dropped his shirt and coat on the far end of the worktable as he made his way toward her, grinning. "Alex? What are we talking about?"

Ask me if I care, Aiden. She sighed, tore her gaze from

him, and collected what she could of her scattered wits. "Going back to India or staying here." Her heart racing, she rose from her seat and pointed to it as she went to retrieve Preeya's tin of medicines. "You were saying something about how I saw the decision differently than others."

Damn, he'd been hoping she wouldn't be able to remember. But since she had, he didn't have a choice other than to continue. He sat where she'd indicated and watched her take a small metal box from a shelf on the far wall. "On the one hand is India," he began again as she returned to stand between his knees, "and the expectation to fully experience life and all the emotions and sensations that go with it. Fairly put?"

She placed the tin on the table amid her silver and pulled open the lid. "Yes."

"On the other hand, there's England," he continued while she took out a small, wax-sealed jar, "which tends to glorify cold rationality and frown upon any sort of emotional demonstration whatsoever. Stiff upper lip, carrying on, and all of that. Would you say that's a fair summation?"

"In a most general way," she admitted with a shrug as she removed the seal. She dipped her fingers into the salve, set the jar aside and turned to him, reaching to cradle his chin with her free hand.

He caught both of her hands and gently stayed her. "Now for the most complicated part," he said quietly, searching her eyes. They were dark today. A deep, still-water blue. "The heart of the problem for you, actually."

She arched a brow in wordless query and he took a steadying breath. "You'd like to surrender to the temptation of the Indian way of living life but you're afraid to, Alex. There is, after all, a great deal of protection to be had in the English practice of being intellectually distant and emotionally numb. You can't be hurt if you don't care and don't feel anything."

She blinked and the pulse beneath his fingertips jolted.

The betrayals were small and all she allowed him to see. Her smile was placid, her voice calm, as she eased her hands from his grasp and said, "Yet another difficult choice."

"Is it really?" he pressed, allowing her to turn his face and apply the salve to his abraded skin.

"Of course it is." Her touch was gentle, light, and she winced when he did. "Let's say, for the purposes of discussion," she added, lifting her fingers and looking away to take up the jar again, "that I decide that it's perfectly fine to accept and act on a strongly felt emotion."

"Let's pick desire," he proposed, slipping his hands to her waist and smiling up at her. "Just for the sake of an interesting discussion."

"All right, desire," she allowed, a tiny smile flirting at the corners of her mouth as she turned back, her fingertips dabbed with more of the ointment. "What happens if I act on those urges?"

He briefly considered a conservative reply, but just as quickly decided against it. She was going to be his lover and they both knew it. There wasn't any reason to pretend ignorance. "Surrender and we'll both be extremely satisfied. Repeatedly. And often."

Her smile broadened. "And what will you think of me?" she asked, trailing her fingers along the tender spot on his shoulder.

"What I already think of you. That you're the most incredible, interesting woman I've ever met."

"And what will your friends think of me?" she asked, stepping out of his hands to catch his right one. "Sawyer? Barrett?"

"A gentleman doesn't go about sharing that kind of information," Aiden assured her as she got more of the balm from the jar. "Not even with his friends."

She paused, her fingers over his knuckles, and met his gaze. "This might hurt a bit. I'll try not to let it."

"I'll survive."

"Why wouldn't you tell them, Aiden?" she asked as three sharp pangs, one rapidly after the other, shot up his arm. "If you're satisfied, if you think I'm incredible and interesting, why not share your joy with your friends?"

"That's a low blow, Alex."

"No, it's honest," she countered, taking a narrow roll of white cotton from the tin. Wrapping it around his hand, she went on, saying, "You wouldn't tell them because you wouldn't want them to think poorly of me and thus, through association, of you. They'd consider me less than a proper lady. Proper ladies don't have such base desires."

He laughed softly. "Would you care to bet on that?"

"Oh? And just how many proper ladies have you ever known, Aiden?"

"My mother," he instantly countered, "my grandmother, my six sisters, Seraphina Reeves. And maybe Emmaline, although I don't really know her all that well. Nine. With a possible tenth."

"Family doesn't count."

"It does, too."

"All right, Aiden," she said, tying off the ends of the bandage and squaring up to him with a smile and her hands on her hips. "Just to avoid the argument I'll allow you all ten and throw in Preeya for good measure. Eleven out of how many women?"

"Alex, darling," he crooned, sliding his arms around her waist and drawing her closer, "what's the point of this? You've made the decision. I've seen it in your eyes. You've been dancing on the edge with me all day."

Her arms slipped around his neck. "Humor me. I'm being English. My decision notwithstanding, the point is that acting on one's urges isn't a particularly wise thing to do. Tempting? Oh, yes, most definitely. But it's not wise. The consequences can be forever."

"Or not. If you're careful."

"Perhaps for a man," she allowed, smiling at him, playing with the hair at his nape. "But for a woman there are always, always consequences."

"Such as?"

"Unexpected children."

"Sheaths are known to prevent them."

"Reputation."

"Discretion," he countered. "You don't make love in public view and you don't send an account of it to the *Times*."

"A husband's outrage."

"Only if he catches you," he pointed out, grinning, enjoying their game. "A healthy dose of caution is usually sufficient. And in your case, the point is moot. You don't have a husband."

"I meant a husband who discovers that he isn't his wife's first lover."

"If he came late to the dance, then it's his fault for tarrying. But that concern's moot as well because you don't intend to ever marry."

"I'm speaking in generalities, not about myself."

Oh, yes she was and he was done playing. "Well, I'm talking about *us*, darling. You and me."

"I won't deny that there is an *us*, Aiden," she conceded after a moment, a curiously satisfied shadow in her smile. "But I won't pretend that it's more than it is. It's of the moment and won't survive time."

"True. But what's wrong with enjoying it while we have it?"

"You have a point."

"I do?" he said, stunned that she'd so readily admitted it.

"Only from a decidedly Indian view of the world."

He'd take it and be damn grateful. "Will you be feeling Indian or English tonight?"

"I don't know. Tonight's not here yet."

"Which are you feeling right now?"

"I'm not sure. Perhaps a little of both. Mostly, I'm feeling terribly warm."

It wasn't an engraved invitation, but it was close. "I can help you with that," he offered, reaching up between them and slowly, very deliberately opening a button on her bodice.

Alex held his gaze, knowing that she should step away. Or at the very least offer a protest, feeble and dishonest as it might be. He opened another and she kept her silence, stayed right where she was. Another and her blood was singing, her pulse thundering. Another and she was struggling to pull air into her lungs. Another and another and then he was done, leaving her unbuttoned to the waist and trying to keep her knees from buckling.

He eased the fabric to the sides and blew a soft stream of air across the swells of her breasts. Twining her fingers through his hair to anchor herself, she asked on a ragged breath, "Do you honestly think that's helping?"

His smile was quirked and soft but no less rakish for it. "I'll bet being warm isn't quite as distracting as it was."

"It's certainly not as unpleasant for some reason."

Devilment danced in his eyes and he lightly trailed his fingertips along the edge of her corset. Sweet tendrils of warmth swept through her and coiled into her core. He did it again, his touch bolder this time, more deliberately inflaming. She smiled and moistened her suddenly too dry lips.

And then his fingers slipped into the lacy confines to tease her hardened nipples. "Oh," she breathed, swaying on her feet, her head light as she leaned into his caress.

"Like that, do you?" he whispered, smiling knowingly up at her.

"Far more than I probably should," she confessed, her heart overfilling, her core going molten. "Far more."

"There are no shoulds to desire, darling. If you like it, you ask for more."

It was a challenge, a dare, a plea. If she stepped back from it, he wouldn't chastise her or think any less of her for the timidity. If she accepted it, there would be no more hesitation, no restraint, no thinking. He would give her the moon, the stars, and all the pleasure she could bear. "More, please. Now, if you wouldn't mind."

His grin was unholy and sent her heart soaring. "Not at all," he murmured, slipping his hands to the underside of her breasts. His thumbs scraping her nipples, he lifted them from the confines of her corset and lowered his head.

"So luscious," he declared, kissing a swell, moving slightly lower, kissing her again.

Alex closed her eyes, awash in the waves of potent sensation, holding her breath, afraid she'd die of waiting. "Oh, Aiden," she gasped.

Had any woman ever whispered such an earnest plea? It thrummed over his senses, igniting his blood and fraying his gentler intentions. He closed his eyes and paused, determined to hold his course, to keep their progress under control. Alex deserved tenderness and a slow, reverent hand. He couldn't let the seduction go too far, too fast. Not here. Not right now.

"Please, Aiden."

The muscles in his loins tightened and grew hard. They were in the kitchen, he desperately reminded himself. The others were due back within minutes. He wanted to go slowly enough to savor the little quivers of her pleasure, take her low moans into his mouth and make her squirm with wanting, make her whisper his name and plea for release. But not now. He couldn't now.

She threaded her fingers into his hair and arched back to boldly offer his lips a dark, pebbled treasure. Through the pounding roar of his heartbeat he heard the rasp of his own labored breathing, heard the high-pitched snapping of his restraint.

A glorious bolt of heat and desire shot through her, full

and wide and deep. Alex gasped in surprised delight, accepting both the incredible pleasure Aiden gave her and the need that drove her deeper into his arms. A second wave of pleasure, far more powerful than the first, rolled over her, filling her senses, propelling her into a realm of demanding hunger and unrelenting need.

"Aiden!" she cried, her legs melting under the glorious fire consuming her.

He pulled her up and, wrapping her tightly in his arms, drew her full against him. The feel of her breasts against his sweat-slickened chest, of heated skin against heated skin, her hips cradled hard and close between his thighs, the fit magnificently perfect, arousing . . .

Driven by the promise of it, he kissed her—deeply, ravenously—and intoxicated by the unstinted passion of her welcome, the ache in his soul bloomed into overpowering desire. There was only the throbbing hardness in his loins and the desperate thundering of his heart, the aching need to lay her down and lose himself in her.

His conscience weakly struggled against the tide, and in the frantic heartbeat he took to tamp it down, the world beyond them stridently intruded.

"Peacocks," Alex whispered, gazing at him, her breathing ragged, her lips swollen from his kisses.

Someone was here. The realization brought rational thought crashing back to the front of his brain. "They can live after all," he proclaimed, abruptly setting her away and solidly on her feet. He couldn't resist and kissed her soundly, quickly, one more time as he stepped around her. Snatching up his shirt, he rammed his arms into both sleeves at once, saying, "I'll distract and delay while you put your clothes back together."

She didn't say anything and he looked over at her while frantically buttoning up. She stood there, watching him, a dazed, contented smile on her face. "Dress, darling," he commanded, ramming his shirttail into his waistband. He snatched up his coat and her smile slowly grew.

Jesus, she was too delicious to leave. He was too damn tempted to go anywhere near her, but if he didn't jolt her out of her reverie . . . "Alex!"

With a slight start, her gaze came to his, focused and aware. He backed toward the door, feasting on the sight of her for as long as he could. "I'll see you at dinner." With a wink, he added, "Preferably not that much of you. Not then, anyway."

She covered her breasts as best she could with her hands and laughed.

Exhaling long and hard, he turned around and walked out before she shredded what little of his common sense she'd left him.

Chapter 15

Aiden stood in the shadows just outside the carriage house, letting the afternoon air cool his blood and draw his senses down from the heights. Inside, Mohan and Barrett talked, their voices made low and their words made indistinct by their distance and the stable wall. He didn't care what they were saying. What they were doing and where they were in the stable wasn't important unless they started toward the door.

Until they did, though, he needed the time to close away the delicious memories of Alex, to let the hardness in his loins ease. The last thing in the world he wanted was to have to deal with Barrett before he had the mask of cool composure firmly in place. His relationship with Alex was private and personal, intensely so, and was going to remain that way. It wasn't something he was willing to share with Barrett. Or anyone else for that matter. Alex would die of mortification if she thought anyone knew.

Aiden narrowed his eyes and stared absently at the back of the house, considering his squirming conscience. All right, so dying of mortification was a bit of an overstatement. She'd be embarrassed and then in the way that was so stunningly, uniquely her, she'd move past it, smile wickedly, say something about experiencing the divine, and leave him standing there blushing and breathless.

And, as long as he was being disgustingly honest with himself, it wasn't any abiding concern for Alex's reputation that motivated him to keep what passed between them a secret, either. If he'd cared all that much about it, he'd have kept his wits about him and wouldn't have let their interlude in the kitchen go as far as it had. They were damn lucky that no one had walked in on them. If it weren't for the peacocks' warning . . .

He shook his head to dispel the image and raked his fingers through his hair. No, how badly he'd wanted her—craved her—had been his overriding thought as he'd unbuttoned her bodice. And at her first gasp of pleasure . . . He hadn't deliberately abandoned control; he'd lost it. And that was the problem, what he didn't want Barrett or anyone else in the world to know.

Yes, it was selfish. Yes, it was self-centered. And it was most definitely shallow. But it was the unvarnished truth. Alex was so very different from any other woman he'd ever known. Being with her was so very different. And if he had to, he'd sell his soul to make love to her. Somewhere along the way, he'd become a desperate, starving man. One of those pathetic males for whom other men—rational, self-possessed men—felt acutely sorry. One of those men that other men considered an embarrassment.

And the truly pathetic thing was that he didn't really want to stop hungering for her the way he did. As odd and inexplicable as it might be, there was a kind of rightness to it. And if the pleasure in the foreplay was so magnificently intense, then Lord knew the culmination probably would be, too.

Probably? Hell, there wasn't any doubt. Alex was going to reduce him to a heap of sated, grinning cinders. He wasn't about to walk away from the chance for such soul-searing ecstasy. Not just to avoid the risk of male social censure. He was selfish—and maybe a little vain, too—but he wasn't stupid. All he had to do was carefully, deliberately manage the impressions of everyone and he could have all his fantasies come true *and* avoid the pity of his peers.

Barrett's would be the most important and most difficult impression to control, he knew. The trick was to keep their conversations focused strictly on business and well away from the personal. Barrett had an uncanny ability to see through denials and attempts to camouflage the truth. That and absolutely no restraint when it came to asking pointed, probing questions.

Which is what made him a good investigator, Aiden had to admit. And a worthy friend. You didn't lie to Barrett. Not about the big things, anyway. If you did and got away with it, it was only because, for one reason or another, he'd let you for the time being. Eventually there'd be a reckoning.

Aiden stood up a bit straighter and rolled his shoulders. Thankfully, there was a great deal they needed to talk about and all of it revolved around his professional concerns for Alex's safety. He'd delayed long enough to be able to focus on it, too.

Stepping out of the shadows, he strode toward the open carriage house door. Barrett and Mohan were just on the other side of it, heading his way.

"I thought it might be you the peacocks heralded," Aiden began, stopping them at the threshold. At his friend's half-smile and cocked brow, he continued, "Good news, Barrett. On the seat of your coach, you'll find the Westerham silver service for twelve. Less one butter knife. And you'd better still have it because if you think I'm going back out in search of a replacement, you're out of your mind."

"You actually found it? How much did it cost you?"

"Alex found it," he corrected. "All two hundred. And that took work. The old woman was vicious."

Barrett's gaze fell to his hand and his smile quirked higher. "You didn't have to hit her, did you?"

"I was suckered into a rugby game this afternoon," he replied, lifting his hand, flexing his fingers, and wondering what was in the salve Alex had used. The pain was gone. Absolutely gone. "Against Blackthorn. Walker-Hines plays for them."

"Oh, let me guess," Barrett replied drolly. "With his usual sorry lack of good judgment, he cuddled up next to Alex and made an indecent proposal."

"If he'd actually touched her, your solicitor would be posting bond for me because I would have killed him."

Mohan grinned. Barrett shook his head slightly, saying, "Damn shame he exercised a smidgen of good sense today." He brightened and his brow went back up. "So was Blackthorn finally defeated?"

"Five to two."

"Resoundingly. Good show, John Aiden," he congratulated, clapping him on his shoulder. "But I must say that you don't seem appropriately pleased by the day's successes. If I had to guess, I'd say that something's niggling at you."

Aiden looked down at Mohan and smiled. "Preeya's off to market with Sawyer and I think Alex is in the kitchen seeing to the start of dinner. Would you please go see if she needs any help?"

The boy sighed, pouted for a moment, and then nodded. He'd barely walked off toward the kitchen when Barrett said, "You *think* Alex is in the kitchen? You don't *know*?"

Aiden ignored the bait and kept to his purpose. He rammed his hands into his pockets and squarely met his friend's gaze. "What do you know of India?"

"Not much. Why?"

"Let's walk toward your carriage while we talk," he suggested, turning even as he did, forestalling any objections

Barrett might have. When he fell in beside him, Aiden began. "I keep collecting puzzle pieces and I don't know enough about India to know if the picture they're forming makes any real sense or not."

"Apparently what you think you're seeing troubles you. Toss the pieces out on the table and we'll look at them together."

"I don't even know where to begin," he admitted.

Barrett chuckled. "I seem to recall Alex Radford saying something in the same vein the morning she walked into my office. And as I further recall, you weren't the least interested in accommodating her confusion."

Well, he'd been working at being an ass that morning. It was a testament to Alex's inherent sense of fairness that she'd allowed him to redeem himself. "I didn't understand then how complex her world is. Or how complicated she is. Even if I had forever and a day, I'd never fully know her, Barrett. Never. She'd always surprise me."

"But you don't have forever and a day."

A reminder, unusually subtle for Barrett, that Alex was a temporary relationship both professionally and privately. "Correct," he agreed, admonishing himself to keep to the public side of his intentions. "And if I'm right about the puzzle, Alex doesn't, either."

"You're still gnawing at the notion that she's the one in danger, not the boy?"

"She's the one who was almost kidnapped. She's the one being followed. I caught a glimpse of him this morning at the auction and again this afternoon. He's the same man who was at the window that morning. Alex didn't recognize him but she says that he's probably of the same caste as Mohan and his father."

"And is that important?"

"Hell, I don't know," Aiden confessed with a frustrated sigh. "The subject of caste comes up frequently enough, though. Mostly in connection with what one can and can't do. I swear, they have more rules than we do."

"For instance?"

"You'd better fall in love with someone in your own caste because you're not going to be allowed to cross the line for them."

Barrett nodded and stuffed his hands in his pockets, too. "I'd suggest that British expectations aren't all that much different except that my mother is now willing to consider a daughter-in-law from the untitled class if I'd just get on with seriously looking for one. Apparently they're more patient about the production of grandchildren in India."

Aiden looked at him askance. "How is that relevant?"

"It's really not," Barrett admitted with a weak smile. "Just my personal cross of the moment. Who fell in love with whom and couldn't be together?"

Barrett and his questions. He was a lot like Mohan. Except considerably more dangerous. "It was merely an illustration," he lied, honoring his promise to Alex. "I wasn't speaking about anyone in particular."

Before Barrett could call him on it and press, he tossed out the next piece he'd collected since they'd last talked. "Alex tells me that Kedar—that's Mohan's father—has two main rivals for the throne. His cousin and his younger brother. Both of them are presumably still in India and under his watchful eye. Now, according to Alex, neither one of them would have the slightest interest in seeing her come to any harm. They're more interested in removing Kedar from the throne and Mohan from the line of inheritance."

"So why is someone following her?"

"My question exactly," Aiden countered as they reached the parked carriage and stopped. "Mohan's whereabouts is no real secret. They don't have to follow Alex to find him. And that business about her marrying the raja someday . . . Alex assures me that Mohan doesn't know what he's talking about. That it could never happen. They're of different castes."

"Well," Barrett replied, frowning as he stared off into the distance, "so much for the possibility of someone wanting to keep her from producing half-English heirs to the royal throne. Which is rather disappointing, actually. I was favoring that theory."

"It was the only one I had," Aiden groused. "Dammit, Barrett. I can feel it, I can smell, but I can't see it. What threat can she pose? To whom?"

"Maybe she knows something she isn't supposed to know or saw something she wasn't supposed to see."

"Then you'd think she'd be aware of it," he countered, his chest tightening. "She insists that there's absolutely no reason anyone would want to harm her."

"Maybe Preeya knows," Barrett ventured. "Have you asked her?"

"I didn't figure out that Alex was actually the one in real danger until this morning. We've only been home a little while and Preeya's still off to market with Sawyer."

"It's a little late in the day to be at the market, don't you think?"

"This household doesn't run on a clock. Not a British one, anyway. When she gets back, I'll ask. But honestly, Barrett, I don't think she knows anything. If she thought Alex might come to harm, she wouldn't keep quiet. She'd come to tell me why and who."

"I don't know that it would do any good to ask Mohan. He's proven himself to be a somewhat dubious source of information. Besides, how much could a ten-year-old know?"

"I'll ask anyway. It can't hurt."

They fell into silence, Barrett staring off into the city and he scowling at the toes of his boots and feeling a growing sense of unease. A question, unformed and unaskable, taunted him from the edge of his awareness, beyond his reach, beyond his frustrated grasp. If he focused, though, and stretched—

"Alex's mother and the raja?" Barrett asked abruptly.

His brows knitted, Aiden considered his friend in confusion. "Where the hell did that come from and what does it have to do with the price of tea in China?"

"The two who fell in love and couldn't be together," Barrett explained, still looking off. "Were they Alex's mother and the raja?"

Christ. Give the man just the tiniest little crumb and he could build the perfect cake from it. "I didn't tell you that."

Barrett looked over at him and grinned. "You didn't have to. I can—every now and again—put two and two together and come up with a reasonable conclusion."

"It's supposed to be a secret. I promised Alex that I'd keep it."

"It's safe," he assured him.

Which was far more than could be said about Alex, Aiden realized. "Well, I wish you'd put that incredible deductive ability to work on my problem. It's been days. Why again today?"

"I'm afraid I didn't follow that. Deductive genius only goes so far."

Aiden sighed heavily as the unknown question flitted past his awareness again. "He was at the window of the Blue Elephant the day Alex was almost kidnapped," he said, crisply laying down the pieces that felt relevant. "And then he disappeared from sight. Why did he appear again today?"

Closer, he thought. But still not the important, elusive question.

"I assume that we're talking about the stranger?"

Aiden nodded, staring off blindly, straining to see inward. "I call him the shadow warrior."

"Has Alex been out of the house since that morning? Other than today, I mean."

"No." Closer still, but not yet close enough. "But she

wasn't out that morning, either, and he was there. Why was he there—twice—today?"

"Good questions. I wish I could conjure the answers for you. The only way I can see to get them is to force them out of the Indian."

"But he has to be caught first and he's quick," Aiden supplied. "You never get more than a second's glimpse of him before he's gone."

"Even the best make a mistake eventually, John Aiden," his friend assured him, clapping him on the shoulder. "When he does . . ." Barrett opened his carriage door, called up to his driver with instructions to take him to his club, and then climbed inside.

The door was closed and the driver had the reins in hand when the question danced close enough for its outlines to be faintly seen. It was sufficient. Aiden groaned at the simplicity of it and understood both the implications and the path it necessitated.

"Barrett! Wait!" Gripping the edge of the open window, he asked, "Can you come back here around two in the morning?"

"If you need me to, yes. What do you have in mind?"

He needed time to think the specific details through, but the central task was crystalline clear. "Leave the carriage at home," he instructed simply. "Wear your London hunting clothes and bring your gun. I'll explain it all then."

"Two it is."

Aiden stepped back and signaled the driver. Watching the carriage roll away, he couldn't help but think that he shouldn't have spent that year drinking himself into a blind stupor. Now that he needed and wanted to see clearly again, it was damn hard to do. And it took far too long. He was always two beats behind the music. So far, he'd been able to recover from the deficit quickly enough that no harm had come to either Alex or Mohan. And maybe, just maybe, and if he were truly lucky, by morning the general dullness of his brain wouldn't matter anymore.

Where, exactly? he wondered, turning slowly to survey the buildings and alleyways around the Blue Elephant. He was there, watching; Aiden could feel it in his bones. It was part of his unease. But only a small part. The largest part of it came from the gut feeling that time was quickly running out.

He moved to the edge of the yard, widening his visual search of the neighborhood. Somewhere . . .

A rented hack eased up to the curb just a few feet away, interrupting his quest. The door opened and Sawyer, market basket in hand, stepped out. He immediately turned back and offered his hand and Preeya gracefully joined him on the walk, accepting his arm. The hack rolled away and Aiden watched, fascinated as the two servants made their way toward him. Oblivious to his presence, he realized.

"Sawyer," he said in greeting as they drew close enough that he didn't have to raise his voice. "Preeya."

Sawyer actually started. Then, his composure back in place, he cleared his throat and affably said, "Good afternoon, sir," as he led Preeya past without so much as a hitch in his stride.

Aiden pivoted, watching and grinning as a surprising possibility took shape. "Sawyer?" he called after the butler. "Are you . . . wallowing?"

Sawyer stopped in his tracks and turned back, a silvery brow raised. He seemed to consider and discard several responses before he smiled and replied, "Your shirt is misbuttoned, sir."

Aiden looked down. What he could see looked just fine to him. There weren't any gaps, no holes missed. He reached up for the collar. His stomach rolled over as his heart slammed into the base of his throat. One side was a button higher than the other. And he'd stood there all that time, talking to Barrett, with it like that. He might as well have had a sign hanging around his neck proclaiming his guilt. Barrett had known. He'd've had to. There was no way he couldn't. And the son of a bitch hadn't said a single goddamn word about it.

The floodtide of embarrassing realization was abruptly stemmed when Preeya stepped closer and reached up toward the center of his chest. He looked down at her hand, acutely puzzled. Until he saw the long, raven-dark strand of hair she slowly, gently pulled from a buttonhole. When she had it free, she held it up between them, smiling at it, then handed it to him, her grin knowing and wide as she met his gaze.

"Thank you, Preeya," he managed to choke out as he took it from her.

"If you have no objections, sir," Sawyer said, obviously fighting a smile, "Preeya and I will be dining privately in the kitchen this evening."

As though he were in any sort of position to mention, much less lecture on, the value of propriety. "None at all. Enjoy."

"Thank you, sir." And with that, he presented his arm to Preeya again and guided her off toward their private world.

Aiden watched them go, shaking his head, thinking that the kitchen seemed to be a place with considerable romantic influence. First Alex and him, and now apparently—

He growled and closed his eyes. He'd pickled his brain in brandy. There was no other explanation. Otherwise, he wouldn't have forgotten that he'd all but bluntly asked Alex to share his bed tonight. And there was no waving Barrett off and postponing the hunt until tomorrow night. The threat was there and, he suspected, drawing closer. It had to be nipped before it bloomed into real harm.

Two beats behind? he thought. More like six. He could only hope that Alex was not only the most ravishing, breathtaking woman he'd ever met, but also the most patient and understanding.

Chapter 16

All things in their time, Alex reminded herself as she brushed her hair. That dinner had been very late and that Sawyer had lingered with Preeya in the kitchen this evening couldn't have been helped. Just as Preeya couldn't have been hurried off to her room once he'd gone. A warmer bath certainly would have been nice, but she hadn't been capable of being quite so philosophical at that particular point. In her head, she'd heard each and every second as it ticked away into the past. An abiding sense of urgency and the heat of the kitchen had made tepid bathing perfectly acceptable.

Now, though . . . Alex laid aside her brush and looked at her reflection in the dressing table mirror. She was bathed, oiled, powdered, scented, and as coiffed as a woman needed to be when going to bed with a man. But not just with any man. No, with Aiden Terrell. Who, she sighed, had no doubt given up any hope whatsoever that she'd appear at his door tonight.

She wanted to do this; knew that for the absolute certainty it was. If she didn't, she'd spend the rest of her life wondering and wishing she had a chance to live this night over again. Although, if she were being honest, she'd have to admit that she'd prefer to have Aiden come to her door. It was a quibbling point, but still . . . There was something so terribly unemotional and deliberately rational about presenting herself and asking if he might still be interested in making love with her.

Alex smiled, realizing that Aiden probably felt exactly the same way about the possibility of making his way down the hall. Only for him there would be, in the aftermath, a sense of having forced the decision and himself on her. Given the ease with which he regretted, though, he probably would feel that way regardless of who arrived at whose door.

She arched a brow and met her own gaze resolutely. There was only one way to keep him from doing that to himself. She was going to have to summon everything she'd ever heard in the women's quarters and everything she'd ever read in the ancient texts and take the lead from him. When Aiden looked back, as he inevitably would, she wanted him to exhale long and hard and marvel at how he'd been so absolutely powerless, thoroughly seduced, and sweetly ravaged. By a virgin.

Alex laughed, rose from her seat, and took her wrapper from the end of the bed. She was ready. It was time. Hopefully, he was still awake and everyone else was blissfully slumbering and completely unaware. And if the gods were truly benevolent, somewhere early in the course of things it would all stop feeling so terribly formal.

A candle burned on the other side of the door; she could see the faint flickering line of light on the floor in front of her toes. She closed her eyes, lifted her chin, and forced her hand up from her side. Mindful that Preeya and Mohan slept behind doors only a few steps away, she rapped softly and just twice. Then opened her eyes and held her breath.

The knob turned and the door swung fully open on soundless hinges. Aiden stood there, a satin sheet barely twisted around his hips, his wide shoulders bare and bathed in the soft light. His hair, as always, was untamed, tumbling down over his forehead in a decadent invitation to touch. And his eyes . . .

The coolness in her stomach eased as she studied him. He'd been waiting for her, afraid that she had changed her mind. Wonder and appreciation and adoration shone in his eyes and she knew that for as long as she lived she'd measure the devotion of all men against the light she saw in his eyes as he smiled at her now. Wherever this night led them, she'd always remember this moment, this feeling of having at long last come home. Part of her wanted to throw herself into his arms and tell him that she loved him. Another part simply wanted to stand there and appreciate the incredible gift that he was.

He could see it in the tilt of her chin and the shallowness of her breath: she was unsure of what to say, what to do. His innocent, daring duchess. "Alex," he whispered, offering his hand. She accepted it and let him draw her across the threshold and close the door behind her.

Turning, still holding her hand in his, he thought to toss out some jaunty comment that would make her smile, would ease her trepidation. But he couldn't do anything but drink in the sight of her. God, she was the most beautiful woman he'd ever seen. Her eyes were dark in the candlelight, her skin so softly burnished. He lifted his free hand and gently trailed his fingertips over the smooth arch of her cheekbone. He'd always thought that heaven would smell light and flowery sweet. He'd been so very wrong. Heaven was rich and deep, heady and spicy.

"You asked me this afternoon," she said softly, "whether I'd feel English or Indian tonight."

"And you said you didn't know." That angels were golden-haired. "I gather that you've decided?"

"Actually, no," she admitted with a tremulous smile. She moistened her lower lip with the tip of her tongue and took a breath that might have steadied her, but made his knees go weak with anticipation. "But I am certain about a few other things. I like how I feel when you hold me, when you kiss me and touch me. And I want—more than anything else in the world—to know what it feels like to fall asleep in your arms."

His heart was trying to hammer out of his chest, but that was all right. Such perfect lips, so full and ripe. He traced them with trembling fingers, marveling in the softness, remembering the taste of them, the passion in touching them with his own. "I can't promise you sleep."

She kissed his fingers, lingeringly and so reverently that his heart slowly skipped a beat, then settled deep into the center of his chest, its tempo even and so hard that he felt it in every fiber of his being.

"I don't want any promises, Aiden," she whispered, the doubt gone from her eyes as she looked up at him. "What there is between us in any moment is all that there is. I don't require anything more."

He released her hand to cradle her face in his palms. "Do you know how very rare and special you are?"

The smile that curved her lips was soft, but no less seductive for it. "Show me."

God give him the patience and the skill to be the lover she deserved. "There'll be pain, darling," he warned, knowing what would have to happen and his soul aching for his necessary role in it. "Brief, but unfortunately unavoidable."

"I know, Aiden." So serene, so accepting. And then her eyes sparkled with a quiet joy and a confidence so sure that it stole his breath. "I was raised in the women's quarters. I might not have had anything to contribute to their conversations, but I did listen. Attentively."

Her certainty, her happiness flowed into him, filling him to the marrow and, oddly, both lifting and settling his spirit. There was no wrong way to make love to her, he realized.

However it happened, it would be right. That's what Preeya had been telling him that night in the kitchen.

"So you think you know what you're doing, do you?" he teased, releasing her face to gently slip free the sash that held her wrap closed.

"I have a general idea," she replied, shrugging and letting the silk slip down and puddle around their feet. "I was rather hoping you'd be willing to teach me the finer details."

Angels didn't wear long white robes, either. They wore nothing at all. God, she was his every dream. Full, firm, and high breasts, her nipples sitting enticingly dark and taut. Long sweeping lines of torso, hips, and legs, so sumptuously curved and so perfect for holding. He willed his hands at his sides and fought for enough air to warn, "You're at the line, Alex. Think before you cross it. There's no going back once you do."

She held his gaze as she reached out and neatly undid the sheet around his hips. He was forcing himself to swallow when she gently stepped up against him, slipped her arms around his neck, smiled softly and said, "I'm done thinking. Will you make love with me, Aiden?"

There was no denying her. Or himself. He bent his head and kissed her waiting lips, nibbling at her lower one, teasing the inside curve of it with the barest tip of his tongue. She moaned softly and melted into him, her breasts hot and tantalizing against his chest, the feminine pillow of her abdomen cradling the hardened length of him.

Alex stifled a cry of disappointment when he drew away and lifted her arms from around his neck. But the look in his eyes reassured her even as it took her breath away and ignited a fire deep in her soul. Her hands in his, he backed toward his pallet and she went, her heart hammering wildly and her core going molten.

He stopped, placed his hands on her shoulders, and smiled as he leaned down and kissed her again. She tried to reach for him, to close the distance between them, but he stayed her gently and bent his head even further to plant a lingering kiss to the side of her throat. Tilting her head back, she granted him free passage, surrendering her body to the sweet mastery of his touch, the certainty of his intent.

Her mind lingered, vaguely present beneath the heady delight of physical sensation and the swift burgeoning of an elemental hunger. He kissed the hollow at the base of her throat, languidly tracing the curve of it with his tongue, before he moved lower. Oh, yes, she knew where he was going and the sweet torture he could inflict in getting there.

She arched back to tempt him, impatient for the pleasure she remembered. His hands tightened on her shoulders and he groaned, but he conceded to her wordless plea. She gasped as his mouth closed over the tender peak of her breast, staggered as he suckled hard and the bolt of blinding pleasure shot into the swelling tide of need. The fire was instant and consuming and she grasped his forearms, hanging on, breathless and weak in the delight of it.

But he didn't leave her time to fully explore it, to find a comfortable place for herself among the waves. With a long, hard pull, he surrendered the prize to press a kiss to the inside curve of her breast. And then move lower still.

"Oh," she breathed, her mind lushly whispering of his destination. His hands slipped off her shoulders to slowly skim over her breasts, to gently pinch her nipples as he planted a kiss at the juncture of her ribs. His palms heated, his fingers firmly gentle, he stroked her sides to her waist as he bent to one knee and laid a trail of branding kisses to her navel.

Her body quivering, Alex threaded her fingers through his hair, desperate to endure, and then arched her back in a silent plea for deliverance. His tongue traced the edge and she tensed in anticipation, shuddered in delight as he dipped in—once, twice—and then moved lower, his kisses slow and incendiary.

"Aiden," she groaned, a molten heat surging into her

thighs and her knees trembling, weakening with every frantic beat of her heart.

He ignored her, slowly, gently, relentlessly kissing his way into her curls. Her mind marveled at the thrill of the intimacy. Then there was no thinking at all, no conscious awareness of anything other than the bolts of luscious fire arcing through her, slowly, singly at first and then faster until they came one on the other, spiraling her senses upward until her world narrowed into only an urgent, burning desperation to reach the top.

And then the pleasure and the need became one and she was hurled upward, gasping and quaking until it exploded in and through every fiber of her body, overwhelming and possessing all that she was.

Aiden smiled, savoring the moan that came, low and quietly, from deep in her soul as she collapsed by small, quivering degrees into his arms. Her face buried in the curve of his neck as she raggedly gasped for air and her arms draped limply over his shoulders, he gently laid her down on his pallet and took the sheath from the night table.

Her unstinted embrace of passion, the wholeness of her surrender to pleasure . . . He brushed a tendril of dampened hair from her cheek, knowing that he'd never lain with a woman like her. Pleasing Alex was an unbelievably potent pleasure in itself.

She sighed against his lips when he kissed her, murmured his name against them while he settled between her thighs, and then gently sucked the air from his lungs as he pressed against the gate of her citadel. His hands deep in the feather pillow on either side of her head, he waited, gazing down at her and marshaling control until her eyes fluttered open and she met his gaze.

Her eyes sparkled and then she arched a brow and smiled in the deliciously wicked way that was hers alone. "Would you think it too terribly selfish of me to ask for more?"

She was, without question or doubt, the most delightful creature who had ever come into his life. How she could make him laugh and burn with need at the same time . . . "I absolutely adore you," he confessed, laughing and leaning down to feather kisses at the corners of her mouth.

Twining her arms around his neck, she caught his lower lip with her own and gently suckled it. His amusement faded beneath a rushing wave of heated desire and he pressed his hips closer to hers, needing her, profoundly wanting her to need him, too.

She shifted, lifting her hips and fitting them, taking him in with a slow, luxurious ease that tore a moan from deep in his soul and sent heated pleasure rippling through his body. Clinging resolutely to conscious thought, he held the speed of his advance in check, determined to give her as much enjoyment as he could before she had to endure the pain.

Her flinch was abrupt and involuntary and he instantly eased away from the barrier. The friction was exquisite and he gazed down at her, stunned by her beauty, by the pureness of the joy in her smile. He stopped and then gently swept forward again, mindful of the limits of her body, reveling in the heat of her welcome, in the sound of her languid, luscious gasp.

Again he stopped short; again he withdrew. And yet again, always watching her, ever aware of her rising ardor, ever aware of his swiftly building need. At the edge of his control, he drew back one last time and slipped his hands lower on her hips.

"No," she declared softly, pushing her hands against his shoulders to stay him.

Aiden froze, straining to hold back, understanding her command but knowing that delaying or even slowing wouldn't make it any less painful for her. Willing himself to be patient, he leaned forward and brushed his lips over hers, murmuring, "You tell me when, darling."

She kissed him while shifting slightly beneath him and hooking her leg over his. He groaned as their fit changed and he lost the angle he needed, but resolving to let her have the time she required, he didn't resist. He closed his eyes, hoping to God she didn't make him wait too much longer.

"What the—" He gasped as she arched up and neatly flipped him over on his back. She looked down at him with a sultry smile and, fitting them just as perfectly as before, settled herself astride him.

"What are you doing, Alex?" he whispered, his hands on her hips as he gently tried to keep her from inadvertently going too far and bringing the pain upon herself.

She reached down and took his hands, threading her fingers through his own. "Making a choice," she murmured as she pushed his elbows into the bedding at his side. She leaned forward, her weight borne on his hands, the deliberate, changing friction intoxicating. He sucked a breath as his heart raced and his blood shot like fire into his loins.

Rocking gently back, she stroked him again, stopping short of her maiden's barrier, then leaned forward again, this time more quickly. He clamped his teeth and tightened his grip on her hands, struggling to keep his awareness from being swept away in the maelstrom of exquisite sensation.

"More, Aiden?"

"Alex," he growled through clenched teeth, straining to hold himself in check, desperately wild with wanting.

She rocked back again, so fast, so hard that he was paralyzed by the pleasure, that his frantic effort to draw her forward came too late. For a second there was the ecstasy of being fully joined and then it was swept away in the realization of the price that had been paid. The cry started low in her throat, rolling upward and slashing at his heart. He bolted upright and pinned her arms behind her, covering her mouth with his own and taking what he could of her pain into himself.

The sound of it slowly ebbed away and she relaxed against him, gently tugging her hands from his grasp. He held her close, trailing tender kisses along the curve of her neck as her hands came to rest on his shoulders.

Her eyes closed, Alex threaded her fingers through the warm silk at Aiden's nape, acutely aware of the pulsing beat of their hearts, the feel of her breasts brushing against his chest as they breathed, the little spirals of enchantment cascading down from her shoulders and into the thrumming heat and potent promise of their union.

"Your move, darling," he whispered, working his way up to her earlobe. "Whenever you're ready for more."

She tilted her head back to look up at him and bathe in the wonder of his gently patient, reassuring smile. Was there a more magnificent man on earth? How could she not love him with all her heart? Her move? Oh, yes, to accommodate his hopes and expectations. And more. To thrill his senses and take his breath away. To hear him gasp in sweet surprise, moan from the depths of bliss. It would be her extreme pleasure to move.

She smiled and the light in his eyes darkened, deepened, and she heard the catch in his breathing, felt the jolt in his heartbeat. With deliberate purpose, she pulled her fingers through his hair one last time and then moved her hands to his shoulders to firmly, gently push him back and down, her hips still and holding him fast within her, her hands gliding over his chest as his shoulders slipped beyond her reach to settle into the satin sheets.

His heart was hammering. She could see it pulsing frantically along the length of his well-muscled neck, feel it thrumming against the palms of her hands and hard and hot deep inside her. Slowly, ever so intentionally, she shifted her hips, moving them in a languid figure eight. He sucked a hard breath and his eyes darkened another degree as the corners of his mouth drifted upward.

The friction was deliciously provocative and Alex moved again, reveling in the heady delight of it and in the hunger that came into Aiden's eyes. Emboldened, pleasured, she smiled at him and drew the figure again, this time as she lifted herself slowly upward.

"God, Alex," he groaned, his hands gripping her hips, his breathing ragged, his smile stunned and wondrous. "Where did you learn . . . ?"

And then down, caressing the length of him in unhurried devotion.

"Oh, darling, yes," he gasped, arching up to meet her.

She did it again, slower on her upward stroke, faster at the downward and ever so much harder, more deliberate at the end. And he met her, arching up and drawing back, matching her tempo, sending searing currents of pure pleasure rippling deep into her womb and igniting the hungry fires of need and want. As before, conscious thought drifted away on a wave of decadent enchantment, and with a smile of sweet anticipation, she closed her eyes and surrendered all of herself to the swiftly gathering, spiraling storm.

He was close, so close to the edge; the rhythm was perfection, the friction savagely exquisite and compelling. Aiden growled, desperate to hold back, to keep himself from tumbling over before she did. But, Jesus, she was good. So goddamn good. If he had to endure even one more luscious stroke . . .

The intoxicating ripple of her low moan shot through him, heralding their imminent deliverance. She faltered as her muscles fluttered around him and she gasped for air. Aiden arched up and drew her down hard against him and then rolled her onto her back. Kissing her fiercely, he renewed the motion of their exotic dance. And moaned in unholy gratitude when she picked it up and moved with him, stopped breathing when she arched up against him and quickened the tempo.

Craving her, desperately hungry, mindlessly consumed by the extraordinary intensity of the pleasure, he filled her harder, faster, deeper and completely. The quivering in her thighs deepened to sweetly violent quakes that held him hard and fast deep within her. Her cry was part gasp, part moan, and wholly unbridled in its measure as the waves pounded through the whole of her body, as she reached her culmination and pulled him unrelentingly, gaspingly beyond control and into his own.

Alex blissfully floated in a sated sea, aware but not caring that her heart was racing and that she was barely breathing. Sweet shadows of pleasure rippled through her, their procession random and slowing, easing her drift down from the dazzling, wonderfully shattering heights. Oh, to have the strength left to return there, to surrender to the thrill of another ride to the glittering stars. Perhaps later, if she asked nicely, Aiden would oblige her ever so selfish desire.

Aiden heaved a sigh as his senses settled back to earth. Easing onto his back, he drew Alex with him, holding her tight in his arms. Her breathing still as ragged as his own, her heart still racing in cadence with his, she came along willingly, fitting the pillow of her abdomen against his hip, draping her arm and leg over him and nestling her head into the curve of his shoulder. Aiden smiled up at the ceiling, his mind staggering with the sheer magnificence of it all.

"As soon as I get my wits back," he said when he could finally breathe and make his tongue work at the same time, "we're going to do that again."

She chuckled quietly and pressed a kiss to his skin. "Hopefully mine are with yours and they'll turn up at the same time."

Hers were scattered, too? Good. Knowing that deepened his own sense of fulfillment. Which he would have said was utterly impossible. "Alex?"

She snuggled closer to his side, nuzzled her cheek into

his shoulder, and made a delightful little purring sound. If he had the strength, he'd roll her onto her back and start all over again that moment.

"Honest to God, darling," he confessed, summoning all that he had left to turn his head and press a kiss into her hair. "I can't remember ever in my life being this incredibly satisfied."

"Good," she offered on a sigh that was pure contentment. "I wouldn't want to be the only one."

Oh, he could get used to this. So easily. The next few weeks or so were fairly well a certainty. He didn't plan to do anything that would drive her from his arms. And after Lal's replacement arrived and he wasn't needed to guard anyone . . . Haven House wasn't that far away. And there was a great deal to be said for the privacy to be had there. If he could keep Alex blissfully smiling like she was right now, she'd be willing to visit. Every day would be nice. Very nice. Twice a day would be even better.

The longer term was the problem. How to keep her here when Mohan and Preeya went back to India? He was going to have to give that some thought. Tomorrow. Right now, he was just too damn sated to plot and plan.

He gathered Alex closer in his arms and pressed another kiss to the top of her head. His name slipped past her lips on a dreamy sigh and he smiled as his eyelids drifted closed. Life wasn't just good; it was perfect.

Alex awoke with a start, her heart racing, Aiden's arms tight around her, and the peacocks screaming murder into the night.

She'd barely wrapped her awareness around all of it when Aiden growled, "Jesus, I forgot," kissed her quickly and hard, then practically dropped her into the bedding as he rolled off the side of the pallet and onto his feet. "Barrett's here," he added, grabbing his trousers and yanking them on. "I have to go."

"Go where?" she asked, groggily watching him pull on his boots. "It's the middle of the night."

"Don't worry," he answered, his words slightly muffled as he roughly tugged a thick black sweater over his head. His head popped through the top opening in the same instant that his hands emerged from the sleeves. In the next, he snatched his gun off the nightstand. "I won't be gone all that long and I won't be all that far away," he assured her, tucking the weapon into his waistband at the small of his back.

He snatched up a short black coat and was at the door before he paused. "Wait for me, Alex. Right there. Just like that. Please."

Clearly, there was no stopping him. "If you'll promise to be careful."

"Promise." He was in the hall and drawing the door closed when he poked his head around the edge, grinned and added, "Sleep while you can, darling."

Alone, she listened to the peacocks and sighed. If it weren't for them, Aiden would have slept through whatever appointment he had. Barrett would have arrived and at some point departed and she'd still be sleeping in Aiden's arms, wrapped in the warmth of his body and his tender care.

Aiden was right; the peacocks had to go. And definitely before tomorrow night. Alex slipped over to lie in the depression he'd filled only moments ago. Burying her face in his pillow, she wrapped her arms around it and held it tight, breathing deep the heated, lingering scent of him. Missing him, she wished him safe and back at her side.

Lord, she hoped it was at least a year before Kedar sent for them. Two would be even better. A lifetime, heavenly.

Chapter 17

The peacocks had settled back into silence by the time he reached the lower level. Knowing that they'd still be screaming bloody murder if Barrett were on the back side of the house, Aiden slipped out the front door and carefully locked it behind him. He found Barrett in the shadows on the far side of the street, dressed in black and smoking a cheroot. It was the quick, hard red pulsing glow that gave him away. As Aiden walked up to join him, his friend declared, "Those peacocks are a public nuisance," and flicked ash onto the pavers at their feet.

"Obnoxious, aren't they?" he agreed. "I was going to shoot them yesterday morning but was attacked by a rampaging herd of kittens along the way."

Barrett snorted. "You're certainly chipper for two-thirty in the morning."

Two-thirty? Damn, that was a gaffe. "Sorry," he offered sheepishly. "I fell asleep."

"Apparently rather soundly," the other countered, the tiniest hint of amusement rippling under the censure. "Since I all but threw a rock through your window—without effect—you didn't leave me with any choice but to set the damn birds to screeching."

"Well," he countered, looking for a bright, but very neutral, spot, "at least they didn't go on forever like they sometimes do."

The end of the cheroot glowed bright red. After expelling a long stream of smoke, Barrett said, "I didn't know that you'd taken to sleeping with a candle lit. Monsters in the dark?"

"No." There were times when he hated the way Barrett could add things up and come to accurate conclusions. Secrets were damn near impossible to keep around him.

"Then the book must not be a particularly good one. Not if you're nodding away while reading it. What's the title? So I can avoid it."

He couldn't think of a single one; his mind wasn't so much a blank as it was awash in the memory of holding Alex and drifting off to sleep with her curled against his side, too sated to even think of blowing out the light. He deliberately but tenderly closed the images away for another time and met his friend's gaze with a brow cocked in warning.

"Welcome back, John Aiden," Barrett said, laughing quietly. "It's good to see the old you again. You've been missed."

The *old* him would have grinned and suggested that when he tired of his lover, he'd pass her along to his friend. The *old* him had been a pleasant but largely indifferent rogue. "We're not going to talk about it, Barrett. It's not for sharing." *Alex isn't for sharing. You're not going to touch her. Ever.*

"Understood." He took a hard pull on the cheroot, then dropped it to the walkway and ground it out under the toe of his boot. "So where are we going tonight? Or this morning as the case may be."

Good. He'd drawn the line and Barrett had agreed to respect it. "Hunting," he replied, his brain practically clicking as it settled into the course he'd set that afternoon. "I'm betting the shadow warrior is hunkered down in a nest he's built somewhere close by. A place out of the cold where he can see the house and keep watch."

"It makes sense. And I suppose you have some vague idea where that might be?"

"If I were in his shoes, I'd take up residence in a dark corner of someone's carriage house. Someone who's at their country estate for the winter and isn't likely to notice the uninvited guest. I figure we'll start along the alley behind the Blue Elephant and work out from there. He can't be too far."

Barrett nodded and, scanning the houses along the street, muttered, "I hope to hell you're the only one who has peacocks."

They slipped into yet another darkened yard, moving in the shadows and Aiden thinking that if ever Her Majesty's Royal Army or Marines needed to invade a carriage house, he and Barrett were the men to teach the finer points. After a good dozen or so, they'd refined it to a silent, flawless art. They would scan the ground around the entire structure for signs of recent human footprints, pause beside the door and listen, look for the telltale flicker of lamplight, and slowly, quietly open the latches. And when that was done, Barrett would hold up three fingers, then tick them down one by one. As the third dropped, Aiden would open the door and Barrett would dart in, low and with the muzzle of his revolver sweeping in a wide arc from center to left ahead of him. Having lost the rock-paper-scissors contest, Aiden would follow on his heels, high and sweeping from right to center.

And they would find nothing except cobwebs and half-frozen muddy patches where the snow had melted and poured down through the shingles. Honing the precision had been entertaining the first half-dozen times they'd gone through the exercise. The thrill of possible danger had lingered a little while longer. But not much. It existed for a few seconds each time they came up on a structure, but the absence of footprints had a considerable dampening effect on it.

Still, they were doggedly, albeit not hopefully, persistent and consistent. Holding their guns at the ready, walking wordlessly together, they circled the stone stable, their heads bowed as they carefully sorted through the shadows in front of their feet.

"Got him," Barrett whispered, abruptly halting, pointing off to his immediate left. "He cut an arc from here to the rear door."

His blood pumping hard and fast, Aiden flexed the warmth into the chilled fingertips of his left hand and visually followed the line of footprints around the perimeter. Nodding his acceptance of Barrett's conclusion, he turned and looked along the sight line that could be had from the side windows of the building. Across the street, a half block down, he could see not only the entire western and back walls of the Blue Elephant, he could also see the kitchen, the western side of their carriage house and the yard in its entirety. The light still flickered through the iron grills of his bedroom windows. The peacocks were sound asleep, huddled together in the corner of their pen.

"It's the perfect vantage," he whispered, turning to Barrett. "Back door or the front?"

He answered by setting silently off for the rear side of the building, following the trail that had been laid down for them. Aiden went along, scanning the windows on the lower level. No light, no movement. He glanced up, noting the height of the roof and pitch. There was enough that a loft was likely. Would their quarry be on the main level or up above? In his mind's eye, he pictured the views of the Blue Elephant from the northern and southern ends of the structure. He'd be on the lower. Probably at or very near the midpoint.

The latch lifted smoothly and without a sound. Barrett's hand went up and, in rapid succession, his fingers went down. Aiden pulled the door back just enough to let Barrett scramble through and then vaulted inside behind him.

And froze just as Barrett had.

Straight ahead of them, in the darkness, stood the man he'd seen at Alex's window, at the carriage line outside Christie's, and climbing into the cab on Fleet Street. Only those times he hadn't been obviously armed. Now he held a gun in each hand with a muzzle steadily aimed at each of them.

So much for the element of surprise, Aiden thought darkly. And for Alex's early assurances that a native assailant wouldn't use a firearm. The only course left now was bluff and luck.

Never taking his eyes off the man, he eased sideways to make himself a smaller target and fixed the man's chest squarely in his sights. "I hope," he drawled, "you speak English because I have a helluva lot of questions you'd better be able to answer. Let's start with who you are and why you're here."

"My name is Vadeen," he replied, his words carefully pronounced, his accent strong. "I am the bodyguard of Prince Sarad, the younger brother of the raja, Kedar. I was sent to protect Kedar's children from harm. I have seen you with the prince and princess and know we share the same task."

The puzzle pieces—every single one of them—tumbled into place perfectly, swiftly, and with stunning ease and clarity. If the man's intent was to knock the pins from under him, he'd succeeded. In spades. Jesus. Sweet Jesus. His heart was pounding and frantically urging him to turn around and walk away, to pretend that the stable had been just as empty as all the others. But his feet wouldn't move and the ragged, sad voice of reason said he couldn't walk, couldn't run, far enough, fast enough, to escape the truth.

"Princess?" Barrett repeated, very slowly straightening to his full height, his movement mercifully distracting and drawing Aiden from the swirl of horrible realization.

Vadeen lifted the muzzle of his weapon to follow Barrett's progress, but the larger part of his attention remained on Aiden. "There are many things you do not yet know. I will put down my weapon if you and your friend will set yours aside, as well."

"We'll lower them," Aiden conceded, his stomach cold and hard. "But that's as far as we're going to trust for the moment. You'll have to earn any more than that."

"A wise and acceptable compromise," the other said, his smile revealing bright white teeth. The muzzles of his guns inched downward at precisely the same angle and time that Aiden and Barrett's did. "Do you have a name?" he asked when all the weapons were aimed at the floor.

"Aiden." He barely motioned with his head. "My friend is Barrett."

He made a similarly restrained nod of his own, indicating several mounds of hay and some barrels against the wall on his right. "My home is a humble one, but I invite you to sit and make yourselves comfortable. The story is long and will take some time."

It wasn't too late to go. If he turned around and left, supposition and educated guesses would be all he really had. He could go back to Alex and . . . pretend that there was no danger. Pretend that he knew enough to keep her safe. Pretend that they were the only people in the world and that they alone shaped their fates. He could pretend that he wasn't living a lie. A lie that could well get Alex killed.

The three of them moved, the Indian backing, the two of them advancing; always at the same time, never glancing away from the gun in the other's hand.

"All right," Aiden said, easing down on a barrel opposite Vadeen, the gun resting in his lap, his hand still wrapped around the butt, his finger lying along the side of the trigger. Barrett settled likewise on a barrel to his right, and Aiden nodded crisply and added, "Start talking. I'm listening."

"With great suspicion," the other pointed out, his smile even brighter with the distance closed.

"Can you blame me?"

His smile disappeared. "No, I cannot. A suspicious man lives longer than one who readily accepts."

"Begin the story, Vadeen."

"And start with the princess part of it," Barrett added.

"It is too soon for that," Vadeen replied, his gaze darting to Barrett only momentarily. "I will come to it when it is right to do so."

"Fair enough," Aiden allowed, resolutely willing his emotions to the farthest, darkest corner of his awareness and then sternly admonishing himself to concentrate on the details. Being able to separate truth from deceit depended on his ability to sort it all quickly and accurately, to match what Vadeen said with what few facts he already knew. If there was a way out of the maze, he had to find it. The alternative was too dismal to even contemplate.

"Five weeks ago," Vadeen began, "the enemies of Kedar at last moved against him, their goal to murder him and seize his throne. By the power of Vishnu, they failed. One of the conspirators was killed. His name was Kalin. He was a cousin of Kedar. The other escaped in the chaos. His name is Hanuman. He is the younger brother of Kedar and of Sarad."

They were the right names, the same ones attached to the same relationships that Alex had given him yesterday afternoon as they'd rolled down Fleet Street.

"Kedar does not know where Hanuman has fled, but fears he may come to London to take the prince and princess prisoner or do them grave harm. I was sent here to find Hanuman and to see that he dies before he can act again on the evil in his soul."

Or so he claimed, Aiden silently countered. Vadeen could just as easily be Hanuman's agent and here to see that Alex and Mohan died. "Speaking of death and evil . . . Did you know the two bastards who tried to take Alex out the back door of the Blue Elephant?"

"No, I did not," came the instant, easy response. "I came here on the ship that brought the crates for Princess Alexandra. The men who delivered them to her told me of Lal's return to India. They also told me of your presence in her house. As I did not know of your ability, I feared I might be required to abandon my search for Hanuman to take up the duty of Lal. Not certain of what to do, I chose to watch and wait.

"In the night I found this place and in the morning I saw the two men make their way along the walk and toward her shop. I did not like the look of them, and thinking they might enter, I went after them. It was my thought to intervene if they proved to be immoral."

Immoral? That was one way of putting it. A rather too polite way.

Vadeen's smile grew by slow degrees and then he added, "It was through the window that I learned you are a most capable man and understood that the prince and princess would be best served if I kept to my duty to find Hanuman."

Flattery was nice, but it didn't necessarily mean a man was telling the truth. Even gilded words were still nothing more tangible than air. "The last bastard standing looked past me. I think he saw you at the window and recognized you."

"He did see me," Vadeen admitted, his smile fading as he nodded. "As I saw him. But in his fear, at a distance, and in the truth that to Western eyes all Indians look alike . . . I believe it was Hanuman he thought he saw. It is his way to use others to achieve his depraved ends. I cannot prove it, but I am certain those men were serving him."

"All right," Barrett fairly growled, inserting himself into the exchange. "Since you can't prove it, we'll let that go for now and move on to the next obvious question. Why did Kedar send his brother's bodyguard? Why didn't he send one of his own?"

"Many of his trusted men were killed in protecting him," Vadeen answered, his gaze holding Aiden's. "Those that lived were needed where they were. I was chosen from Sarad's men because I speak English and can be trusted."

"And the next one," Barrett went on. "If you're supposed to be looking for Hanuman, why are you following Alex?"

Again, Vadeen didn't look at Barrett when he replied. "It is the princess he wants. As he comes to her, he will come to me. I have followed her to keep watch and to stand between Hanuman and you, Aiden. I know what Hanuman looks like. You do not. I am the one who will see the danger first. It is my thought that should I fail to stop him, you will be warned in it and more prepared to protect her."

Aiden cocked a brow. "Aren't you at all worried that Hanuman will come after Mohan?"

"I mean no disrespect to Prince Mohan, but the princess is the most valuable prize. She is the one that Hanuman most wants."

Barrett asked the question before Aiden could. "Why?"

"The throne is lost to Hanuman now, but he will not accept his failure with grace. He seeks to cause as much pain as he can. Prince Mohan is the first son of Kedar's first wife and he will be the next raja. His death would be tragic and he would be mourned. But there are other princes and there will be another raja after Kedar. Princess Alexandra is the daughter of Kedar's heart. She cannot be replaced. Her death would tear the soul from his body."

"And we're to the story of the princess," Aiden said, wishing they weren't but knowing deep in his gut that the truth couldn't be ignored. God, his heart was beating so hard and fast it was going to fly apart.

Vadeen considered him for a long moment and then nodded. "When Kedar was a young man and not yet the raja, he was sent by his father to live for a time with his mother's brother in Delhi. He was to learn what he could of British ways so that when his time came to lead his people, he could do it well."

Just as Mohan had been sent to live in London, Aiden silently added. A family tradition.

"It was in Delhi that he met a young English woman. She was the daughter of a British East India officer. They fell in love. Her father discovered their love and, being a man of narrow thinking, sent his daughter away in the night. Kedar looked for her for many years in many places, but could not find her.

"When his father died, Kedar had to put away his yearning and fulfill his duty. He became raja and took a wife. Then, in accordance with our customs, he took another and installed mistresses. Prince Mohan and the others were born. The kingdom was preserved into the future. But Kedar never forgot the English woman. She remained in his heart."

"And then one day in a temple . . ." Aiden supplied, sighing and easing his finger off the side of the trigger.

Blinking, Vadeen stared at him. "You know the rest of the tale?"

"Only bits and pieces Mohan shared," he admitted, his stomach knotted and cold. "And a few guesses of my own based on comments Alex has made. You might as well tell me all of it."

"In the temple was an English girl stealing the offerings of food. Kedar saw her and knew the face of the English woman he had loved in Delhi. The girl ran away from him but he sent his soldiers out to find her. They returned with the girl and her mother."

Being found in a temple and looking like your mother didn't make a girl a princess. There was more to the tale than that. Not that it was all that difficult to guess what it was. The pieces had been there all along. He just hadn't wanted to see the picture they formed.

"And Kedar was happy at last," Barrett summarized cynically. "The angels broke out the harps and all was finally right in the kingdom."

Aiden snorted and shook his head. It was bad enough that Barrett seemed determined to be as unpleasant as humanly possible, but he was pursuing the course without having the slightest idea of all the intricate requirements of caste and race in India. He hadn't understood, either; not until Alex had explained the basic outlines of them. And all that she'd told him squared with what Vadeen was saying in the darkness.

"Ah, I see, Aiden, that you have some understanding of his dilemma," Vadeen said. "No, he could not be happy. He was the raja and knew there were enemies who sought means to remove him from power. His love for the English woman would have been seen by some as a sign that he was unfit to rule and he knew that if he were foolish enough to provide his enemies with such a weapon, they would use it against him. And against the English woman. He had no choice but to hold her secret in the shadows of his heart."

"And Alex?" Aiden asked, already knowing the answer, beating back the rising tide of despair. "Was she a secret, too?"

"You are a most perceptive man, Aiden. The English woman knew of the dangers in Kedar's court. She swore the girl was the child of her husband. But Kedar can count and he can see. He has always known that she is his. Just as he has always known that he did not dare to declare her his firstborn child, his daughter, until his enemies were vanquished."

"Which they will be as soon as you find and kill Hanuman," Barrett offered.

"Yes. When it is safe, Kedar will acknowledge her as a royal princess."

Aiden clenched his teeth. He was going to lose her. She'd have no choice but to go back to India. Princesses never had choices. They existed only to serve the needs of the kingdom. Alex deserved a better life than that.

"Does Alex know that she's Kedar's daughter?" he heard Barrett ask.

It was a pointless question. At least to his mind. He knew Alex. If she'd even suspected that she was royal, she wouldn't have dithered for a single second over the decision to go back or to stay in England. Not one single second. She'd take up her duty without hesitation. Alex knew more about obligation than the Queen.

"No. She looks fully English and so the truth was kept from her so that she could not endanger herself or the throne with a careless slip of the tongue."

Aiden swallowed down the painful swelling in his chest to ask a question that did matter. "But Hanuman knows, doesn't he? If he didn't, Alex wouldn't be in danger."

"He suspects," Vadeen answered simply. "For Hanuman, it is enough."

"Pardon my skepticism, Aiden," Barrett said, apparently not even trying to hide his sarcasm, "but has it occurred to you to wonder how the bodyguard of Kedar's brother knows all of his master's brother's secrets?"

No, that Vadeen did was sufficient. He didn't fathom the ways of India and he never would. But all the facts seemed to add up. Either Vadeen was telling the truth or he was the most accomplished liar the world had ever seen.

"When I was chosen as the one to seek Hanuman," Vadeen explained, "it was decided that I must know the truth so that I would understand the importance of my success. It was Kedar himself who told it to me."

"Oh?" Barrett rejoined. "And how do you think he'd feel about your telling it to us?"

For the first time since they'd come into the stable, Vadeen turned his full attention to Barrett. "Aiden is the protector of Princess Alexandra's choice. I have watched him and know her judgment to be sound. If I fail and Hanuman kills me, it is important that Aiden knows the danger that stalks her and why he must succeed. You are his friend. As you came with him tonight, you will help him protect the prince and princess. So it is right that you too know the story."

Aiden silently congratulated the Indian on having—at least for the moment—put a halt to Barrett's sardonic interrogation. "When were you planning to tell me all of this, Vadeen?"

"You saw me today as we were out in the city. And I saw you in the yard searching for my hiding place as the sun was going down. I had thought in the morning to present myself and the explanation." He smiled, broadly. "But when the peacocks raised their cry in the small hours, I knew that you had a different sense of time. I waited here for you."

"I hope we didn't keep you waiting unduly long," Barrett offered dryly.

"You did not," the other replied, laughing softly. "You are very efficient in your work, Barrett. Should you ever wish to enter the service of my master, I would be willing to speak in your behalf."

Barrett growled and muttered about sledding with Satan. Aiden let him. "When is Alex supposed to know the story, Vadeen? Were you going to tell her in the morning, too?"

"Kedar placed the decision in my hands. I had intended to speak with you alone." He paused for a second or two, then crisply nodded. "I am going to reach into the folds of my coat," he said, leaving his guns in his lap and lifting both hands, palms out so that they could clearly see them. "I will do it carefully and slowly so you know that I am not searching for a weapon."

"Careful men do tend to live longer than reckless ones," Barrett sniped.

"Yes, they do." A man of his word and apparent good sense, Vadeen very deliberately slipped his right hand into the front opening of his jacket. And then just as cautiously withdrew it, a sealed parchment packet held between his forefinger and thumb. "As Kedar told me the story, it was written down," he supplied. "The seal is his. He instructed me to give this to the princess when I thought she should know who she is."

Aiden had to swallow and take a deep breath before he could ask, "When will that be?"

"I give the choice to you, Aiden," he replied, extending his arm and the packet. "I have seen that you know her well and that she trusts you."

Aiden considered the packet, the ticking away of precious seconds louder than the painful thunder of his heartbeat. Reaching out, he took it and then slid it to the outside pocket of his coat. "Alex once told me that they'd be summoned back to India when Mohan's father thought it was safe for them to return."

Vadeen nodded. "Prince Sarad will be here in one week. Perhaps a few days sooner if the winds are good. He is to take Kedar's children home without delay."

Days. Only days. He wanted to cry. And not sure that he could keep himself from it, he rose to his feet, asking, "Are you going to stay out here or do you want to come into the house?"

Vadeen shook his head as he and Barrett also gained their feet. "One can often see more clearly from a short distance away. I will remain here."

"If you need anything—"

"I will ask," he promised. "You must do the same."

Aiden nodded and turned away, moving resolutely toward the door and desperately hoping that Barrett had enough sense to leave him alone for a while. He wasn't quite sure whether hitting someone would make him better or not, but if Barrett offered the chance to find out, he'd take it.

He had managed to get halfway back to the Blue Elephant, through anger, through dismay and disappointment, and all the way to a burning mixture of self-loathing and burgeoning panic before Barrett trotted up beside him.

"Talk to me," his friend said without preamble. "What are you thinking?"

Aiden didn't slow his stride or look over at him. "Not much beyond your basic 'Good God Almighty! I've bedded a princess!' "

"You didn't know at the time that she was a princess."

"And that makes it all right? That takes away all the ugly consequences for her?" he demanded, thinking that perhaps he wasn't quite done with the anger after all. "When it comes to doing the worst possible, most outrageously wrong thing, no man picks them better than I do. No man! Hell, I can do it without even trying. All I have to do is breathe and think to myself, 'What could be the harm?' Jesus!"

Barrett didn't say anything more until they reached the front door of Alex's shop. Aiden was fishing the key out of his pocket when Barrett caught his arm and asked, "What are you going to do?"

"I don't know," he admitted hotly. "Do you have any pearls of wisdom you'd like to cast my way?"

Barrett let go of him and with a sigh looked back the way they'd come. "It's too late for the only one I could have offered you."

Way too late. And suddenly he was plunging back into despair, his chest tightening and the tears clawing their way up his throat. Ramming his fingers through his hair, he closed his eyes and snarled, "What a goddamn disaster."

"It could be worse," Barrett offered weakly.

"You're right," he agreed, his anguish and despair evaporating in the heated surge of returning anger. "Deflowered Indian princesses might be expected to kill themselves."

Barrett expelled a hard breath and squared his stance. "Don't give her the letter right away, John Aiden. Hold on to it for a few days. Give yourself time to think. Give both of you time to come back to ground."

"In a few days Sarad could be walking in the door of the Blue Elephant," he countered through bared teeth. "What am I supposed to say then? 'Excuse me a moment, your highness. If we could possibly delay the reunion, there's a little something I've been neglecting to tell my lover, your niece'?"

"Aiden, don't do anything gallant tonight," his friend replied, trying, Aiden knew, to be the voice of calm and reason. "You'll regret it in the morning."

And that mistake would be bigger, more significant than the one he'd already made? What was one more regret? "Thank you for coming along, Barrett," he said tersely, stepping up to the door and inserting the key in the lock. "We wanted answers to the questions and we got them. God-awful as they are."

He had crossed to the other side of the threshold when Barrett quietly asked, "Are you going to be all right?"

Aiden slipped the key into the lock on his side. "It's Alex you need to be worrying about."

"Alexandra Radford isn't my friend."

He looked up to meet the other's gaze. "That, Barrett," he said, "is your great loss. Good night. Thank you again." Then, before Barrett could say one more word, before he could shove his foot in the door and persist in angering him, Aiden closed the door and locked it.

Alone in the dark on the other side, he gazed up the stairs, knowing she was waiting for him. His beautiful, breathtaking, passionate Indian princess. His mistake had been committed unwittingly, but committed it he had. He'd do right by Alex. Whatever he had to do to shield her, he'd see it done.

Chapter 18

Alex opened her eyes, listening for the sound that had awakened her. It came again, from over by the windows, part groan, part sigh. She moved her head on the pillow just enough to see. Aiden sat on the trunk, dressed as he'd been when he'd left her, his elbows on his knees, his face buried in his hands.

"Aiden?" she called softly, sitting up, holding the sheet over her breasts.

He looked up, clearly startled. He took a quick breath and offered her a fragile, stiff smile. "I didn't mean to wake you, darling. Go back to sleep."

When he was in obvious agony? "Aiden, what's wrong?" Dropping the sheet and gaining her feet, she crossed the short distance and then knelt at his feet, her hand on his knee as she gazed up at him. "What's happened?"

He closed his eyes and fell back against the wall. Softly, quietly, he asked, "Who is Sarad?"

Her heart skipped a beat. "Mohan's uncle," she supplied, her mind frantically racing. "Kedar's younger brother. He's the one who sends me the things for the Blue Elephant. How—"

"Do you trust him?"

"Kedar trusts him," she answered, her stomach growing colder with every beat of her heart. "How do you know about Sarad? I never told you his name."

His eyes still closed, he cleared his throat and asked, "Have you ever heard of a man called Vadeen?"

"It's a fairly common name, Aiden."

"This one is Sarad's bodyguard. Do you know him?"

"The last time I actually saw Sarad," she replied, desperation welling up inside her, "I was a child not much older than Mohan. I certainly wouldn't know his bodyguards."

"Have you ever met Hanuman? Would you know him if he walked up to you?"

Hanuman? Oh, God. Certainty slammed down over her. "Yes and yes. Is he here in—"

"If a man walked into the store and told you he was Sarad, how would you know if he was lying or not?"

She was at the end of patience, at the end of endurance. "I'm not answering another one of your questions until you answer mine, Aiden. What happened tonight?"

He opened his eyes with a sigh and sat away from the wall. From his pocket he took a parchment packet. Handing it to her, he whispered sadly, "The bottom fell out of the world."

She took it from him and flipped it over. And then dropped back onto her heels, her heart skittering madly and her stomach frozen with dread. Kedar's seal. Her name, in Hindi, scrawled over the face. Possibilities flooded over her. Kedar was summoning them back to India. The messenger, the man named Vadeen that Aiden had asked about, was downstairs, waiting. Kedar was writing to say that he'd been taken prisoner and it would never be safe for them to return; she should take Mohan far away and keep him safe. That he was dying. That Mohan's mother was dying.

She closed her eyes and took a deep breath, willed her mind to still and her panic to ease. With trembling fingers, she broke the wax and opened the folds. Then opened her eyes. And began to read.

The first words were an instant comfort. Kedar was well. All in his house were well. His enemies had been defeated. Alex sagged in relief and read on, hearing the richness of his voice in each and every word. And the whispers that had followed her all of her life in the palace. She reached the end and stared at the closing salutation, at the call for divine blessings upon his daughter. *Daughter.* She had a father. A living, breathing, loving father. Kedar. The man her mother had loved with all her heart.

"Is it Kedar's seal?"

She blinked and looked up from the letter, up into Aiden's sad eyes. "Yes," she answered, wondering why he considered this to be bad news. The bottom hadn't fallen out of the world at all. If anything, it had come wondrously right. "And the pen of his scribe. I recognize both."

"You didn't know, did you?"

She shook her head, marveling at the web of deceit that had always been her life. "When I was a child, I secretly hoped and pretended. And then I put it away and accepted what my mother said was the truth."

"What happens now?"

Alex looked back at the letter. Yes, she'd read it correctly. "Vadeen dispatches Hanuman and Sarad comes for Mohan and me within the week and we return to India."

"And what happens in India when your father learns that an English cad has bedded his princess?"

The gentle sense of happiness shattered as two realizations crashed over her. She was a princess. And for Aiden that changed everything between them. Her mind reeling and her heart hammering, she refolded the letter with great care, desperately searching for her way, for the right words. Putting the letter aside and turning to place her hands on his knees, she smiled up at him. "In the first place," she began, "I can't see any reason for him to ever learn of it. And in the second, I would think that I'm proof that he fully understands the power of temptation and passion."

She could see the struggle between temptation and reason in the hard line of his jaw; he wanted to believe her, wanted to reach for her. "Will you be a lesser princess because you're half English?"

She couldn't lie to him. "In the eyes of some. But not Kedar's. You'd like him, Aiden. He's a good and kind and fair man."

He sighed and swallowed. And then, blessedly, his eyes lit with sparks of anger. "In England princesses are married off—as the expression goes—advantageously. Is that what's going to happen to you, Alex? Are you to be married off to the highest bidder?"

"The choice of husbands will be mine. And—"

"Will he mind too terribly much," he interrupted bitterly, "that I danced with you before he did?"

"I'll never choose one, Aiden," she finished calmly, hoping to soothe him. "No one will force me to wed."

"So you'll go through life alone."

His tone made it an accusation. Her own anger flared. "As I recall, it's what you intend to do. Why is it a situation appropriate for you, but not for me?"

He rammed his hands into the pockets of his coat and stared off over her head, the muscles in his jaw pulsing furiously. "You could stay here, Alex. Keep the Blue Elephant. I'll run the shipping route for you and bring you all that you need."

And she would be alone, waiting for him to come into port, living for those few days a year, praying all the others that nothing horrible had happened to him, and always waiting for the day when he'd tell her that he wouldn't be coming back, that he'd fallen in love with another woman. No, that wasn't the life she wanted with him. If she couldn't be his wife and the mother of his children, then it was better that they break it cleanly. Better that they part with sweet memories than to linger for years, trying to sustain hopes that would eventually wither away.

She knew that she could ask him to come back to India with her, but she also knew that even if he accepted, there would come a day when he wished he hadn't. He had too much pride to be a kept man, too much energy to wander the halls of the royal court, day in and day out, without purpose. No, he had peace to make with his father and a shipping company to someday lead. His path lay to the west, hers to the east. In loving him, she had to let him go.

"As a princess, I have responsibilities," she began, her heart tearing, her soul aching, her mind certain that she was choosing the only path she could. "In addition to those of being the royal tutor. I can't stay, Aiden. The decision's been made for me. In a way, it's a relief."

He leaned back against the wall and pulled his hands from his pockets to scrub them over his face. "God," he groaned, letting them fall into his lap as he stared off over her head again. "I knew you'd say that. Duty before all else. It's so damn British."

"Please don't be sad, Aiden. Or angry." She reached up and took his hands in hers, loving him so much, unwilling to let him go a single moment before she absolutely had to. "We've known from the beginning that there was no forever for us. Only the length of time we have together has changed. It's now just shorter than we'd hoped."

Forcing a buoyancy into her voice she didn't feel, she smiled up at him and added brightly, "Which, to my mind, anyway, suggests that we should probably make every second of it count."

He didn't move, didn't make a sound. As though he hadn't heard a word she'd said, he continued to stare at the other side of the room, blinking, looking for all the world like a caged animal. Part of her wanted to gather him into her arms and rock him gently, to assure him that all wasn't as hopeless as he thought. Another part of her wanted to take him by the lapels of his coat and shake him until his teeth rattled. She decided on a middling course.

Releasing his hands, she rose to her feet, and then reached down for his foot, one hand on the heel of his boot, the other around his instep.

"What are you doing?"

At least she finally had his attention. "Making a choice," she answered, pulling. The boot didn't budge and she adjusted her stance for better leverage.

"Alex, you're a princess," he said as she tugged—without effect—again. "I know that it shouldn't make any difference, but it does. It makes a big difference."

She gritted her teeth and, trying a third time, replied, "I'm the very same woman I was at midnight, Aiden."

"Alex, darling, stop." And then he took the choice from her by gently but firmly pulling his foot from her grasp.

Turning, she found him still slouched back against the wall. But the caged look was gone. One corner of his mouth was quirked up in a smile that seemed slightly more amused then it did sad. It gave her just enough hope to press him for more. Kneeling down between his thighs, she cradled his face in her hands and met his gaze squarely, lovingly. His hands came up off his thighs and then he started, sucked a hard breath and forced them back down. The smile disappeared, replaced by a thin line of resolve.

Alex ignored it all and quietly asked, "Is denying ourselves pleasure going to make me a virgin again?"

"I wish it could."

So softly, so earnestly, from so deep in his heart. "You regret far too easily, Aiden," she countered, loving him for the tender soul that he was, wanting with all of hers a forever they couldn't have. "The past is over and gone. It can't be changed," she went on, pouring all the hope that she could have into her words. "What will come in the future can't be known. All that exists is *now,* Aiden. This one moment in time. Live in it with me. Please. Make love with me."

His confusion tore at her heart, but she waited in silence, watching temptation and wonder struggle against his sense of right and wrong, praying that desire would win the battle. Then suddenly the haunted, desperate look flickered through the depths of his eyes. His breathing ragged, his pulse hammering against the palms of her hands, he forced himself to swallow. "If I asked you to—"

She pressed her fingers to his lips, silencing him. "This moment, Aiden," she whispered. "Don't look forward. Don't look back. Look at *me.*"

He couldn't fight any more, couldn't breathe, couldn't do anything except feel a relentless, utterly overwhelming sense of desperation. It wasn't right. Or noble. Or honorable. It was need; raw, primal, and undeniable. A need to escape the pain, a need to lose himself in the sated, mindless oblivion that only she could give him. He needed her. And God help him, he wanted her more than life itself. For just this moment . . .

The floodgates opened and he surrendered to the unrelenting torrent. He reached for her, wrapping her in his arms and hauling her hard against him, crushing her lips under his own. She met his advance with a cry of joy and a ferocity every bit the equal of his own. With a grateful moan, he spiraled away into the searing salvation of passion.

Alex awoke with a smile and Aiden curled around her. There was, she knew, no happier, more deeply and thoroughly satisfied woman on earth. It was a miracle that she had any mind left at all. And if she could ever possibly want again . . . She'd be extremely grateful, she admitted, grinning. And she most certainly wouldn't squander the opportunity. God, what she wouldn't give to spend the rest of the day right where she was. She glanced toward the window and, with a resigned sigh, accepted that she couldn't keep life from intruding on bliss.

Easing her leg out from under Aiden's went smoothly. But she'd barely started to slip out from under his arm when he tightened it and drew her closer, nuzzling into her neck and murmuring, "Don't go."

"It's daybreak," she murmured back, kissing his forehead before resolutely slipping out of his embrace. "Mohan will be rising soon. Sleep a while longer. I'll wake you later."

He rolled onto his back, and then to his other side to watch her walk around the end of the pallet, stoop to pick up the letter, and then make her way toward where they'd left her wrapper and one of his sheets the night before.

His head propped in his hand, he watched her pick up her silk cover. "I know that there'll be a reckoning for it later," he said softly, "but I want all the moments together we can have."

Relief weakened her knees. She'd won. She wasn't going to have to give him up too soon. "So do I," she confessed, drawing on her wrapper as she tucked away the parchment and moved back to the bed. Kneeling down beside him, Alex ran her fingers through his tousled hair and added, "But there isn't much chance of stealing any moments around here. Not during the day."

He cocked a brow and gave her a quirked, rakish smile. "We could go to Haven House."

"Oh, now there's an attractive possibility. Under what pretext?"

"A riding lesson?" he suggested, trailing a fingertip down her throat.

"That would work rather nicely, wouldn't it?" she offered, keenly aware that he was veering off course and drawing her wrapper down off her shoulder to bare her breast.

"My mother warned me that men and horses were a combination to be avoided at all costs, you know."

"Why?"

"I don't know," she replied, her breath catching as he trailed his finger back along her shoulder and then down. "But she was very emphatic about it."

The corners of his mouth twitched and his eyes sparkled. "Is that why you've used every excuse to get out of it?"

"Yes," she admitted, as he drew a slow, tantalizing circle around her hardened peak. God, if she didn't stop him, she wasn't going to be able to leave.

"Why the sudden change of mind?"

And Mohan would have his young sensibilities shredded. "Because," she answered, leaning forward to kiss him quickly before scrambling to her feet and beyond temptation's reach. "There's something at the end of the ride that I want." She covered herself and tied the sash, grinning at him. "And I want it madly enough that I'm willing to take incredible chances to get it."

"What time do you want to go?"

"After Sawyer gets here."

"I'll meet you in the yard, with horses saddled," he offered, his smile wicked and ever so deliciously promising. "If you have boots and a split skirt, wear them."

A split skirt? She didn't have one, but she could modify one of her other ones easily and quickly enough. But why it was necessary and why he seemed so delighted by the prospect . . . "You know why my mother warned me against riding, don't you?"

He laughed, mischief dancing in his eyes. "Nine-oh-five, darling. A split skirt."

"I'll be there," she promised as he abruptly sat and reached for his trousers. "Aiden, please don't get up," she cajoled, knowing that he couldn't have had more than three hours of sleep in the course of the entire night. "You need to sleep a bit longer."

"No I don't," he countered, trying to both undo the tangle of his pants and turn them right side out. "I have to find an apothecary shop. I'm out of sheaths and I'm fairly sure that you won't want to stop with me for them on the way to Haven House."

No, she didn't. "They aren't necessary," she pointed out. "The count of my days isn't right for conceiving."

His hands stopped, his brow shot up, and his smile turned unholy. Barely moving his head, he looked at her askance. "Really?"

"Really."

He tossed his trousers aside and drawled, "Oh, darling, today is your day for delightful discoveries."

"Nine-oh-five," she reminded him, moving to the door, her pulse lusciously fast and warm. "Please don't be late."

He was laughing when she pulled it closed behind her. She lingered for just a moment, closing her eyes and committing to her memory the wondrous sound of it. Only when the dreary shadows of what was to come drifted up to the edge of her awareness did she turn and walk away.

Preeya glanced up from her pan as Alex came to stand beside her at the stove. "Much has happened in your night," she observed, smiling and going back to her stirring.

Since Preeya somehow knew that already . . . "I'll tend the eggs," Alex said, removing the letter from her pocket, "while you read this."

Preeya traded the slotted spoon for the folded parchment. She opened the folds, read, then pursed her lips and reached out to pull the pan off the fire. "Breakfast will be late," she announced. Holding the letter between them, she asked, "How was this delivered into your hands?"

"One of Prince Sarad's bodyguards is here in London. He gave it to Aiden. Aiden gave it to me. You don't seem to be overly surprised by the news, Preeya."

"We will come to that in time. First, I would ask why you have brought it to me."

Alex gave her the obvious reason first. "So that you can help me decide how I should tell Mohan. He has to know at some point, Preeya. And fairly soon."

"Is that the only reason?"

Alex carefully put the spoon in the pan. "When I look past today, I want to cry."

Preeya took her hands and led her to the stool at the work-table, saying, "Your world has been changed, dear Alex. So quickly, so greatly. And in so many ways. All in the passage of one night. It is understandable that your feelings are in turmoil." She laid the letter aside and poured them cups of tea and allowed Alex several sips before she asked, "Your Aiden . . . He was good to you? He loved you tenderly?"

Alex smiled around the china rim. "Tenderly" wasn't the word she would have chosen. "Well" and "perfectly" came much closer to being accurate. But that wasn't what Preeya really wanted to know. "That I had forever to be in his arms."

"If it is destined, it will be. You know that."

She nodded, also knowing that what no one ever said was that if it wasn't destined, it wouldn't be. "Aiden's doing better this morning, but . . ." She sighed and shook her head, remembering. "He didn't take the news at all well last night. He's very good at regretting."

"That is because he is a good man with a caring heart," Preeya observed. She took a sip of her own tea before adding, "He wishes no one to ever suffer. He would cradle the world if he could. That he has come into your life is a great blessing."

"I know you're right. But at the moment, Preeya, I don't feel especially blessed."

"Why? Have you quarreled this morning?"

"No," Alex assured her. "Not at all." Holding her cup in both hands, she took a long, slow taste of tea, trying to find words that didn't sound self-pitying. And gave up. "I'm going to lose him, Preeya. He's mine only until Sarad arrives."

"Oh, Alex," Preeya offered with a shake of her head. "Your life has been difficult from the beginning. I knew in the first moment I held you that your journey would not be an easy one. But I have also known that at the end of the journey would be a reward worthy of your struggle."

Suddenly Alex understood why Preeya hadn't been the least bit surprised to learn that the royal tutor was also a royal princess. "You were a part of this, weren't you?" Alex asked, pointing to the letter with her cup, her mind reeling. "Your husband was Kedar's uncle. You knew my mother before we came to court, didn't you? You knew about me."

Preeya nodded, a satisfied smile playing at the corners of her mouth. "I had become the third wife only weeks before Kedar was sent to join the household. We were of the same age and we were both strangers in a place that was our home. In our loneliness, we became friends. When Kedar met your mother, he shared his happiness with me. And because I was happy for him, I did what I could to help them be together. Your mother became my friend, as well.

"Then she was sent away by her father and lost to Kedar. She was lost to me, as well. But only for a while. She sent me a message, asking for my help, and I secretly went to her. I was there with the midwives when you came into this world, my Alex. I was there when they left and your mother hovered close to death. You were in my arms when she told me that you were the child of Kedar, the child of their love."

"You've always known," Alex mused aloud, still stunned by the revelation. "Always."

Again Preeya nodded. This time, however, she didn't smile. "I made your mother many promises that day when we thought she would not live. I promised her that I would take you away and care for you if she could not. I promised her that if she lived, I would not endanger Kedar by telling him of your birth or of your mother's marriage to the man who would be called your father. I promised her—with great sadness, but in respect for her love of Kedar—that I would let her, and you, remain among those lost to him."

"And she lived and we were lost."

"Never lost to me, my Alex," Preeya said gently, reaching out to pat her arm. "I have always known where you were. I watched from a distance, prepared to take you away to safety if your mother could no longer protect you. I had promised. But when the man was killed and your mother took you and fled, I didn't know what to do. Fearing for you, for your mother, I set aside one of the promises I had made her. I went to Kedar and I told him everything."

What courage that had taken. Courage born of love. "Was he angry with you?"

"No. He understood why we had chosen as we had. And he was too concerned with finding you and your mother to care about the past. He wanted to hold again the woman he loved. He wanted to gaze upon the face of their child. Nothing else mattered. Kedar is not a man to waste today or tomorrow by regretting yesterday."

"As Aiden is wont to do," Alex admitted.

"He will change. Kedar was not always so wise. In many ways your Aiden reminds me of Kedar when he was of the same age."

The comparison teased her curiosity. "Preeya? You knew from the moment Aiden and I came into this kitchen together that first day that we would be lovers and you encouraged me to make that choice. Why?"

She chuckled softly and shook her head as though it were the silliest question she'd ever been asked. "Because I want you to be happy and your Aiden fascinates and delights you." She took a sip of tea. "Can you deny that?"

"No."

Apparently something was lacking in her answer because Preeya arched a brow, sighed, and then asked, "Which is the greater destiny, my Alex? Being a princess? Or loving and being loved?"

"Loving and being loved," she supplied, the answer obvious.

"Life brings enough sorrows without our making them for ourselves. Love your Aiden and let him love you. Embrace the happiness you have today." She finished her tea, set aside her cup, and slid off the stool. Pausing as she passed on her way back to the stove, she placed a kiss on Alex's cheek and whispered, "If it is destined, it will be."

Alex smiled wanly. At least there was now an explanation for why part of her believed in the invisible hand of fate and part of her believed that the course of life was within her power to shape. Unfortunately, neither perspective seemed to offer any better chance of lasting happiness than the other. Although, in the short term, she had to admit that she and Aiden had planned a promising day for themselves. And fashioning a split skirt was a necessary part of it.

"Aiden is going to teach me to ride today," she announced, setting her cup aside and getting up from the table.

"Good." Preeya glanced over her shoulder. "You will be leaving Mohan behind?"

It was more a statement than a question. Alex nodded. "If there's some great calamity that requires our presence—"

"It is called Haven House for a reason," Preeya asserted, smiling broadly. "We will manage calamity without you."

How on earth did Preeya know that's where they were going? How? She'd said nothing to her. And she and Aiden had been speaking quietly as they'd made their plans. Even if

Preeya had had her ear . . . No, Preeya wasn't the sort to eavesdrop. Not at all.

"And while you are gone, I will tell Mohan the story of his sister."

"Thank you."

"Go. Be happy today."

Alex smiled and left the kitchen shaking her head. Who could fathom how Preeya knew the things she did? She just did. And given the huge secret she'd kept perfectly for twenty-four years, it was a given that no one else was ever going to know where she and Aiden spent their day. She grinned. Or days. If the gods were feeling benevolent.

Chapter 19

He'd reluctantly returned to the Blue Elephant yesterday afternoon. More reluctantly—and later—than he had the afternoon before. Today . . . From his vantage in the window seat, Aiden watched as Alex tried to reason the short bit of knotted rope from Tippy's mouth. Tippy didn't seem to care one whit what good dogs did, didn't seem the least impressed by the argument that she had to let it go before she could run after it and fetch it back to the parlor again. Alex, ever Alex, wasn't the least frustrated by the dog's lack of cooperation. She just kept smiling at her, tugging gently on her end of the rope toy, and explaining the rules of the game in the most patient voice and rational terms.

No, today he didn't want to go back to the Blue Elephant at all. At Haven House, Alex was his alone; he didn't have to share her with an adoring younger brother or a sweetly doting Preeya. He didn't have to worry about little ears when they talked or be mindful of little eyes when he wanted to touch her. At Haven House the world was British to the core, well ordered and predictable. There were no screaming peacocks, no strange combinations of food, no clock ticking away precious minutes and hours.

At Haven House, Alex wasn't an Indian princess or even

the royal tutor; she was his lover, his friend, his companion, his absolute delight. No one was going to walk through the front door and take her away from him. Not Sarad, not Hanuman. Reality couldn't touch them here.

It waited for them at the Blue Elephant. With every day that passed, it drew closer, grew darker and more certain. Time was running out. He could feel it. And he knew that its end would come in the little shop in Bloomsbury.

But if he didn't go back there . . . If he kept Alex tucked away within the thick walls of Haven House . . . If Vadeen accomplished his task neatly and cleanly . . .

It wouldn't change the end. Sarad would still arrive. The gangplank of his ship would be lowered and Alex would walk up it, her chin held high and her shoulders squared, resolved to fulfill her duties, to meet her obligations.

There was nothing he could offer her that would make her stay. He wasn't a poor man by any means. But he wasn't a prince, either. He didn't own a house, much less a palace. Hell, he didn't even have a ship these days. Life with him would be a great deal less than royal. And always would be. Alex deserved to be a princess. And someday, down the road of her life, there would be a prince who fully understood just what a rare treasure she was and who would live his life only to make her happy.

And since he wasn't that prince . . . Since he was the bodyguard responsible for keeping her alive for that someday wonder, he needed to get her back to the Blue Elephant before dark. He picked up the gun from the seat beside him and, tucking it into the small of his back, rose to his feet.

"Tippy, sit," he commanded as he advanced toward Alex and the still recalcitrant dog. Tippy instantly dropped down on her hind end. "Release."

Alex staggered back as the resistance on the other end came to a sudden end. "Oh, you could have told me how to do that," she laughingly chided.

"And ruined your half of the game?" he countered with what he hoped looked like a carefree smile. "It's time to go home, darling. We're later than usual."

She nodded and put the rope in the basket in the corner. She paused to scratch Tippy behind her right ear, say, "We will pick this up tomorrow where we've left it. Be a good dog while I'm gone," and then headed for the foyer and the cloak tree.

Tippy followed her departure with a notably forlorn and disappointed look. Walking past the animal, Aiden muttered, "Me too, girl."

How incredibly right her mother had been about the combination of men and horses, Alex mused, grinning, as they cantered through the twilight, side by side. Riding at a walk was comfortable and the gentle roll to the gait was a bit like flirting from opposite sides of a crowded room. There was a vaguely carnal promise to it, but it was distant at best. The vagueness, she'd discovered that first day of instruction, disappeared when the horse broke over into a trot. The rhythm was clipped, but undeniably sensual in a somewhat rugged sort of way. It was a prelude; rather like the first moments after locking the door and trying to discard layers of clothing while kissing.

Cantering, though . . . Oh, Lord, cantering was her favorite gait. It was easy and smooth and always made her think of Aiden and the erotic pleasures to be had once they tumbled down together. Alex chuckled softly. He hadn't let her gallop the horse yet, but she suspected that she was going to enjoy that even more than the cantering.

Yes, riding was indeed dangerous for a woman committed to sterling virtue. Riding with a man like John Aiden Terrell was especially so. And she wished she'd taken it up sooner than she had.

Beside her, Aiden raised his hand in silent signal and Alex

reined in her mount, mindful of the rules he'd laid down the first day: they were to walk their horses for the last block and, as they neared the corner and the rear yard of the Blue Elephant came into sight, she was to fall slightly back so that he preceded her into the open space. Why, she didn't know. He hadn't explained and she hadn't questioned. It was the way he wanted it done and she trusted him and acceded. How far they'd come since that first day, she mused.

Alex studied his back as he moved ahead. Her heart both melted and twisted as it did every night at this time. For three straight days she'd watched the sun drop toward the rooftops and hoped that Aiden would suggest that they stay at Haven House for the night, for eternity. If the gods demanded all she had, all that she was, for a forever with him, she'd pay it and never regret the decision. But he hadn't asked and he never would. The ghost of Mary Alice Randolph didn't leave any room in his heart for her.

It wasn't good or kind to envy and resent a dead woman, but she did. Mary Alice couldn't make Aiden laugh anymore, couldn't make him gasp and moan in pleasure. She couldn't be his wife or the mother of his children. That Aiden clung to "what was" and "what might have been" so tenaciously . . . Alex swallowed down the tears tickling her throat, reminding herself that what he could give was all that he could give and that it would have to be enough. She couldn't change his past, couldn't change him, couldn't make him love her more than he loved his Mary Alice.

Ahead of her, to the accompaniment of the peacocks' high-pitched heralding, he rode into the yard and reined his horse to a halt in the pale shadows at the front of the stable. Alex did the same, and as he swung down and strode back to assist her in dismounting, she deliberately put away her melancholy and summoned a smile for him.

"Time to come back to earth," he said, reaching up and slipping his hands around her waist.

"I don't want to," Alex admitted even as she placed her hands on his shoulders and leaned out. "Let's take a ride in the moonlight. It's not that cold." She glanced toward the kitchen and noted the bright light spilling through the windows. "Preeya's still preparing dinner. We have time."

He set her on her feet in front of him and loosely wrapped her in his arms. "You make the little voice of common sense hard to hear, darling."

"It's not me," she countered, smiling up at him, twining her fingers through the hair at his nape. "It's the peacocks." He laughed and she added, "What would be the harm, Aiden? I don't want to go back inside. Not yet."

He kissed her lightly and quickly; a prelude, she knew, to refusal. "Then keep me company while I put away the horses," he offered as he stepped back and eased her arms from around his neck.

It was the best reprieve she was going to get and she knew it. Better a little more time alone together, she consoled herself as she drew the reins over her horse's head, than none at all.

The reins of his own mount in hand, Aiden reached for the door latch and froze. Alex abruptly halted behind him, puzzled. "What is it, Aiden?"

"I closed the latches when we left this morning," he replied, drawing the gun from the small of his back. "Move off and put that horse between you and the doorway."

"Maybe Sawyer took the carriage out while we were gone," she posed even as she stepped to the other side of her mount, partially obeying his command. Looking under the animal's neck, she added, "And forgot to latch the doors when he returned."

He shook his head while pushing his horse to the side. "If this goes badly, get on that horse and get to Barrett's as fast as you can."

Alex didn't argue with him, didn't tell him that, no matter

what happened, she wouldn't leave him. His mind needed to be focused on what lay ahead, not what might happen behind him. He reached for the handle with his left hand and Alex drew a deep breath and held it, her heart racing and her pulse skittering. She didn't hear the door open, but she felt the rush of air.

And then reality twisted and shifted, the images and realizations somehow both lightning fast and excruciatingly slow as they tumbled, in heart-wrenching detail, one over the other. Aiden, his gun in hand, searching in the shadows. The quick movement on his left. Aiden's curse. Hanuman. His clothes bloodied, his face contorted with rage and determination. The feral snarl, the dull glint of bloody steel as he charged Aiden.

"No!" she shouted in Hindi, dashing from behind her horse. "It's me you want!"

The hatred in his eyes as his gaze met hers, as he turned the direction of his attack. The bright fire of explosion and the choking smoke. And Hanuman staggering backward, the rage still in his eyes, the blade arcing harmlessly down and then slipping from his fingers as the darkness spread across the center of his chest.

As he crumpled into the straw, time clicked and settled. Perception, however, remained slightly askew. Alex couldn't feel herself moving, but could see that she was. She could hear her heart thundering, but it seemed to come from a great distance. Hanuman lay sprawled on the floor, gazing up at the rafters, his vision unfocused, his breathing shallow and irregular, each labored exhalation producing a bubble of blood between his lips. Her uncle, she realized dully. Her uncle had meant to kill her, to kill Aiden to get to her.

She watched as Aiden kicked the sword away and knelt down to snatch Hanuman's blood-soaked shirtfront with his free hand. Lifting the limp form slightly, he leaned forward to growl, "Where's Vadeen?"

A haunted look and another bubble of blood were

Hanuman's only response. Aiden lowered him back to the floor and rose to his feet. "Look in that line of stalls, Alex," he instructed, pointing to those on his left as he quickly moved to check those on his right. "He's here or close by."

She went, mindlessly and mechanically, vaguely aware of Hanuman's sudden silence and her stomach coldly churning. The mercy of the dullness ended suddenly as she pulled open a stall door and gazed down on the slashed and bloodied Indian propped against the inside wall.

"Aiden!" she called, dropping to her knees and pressing her fingers to the side of the man's neck, desperately searching for the telltale thrum of life. It was there; just barely. His eyelids fluttered and opened just as Aiden slid into the stall and went to his knees beside her.

"Christ Almighty," he said softly, as he made a quick inspection of the wounds to his arm, legs, and side. Vadeen dragged a breath through his clenched teeth and tried to straighten his back.

"No, don't move," Aiden commanded, pressing his shoulder back against the wall. "Where's the closest physician, Alex?"

"Six blocks."

He stripped off his jacket and thrust it at her, saying as he rose to his feet, "Stanch the worst of the bleeding while I hitch the carriage."

He was gone in the next second. Over the sound of his getting the horses from their stalls, Alex righted his jacket and surveyed Vadeen's leg. Going clear to the bone, it was, by far, the worst of his injuries. If he lived, he might never walk right again.

"Hanu—"

"Aiden finished the task you began," she assured him in Hindi. "All is well. We're taking you to a doctor. This is going to hurt, Vadeen, and I'm sorry to add to your pain, but I must or you'll bleed to death."

He nodded and sucked one hard breath as she tied the sleeve of Aiden's coat hard over the cut that had opened his upper thigh from one side to the other. And then, thankfully, he went limp and his awareness of the pain passed into the oblivion of unconsciousness.

"Mr. Terrell!"

Sawyer. In the doorway and sounding as though he'd sprinted from the house.

"We're all right," Aiden replied over the sound of clinking tack while Alex tore off the shredded lower portion of Vadeen's pant leg and used it to bind the gaping wound on his right arm. "And that bastard deserved to die. Kindly drag his body out of the way for me."

"What else can I do, sir?"

"Keep Preeya and Mohan out of here," Aiden answered crisply. "In fact, take Preeya into the house and don't let either one of them out of your sight until we get back. Here," he added. "Take this and don't think twice about using it if you have to."

Alex was removing what was left of Vadeen's sleeve and puzzling that part of the exchange when Aiden snorted. "For God's sake, man, hold it firmly by the butt and at least look like you know what you're doing with it."

Aiden had given him the gun, she realized as she packed the fabric into the grisly gash on Vadeen's side and Sawyer asked, "And where are you going, sir?"

"Tell Preeya we'll be late for dinner," was the only answer the man got.

"Very good, sir."

The horses snorted and pawed and then there was the heavy slap of leather against wood. In the next second Aiden was striding into the stall. "Good," he muttered, reaching down and sliding his arms under Vadeen's. "He's not going to feel the rough handling."

Alex watched in amazement as Aiden hefted the man's

dead weight up the stall wall and then bent down to plant his shoulder in his midsection. Vadeen groaned as he was bent double and pulled over Aiden's shoulder. She trotted after him and then dashed ahead to open the carriage door before he reached it.

Depositing Vadeen on the front-facing seat, he stepped back and vaulted out to stand in front of her. "What the hell were you thinking, Alex?" he demanded, his eyes flashing with anger. "I told you to keep that horse between you and the barn. Were you trying to get yourself killed?"

"Better me than you," she replied honestly.

He rocked back on his heels and then instantly leaned forward, his brows knitted. "I could turn you over my goddamn knee," he seethed. "Don't you *ever* do anything like that again. Do you hear me?"

"Yes, I hear you," she countered, her own anger flaring and her hands going to her hips as she met his gaze unflinchingly. "But it doesn't mean that I'm going to blithely obey."

He swallowed and the muscles in his jaw ticced furiously. "When we're alone tonight," he said evenly, emphatically, "you and I are going to have our first significant row."

"Good," she retorted, pushing past him and hopping up onto the step. "I'm looking forward to it."

He caught her around the waist and hauled her hard against him. "Fair warning," he whispered. "I'm going to win."

His kiss was fierce and harshly, utterly consuming. And beneath the heat of his anger, she felt not only the eddying currents of his fear and his relief, but also the depth of his caring. It was a precious gift she'd thought she'd never receive and with a grateful sob she accepted it, melting into him and surrendering.

He set her from him as abruptly and roughly as he'd seized her. "We're not done discussing it, Alex," he warned.

Ah, but the sparks in his eyes weren't just those of anger

anymore. Desire and amusement flickered there, as well. She turned and climbed into the coach, saying, "I'm willing only if you promise to kiss me like that again."

Grinning and shaking his head, he closed the door behind her.

God, if he hadn't known before that Alex had a backbone of steel, the last few hours would have convinced him of the fact. Both he and the doctor had tried to send her out of the surgery, but she'd adamantly refused. And then scrubbed her hands and lent her strength and resolve to the suturing and bandaging. Aiden had seen some men faint dead away at less, seen others heave the contents of their stomachs on their feet.

But not Alex. Her dress was ruined, stained with Vadeen's blood, and she didn't care. Her hands had cramped from the exhaustion of holding the torn flesh in place while the doctor sewed the wounds closed and all she'd done was silently flex her fingers before moving on to the next. Vadeen had cried out in pain and she'd tenderly spooned the opium tincture into him and whispered encouragement until the drug dulled the edges of his pain. And now . . . Now she was bearing a fair portion of Vadeen's weight as they gingerly guided him toward the rear door of the Blue Elephant.

"It is not appropriate," Vadeen said with a lopsided, drug-induced smile, "for a princess to assist a man in walking."

"And it is appropriate," she countered, "for her to stand idly by and let him fall flat on his face?"

Aiden chuckled. "Surrender the point now, Vadeen, and get it done. You're in no condition to use the only tactics that will win the contest. And if you were and did, I'd kill you. I'd rather not have to do that."

His head lolled on his shoulders as he tried to turn it to look at him. "You have tolerated much, Aiden."

"Don't tell her, but I really haven't been all that miserable." He stopped as a sudden realization struck. "The peacocks."

Alex looked back over her shoulder. "They're gone."

Thank you, Aiden offered up to the stars. "The neighbors must have finally had enough and taken matters into their own hands," he ventured. "Frankly, I'm surprised they didn't dispatch them long before now. Lord knows, I've been tempted."

"They do smell good," Vadeen contributed, grinning. "Have you ever eaten roasted peacock, Aiden?"

"Can't say that I have," he admitted, starting them forward again and wondering why he hadn't noticed the silence and the delicious scent the moment he'd driven into the yard. It was almost as though, with the death of Hanuman and the doctor's assurance that Vadeen would live, the larger part of his brain had decided to go on holiday.

"They taste much like chicken. Only wild."

Of course they did. Everything supposedly tasted like chicken, only different. Quail. Pheasant. Partridge. Dove. Pigeons. And none of them came even remotely close to tasting like chicken. And he knew that because he'd been lured into trying each and every one of them on the same empty promise. Aiden shook his head and expelled a long breath. Lord, the part of his brain that had remained behind was frightening in its devotion to the consideration of the irrelevant minutiae of his experience.

The back door of the store opened and the brightness of the lamplight on the other side blinded him. He blinked into it, his pulse quickening with apprehension as he realized that on the other side of it were a good half-dozen large men. He reached back for his gun, remembering that he'd given it to Sawyer just as Vadeen spoke in Hindi and lurched forward, threatening to pull all three of them off their feet.

"Your highness," Alex translated, gasping and struggling to keep her balance.

His brain returned with an almost audible snap. The man holding the lantern was an Indian and clearly a servant of the regally dressed, somewhat older version of Hanuman advancing toward them. Mohan walked at his uncle's side, followed by three other men who Aiden guessed were Vadeen's comrades-in-arms.

"It is not necessary, Vadeen. Please do not add to your injuries in trying," the man replied, his English studied, his accent fairly light. He motioned to the men behind him and they quickly moved forward to take Vadeen from him and Alex, as their master went on, saying, "I have seen the proof of your success. Take your rest, Vadeen. It has been earned."

Relieved of the burden, Aiden squared up to the man and resolutely faced the inevitable reckoning. "I gather that you're Prince Sarad."

"I have been told that you would be John Aiden Terrell."

"I am."

Sarad slowly, deliberately took his measure and then brought his gaze back to meet Aiden's. "I have also been told that you have been the protector of my brother's children in recent weeks."

He nodded, knowing what was coming next, his heart growing more leaden with every beat.

"On behalf of my brother Kedar," Sarad went on, apparently oblivious to the pain his words were inflicting, "I thank you for all that you have done. I have entrusted the payment for your services to your man, Sawyer. He has removed your belongings and awaits your return to your own home. Prince Mohan," he added, motioning offhandedly to the boy, "has indicated that he would like to gift you with the horses and the carriage you assisted him in acquiring."

"Thank you, Mohan. That's very generous of you."

"It is my pleasure, Mr. Terrell." He smiled sheepishly and shrugged. "And I cannot take them with me on the ship."

"Well," Aiden replied, forcing himself to chuckle, "when you're done with them, let me know and I'll come collect them."

"You should take them now, Mr. Terrell. We sail in the morning."

"In the morning?" Alex gasped, her hands pressed hard against her midriff, the anguish on her face the mirror, Aiden knew, of that tearing him apart on the inside. "Why so soon?"

"The danger is past and your father wishes to have his children home," her uncle replied. "Were it possible to have the ship ready to sail before then, we would not spend even a single night."

"But," she stammered, her voice edged with barely contained tears. "My shop. Our home. All the things in it . . ."

"Preeya is directing my men in the packing. She is upstairs if you wish to speak with her concerning the task."

Aiden watched Alex swallow, saw her look past her uncle and into the open back door of the Blue Elephant. She was close to tears and in a few more minutes she was going to lose the struggle to hold them at bay. He knew exactly how she felt. The only thing he could think to do was to get their parting done as quickly and as cleanly as possible. The rug had been pulled out from under their feet and the next blows would hurt less if they came while they were both still stunned and reeling.

"You'll tell Preeya good-bye for me, won't you?" he asked, turning to her and offering a smile. It was tight, but it was the best he could do.

"Of course," she offered, clearly dazed, the smile she gave him in return vacant and weak.

"Behave yourself, Mohan," he said briskly, reaching out to ruffle the boy's hair.

"I will. Thank you for all you have done for me. I am honored to have known you, Mr. Terrell."

"The honor's mutual." He started to turn away and then stopped to look back over his shoulder and jauntily ask, "You are taking the cats with you, aren't you?"

Mohan grinned and nodded. "Yes, sir. Sawyer insisted."

"He's a good man."

"Aiden, please," she said softly, catching his arm and staying him.

Tears welled along her lower lashes and tore at his heart. "Good-bye, Alex," he whispered, lifting her hand and pressing a light kiss to the back of it. He released her with a wink and managed to clear the lump from his throat to say, "You'll be the best princess India ever had."

"Aiden . . ."

"Take care of her," he instructed Vadeen as he walked past, determined to be gone before Alex's tears shredded what little was left of his dignity.

"With my life."

He couldn't speak; not and keep hidden his ravaged emotions. He nodded instead and kept walking, willing himself to keep his gaze on the carriage and his mind focused on the task of getting the horses tied to the rear of it, on getting back into the driver's box and setting it all in motion, on getting the hell gone before he made a complete, blubbering fool of himself.

Alex fought back the tears and turned to her uncle. "I will join you in the house in a moment. For now I wish to say my farewells privately."

"Narain will wait for you here," he declared, turning away. "Do not tarry, niece."

She didn't have the time or the energy to protest. And she'd tarry if she damn well pleased. Gathering her skirts, she hurried out toward the rear of the carriage, her heart lodged high in her throat and her thoughts a confusing jumble of words and swirling emotions.

"You're not leaving with regrets, are you?" she blurted as she reached his side. "You have nothing to be sorry for, Aiden."

He looked down at her and blindly finished tying the

reins of her horse to the ring. "Well," he drawled, "I never did teach you to dance."

His voice was tight, too tight, too controlled. He was hurting just as deeply as she was. Desperate to prolong her time with him, wanting with all her heart and soul to ease his conscience in his leaving, she raised her hands in the pose her mother had taught her long ago. "Teach me now," she pleaded. "Show me how to dance, Aiden."

He swayed on his feet and then stiffened, expelling a hard breath. Offering her a brittle smile and a cocked brow, he asked, "Does an Indian princess really need to know how Englishmen dance?"

"There's a difference between needing and wanting," she countered, her heart tearing. "I want to know what it's like to dance with you. I want that memory to tuck away with all the other treasures that have been ours."

He looked over at the door, to where Narain waited silently for her in the shadows. Then slowly, almost hesitantly, he stepped close and took her hand in his and slipped the other to the small of her back. "Keep the distance between us as we move," he whispered, his voice catching.

Alex nodded, afraid her sorrow would overflow if she tried to speak. He guided her smoothly backward and she looked up at him, memorizing his face as it looked in the moonlight, remembering the way he smiled, the sound of his laughter. *Ask me to stay, Aiden,* she silently begged. *Ask me to love you. Tell me that you'll try to find room in your heart for me, too.*

He stumbled and stopped, then deliberately released her and stepped back. "I can't do this, Alex. I have to go." He moistened his lower lip with the tip of his tongue and took a ragged breath. Cupping her cheek in the palm of his hand, he gazed down at her and murmured, "Stay safe, my beautiful princess. Think of me from time to time and know that I'll never forget you."

"I will always remember you, Aiden. Always."

And then he was gone, striding past her without another word, without another touch. She couldn't turn and watch him disappear from her life. It was all she could do to stand where she was and keep silent with the tears coursing over her cheeks. The springs of the carriage creaked. The leather of the reins popped. The horses snorted and then their hooves pounded over the hard-packed earth of the yard and onto the brick pavers of the street beyond.

She stood in the darkness, listening to them fade away.

"Princess?"

The sob broke from her soul and tore up her throat. Gathering her skirts, she fled toward the house, past the startled guard, and up to the sanctuary of her lonely room.

Chapter 20

The knock at the door was soft, but it arrowed past her grief and flared into a wild, surging hope. Alex scrambled to her feet and darted forward, afraid that if she delayed he'd change his mind and leave her again. She flung the door open, her heart bursting with happiness.

"Preeya," she whispered, staggering back, her hope crushed and new tears flooding down over her cheeks. Collapsing on the edge of her mattress, she tried to apologize for the rudeness of the greeting, but only a choking sob rolled past her lips.

"You do not have to explain," Preeya offered, advancing into the room and softly closing the door behind her. "Almost twenty-five years ago I found your father as I find you now. His heart was as broken, his pain as deep."

"Aiden's gone, Preeya," she sobbed, wrapping her arms around her midsection and rocking forward and back. "I'll never see him again. I'll never hold him. And I love him so much. I'd rather die than spend the rest of my life hurting like this."

"As your father said the same words to me," Preeya went on, settling on the bed beside her, "I will say the same to you as I did then." With a gentle hand she tucked an errant strand of hair behind Alex's ear. "Great loves are destined. But such a love always comes with a trial equal to the glory and promise of happiness. If you fail the trial, you deny what destiny has deemed your course. But if you have faith and trust that what was meant to be will be, you will endure the trial and be rewarded."

Alex dragged a wracking breath into her body, desperately willing Aiden back, willing him to come striding in the door, his green eyes alive and bright with love and devotion, hard with a determination to find a way for them to be together.

"You have a choice, Alex," Preeya admonished, taking Alex's chin in hand and tenderly turning her head so she was forced to look into her eyes. "You can wish yourself dead and that is how Aiden will find you when he returns for you. You can surrender to despair and break his heart. Or you can dry your tears and believe that love is eternal and that the hope of it is never lost."

"We leave in the morning, Preeya," she countered, unable to stop the tears, unable to summon resolve. "Am I supposed to hope for a miracle by then?"

Preeya arched a dark brow. "Kedar searched ten years for your mother. Your mother endured ten years before she could be again in the arms of the man she loved. Did their daughter not inherit their strength, their faith, their courage?"

Ten years of misery, of being apart. Then ten years of hiding their hearts and their love. That was a reward for enduring? "No, she didn't," she declared, turning away. "I want more in my life. And I want it now. I want Aiden and a home with him. I want to be the one to bear his children."

"Aiden will find you no matter where you are," Preeya assured her. "No matter how long it takes."

Dreadful certainty closed inexorably around her heart. There would never be a life with Aiden. No home. No children. She could want as desperately as any woman ever had, but wanting wouldn't change the course ahead, wouldn't change Aiden. She scrubbed the tears from her cheeks and took a ragged, but steadying breath. "He walked away, Preeya," she said, lifting her chin. "Sarad dismissed him and he walked away. He's not going to turn around and come after me."

Beside her, Preeya sighed and shook her head. "It is the rare man who sees his course at first glance, Alex," she said with obviously strained patience. "Give your Aiden time to stumble around in his darkness. Eventually he will understand what it is that he seeks. You must not only have faith in love itself, but also in the one you love. If he were not worthy of it, you would not have given him the precious gift of your heart."

"He doesn't know that I did. I never told him that I loved him."

Preeya snorted in a most unladylike fashion and slid off the bed. She was halfway to the door when she stopped and turned back. "And do you think that love exists only when put into words?" she asked, her arms akimbo, her tone kind but firm. "That he does not know by your actions? That he did not feel love in your touch? See it in your eyes? In your smile? That he did not hear love in your voice when you whispered his name and reached for him in the dark?"

For his sake, she hoped he hadn't. What regrets he carried from his time with her would be ever so much deeper if he knew that he'd broken her heart.

"Faith, Alex," Preeya declared as she left. "You must live in faith."

Alex closed her eyes, hearing the slow painful beating of her tattered heart and the pounding of hammers as Sarad's men coolly, methodically crated up her world. By morning's light it would all be stowed away in the hull of an India-bound vessel. The Blue Elephant would cease to be. And all the life, all the hope, promise, and happiness within its walls would slip forever into the past.

. . .

Aiden leaned back in the dining room chair, his legs stretched out under the table, his arms folded across his chest. In front of him on the table sat three things: the ornate white velvet-lined gold box containing a heaping mound of finely cut gemstones, a bottle of Carden's best brandy, and an empty glass. The box was beautiful. The stones were worth a king's ransom. Or a princess's, depending on how he looked at it. But it was the brandy that largely occupied his attention and his thoughts. And had been for the better part of the last two hours—since he'd walked into the house and decided that there was nothing to be done but get himself blindly, roaringly drunk.

He'd gotten the bottle and the glass off the caddy in the study, carried it here where Sawyer had left a lamp burning, set them on the table within easy reach, and then resolutely planted his sorry carcass on the chair. And he hadn't moved since. He'd looked at the box of jewels, thought about why he'd been given them, remembered the look in Alex's eyes as he'd put her from his arms in the yard, and that had been the end of his purposeful thinking. He'd spent God only knew how long wandering through his memories of the past weeks, alternately smiling, laughing, and thinking about drowning his pain and sorrow in the brandy.

But he hadn't been able to reach out for it. He just sat there, staring at it. Which, he admitted with a sigh, was truly pathetic. He was genuinely miserable. There wasn't a part of him that wasn't weary and didn't ache. He didn't want to think and he shouldn't have wanted to feel anything—especially the searing, pounding ache deep in the center of his chest. But he didn't want to sleep, didn't want to eat. And, apparently, he didn't want to drink, either. It was the strangest, most confounding, inexplicable thing. Not the least bit rational. It wasn't as though he didn't know the kind of blissful forgetfulness to be found in swimming in alcohol.

Why he didn't want to escape, to forget, was the root of it, he knew. The answer to that central, all-important question had been eluding him for the last hour. Although "eluding" wasn't the least bit accurate, he knew. It implied that he could sense an answer and simply couldn't grasp it. The truth was that he didn't have so much as an inkling that one actually existed. And it was a given that he wouldn't find it waiting to fall out of the bottom of a well-drained glass.

"You reach for that bottle and I'll break your hands."

Aiden looked up at the familiar voice and watched his friend advance to the table. Proof, Aiden silently growled, that if you didn't lock the door behind you, trouble was free to wander in off the streets. "What are you doing here?" he asked not at all politely.

Barrett stripped off his greatcoat and dropped it over the back of a chair, saying, "I went by the Blue Elephant to see you, was told—rather summarily—of your departure, and was afraid you'd do something shortsighted. I came by here on my way home hoping to keep you from it. Have I arrived in anything approximating a timely fashion?"

"Actually," Aiden drawled, his gaze going back to the bottle, "I've been sitting here for quite some time, trying to figure out why I spent a year drinking myself into oblivion. That's good brandy. All I have to do is reach out and I can have it. And God knows I feel so damn empty I hurt clear down to the soul. But I don't want to drown the pain. I'm not even tempted to pour myself a drink." He looked up to meet his friend's gaze. "Why is that, Barrett?"

"Maybe you're a year older and a year wiser," he offered.

Aiden snorted.

Barrett considered him for a long moment, his lips pursed and his brows knitted. Finally, he quietly asked, "How honest do you want me to be?"

If Barrett had an answer, he was entirely willing to hear it. "Hell, I can't hurt any deeper than I already do."

"All right," he said crisply, leaning back against the buffet and crossing his arms over his chest. "I never met your Mary Alice Randolph. Tell me about her."

Mary Alice? He knew what she had to do with wanting to drink himself blind. But what did she have to do with Alex? Leaving Alex behind was why he was sitting here asking himself pointless questions instead of being at the Blue Elephant, rolling around on black satin sheets in the throes of mind-staggering passion. Even as he considered asking for an explanation, he decided that he didn't care. He was too tired to try to make sense of anything. "What do you want to know?"

Barrett cast him a quick look and then shrugged. "I don't know. What did she look like?"

He could see her so clearly. They'd met at a party and she'd been hiding in a corner behind the potted palms. "She was blond and blue-eyed and petite. A tiny little slip of a thing. She always wore pink."

After pondering that information for a moment, Barrett nodded and asked, "What made her special?"

Aiden frowned. He'd found himself in the same corner in trying to evade an encounter with his former—as of that afternoon—lover, Rose. He couldn't pretend that he wasn't sharing it with someone else. They'd struck up a conversation and . . . Damn if he could remember about what, though.

It was odd and more than a little troubling to be able to look back and see Mary Alice but to have no recollection of anything she'd ever said, of her thoughts on anything, or of her hopes and dreams beyond those of getting back to Charleston.

"Don't you remember, Aiden?"

"No, I don't," he admitted, frustrated with himself and irritated that Barrett was pressing the point. "Consuming a massive amount of alcohol tends to pickle your brain, Barrett. Some things get lost. Most of the time it's a mercy. That's the attraction of being a drunk."

The clock struck the hour of three. Only when the notes of the third chime faded away did Barrett quietly ask, "Did she make you laugh?"

"Not intentionally," Aiden supplied wearily, willing to answer for no other reason than to get the inquisition over and done. "She was shy and rather serious."

"You know, we always wondered, Carden and I . . . Why didn't you ever bring Mary Alice around and introduce her to us? To Seraphina?"

"Because . . ." Oh, hell, there wasn't any point in lying about it. And he was too exhausted to even make the attempt. "I didn't think she could hold her own against you and Carden. That she'd be flustered and uncomfortable and that you'd think she was nothing more than a brainless bit of fluff. And I knew that Seraphina would intimidate her. Not intentionally, of course. Sera wouldn't do something like that. It's just that Mary Alice didn't have the self-confidence that Sera does."

"Was she good in bed?"

Aiden groaned and leaned back in his chair to stare up at the ceiling. Were the questions endless? Was there any purpose to them at all?

"She's gone, John Aiden. There's no reputation to protect."

Christ, he knew that. He didn't need Barrett to point out the obvious. "I have no idea," he admitted on a sigh, still staring at the ceiling. "I never made love to her."

"Really," Barrett said dryly, the single word a voluminous statement, an admission of a long-known fact. "Why not?"

"I wanted to marry her." It was a superficial answer and he knew it. But he was suddenly tired of looking back, tired of thinking, and especially tired of being uncomfortable with what he saw when he did.

"So?" his friend pressed, his tone edged with just a hint of sarcasm. "What does the one have to do with the other? Most men want to make love to their wives, Aiden. And, in the event that you haven't noticed, most of them don't wait for the legal blessing. Why were you willing to?"

"She asked me to. I respected her wishes. I respected her."

"Why?"

"Jesus, Barrett," he groaned in exasperation. "I couldn't take advantage of her. She was young and homesick and innocent and fragile and—"

"She needed you," he supplied.

"Yes."

"So you took care of her," Barrett summarized. "She was a damsel in distress and you happily stepped up to play her knight in shining armor."

A tiny spark of indignation pulsed deep within him. He brought his gaze down from the ceiling to meet Barrett's. "That makes it sound shallow. It wasn't."

Barrett slowly came off the buffet to place his hands flat on the table and lean down. "I beg to differ, John Aiden," he said firmly, his brow cocked and his jaw hard. "I'm sorry to be so blunt, but it's long past time you squared up to it. You didn't love Mary Alice Randolph. Yes, you certainly liked her. She was undoubtedly a good person.

"No," he said, holding up his hand to forestall the objection. "You didn't love her. What you *loved* was being her hero. That's why you looked down into those tearful blue eyes of hers and promised you'd get her past the blockade and home to Charleston. If you'd loved *her,* you never would have considered it. You would have made her stay in England where she was safe."

His heart felt like it was in his stomach and his stomach was somewhere in the vicinity of his feet. It was hard to tell anything for sure; his brain was numb and there were little silver gnats swirling at the outside edges of his vision. Nothing was wrong with his memory, though. He could see his parents standing in the parlor, the look of anguish on his mother's face, the rage on his father's. And he could hear every word, feel each one of them tearing through him.

"And I'm guessing," Barrett went on, his voice sounding considerably kinder than the one coming from his memory, "that your father said as much to you when he finally managed to get you back to St. Kitts."

"That and a great deal more," he admitted, raking his fingers through his hair.

"I'm also going to guess that somewhere in that conversation the fog in your brain lifted and you had a flash of understanding of exactly what you'd done and why. And rather than face the guilt of having put being a hero before your responsibility as a ship's captain, you threw yourself into the nearest bottle and obliterated the world. God forbid that you gracefully accept that you're human and did something stupid."

Aiden stared down at the table. Barrett had it spot-on. It was as though he'd been standing there in the parlor, listening, watching. As though he'd been able to open the top of his head and look inside to see that hideous realization explode through his awareness. He *had* climbed into a bottle to escape it. And, until this moment, he had managed to forget it all.

"John Aiden, trust me on this," Barrett said with a sigh. "*All* twenty-four-year-old men do stupid things. It's the nature of the beast."

It was a nice sentiment and clearly intended to make him feel, if not better, then at least part of a very large club. "Did you?" Aiden asked, leaning back in his chair and scrubbing his hands over his face.

"Hell, yes," Barrett replied with a snort. "You're an absolute amateur."

He couldn't say why in any specific way, but Barrett's membership in that club—and apparently elevated status—lifted a horrendous weight off his shoulders. It felt so damn good to have it gone that he couldn't keep from chuckling. "Did you spend a year drinking your brain to mush?"

"No," Barrett drawled, straightening with a chagrined smile. "I enlisted in the army hoping to leap in front of a bullet."

"You obviously failed."

His smile was weak and just a bit cynical. "I assure you that it wasn't for a lack of trying. The only reason I'm still alive is time, sheer luck, and the friendship of Carden Reeves."

And he'd managed in the process, Aiden knew, to come to terms with whatever it was that had driven him to the edge and the desire to throw himself over it. Aiden sighed and looked back at those days and months of his own life. But not in exhaustion this time. And not through a haze of overwhelming regret or despair. Barrett was right. His father had been just as right a full year ago. He hadn't loved and wanted to be a husband as much as he'd wanted with all his heart to be Mary Alice's dashing, daring hero. And he'd failed her and his glorious illusions in a most spectacular way. It was a fact, undeniable and irrevocable. It was also in the past.

"I can't undo what's been done, Barrett," he said as acceptance wrapped around the memories and laid them into silent rest. "I can regret it forever, but I can't undo it. The only choice I have is to accept that and live or to lie down and die. And I've discovered that living, even with regrets, is preferable."

Barrett sagged and expelled a long, hard breath. "Those of us who manage to survive ourselves long enough usually get around to understanding that," he said, smiling as he leaned against the buffet again. "I'm glad to know that you've arrived in one piece. How did you happen to finally do it?"

Aiden chuckled. "Time, sheer luck, and the friendship of Barrett Stanbridge. You forced me to live for a while. Thank you."

"The only thing I did was agree to your father's request and get you sober. If you owe anyone a debt of gratitude, it's Alexandra Radford. She's the one who made you *want* to live again."

"Yes," Aiden countered as the center of his chest tightened painfully, "but you're the one who set me up. You sent me off with her knowing damn good and well that I'd notice how beautiful she is and want to seduce her. You shamelessly used her to salvage me."

"I'll admit it," he replied. "Not the least honorable, but after four weeks of trying to talk some sense into you, I was desperate. And you have to admit that, in the end, it's worked out largely as I intended. Your head's, more or less, back on your shoulders."

Oh, yes, Aiden thought derisively. His head was moderately centered again and because that had needed to happen, he couldn't complain. But, unfortunately, the rest of him felt twisted and battered and decidedly off-kilter. "That's only because you're looking at it all from the outside," he groused, considering the brandy bottle and his original puzzle again.

"Well, I didn't count on you handing her your heart," Barrett rejoined, sounding both a bit defensive and marginally disgusted. "I really thought that you'd been burned recently enough to scramble away from that."

"Apparently once a hero, always a hero," Aiden chuckled wryly. "At least it turned out better this time than it did the last." He snorted and added, "I'm going to have to get myself a white horse. Maybe even have some business cards printed."

Barrett rubbed his jaw with his hand and heaved a sigh. After a long moment, he shifted, crossed one ankle over the other, and drawled, "Just out of idle curiosity . . . Did Alex make you laugh?"

His mind arrowed back with startling speed and clarity. "All the time," he supplied, grinning. "Not that she tells jokes or amusing stories, you understand. She has such a different, unexpected way of looking at the world, at life. I can't explain it any other way." He laughed softly. "It's just her. Alex being delightfully Alex."

Barrett seemed to digest that for a moment, then hummed and ventured, "What do you suppose it was that made her special?"

"Everything," Aiden instantly replied. "She's independent and strong but she also knows how and when to bend. She's a survivor and . . ." He stopped and shook his head, then turned in the chair to square up to his friend. "No, that's not quite right," he amended. "You see, Alex *knows* that she's going to survive whatever comes her way so nothing really frightens her. She accepts what is, adapts, and goes on with such extraordinary grace and serenity.

"She's not passive, though," he hastened to add, not wanting Barrett to have the wrong impression. "Alex is anything but passive. Or coy. I've never known a woman who was so honest, so unaffected. You can't imagine what a difference that makes. Take flirting, for instance. You know how most women do it. They bat their lashes and say something that you can interpret as an invitation or not. They make you do the hunting, take all the risk. But Alex . . . Honest to God, Barrett. She can smile—*just smile*—and it'll curl your toes. You can forget about breathing. Not that you even care about such things."

Obviously working at containing a smile, Barrett nodded and observed, "Sounds as though she was an interesting lover."

"Oh, sweet Jesus," he whispered, the memories, the inconceivably wondrous feelings deluging him. How she looked in the candlelight, the scent of her, the creamy satin of her skin, the cascade of her hair, the unstinted measure of her passion, and the joy that she so sweetly poured into his soul. The extraordinary satisfaction, the rightness of joining with her and surrendering himself to the unimaginable, indescribable pleasure she gave him.

"God," he groaned, knowing that even if he lived for a thousand years, he'd never meet another woman like Alex. His beautiful, passionate, giving Alex.

"Do you know what makes Alex really special?" he murmured, staring blindly at the carpet between his feet as realization wormed slowly through his brain and his heart swelled with aching.

"What?"

"She loves without condition. There are no strings, no hidden traps. She gives everything—every bit of her heart and soul—and asks for nothing in return. Absolutely nothing." He looked up at his friend. "Do you have any idea of how powerful that is?"

Barrett shook his head. "I've never been that incredibly fortunate."

Aiden stared off into his future, knowing that every time he lay with a woman he was going to close his eyes and pretend she was Alex. He'd rise every morning, reaching out to touch her, turning to talk to her. He'd retire to his bed every night thinking he'd find her there. A thousand times a day he'd listen for the sound of her voice, the sweetness of her laughter, hope to see the delightfully wicked sparkle in her eyes. And it would never be there. None of it. Alex was gone. He'd let her go and walked away.

The emptiness of his heart overflowed and flooded his soul, washing away all the pretenses, all the denials, all the shoulds and oughts of his existence. And there, under it all, stripped bare and obvious, was the solid bedrock of a stunning, utterly indisputable truth.

Aiden again met his friend's somber gaze. "I love her, Barrett. *Her*."

"I know," he said, barely nodding. "I've been watching you for the last few weeks. I've been standing here listening to you pour your heart out and hoping to hell that you'd finally see it for yourself. There isn't a doubt in my mind that you've found the great love of your life, John Aiden. The question right now is what you're going to do about it."

Aiden stared off into the distance, listening to the rapid hammering of his heart and knowing the decision was already made. The course was set.

Barrett picked up the bottle and filled the glass, then shoved it closer, saying, "If you don't go after her, you might as well climb back in because you are never again in your life going to be as alive and happy as you were when you were with Alex. No man is that lucky twice."

"Very true," he agreed, rising as he picked up the glass and threw the contents down his throat in one smooth, quick motion.

"Goddammit, John Aiden," Barrett snarled. "Don't you ever learn?"

"Only the hard way," he admitted, slamming down the glass and heading for the door. "I'll talk to you later today," he called back over his shoulder. "Much later."

"Where the hell are you going?"

"To buy myself a big white horse," he called out, not looking back, the liquor searing its way downward and blessedly warming the dread churning in the pit of his stomach. "That's going to be something of a bitch to get done in the middle of the night."

Just ahead of him, the brandy bottle shattered against the wall beside the front door. Aiden ignored it and kept going.

Chapter 21

Alex walked along the bustling wharf in the early morning light, carrying her parasol and valise, and trying very hard not to rain on everyone else's happiness. In the tradition of royalty the world over, Sarad, flanked and backed by his bodyguards, led the procession toward the brightly pinioned ship anchored just ahead. Behind Sarad, borne in the canopied and gaily festooned royal litter, went Vadeen, his bandages concealed by a new and resplendent set of clothes. Mohan scampered at his side, chattering away in Hindi, his English suit forsaken for opulent silk of royal purple and red. Preeya, in a new, gold-embroidered sari, followed in their wake, her parasol and valise—and Mohan's basket of kittens—carried by the very proper but sweetly smiling Sawyer.

A fair distance back, Alex brought up the rear of the happy little entourage, kicking her English traveling skirt out ahead of her and fighting the urge to look back over her shoulder. Wishing Aiden at her side wouldn't bring him, she reminded herself for the countless time. Looking for him only deepened the pain in not seeing him. No, she had to keep her attention focused on the ship and the gangplank leading up to it. Resolutely looking forward would be the only way she might get through the next few hours without dissolving into yet another sobbing puddle of tears.

Forward, not back, she silently repeated. Sarad had reached the wharf end of the gangplank and was conversing with the man who had to be his ship's captain. The guards were back a short distance, but close enough to shield any one member of the royal party if the need arose. Except her, she noted. She was far enough away that it would take them some time to reach her. They were watching her, though, and talking among themselves. No doubt discussing the princess's silly devotion to English dresses and her tendency to dawdle, she decided. And, judging by their scowls, they weren't feeling particularly tolerant of either predilection.

For a second she considered quickening her pace to please them and then decided against it. These were her last moments on English soil and no one was going to hasten their end. She was a princess and only Sarad would chastise her for the distance she'd allowed to develop between the guards and herself. And, besides, the longer she tarried, the greater the chance . . .

No, she chided, there was a fine line between faith and foolish hope. Dragging her feet and delaying her departure was akin to looking back over her shoulder. If it was meant to be, it would be. How fast or slow she walked wouldn't change her destined course. Aiden either came for her or he didn't.

She reached the knot of her family and stopped. The ship gently rocked in its berth and the soft lapping of the water against the hull seemed oddly out of place amid the jarring, raucous noises of the dock. Alex closed her eyes and focused on the lullaby, hoping it would ease the throbbing ache in her soul.

Vadeen called out sharply in Hindi, startling her and shattering her concentration. Glancing around, she instantly noted the tension in the guards, their dark expressions and the direction of their gazes. She turned to see what had alarmed them.

Aiden, her heart sang. Her delightfully wicked, tousle-haired Aiden was there, riding purposefully toward her, his jaw set and his shoulders squared. There was no more handsome man on earth, no other who would ever claim her heart as he did.

Details flitted past her awareness. He wasn't riding his own horse, but a huge white one she'd never seen before. And everyone around her was watching his progress, their expressions a strange mixture of happiness and what seemed almost to be trepidation. They were wise, she realized as he drew the massive animal to a halt in front of her and swung down from the saddle. To assume that he'd come for any reason other than to say a formal good-bye was a fool's blindest hope.

Unable to stand not knowing, she took the initiative and tossed the biggest gambit of her life. "I'm glad that you came to say good-bye, Aiden."

Standing in front of her, the reins in his hands, his eyes dark and his lips a firm line of resolve, he slowly shook his head. "Don't get on that ship, Alex," he said quietly. "Please."

Her heart fluttered with hope, but she held it in check, knowing Aiden, knowing his ghosts and the limits of what he could offer of himself. And knowing just as well that she couldn't live with less than all of him. She managed a smile and began, gently saying, "I have responsi—"

"If anyone knows the price of responsibility and the value of love, it's Kedar. He'll understand if you choose love, Alex."

Her knees went weak with the wildness of her surging hope. "I don't want to be alone," she confessed, her body trembling, "waiting for your returns, praying that nothing's happened to you. I can't live like that, Aiden."

"Then I won't go."

So calm, so certain, so impossible. "It's what you do for a living. What your family does. You sail. That requires you to go."

"Then you'll come with me," he countered without hesitation, his resolve clearly unshaken, his gaze searching hers. "We can run a regular India-to-London route. I sail, you buy. And whenever you want, I'll take you to see Preeya and Mohan. I promise. Please say you will, Alex."

No pledge of forever. No declaration of his feelings. But it was a life together. And, in that, a chance that he might, over time, grow to love her. It was enough for her heart, enough to give her hope.

His brow shot up and his gaze slid away from her as he asked, "What did Vadeen say?"

Alex blinked, startled from her reverie and realizing she hadn't the foggiest awareness that Vadeen had said anything at all.

"I said," Vadeen answered, grinning, "that I had despaired but am now hopeful again. You have, Aiden, in the English way of circling and circling, finally approached the point of asking Princess Alexandra to marry you. I beg you to have mercy on us all and to circle no more."

His smile was instant, bright and broad. Her heart soared with certainty and unbridled joy as he turned back to her.

"She is a princess," Mohan interjected. "The permission to marry must come from the raja, from our father."

His smile faded and then he shrugged and said, "All right. If that's how it has to be, then that's how it has to be."

Her jaw went slack in astonishment as he turned and walked over to her uncle.

"I request passage on your ship, your highness. I'll pay whatever price you ask. I intend to go to Kedar and formally ask to marry his daughter, the Princess Alexandra."

He hadn't asked her yet! She hadn't agreed to be his wife.

Not that she had the slightest intention of refusing, but to have it all negotiated without her consent . . .

"My brother will expect a bride price," Sarad countered, folding his arms across his chest. "Unless you have something of great value to offer, there is no point in making the journey."

"What will he want? I'll get it."

It had better be a white horse because, as far as she could tell, it was the only thing of any value he'd brought with him to the dock. And if he thought for one minute that she was going to sail off and wait for him to come on the next ship—

"It is difficult to say," her uncle mused aloud. "She has a special place in his heart and there will be many suitors willing to offer great riches for her."

Aiden bristled; she could see it in the widening of his stance, the squaring of his shoulders. "Then we'll go to Kedar," he replied, his tone flinty, "tell him to name his price, and I'll send for it."

"I think it would be best if you waited for him to—"

"Excuse me, gentlemen," Alex interrupted, dropping her valise and parasol and stepping up to stand with them. "But I haven't gone anywhere. I'm right here and I will not be removed from this matter."

Before either of them could muster a protest or an apology, she planted the palm of her hand in the center of Aiden's chest and backed him away from her uncle. When she had him a sufficient distance, she took the front of his shirt in hand and drew him to a stop. "John Aiden?" she said, looking up into sparkling, laughing green eyes.

His grin was wide and bright. "You never call me John Aiden."

Her anger dissolved in an instant. God, how she loved him. How impossible it was to think of living without him. "That's because," she admitted, laughing softly, "I'm so very rarely irritated with you."

She was his; the love of his life. She always had been. She always would be. He knew it in his heart and deep in his soul. Mindful of those watching them, Aiden slipped his arms around her waist and drew her close. "You are absolutely beautiful," he said softly, his words for her ears alone. "You take my breath away every time I look at you. Alex, you're everything to me. My happiness, my heart, my life. I can't live without you. I don't want to live without you. I love you." He bent his head and brushed a kiss across her lips, then straightened to solemnly ask, "Will you marry me, Alex?"

She twined her fingers in the hair at his nape and arched a brow as a smile tickled the corners of her mouth. "Will you remember tomorrow your solemn vow to never be happy?"

He'd been a such a fool for so long. God only knew why Alex had as much patience with him as she did, but he'd be forever grateful for the incredible gift of it. "Sometimes what you least expect comes to you from where you least expect it when you least expect it. And sometimes, Alex, the gift is so brilliant, so magnificent, that it completely changes the way you see the entire world. I've set that vow aside. In loving you I've realized that I made it for the wrong reasons."

"And will you someday set aside your vows to me?"

"Never," he promised from his heart. "I'll make them for every reason that's right. I'll stand before God and swear on my soul to hold them sacred. There will never be another woman, Alex. I will love only you, hold only you into all eternity. Please stay. Please tell me that you love me."

Her joy was boundless and complete. "What will come, will come, Aiden. We can't know what it will be. But I do know that I love you with all my heart and that I'm destined to face whatever life brings always in your arms, always protecting your heart and our love. Yes, Aiden. I'll marry you."

"Thank you," he murmured, bending down to kiss her slowly and with a reverence that filled her soul to overflowing.

Only when the fires of passion flared, when their breaths caught, did he draw away. Grinning, he cleared his throat and asked, "So what do we do now, darling? Do we go to India and ask your father's blessing?"

She shook her head. "Kedar knows that love is the blessing," she assured him, smiling and easing out of his embrace, certain of her course. "We bid the others a safe journey."

Hand in hand, they turned and made their way back to her family. Sarad was the only one who didn't look supremely pleased and so Alex deliberately began with him. "Please tell my father that I have chosen love and that I will bring my husband to meet him before the year is out."

He snorted, but one corner of his mouth twitched upward. "Kedar will be disappointed. But he will also understand your choice as no one else can. Mark the days of your promise well, my niece. Your father will."

Alex nodded and turned to Mohan. Aiden released her hand and she reached out to smooth his dark hair as she said, "I'll always be your sister, you know. If you need me, I'll be there for you. I'll watch you and remind you to be a good and honorable ruler. And I'll pray that you someday find a love as perfect as I have."

"I am happy for you, Alex. I am glad that I was able to play a small part in making Aiden see the wisdom of loving you. I think the ploy to make him jealous of other men was a masterful one. Do you not agree?"

"It was absolutely brilliant." She bent down and hugged him close and pressed a kiss to his cheek. "Thank you, little brother."

"I will see you in one year?" he asked, his bravado cracking as she straightened and drew away.

"If not once or twice before," Aiden assured him, reaching past her to ruffle the hair she'd just smoothed.

To the sound of his laughter, she turned to face the hardest of her farewells. "Thank you, Preeya," she said, the tears welling in her eyes as she took her hands in her own. "For always watching, for keeping my secrets and hoping for my great happiness. For sharing your wisdom and making me be strong when I didn't think I could be. If Brahma sees fit to bless me with children, I will have Aiden bring me to you so that your love can see them safely into the world."

"No tears at our parting, Alex," she gently admonished, her smile soft and gentle. "You have chosen well and wisely. Aiden is a good man. A strong man. There will be many, many children, Alex. You will be in India often. It will please your father to hold his grandchildren. I will see you again before the year is gone. And I will be prepared and waiting for you."

Alex hugged her close and kissed her, lingering for a while, reluctant to let her go, determined to banish the welling tears before she stepped away and Preeya could see them. After several long moments, she gave the effort up as futile. With a chagrined smile, a sniffle, and a quick brush of her eyes with her fingertips, she stepped away and turned to the man standing at Preeya's side.

"At least we don't have to say good-bye, Sawyer. I will miss having you around the house, though. I've enjoyed your company."

He cleared his throat. "Thank you for saying so, Miss Radford. I am sure that our paths will cross in the days ahead. And most assuredly when you and Mr. Terrell visit in India."

"Whoa!" Aiden exclaimed from behind her. "Did I hear that correctly? You're going to be in India when we get there?"

Again Sawyer cleared his throat. "You understood correctly, sir. When his lordship returns, I intend to submit my notice, and immediately leave my life here to become a part of Preeya's."

Stunned, Alex looked back and forth between them. "How—"

"I was asked to translate one conversation," Mohan quickly explained. "I assure you that I learned nothing of an untoward nature and that I was greatly disappointed."

"Carden is going to kill me." Aiden chuckled. He extended his hand to Sawyer. "Congratulations. The matter of my imminent death aside, I sincerely wish you both every happiness."

"Thank you, sir."

Aiden hugged Preeya and planted a kiss firmly on her cheek.

"Aiden says that he's very happy for you both," Alex translated for the stunned and furiously blushing woman, then took her back in her arms to give her her own congratulatory kiss. "You're very good at keeping secrets, Preeya. I never guessed. But I'm delighted by the surprise and ever so pleased for you."

"My destiny came more quietly, but no less fully than yours." Cupping Alex's cheek, she smiled and said firmly, "The time for farewells is over. Go with your Aiden and be happy. I will see you in a year's time, my Alex."

Yes, all things in their time. And the time had come to walk away. She stepped back and looked at them all, gave them each a reassuring smile.

"Ready to go?" Aiden asked softly, his hand slipping comfortingly to the small of her back.

She smiled up at him and nodded, then let him take her hand and lead her to the horse.

He swung up and smoothly across and then grinned down at her. "Would you like me to sweep you off your feet, princess?"

She laughed, remembering their conversation and suddenly understanding why he'd ridden a white horse today. For just this moment, just to make real that young woman's starry-eyed, impossible dream. "You did that some time ago, my handsome prince."

"And I'm not about to drop you. Ever," he promised. "Turn around, darling, and I'll lift you up."

Aiden settled her sideways across his lap and wrapped his free arm around her waist to hold her close. She slipped her arms around him and curled into him, her head nestled into the crook of his shoulder. His world right, his head and his heart firmly centered, he pressed a kiss into her hair and asked, "Is there anything you need off that ship?"

She snuggled closer and sighed contentedly. "No. What was crated, I ordered unpacked. I simply locked the door of the Blue Elephant and left it all behind. Even my valise was empty."

"Why?" he asked, turning the horse around and letting it amble away from the docks.

"In the depths of my heart, I knew you'd come for me, that I really wasn't going to leave. It was an act of faith."

"You know me better than I know myself."

She laughed softly. "Isn't that the way it should be?"

"Yes, it is."

She sat up a bit, just enough to meet his gaze. "I love you, Aiden. With all that I am."

"I know," he whispered, pressing a languid kiss to her forehead.

"You aren't concerned that I told Preeya our children would be born in India, are you?"

India, huh? He grinned. "I didn't know that you had. No one translated the conversation for me."

"I'm sorry."

"There's no need to be, darling," he assured her, chuckling and hugging her. "I heard my name often enough that I didn't feel the least excluded. And I think the idea of our children being born in India is an excellent one. They should know the world that helped make their mother the incredible woman she is."

"You know," she mused, slowly wiggling deeper and closer into the space between his thighs. "Marrying a princess makes you a prince."

"Prince Aiden? For God's sake, don't tell anyone. It sounds ridiculous."

She drew an arm from around him and trailed a fingertip down the buttons of his shirtfront. "As an Indian prince," she said, undoing the button just above the waistband of his trousers, "you're rather expected to take other wives and mistresses."

"Well, they're going to be disappointed," he managed to say, acutely aware that she was opening the button on his waistband. He hardened instantly and had to shift under her to accommodate it. "I'm not going to have the time or the energy for them," he finished raggedly, his heart hammering.

"That's good to know."

He knew what she was going to do and yet she still caught him by surprise. The rhythm of the horse's gait combined with the slow friction of her hand against his skin was wildly provocative, the bold, deliberate caress of his abdomen setting his blood on fire. He groaned as she slipped her hand lower to create the most exquisite torture he'd ever endured.

"Jesus, Alex," he gasped, smiling down into her upturned face. "Do you want me to make love to you right here on this horse?"

Her eyes lit up and her grin went brilliantly bright, deliciously unholy. His blood sang, his toes curled, and he stopped breathing. If he could just get them as far as the carriage house . . .

He lifted her up, turning her so that she faced forward, and then settled her astride and fully, firmly between his thighs. His arm wrapped tightly around her waist, he pulled her close.

"We're going home," he promised as he kicked the horse into a canter, as the sweet temptation in his arms laughed and claimed every last measure of his heart and soul.

Turn the page for a sneak peek at the final installment in the thrilling *Perfect* trilogy!

THE PERFECT DESIRE

Coming soon from
ST. MARTIN'S PAPERBACKS

Dead women didn't care what happened to their wardrobes. Well, Mignon might, but there was nothing she could do about it except stomp around Heaven, waving her arms and screaming. Not that it was even remotely possible that Mignon had gone to Heaven, Isabella Dandaneau reminded herself, staring out the window of the rented hack.

She exhaled long and hard, brought her gaze down to her lap, and then worked at smoothing a wrinkle in Mignon's skirt. *My* skirt, Isabella silently corrected. And sensibilities—hers *and* Mignon's—aside, desperate situations didn't allow for squeamishness. She needed clothing and Mignon didn't. Not anymore. The constables had turned it all over to her and sending it back to Louisiana would have been nothing more than an exercise in foolish pride. What she couldn't easily alter to fit her more meager attributes, she'd sell. It'd be nice to have enough money to buy food for a while. Knowing that the bounty had come—albeit indirectly—from Mignon might make swallowing it a bit difficult, but she'd manage.

The cab rolled out of traffic and slowed to a stop before a dark gray granite building. The gold-lettered signplate beside the heavy door was the right one and she let herself out of the carriage. Her heart racing, her hands trembling, Isabella considered the five granite steps that led up to the door. Desperate situations didn't allow for cowardice, either, she sternly reminded herself. Still, it took a deep breath and every measure of her self-discipline to gather her skirts and march upward and into the offices of the man the authorities considered Mignon's killer.

The secretary looked up from his desk and only reluctantly rose to his feet to say, "Good morning, madam. How may I help you?"

Isabella took another slow, deep breath and committed herself to seeing it through. "I'd like to speak with Mr. Barrett Stanbridge, please."

"I'm afraid that is not possible, madam," the little man replied, his nose tilted at a disdainful angle. "Mr. Stanbridge has canceled all of his appointments for the foreseeable future."

Of course he has, Isabella thought. *Defending one's self against murder charges would be rather time-consuming.* "Please tell him," she said firmly, unable to let the man's concerns override her needs, "that I am here regarding the woman killed the night before last."

The secretary's eyes narrowed. "Regarding in what manner?"

Hoping that she held all the cards for the next few moments, Isabella smiled and politely, quietly replied, "What I intend to say to Mr. Stanbridge, I intend to say in private. I'll wait here while you deliver my request."

He assessed her, clearly weighing his hope against his employer's instructions. After a long moment, he tugged the hem of his coat and stepped around his desk, saying, "Your name, madam?"

She hesitated, then decided there was a slight advantage in taking Barrett Stanbridge by surprise. "It's not necessary that you know it."

The man hesitated again, but finally knocked on the door, opened it just wide enough to slide through sideways, and then instantly closed it, leaving her alone in the anteroom. Isabella sagged and rubbed her sweating palms along the side seams of her skirt. God, this would be so much easier if she had even the slightest bit of experience at parlor intrigues. Mignon had been one of the best at it and she was dead. What did that suggest about the odds of *her* succeeding?

Closing her eyes, Isabella held her breath and lifted her chin. There was no going back. There was nothing to go back to. She'd simply have to assess the man when she met him and make reasonable judgments as matters went along. The trick would be to tell him no more than she had to, before she had to. And if her instincts even so much as whispered for her to run, she would. Dignity and poise be damned. Staying alive was what mattered.

The twisting of the doorknob warned her of the secretary's return in time for her to slip the mask of cool composure back into place. The door opened wide and the slight man stepped back into the anteroom, moved to the side of the doorway, and gestured to the opening, saying regally, "Madam."

Both relief and trepidation washed over her in a single wave. Not trusting her voice, she nodded her thanks and swept forward, bracing herself and hoping her bold plan didn't turn to disaster. Or suicide.

Resolve and fortitude took her across the threshold and halfway to the desk before wavering. Momentum alone provided two additional steps and then she found herself standing on the Persian carpet, her heart racing and her mind careening through a tumble of observations.

He was a massively shouldered, incredibly long-legged man. Dark eyes, dark hair, a wonderfully hard-chiseled jaw. Wickedly handsome. Of course Mignon had noticed him in a theater crowd. Every woman had. And at any other moment—when he wasn't strangling on curses as he was now—he'd be rakishly smooth and confident. The perfect ladies' man. Which was why Mignon had chosen him.

He blinked, took a deep breath. As he was swallowing, Isabella seized what there was of an advantage. "No, you're not seeing a ghost, Mr. Stanbridge," she said, putting on a soft smile and forcing her feet to carry her forward again.

He'd cocked a brow and begun to openly assess her by the time she reached the edge of his desk, stopped, and added, "My name is Isabella Dandaneau. Mignon Richard was my cousin. Our mothers were sisters. There is—or rather *was*—a strong family resemblance."

He nodded ever so slightly. "Are you here for vengeance?"

Good God, the man's voice had the most delicious rumble to it. If his hands were just half as efficient at caressing. . . . She started, appalled by the direction of her thoughts and stunned by the ease in which they'd not only escaped her control, but also set her heart skittering with a ridiculous kind of feminine anticipation.

"Well, in the first place," she replied as her stomach twisted into a knot, "I never liked Mignon well enough to go through all the effort of avenging her. In the second place, the only thing surprising about her death is that it didn't happen long before now. And in the third . . ." She considered him and listened to her instincts. "You're not the one who killed her."